The
Davenport Daughters

Also by Betty Kerss Groezinger

The Davenport Dilemma

The Davenport Daughters

Davenport is back from the dead…
But can he live long enough to save his
daughters and grandchildren?

Dear Toni —
I remember so many fun times with your Happy days. I wish I could be with you for this celebration.
I hope you enjoy story and learn a little more about your cousin Bill —
Love, hugs and Happy 100 Birthday!

Betty Kerss Groezinger

Betty

Psalm 91

gatekeeper press™

Columbus, Ohio

The Davenport Daughters

Published by Gatekeeper Press
2167 Stringtown Rd, Suite 109
Columbus, OH 43123-2989
www.GatekeeperPress.com

Library of Congress Control Number: 2021948480

ISBN (paperback): 9781662918810
ISBN (eBook): 9781662918827

For my family with love
Kim, Teresa, Patrick, Lauren, Aaron, Ashley
Meghanne, Connie, Pam, Bob, and Tom

And my great grandchildren
Peyton, Lucy, Eli, and Sienna

and

In memory of the two men in my life
Bill, whose life inspired the stories
and
Ray, who encouraged me to write them

Acknowledgments

ONCE AGAIN, I'M SO grateful for the special people who took time to read and critique this story.

To Kitty and Jerry, who read the first draft and encouraged me every step of the way. To Gary, who read an early draft and talked to me about weapons and landmines. To Burt, who read bits and pieces and talked to me about the Mafia. To Kim Clark, who found the time to read and edit the story—even when she didn't have time—*Thank you for making the story so much better.*

To the readers of my first book, ***The Davenport Dilemma,*** who have waited so long for the sequel, and who kept asking when it would be finished—*Thank you for the encouragement, it's been a long road with a move from one home to another and a myriad of problems including a publisher who went out of business!*

Special thanks to all my family, for your continued love, support, and listening ears!

Thank you for choosing to spend your time reading this book. I hope you'll visit me on my website, ***bettykerssgroezinger.com*** and Facebook at ***The Davenport Dilemma.***

Happy reading!
Betty Kerss Groezinger

"We will take America without firing a shot … We will BURY YOU! We can't expect the American people to jump from Capitalism to Communism, but we can assist their elected leaders in giving them small doses of Socialism, until they awaken one day to find that they have Communism. We do not have to invade the United States; we will destroy you from within."

— Nikita Khrushchev
From an address by Khrushchev to the
Western Ambassadors at the Polish embassy in
Moscow on November 19, 1956.

"America will never be destroyed from the outside.
If we falter and lose our freedom, it will be because we destroyed ourselves."

— Abraham Lincoln
16th President of the United States.

Chapter 1

Sunday
October 23, 1983
SOMEWHERE SOUTH OF FORT WORTH, TEXAS

ABULLET RIPPED THROUGH the man's throat…
The woman turned toward the gunshot, eyes glued on the scene as color drained from her face. She stifled the scream that wanted out and hid behind a car. Crouching down low, she grabbed her child and ran for her life.

THE YOUNG WOMAN RAN faster as the scene bombarded her mind. She kept seeing Joey fall when the man shot him, there was so much blood.

"Lord, help me," she cried when she looked back to see if anyone was following them. She tripped on the rocky edge of the road and almost dropped her daughter. Screaming and struggling for balance, she tightened her arms around the wailing child.

She stood still trying to quit shaking. Every sound was magnified in her ears, gravel crunching under her feet, cars roaring by, and thunder cracking in the distance, and all the time her mind replayed the gunshot over and over again. She was terrified the killer would catch her. Their eyes met when she looked back, she knew what he looked like.

"Just run, one foot in front of the other, one foot in front of the other…"

Her daughter had quit crying, but now she had the hiccups. "I know you're hungry and thirsty, baby, breakfast was so long ago." Sophie grew heavier with each step. Tears blurred the woman's vision and she stumbled again.

Shifting Sophie to her other arm, she stared across a wide field. Several houses were on the far side; someone might help them if she could get over there. Thunder rumbled around the threatening clouds, it would soon be dark and raining. She had to find somewhere to hide. Her stomach churned and came up in her throat. Oh, dear Lord, she was going to be sick again. She slid down the incline from the road into a clump of bushes.

"Don't move, baby," she told the three-year-old when she put her on the ground. Dry heaves racked the woman's body once more.

Queasy and shaking, she crumpled to the ground. Sophie crawled into her lap crying. Holding her daughter with one arm she dug in her pockets trying to find something to get rid of the nasty taste in her mouth. Then she remembered she did that the last time she was sick. Her pockets were empty. *If I just had my purse… if I had change for a phone call, if, if….*

Tears rolled unchecked down her face.

"Don't cry, Mommy," Sophie wiped at her tears. The young woman rocked her daughter back and forth as she listened to cars speeding by.

One of the houses across the field had a porch light on. She wanted to get there, but her legs were like dead weights. She'd been running for hours, she didn't think she could make it. Her head throbbed and she was having trouble seeing.

"I can't do it, baby." She held Sophie tighter and burrowed deeper into the dense foliage praying no one could see them. Maybe if she rested a little while she could get to that house. She had to try, Sophie needed food.

She rubbed her eyes trying to focus then stared down the highway. Her sister should have been following her, but she hadn't seen her. She was so afraid that man shot her like he did Joey.

Exhaustion and fear overtook the young woman…she broke into gut-wrenching sobs.

Chapter 2

Early Sunday Morning
October 23, 1983
DALLAS, TEXAS

RESPONDING TO A FRANTIC call reporting gunshots, two squad cars rolled to a stop in front of a house in the northern suburbs of Dallas. Nothing appeared out of the ordinary to the four officers exiting the vehicles. It was Sunday morning and the neighborhood was quiet. The only sign of life was an elderly woman watching from a window in the house next door.

"That's probably the neighbor who reported the gunshots," said an officer as he got out of the car.

Two officers ran around the house toward the back yard, the other two went to the front porch. Peering through the stained glass window in the door, an officer knocked and called "Police."

There was no response, he twisted the doorknob and pushed it open. Guns leading the way, the men entered shouting, "Police." A small table was knocked over and a lamp lay on its side with the shade crushed, books and papers were scattered around the room. Something had happened, a struggle or fight. It was more than rowdy kids playing.

"Clear," the men called out going from room to room. The house was empty. They continued through the kitchen and joined the officers in the back yard.

"Officer down," shouted the man kneeling beside a body near the open garage. He checked the pulse in the man's neck. "Mac, call it in, he's still alive. It's Jackson, one of our men."

The officer stood up. "There's a trail of blood on the sidewalk, looks like someone kept going after he was shot."

The men followed the trail to a detached garage at the back of the lot. They approached the car with caution, two officers on each side.

"Man down over here," called the officer on the driver's side of the car. "Looks like he was trying to get in the car, door's open and keys are in his hand."

He checked the man for a pulse. "He's still breathing, but bleeding profusely."

The officer moved the man enough to pull his billfold out of his pocket. "ID says Jeffrey Williams. He was trying to scribble something on the concrete with his car keys, but I can't read it."

"Mac, talk to the neighbor who called in and find out what she saw."

"The ambulance is here," Mac yelled as he ran to the house next door and knocked. An elderly woman peeped through a slight crack in the door.

"Police, you called in a report saying you thought you heard gunshots." He showed her his badge. "Did you see anything?"

She opened the door and the officer asked again, "Did you see what happened, ma'am?"

"Not really. I heard what sounded like a car backfiring, and I went to the window. A van was parked in front of my neighbor's house and a man was dragging her down the sidewalk. He shoved her in that van, that's when I called the police. She didn't want to go with him. She kept trying to pull away, but she couldn't do much with her little girl in her arms. They were both screaming."

"Did you get the number on the license plate?"

"No, it was too far away, but it was a white van with a sliding door. That man shoved them in there. I'm telling you, they didn't want to go with him. You need to do something…"

"That's what we're doing, ma'am. What did the man look like?"

"I couldn't see him very well; his back was to me most of the time. He was a big man with dark hair and had on a tan jacket. That's really all I can tell you."

"If you think of anything else, please call me," the officer said handing her a card, "Thank you for your help, ma'am."

"Just help that poor woman and her little girl, they didn't even have coats on. It wasn't right to force them in that van. They didn't want to go."

Paramedics were pushing a stretcher into the back of an ambulance just as a second ambulance pulled up. The neighborhood was alive with activity now. People were standing in their yards watching; a few curious ones crossed the street and were trying to talk to the paramedics.

WASHINGTON, D.C.

"**WHAT THE HELL IS** going on out there in Texas?" roared General Thurman in the command center of Army G-2. He slammed the phone down.

Agitated and pacing the room, the general looked at George Reaves, his long-time aide. "That call was from the Dallas police telling me one of the men assigned to guard Josh Davenport's daughters was shot. Both of the daughters, Kris Williams and Laurie Parrino and their two children, are missing. Some kind of struggle went on in the Williams' house and the husband, Jeffrey Williams, was shot. He's alive, but unconscious. Prognosis says he probably won't make it through the night."

The general stopped and closed his eyes willing his pulse rate to slow down. "There's more, Reaves. Joey Parrino, Davenport's other son-in-law, was shot and killed at the scene of a car wreck on the south side of Fort Worth."

The general's mind flew back a few months to when he found out why one of his G-2 agents had gotten so independent and started pulling disappearing acts. It still rankled he was the last to know Josh

Davenport worked for the president. For years his own agent did secret missions for the president and he hadn't known. His own agent, he found that very hard to swallow. As if that was not enough, Davenport had the gall to tell him he was training one of his G-2 agents, Owen Blakely, to work with him.

Following fast on the coattails of that news he found out another agent, Nathan Scott, was selling information to Mason Silverman, the head of the National Security Agency. Both men were informants for the *Brotherhood*. There was no way he would ever understand what caused a man to turn traitor. At least, Silverman was man enough to shoot himself. However, he had the satisfaction of throwing Scott in the brig and that felt good. The traitor would never see the light of day again if he had any say in the matter.

He'd never figured out how he was supposed to manage operations in the dark. INSCOM, the Intelligence and Security Command of the Army, was charged with detecting and preventing treason, espionage and sabotage along with information gathering operations for military and national decision makers. Sometimes in the middle of the night he'd wake up in a cold sweat wondering what else he didn't know and when that bomb would drop. And now, that damned *Brotherhood* had found out Davenport was alive and was determined to kill him.

"Damn it, Reaves, Davenport will be on a rampage. Not only are his daughters missing, but they could be widows. He'll be a wild man. He and the president will demand instant answers."

Anger flooded through the general, he stood up and stormed around the room. His attitude cooled somewhat when he remembered what happened six years ago. Davenport had infiltrated the *Brotherhood* and managed to get to the top echelon providing INSCOM and the president valuable information. When his cover was blown, he agreed to let his family think he was dead in order to protect them from the *Brotherhood*. Since that time, he had taken on some seriously impossible operations. The one that stuck in the general's mind was the time

Davenport went behind the iron curtain and brought two men out. Operating alone exacts a heavy price, and for that the general had a heartfelt respect. He deeply respected all his outriders.

What set the general's teeth on edge was being left in the dark. When Davenport found out his wife married Nathan Scott, he went underground and broke all protocol getting her out of the United States and to his secret hideout. That rankled—he still had no idea where Davenport's safe house was located. All he knew was where it wasn't; it was not in the states. And now this thing with the daughters was likely to send the man over the edge again. A totally out-of-control G-2 agent gone rogue and on a rampage, he didn't want to think about the problems that could cause. The general dropped down and put his aching head in his hands.

His face got redder as his infamous temper rose again. "Reaves, we have to give Davenport all the support we can. Who's available to send to Texas?"

"Al Lindberg just flew in from Russia, his plane landed a few minutes ago," Reaves answered. "He's worked with Davenport before."

"Brief him and get him on the next flight to Dallas, military or commercial, whatever is fastest. We need answers now. We have to find Davenport's daughters and grandchildren, and Davenport, if we can. The man seems to be able to disappear at will."

The general reached across his desk, picked up a bottle of scotch and poured a stiff drink. There were many possibilities, but if he had to guess who abducted the women, his money was on the *Brotherhood*.

Chapter 3

A SMOTHERED SCREAM ESCAPED her lips when something touched her shoulder, she fell backwards against a tree. All she could see through her tears was a blurred face looking down at her. Scrambling to her feet, the young woman thrust Sophie behind her and yelled, "Get away from me."

The man backed up a couple of steps and raised his hands, "I'm not going to hurt you. I thought you might need help."

She picked up Sophie and moved further away from the man. "Who are you? What do you want?"

"I was walking my dog when I heard the child cry." He reached down and patted the head of the golden retriever by his side. "This is Abby, she's very gentle. My wife and I live across the field where you see the lights. Do you need help?"

The dog ran over and looked up at her expectantly, tail wagging.

"Abby wants you to pet her. She won't hurt you or the child."

Maybe he's not one of them, maybe he will help me. She reached down and patted the dog's head. Sophie wiggled trying to reach Abby.

"Doggie, Mommy, want to play with doggie," Sophie said.

"She won't hurt my daughter?"

"No, Abby loves children; she'll sit beside the child if you put her down."

She'd never been a coward. She had always been strong, but that had changed in the last few hours. She'd never seen a man murdered before, her head swirled with the thought and she hung on to a tree. Maybe, just maybe, this man was safe. There was no dog with the men who kidnapped them. She put Sophie down and her daughter giggled when the dog nosed her hand and sat down beside her.

"Who are you? You said you live nearby?"

"I'm Jonathan Crane, pastor of the church you see across the field. My house is right next door to it. It's obvious something has happened to you, I'll help you and your daughter if I can."

Another wave of nausea swept over her, she swayed and grabbed the tree again. She had no choice, it was about to rain and she had to do something soon. Sophie needed food. His house must be the one with the porch light on she was looking at earlier. The young woman took a deep breath and words burst out of her, "We were kidnapped then in a car wreck and I got away. I'm so afraid those men will find us again."

Startled, the man watched the young woman a moment then glanced at the highway. "If you can walk, we should get you away from the road and out of the weather, it's about to rain. My wife is in the house and has a pot of soup cooking. You'll be warm and safe there."

The small blonde woman stared hard at the man in the fading light. He was definitely not one of the men who had taken them; this man had a kind voice. Thunder boomed again, it was closer. Her eyes were drawn to the dark sky and she shivered. She had no money and no idea where she was. She had to trust somebody; her daughter was thirsty and hungry. She closed her eyes for a second then gave a curt nod. "Yes, I can walk. I've been walking a long time."

She grabbed Sophie when the man offered to carry her. "I'll carry my daughter."

Abby ran before them leading the way and turning every other minute to see if they were following, somehow the dog made her feel safer. She looked anxiously across the field at the house; the lights on the porch were beckoning. She hoped she could make it. Sophie's hiccups were gone and she was watching the dog. They reached the front porch just as lightning split the sky and rain started. She turned and looked again for her sister.

The front door opened as soon as they stepped on the porch. "I was wondering how long you were going to walk tonight. I see you've brought company, just look at that sweet baby."

Pastor Crane smiled, "This young woman and her daughter need a little help tonight. I found them hiding in the field; they've had some trouble."

"You're welcome, my dear, I'm Cathy Crane. Come in where it's warm, you look half frozen. You and your little girl don't even have jackets."

They followed Mrs. Crane into the kitchen. The wind was howling loudly and rattling the windows, but it was warm and something smelled delicious. The pine table in the middle of the room was inviting and she collapsed in the nearest chair. Sophie squirmed trying to get down on the floor where the dog sat looking at her.

"I've just made some spiced tea," Mrs. Crane said handing her a steaming cup. "This will warm you up. It's all right to let your daughter down, Abby won't hurt her." Sophie slipped to the floor and giggled when the dog sat beside her. The lady poured milk in a child's cup and handed it to Sophie along with a cracker.

The young woman wrapped her cold hands around the hot cup. When Mrs. Crane sat down across from her, she studied the woman's caring face and it made her want to cry.

"Thank you, Mrs. Crane, it feels so good in here." The hot, fragrant tea was wonderful. At last, the nasty taste was out of her mouth.

"I'm Cathy," she smiled. "Everyone calls my husband Pastor, but they call me Cathy."

"I'm very grateful we're inside. We'd have been soaked and sitting in mud under those trees." She tried to smile, but she couldn't make her lips move so she sipped the hot tea again. "Thank you for letting us come in out of the rain and being so nice to us. I'm sorry I was scared of you," she said to Pastor Crane.

"I knew you were scared, my dear. Do you feel like telling us what happened?"

Fear rose again, wild thoughts flew through her mind. What if he isn't a minister? Are these people who they seem? In a few short hours, she had gone from being a normal person to not trusting anyone. Maybe she could tell how those men grabbed them. If she only knew who the men were, all she knew for sure was they murdered Joey. She didn't even know what happened to her sister or nephew.

"I don't really know what happened. I mean I know what happened but not why, Pastor Crane. My husband had gone to the garage to get the car, and I was trying to get Sophie's shoes on her when the doorbell rang. I opened the door and two men burst inside, I have no idea who they were. They grabbed me and Sophie. I fought, but a huge man forced us down the sidewalk and into a van. They didn't even let me get my shoes or our coats. The car took off fast. When it stopped, the driver pointed a gun at me and told me not to make a sound. A minute later, the van door slid open and that huge man shoved my sister and nephew in with us. I heard my brother-in-law Joey yelling at them. They drove for a long time; I've no idea where we went. We couldn't see out, they made us sit on the floor." Nausea threatened again and she sipped the hot sweet tea.

"That's terrible," Cathy said as she poured more tea.

"Every time our babies cried those men yelled at us. They kept telling us to shut those crying brats up or they would. My sister and I huddled around our babies trying to keep them quiet, but you can't keep toddlers from crying. When the van wrecked, it threw us all around, and we were scrambling to get to our babies when we heard my sister's husband…"

The picture of Joey being shot flashed before her eyes and she couldn't speak, she shuddered and tried to keep from crying. She cleared her throat. Her voice shook when she continued. "Joey tried to help us.

I think he drove his car into the front of the van. When we crashed, the men jumped out leaving the doors open. The next thing we heard was Joey shouting for us to get out and run, so we did."

She reached for the tissue Cathy was handing her. "I didn't wait, I ran with Sophie in my arms. I looked back once when I heard a gunshot. It lifted Joey off the ground; blood was spurting as he fell. It was horrible, really horrible. I froze and couldn't move for a minute, I couldn't quit staring at Joey."

She wiped tears away then cleared her throat again. "We were in the middle of a bridge. I stooped down with Sophie and ran between the cars. When I got to the end of the bridge, I slid down the embankment. Then I ran until I couldn't; that's when you found us hiding in the bushes. I was so scared you were one of those men who kidnapped us, but there wasn't a dog with them. I haven't seen my sister since the wreck. I don't know what happened to her."

"You ran all day carrying Sophie, you have to be exhausted. Did you know these men?" Pastor Crane asked.

"No, I've never seen them before." She looked down at her hands, they were shaking and she wrapped them around the cup. She needed to hear a familiar voice and she really wanted to go home. "May I call home? I need to talk to my husband. He'll come get us."

The phone rang and rang, four, five times then a strange voice answered. It was not Jeffrey, she gasped and hung up. "Someone answered, it wasn't my husband."

Tears flowed again and she bit her lip trying to stop trembling. Where was Jeff? Her mind raced, so many strange things had happened since her dad died. Could this have something to do with mom? Before she went away, she implied dad might still be alive. *That was crazy talk, I saw daddy in the casket. I saw the casket go down in the ground.* Mom did say she couldn't explain because it would put us in danger. "Well, danger found us, Mom, and Joey's dead." She shivered, "I don't know where you are, or my sister, or my husband. I don't even know where I am."

She couldn't sit still. She crossed the kitchen to the window and stared at the heavy rain. She watched lightning streak across the sky and prayed her sister and Nicky were somewhere dry and warm. *If you hear me, please answer me,* she silently demanded of her twin sister. *Where are you? Please answer me.*

PASTOR CRANNE WATCHED THE young woman's shaking hands and knew she was close to the breaking point. He reached over and turned on the television, "It's time for the six o'clock news. Let's see if they tell us anything about the wreck." The sound came up and she listened intently.

> *Good evening, folks, this is World News Today, October 23, 1983...*
> On September 1, 1983, the Soviet Union shot down Korean Airlines Flight 007 in Russian airspace and killed 269 passengers and crew members. This incident remains unresolved and is continuing to create tension between the Soviet Union and the United States.
>
> On October 15, the FBI arrested James D. Harper, Jr., a technician working in California's Silicon Valley, on charges of selling sensitive military research data to a Polish spy for $250,000. Investigation is ongoing.
>
> Two days ago, a terrorist drove a truckload of high explosives through a series of barricades and into the Beirut airport in Lebanon. The explosion demolished the four-story building killing 239 U.S. Marines. Today, in an almost identical early morning attack, two miles to the north another bomb-laden truck smashed into an eight-story building used as barracks by French paratroopers, 58 were killed.

Today's update, October 23, authorities have been unable to find any trace of the crown jewels and other priceless artifacts including the Spear of Destiny stolen from the Hoffburg Palace museum in Vienna, Austria a month ago. The Spear of Destiny is purported to be the one that pierced the side of Jesus Christ; Charlemagne carried it into battle, and, in more recent times, paraded by Hitler in his rallies during World War II. This theft has caused a violent uproar in many circles. The mystery of where the Spear of Destiny is continues.

And that wraps up today, October 23, 1983.
This is Jonathan McFey, World News Today …
Stay tuned for your local news.

THE YOUNG WOMAN FIDGETED getting more and more anxious. *I don't care about all that right now*, she thought. *Tell me about my husband and sister.*

And now for the Dallas news…
The federal government continues to monitor the finance and banking policy implementation to ensure the stability of the saving and loan industry in Texas. County Savings has been taken over by an unnamed financial group under a plan that has allowed a dozen big institutions to acquire 88 locally owned savings and loans.

This is but one of a slew of banking crises around the globe. Since 1980 when the crisis began, fully two-thirds of the 182 nations belonging to the International Monetary Fund have suffered similar problems. Faltering confidence in saving and loan institutions is rampant.

A tragic accident occurred this afternoon south of Fort Worth on a high-rise bridge over I-20 when a car collided with a van. People erupted from both vehicles and a deadly confrontation ensued. One man was shot and killed, and an unidentified woman fell from the bridge to the highway below and is in critical condition. Names are withheld prior to notification of the victims' families. Eyewitnesses say that another woman carrying a small child fled from the scene. There is no news of their whereabouts.

Coming up next is the weather forecast for the Dallas/Fort Worth area …

"**That has to be** my sister. Oh, dear Lord, she fell off that bridge. I knew something happened to her. He didn't mention my nephew, did he fall too?" She rocked back and forth with tears running down her cheeks.

"You have to call the police. They need to know you and Sophie are safe," Pastor Crane said. "They will know what hospital your sister is in."

The young woman looked at him with sheer panic on her face. "There are problems, I'm afraid to call the police."

She couldn't help but think about what happened last spring. Someone, somebody had removed every record of her dad's life, even his grave had disappeared. *Would we have been next? Would my sister and I have vanished like daddy if Joey hadn't crashed into us? Oh, Lord, what is happening?*

"Do you want to tell us about it? Maybe between us, we can figure out what to do. And maybe it's time you tell us your name."

She raised her head and wiped away the tears with shaking hands. "I'm sorry, I can't explain, Pastor Crane. But I do need to tell you who I am. I'm Kris Davenport Williams. My husband is Jeffrey Williams, and we live in Dallas. The man on the news who was shot is Joey Parrino, my sister's husband. That's why I'm so scared, I saw them shoot him.

I've been afraid they would find us, I'm scared they've done something to my husband, he should have answered the phone."

Cathy sat down beside her and held her hand. "How about your parents, maybe we could call them?"

"Oh, I wish I could, but I can't. Mom's out of town and I don't have her phone number," her voice faded as her mind took over again.

Mrs. Crane watched the confusion filtering across Kris' face. Looking up at her husband, she motioned to him. "It's time to eat supper, help me put it on the table. I think Sophie is hungry, she's getting restless. We'll all feel better if we eat."

The soup was hot and good, and Kris' stomach settled down. Sophie had eaten and was back on the floor playing with Abby and the toys Cathy pulled out of a closet. Her daughter was laughing and that helped, it helped a lot.

"That was delicious, Cathy, thank you. Sophie and I haven't had anything to eat since breakfast."

Her daughter was playing with the dog and giggling. Kris stood up saying she needed to be alone for a few minutes. She had to figure out what, if anything, she could tell Pastor Crane. Rain was coming down in torrents when she stepped out on the front porch and looked across the field at the bushes. She shivered and wrapped her arms around her body. She and Sophie would still be out there except for these kind people.

Who would kidnap my sister and me? And why, we're not rich or famous. Is it about daddy, could he really be alive? The only thing mom would say was that whatever happened he had no choice in the matter of his death. And that makes no sense at all.

If only I knew how to reach mom. Oh, sis, I'm so in the dark, I've never been this alone. You've got to be all right. Please, Laurie, I need you to answer me...

Chapter 4

*T*HIS IS A FIRST, *something to write in the baby book. My son actually slept all night.* As grateful as she was for the sleep, she knew she better get up. He would be waking up soon and she would love to have a cup of coffee first. She tried to sit up.

Wow, I'm so stiff it's hard to move. She tried again, but nothing happened. *I must have slept really heavy, or I'm still asleep and dreaming.*

She reached up to push her hair out of her eyes. Her arm didn't move, she couldn't make her fingers move either—nothing moved.

Okay, I'm ready to wake up now.

She struggled to see. She wasn't sure if her eyes were open or not, maybe her hair was covering her face. All she could see was darkness, it must still be night. There were sounds around her. She heard a door open and close and someone walking. She couldn't make her body move. She should be able to see and get up…sheer terror welled up inside her and she screamed.

No sound broke the silence.

"EASY NOW, USE THE sheet to roll her over. Be careful, besides the broken arm, she has internal injuries and cuts and bruises all over her body." The nurse gently smoothed the patient's hair away from her eyes. "She's very pretty. I wish we knew her name so we could call her family. It's not good for her to be alone."

"I haven't seen anyone in a coma before," said the helper in the intensive care unit. "She hasn't opened her eyes since she's been here. Will she be all right?"

"I hope so, she's young and that's on her side. Dr. Reynolds says there's a skull fracture and concussion. If the swelling gets any worse, he may have to operate to relieve the pressure."

The nurse checked the IV in the young woman's arm then pulled the sheet around her. "The police think she either fell or was pushed off the high part of the bridge on Interstate 20 on the south side of Fort Worth. They have no idea how she survived the fall. It's amazing she's still alive."

"That's horrible. Has she been awake at all?"

"No. Not yet."

"When do you think she'll wake up?"

"The doctor hasn't said and there's no way to predict. Comas can last a few days, sometimes longer. The longer a person is in a coma the less likely she'll recover. In the meantime, we have to watch for any signs of waking. It won't happen all at once, maybe a second or two at first. Then the time she's awake will gradually increase. I want you to sit here and talk to her. If you see her eyelids fluttering or any tiny movement, call me at once."

"Can she hear us talking?"

"It's possible she can hear us and, if she can, it could be frightening so talk to her. Tell her who you are, where she is, and we're here to help her. Tell her your name and ask what her name is. Ask about her family, anything to stimulate her mind."

I HEAR YOU, I CAN HEAR you. I'm trying to move my eyes, the young woman cried. *Help me, oh, please help me. I want my baby.*

"I have to check on the man in the next room. I'll be back in shortly, and we'll turn her again. Keep talking to her."

Don't go, please don't go. Coma—is she talking about me? Is that why I can't move? She tried to sit up again, but she couldn't. There was a different voice talking, much too soft. She needs to speak louder.

I can't hear you, please talk louder. Who are you?

"ANY CHANGE?" THE NURSE asked when she came back in the room.

"No, she hasn't moved."

"I'll stay with her for a while. Bring me some crushed ice; I want to moisten her mouth." Patti Coleson had been a nurse in the ICU for years and had worked with a number of coma patients. There was something different about this young woman, she felt like the woman was hearing her. She leaned over the bed talking to her, "What happened to you, honey? If you can tell me your name, I'll call your family. I know it's hard to do, but keep trying and in time you will be able to." She finger combed the young woman's hair and arranged it on the pillow. "You have such pretty hair."

When the helper brought the ice, the nurse placed a small piece on her lips. "Open your mouth, honey. This is a little ice chip and it will make your mouth feel better."

I CAN HEAR YOU. I'm trying to open my mouth, I'm so thirsty. Oh, that feels so good on my lips. She felt the moisture slip in her mouth.

"Who are you, dear? If you can tell me your name, I'll find your family. What is your name?"

Name… Name… What is my name? I don't know. She felt like her heart was going to jump out of her chest. *I don't know my name, but I know I have a baby, a little boy. Where is he? I want my son. I have to find my son.*

She screamed again, but she heard no sound.

Chapter 5

WALKING UP AND DOWN the front porch of the pastor's home in Burleson, Kris wrapped her arms around her body trying to stay warm. There was nothing she could hold on to, no mom, dad, husband, or sister. She'd always had her sister to talk to, no matter where they were. Even if they were apart they could still communicate. This must be how people feel who don't have a twin. She'd never been this alone before.

Everybody had disappeared. She'd heard nothing from her mom's husband, Nathan. She had called his office and gone over to the house many times, but she hadn't seen or heard from him in six months. She had no idea what happened to him, so many unknowns.

"I can't call the police, I don't know who to trust," she moaned aloud.

If mom was right and daddy is alive, she didn't want to do anything to jeopardize his or her mom's safety if she was with him. That was a really big *if*—thinking daddy might be alive, but if he isn't, where was her mother? If he is, whoever was after him could be the one who kidnapped us. Kris froze. That's it; that must be it. They were going to use us to get to dad, that's why they took us. Well, if that's the case, she couldn't explain any of this to these kind people, she could not put them in danger. Cold and shaking and more confused than before Kris went back inside the house.

Pastor Crane was pacing and started talking as soon as she walked in. "Obviously you can't go home. Whoever kidnapped you will know from the news that your sister is in a hospital in Fort Worth. I think you and Sophie are safe here, there's no way they could connect you to a minister in Burleson. However, your sister may not be safe in the hospital. I think you should let the police know about the kidnapping. Can you think of anyone who might help you find out about your husband?"

"Maybe, mom had a friend who's a detective with Dallas police. He was trying to help us last March when mom disappeared, but I don't know his phone number. It's in my address book at home. I guess I could call the police department and ask for him, but I'd probably have to leave a message. That could be a problem."

"We could try looking his home number up. I have a Dallas phone directory in my office or we could also try information," Pastor Crane said as he left the room.

He was back quickly with the directory. "What's his name?

"Herman Wilkens, but I don't think home numbers of policemen are listed."

"You're right. I should have thought of that. Okay, the only thing left is to call the police department in Dallas. Don't tell them this number; just say you'll call back."

Kris picked up the phone and dialed. Her voice quivered when she asked to speak to Herman Wilkens.

"Detective Wilkens isn't here. Can someone else help you?"

"No, it's personal. He's a friend of my family."

"Hang on a minute, the chief just walked by. Let me check with him."

Kris waited anxiously. The operator came back on the line saying, "I'm transferring you to the chief."

"Chief Sanders. You want to speak with Detective Wilkens?"

"Yes, sir, he's a friend of my family and I've lost his home phone number."

"Are you Kris or Laurie?"

Panic seized her and her throat tightened. "I, uh, why do you want to know?"

"I know that both Davenport daughters and their children were kidnapped today. I'll help you if I can."

Silence hung heavy while she tried to decide whether to answer or hang up. There was no choice, she needed Herman. "I'm Kris. I saw the six o'clock news. I'm the one who got away. I need to find Herman."

There was a pause before the chief responded. "I understand, Kris. Are you under any duress? If you are, use the name, Molly, in your next sentence. That's Herman's wife."

"No, I'm not under duress. I'm in a safe place. I can't find my husband and I'm worried about him. I need to know about Jeff and what hospital Laurie is in. "

"Where are you? Give me the address."

"I'm safe, Chief Sanders, but I'm not telling anyone where I am. Please, tell me what you know about my husband and my sister."

"I'll find Herman. Give me a number where he can call you."

"You get Herman for me or get me a number where I can call him. I'll call back in an hour." Kris broke the connection and looked up at Pastor Crane. "I hope I wasn't on the line long enough for them to trace the call."

Sophie was getting fussy and sleepy and Kris picked her up. She curled up in a big rocker hugging her daughter. Holding her daughter and rocking was soothing, but it didn't stop her thoughts. Since hearing the news report, she was having visions of her sister falling off the bridge. *If you can hear me, Laurie, please answer. Just say anything. I need to know you're alive.* She was getting feelings of sheer panic and fear, but she didn't know if it was her own feelings or if it was coming from her sister.

"Kris, I've made up the beds in our spare bedroom for you and Sophie," Mrs. Crane said. "It has a baby bed my grandchildren use and it's all ready. Sophie looks like she is out for the night."

Kris eased up with Sophie tight in her arms and followed Mrs. Crane. The room was pleasant and there was a small night light on the dresser. She put Sophie in the bed. She wiggled, stretched, and was sound asleep when Kris pulled the blanket around her. "Sweet dreams, baby," she whispered. Kris didn't want to leave her and stood in the doorway watching Sophie for a long time.

MRS. CRANE WATCHED ANXIOUSLY, she shivered imagining how she would feel if she had gone through what this young woman did today. *We have to help these two children and also the young woman who fell from the bridge. Please protect them, Lord, wherever they are.*

KRIS HAD TO FIND some answers so she followed Mrs. Crane back to the den, but her stomach churned as she walked away from Sophie.

Her body felt like she had been beaten up. Every part of her either hurt or throbbed or was sore, particularly her feet. She was wearing sandals when they kidnapped her and they were not much better than being barefooted. What she wanted was to take a long hot bath, she wondered if it would be rude to ask. But that had to wait. She had to talk to Herman first and find out where Jeffrey was and why some stranger answered the phone at her house.

Pastor Crane was watching the news when they got back to the den. "They haven't said anything new," he told Kris. "It's been about an hour, I think you should call again. Maybe your detective friend will know about your husband and sister."

Her hands were shaking as she made the call. *Please, please, Herman, be there. Is this what daddy was trying to protect us from?* When his voice came on the line, she broke into tears again. "Herman, oh, Herman, I'm so glad to hear your voice. Do you know where Jeff is? I can't reach him. And Laurie, what hospital is she in? Is Nicky all right? Have you heard from my mom?"

"Whoa, slow down, Kris, take a deep breath. I'll answer what I can, but first you need to tell me where and how you are."

"I'm in Burleson at the home of a minister and his wife. Sophie and I are both okay, just exhausted and scared. Herman, please don't tell anyone where I am, I don't trust anybody except you."

"I won't tell anyone. How did you get there, that's miles from where the wreck happened?"

"I ran for a long time carrying Sophie. After that, I walked until I couldn't keep going. I was exhausted and sick at my stomach so we hid in some bushes at the side of the road. That's where Pastor Crane found us."

"Do you know these people?"

"No, he was walking his dog out in the field when he heard Sophie crying and found us."

"Give me the address, Kris, and I'll come get you."

"Please, Herman, tell me about Jeff and Laurie."

"Let me talk with the pastor first, Kris. I need to be sure you are in safe hands."

Kris handed the phone to Pastor Crane. They talked several minutes before he passed the phone back to Kris.

"Okay, Kris, here's the plan. I have the address and it's about an hour drive. I'll get there as fast as I can, but it will depend on traffic and the weather. Sit down and rest, take a nap if you can. I'll take you and Sophie back to my house. You can't go home, it might not be safe. Kris, Jeff was injured and is in the hospital. As soon as you get Sophie settled at my house I'll take you to him. Molly will be happy to take care of Sophie. We have a baby bed and lots of grandchildren's clothes at the house. I'll leave an officer there so you won't have to worry. How does this sound?"

"Why is Jeff in the hospital? What happened to him?"

"He was shot, Kris. He's in surgery right now."

All the color left Kris' face, "How bad is it, Herman?"

"We can talk when I get there; I need to get on the road. Get some rest if you can." With that, he hung up.

Kris knew her husband was bad or Herman would have told her he was okay. She turned and looked at her new friends and the tears started again. She'd never cried so much in all her life as she had today. She'd never been one who cried when she was sad or when things went wrong, but today changed all that. She had never been kidnapped before—and she had never seen anyone murdered before.

She turned away from the Cranes and stared out the window. Laurie's husband was dead, she knew that for sure. Jeff was in surgery, was her husband still alive? Tears streaked down her face.

A jagged bolt of lightning split the dark sky and Kris saw the clump of bushes she and Sophie had taken refuge in. She shivered as thunder rumbled overhead shaking the house.

Laurie hadn't answered her—her sister had never failed to answer before.

Was she alive?

Chapter 6

JENNIE DAVENPORT SAT STRAIGHT up in bed. She had not had a dream this disturbing since the one she had about Josh when he told her he was alive, and that dream came true. This time was different; it was a nightmare about her daughters. It slammed into her in the middle of the night and scared her. A dark foreboding took hold of her.

Something had happened to Kris and Laurie. She panicked and jumped out of bed. Standing at the window, she watched flashes of light ripple across the lake far below her as a new day began rolling over the mountains. Still trembling from the nightmare that awakened her, she opened the window and drew deep breaths of cold air. She could hear the wind whistling through the trees and the lonely sound of a faraway train. She shivered as frigid air blew around her. She looked at the bed to reassure herself Josh was there, that the man in her bed was really alive.

She closed the window and crawled back under the warm covers and snuggled against her husband hoping to free herself of the nightmare. Unless she was touching him, she still had trouble believing he was alive and she was with him. His arm reached out and pulled her closer.

Josh Davenport tightened his arms around her. "What's bothering you, honey? You've been up and down most of the night and now you're shaking."

"I'm sorry, Josh, I know this sounds crazy. I'm afraid something is wrong with our daughters. It swept over me during the night and I can't get rid of the feeling."

Josh turned on the lamp beside the bed. When he saw Jennie's face he got out of the massive bed and put on a heavy robe. "I'll check right now."

"It's too early, come back to bed. It's only about five o'clock.

"I learned long ago to trust instincts. It's the same as when you feel the wind, it's blowing from somewhere and you'd better pay attention because a storm may be brewing. Wrap up warmly and come to the office with me. I'll make a call and check on our daughters, we'll see if they are okay."

She inched out of the warm bed and picked up her robe. The room was freezing and she couldn't stop shaking, she wasn't sure if it was the cold or if it was fear. Both, she thought. She was still cold from standing at the open window. Slipping her feet in fur-lined slippers, she pulled a wool robe tight around her. She stirred up the embers in the fireplace then took time to add another log. Josh was taking this seriously and guilt grabbed hold of her again. She was really scared now. It was her fault if something had happened to their daughters; she had left them alone. She'd wrestled with this for the past six months. How could she have left her daughters? They knew nothing about the things Josh was involved in. They didn't know about the vicious group trying to kill him. They didn't even know he was alive.

Jennie swayed and caught hold of the bed post. "It isn't right for me to be safe when my daughters are not. Oh, Lord, please, they have to be all right," she cried aloud and ran to Josh's office.

Ever since she left Dallas, she'd struggled with the fear that something might happen to Kris and Laurie. Everything Josh told her had made this fear more real. He'd told her all about the *Brotherhood* and his meeting with the president. He said that after he had agreed to the president's challenge to try and block the *Brotherhood's plans*, he'd realized he would need another identity and a secure haven where he and his family could live in safety someday. Josh understood and accepted this job would put him in danger. He also recognized the possibility of danger to his family and that was something he would never tolerate.

In his off-duty times Josh had hiked in the mountains of Scotland, it was far removed from the stress of his life and it helped to keep him grounded. On one of these excursions, he chanced upon a castle and he knew from the first glance he had found his home. It was exactly like he and Jennie had dreamed of building even down to the small ponies that were wandering around the grassy slopes. He bought the castle under the alias, Alexander Cameron, the name he'd used for years when he needed to disappear. Layers of security had been installed around the castle making it as safe as possible from the *Brotherhood*.

No matter what was happening now, Jennie knew it was time to go home. She couldn't stay here if her daughters were not safe, Josh would just have to understand.

Waiting for the call to go through to the Army Command Center of G-2, Josh watched emotions flicker across Jennie's face. He thought about the problems she had in getting to the Compound last April. She'd shown good instincts when faced with the adversities of changing the plans he'd made for her. She coped well and managed to get to London on her own. She also figured out who the man was the *Brotherhood* sent to kill him. When the assassin found him, Jennie threw herself between them and took a bullet meant for him. That was a bad time, a really awful time, and he never wanted anything like that to happen that again. During the past six months, he'd realized how much she'd changed during the years they had been apart. She was much stronger now. He loved the new woman she'd become.

It took a long time to get through to the command center. It was morning in Washington, D.C. and Josh was relieved when General Thurman came on the line.

"Kidnapped, damn it, General, how the hell did this happen? Where were the guards? Who's out there in Texas? Details, give me details."

"Slow down, Davenport, Al Lindberg is on the way to Texas as we speak. The police chief in Dallas informed me that Kris made contact with Herman Wilkens and is safe. We don't have any firm information about Laurie yet. All we know is that an unidentified woman fell from a bridge and is in a hospital in Fort Worth. We're waiting on our man to find out if it's Laurie."

"What about my grandchildren, Sophie and Nicholas?"

"Sophie is safe with Kris. I've had no information at all about the boy. I don't know if he was taken when they took Laurie. We're trying to find out."

JOSH CHANGED RIGHT BEFORE Jennie's eyes to a man she didn't know. His eyes went feral and cold, even his stance changed. It scared her and she wanted to run away. Here was the man the general had told her about, the one who did missions for the president, the one who rescued Jack Harrell from a prison behind the iron curtain. This was not the man she knew, but she was not going to run away. She had to find out what happened to her daughters. Something was very, very wrong.

"I'm on my way, General. I'll be in Texas before dark. When I get there, I want to know exactly where my daughters are. I'll be in touch later today." Josh slammed the phone down and stormed around the room. If the man known in Scotland as Alexander Cameron had a vulnerable spot, it was Jennie and his daughters. They were his Achilles' heel, the one place someone could get to him.

"What's happened, Josh? The girls …?"

Josh charged out of his office and down the hall. He pounded on the door to Jack Harrell's room yelling, "Get the helicopter ready, we leave for the airport as soon as we're dressed."

Jennie followed and grabbed him by the arm. "What happened, Josh? Tell me."

"Someone kidnapped our daughters yesterday morning. Kris and Sophie got away and they are safe. The general didn't have much information about Laurie or Nicky."

Jennie's legs buckled and she fell on a bench in the hallway. A very rumpled Jack Harrell came out of his room asking what the devil was going on. Owen Blakely showed up a couple of seconds after Harrell.

"My daughters and grandchildren were kidnapped. I'm guessing the *Brotherhood* took them in an attempt to draw me out. Kris and Sophie managed to escape. There's an unidentified woman in a Fort Worth hospital they think might be Laurie, her condition is unknown. No info about my grandson right now. Harrell, have the Learjet checked out, gassed up, and on the airstrip. Blakely, Doc Fitz hasn't cleared you for action yet. You'll have to stay here and be our contact man."

He looked at his very sleepy pilot still standing there, "Move it, Harrell, get dressed."

Josh turned to face Jennie saying, "I want to know exactly what you were feeling last night. Tell me everything that caused you to know something was wrong."

She looked into those cold eyes and stammered, "Crazy, irrational thoughts and pictures bombarded my mind. I really couldn't see much except for blood, lots of it. It was horrible, Josh. The overwhelming feeling was that our daughters were crying. My head hurt like I had been hit, and then confusion. Mostly I felt fear and panic. Muddled sounds came through, like someone trying to call for help, but couldn't no matter how hard she tried."

"Could you see where they were?"

"Not really. It seemed to be high up, maybe a bridge, I saw railings. There were cars and people running all directions. Does that help?"

"Not yet, but it may make sense later. Wake James and Darcy and have them get coffee and food ready for everybody," Josh walked rapidly away.

Jennie raced after him. "I'm going with you, Josh."

Josh stopped so abruptly she bumped into him. "No way, Jennie, you're staying here with Owen. You were shot trying to get here and I will not put you back in danger. You are staying here."

Hands on her hip, Jennie planted herself in front of her husband, "I am not staying here, Josh. You left me once and you will not do it again. Besides, it's been six years and you don't even know what our daughters or grandchildren look like. I do. No compromise, I am going back." Her face was unyielding when she turned and punched the bell to call the staff for food.

"You are not going, Jennie. I have to know you're safe."

"Yes, I am. You can't stop me. You can leave without me, but I will just get there by myself." She glared at Josh for a couple of seconds. "You know I can." She turned her back to him and marched down the hall.

BLAKELY HAD SEEN THAT look several times before. The first time was when she swung her purse at the man who tried to grab her in Chicago, then again in Atlanta when she doubled Nathan Scott over with a well-placed knee jab. He smiled, that traitor deserved that and more. And still again on the presidential plane when she surfaced after hiding out for an hour and demanded the steward prepare her breakfast. This man turned out to be the assassin the *Brotherhood* sent to kill Davenport. The last time was when she stepped in front of Josh and took a bullet meant for him. Blakely couldn't hold back a slight grin when he saw her stalk off in the direction of her bedroom. Davenport didn't have a chance, he had to take her.

"What are you smirking at, Blakely?" Davenport roared. At this moment, Davenport wasn't so sure he did like the new woman Jennie had become.

Chapter 7

SHE FELT A PRESENCE in the room then heard slow deliberate steps, heavy footsteps like a big man, they were coming towards her. It was not the usual brisk ones of the nurses. The young woman in the hospital bed struggled again and again to open her eyes. *You can do it…just open your eyes. Move your hand…press the call button…*

Who's there, she cried. *Help me….*

No sound came from her mouth.

No expression crossed the woman's face when the man walked over and stood by the bed staring at her, his dead eyes boring into her. The heavily built man watched for any sign she knew he was there, he saw no change in her features. Maybe the doctor was right when he said the woman was in a coma and not likely to come out of it. He said the head injury was severe and, coupled with internal injuries, the prognosis was not good.

He leaned over her and blew hard on her closed eyes. He watched for a minute then blew again and touched both of her hands.

Waves of evil flowed over her, she felt hot air on her face then something rough touched her hands.

Her eyelids didn't twitch, there was no movement of any kind and her expression never changed. He rubbed his calloused hand all over her face and head then wrapped his hand around her throat. She didn't recoil when he exerted pressure.

Terror mounted in the young woman as she felt a rough hand surround her throat. *Help me, he's choking me…let go…* she screamed.

Someone help me. Her heart was pounding so hard she thought it would burst. *Help me…*

"Reprieve, you get to live one more day." He pulled his hand away from her throat. "It's best if I let you die a natural death."

Who are you, I know you're here. Are you the one who pushed me off the bridge?

The man walked away then whirled around trying to catch her moving. She didn't stir when he went back to her bed and touched her face again. He leaned down and whispered in her ear.

"The living dead, you are already dead. All I have to do is wait a day or two."

Her insides quivered as she heard that deep rasping whisper and her fear mounted. *Go away, please go away,* she cried. *I'm not dead, I'm alive.*

She listened as slow ominous steps moved away from her. She couldn't breathe.

She heard his footsteps stop… *Keep going, please go away…*

As if he heard her, the man stopped at the door of her room and turned his lifeless eyes on her once again. "Just in case you can hear me, I suggest you don't wake up. You won't like it if you do."

Once more, those unhurried steps echoed in the quiet room as he left. When he left the ICU, he walked a little faster down the long shadow-filled hallway and slipped quietly in the door to the staircase. For a big man, Otto Fleicher moved with almost no sound. He went down the steps and out of the building.

Help me, somebody please help me, I'm alive. She screamed and screamed…

And again, no sound came from the body in the hospital bed.

"**WHAT'S HAPPENING TO YOU,** honey?" a familiar voice asked as the nurse ran into the room. "The monitor is going off."

She checked the equipment hooked up to the young woman, it was working properly. She looked around the room; nothing was out-of-place. She dampened a washcloth and wiped the young woman's face as she watched the monitor. Her heart rate was gradually slowing down.

The nurse lifted the sheets and checked all the connections then covered her up again. "You're okay, just breathe slower." She drew a chair up beside the bed and picked up the young woman's hand and stroked it. "You'll feel better in a few minutes," she said in a soft voice. "I wish you could tell me why you're so upset."

Someone was here. He came in my room and threatened me. He put his hand around my throat...

Her blood pressure was coming down. "I believe you know I'm here. I'm pretty sure you can hear so listen to me. I want you to take some deep breaths and calm down. I think you had a panic attack. I'm going to bring a radio in here and find some nice soothing music to keep you company. I'll be back in a few minutes, keep breathing deeply, slow and easy. I won't be gone long."

Oh, please, please, hear me. I can hear you, why can't you hear me? I'm alive, you have to help me...don't leave me alone.

I'm so scared...

Chapter 8

YESTERDAY KRIS DAVENPORT WILLIAMS thought kidnapping was the worst thing that could ever happen to her.

The drive from Burleson to Dallas flew by in a blur. The phone was ringing when Herman opened the front door of his home. The nurse from the hospital said Jeff was out of surgery and they should come right away, he was critical. Kris started shaking and she sat down on the nearest chair. Her mind flew to the night her dad died, that horrible time when she, Laurie, and her mom had gone to the hospital in the early morning hours before daylight. She'd watched her mother slowly sink to the floor in pain and anguish, and now, it was her husband who might be dying. She looked around the room, she felt so alone, no one except Herman to stand between her and what had become a vicious world. *Laurie, please talk to me, I need to know you're alive…*

The last twenty-four hours had run together in a muddle of pain and sheer exhaustion. She hated leaving Sophie, but it was better for her daughter to stay with Molly. It broke her heart to leave without her and she cried all the way to the hospital. She knew Sophie would be scared and confused when she woke up because that was exactly how she was feeling. The police officer guarding the house assured her he would not leave. He swore he would keep Sophie safe.

As soon as she and Herman arrived at the hospital, the doctor said they had done all they could for her husband. The bullet caused major damage and he lost too much blood. If help had arrived sooner, he might have had a chance.

When she saw Jeff her knees almost buckled, he was so pale and tubes were everywhere. The nurse looked at her then back at the monitor and shook her head, the monitor had stopped beeping. She was too late, he was already gone.

*Oh, Lord, this isn't real, Jeff can't be dead. It's just a nightmare…*she didn't get to say goodbye or tell him she loved him. The room spun around her, her legs gave way and she grabbed hold of Herman. Her anguished sobs were muffled by his shoulder.

HERMAN FOUGHT TO STAY calm. He was not a patient man. He needed to hit something or somebody. This was the last straw. He'd had more than enough of the strange occurrences surrounding Davenport's death and his family. It started with missing paperwork at the precinct then the situation got more serious when his old friend, Carl Kimbrell, found Davenport's Army files were missing. Kimbrell tried to get Davenport's top security file, but someone found out and the next day he was sent to Greenland. Soon after that the situation went from bad to worse, and Davenport's grave disappeared. While Herman was still trying to figure out how and when that happened, Jennie left for parts unknown. She left her daughters without telling them where she was going and he had no idea where she was. It hadn't stopped there, Nathan Scott, Jennie's second husband, vanished a few days after she did and hadn't been heard from. And, if that wasn't enough, Herman still didn't know if Davenport was dead or alive.

There was no doubt in his mind that the players who controlled these incidents abducted Kris and Laurie and murdered Laurie's husband. And now, Kris' husband had died from a gunshot. The twins had become widows, and it was so wrong. They were only twenty-four years old, the same age as his daughter.

"Wherever the hell you are, Jennie, you need to come home. Your daughters need you," he mumbled under his breath as he held the sobbing young woman. He had to find Jennie. If Davenport was alive, the man had to come back and take care of his family.

As soon as Herman could he was calling the Chief of Staff at INSCOM. They pulled him into the middle of this when they ordered him to provide security at Davenport's funeral, and then again when he was assigned to watch the Davenport home for several months. He was there when all this started, and he was going to finish it or die in the attempt.

Yep, I need to hit something or somebody. The former football fullback was way past the end of his patience. He was calling INSCOM, the hell with protocol and the hell with what Chief Sanders said. There was a limit to how much a man could put up with. He wrapped his arms tighter around Kris.

I HEAR YOU, WHO ARE you? I can hear you…

Kris jerked away from Herman, "Did you hear that?"

"Hear what?"

"I heard a voice saying *I hear you, who are you*? If you didn't hear it then it's Laurie trying to talk to me."

"I didn't hear anything except hospital noises and the PA system paging a doctor. What do you mean, it's Laurie?"

"Laurie and I can talk, Herman. We've always been able to hear each other in our minds, it's a twin thing. I haven't heard anything from her since the car wreck and I've been trying to get through to her. Why would she be asking *who are you*? She knows it's me."

Herman's face darkened, his brows drew together in confusion. "I haven't a clue, honey. If you can do that, ask her where she is and I'll go get her."

"She's not making any sense, she's just mumbling," Kris could not take her eyes off Jeff. She kept watching him and praying he would open his eyes or move. Maybe the monitor had malfunctioned. Kris turned away wondering if this was real or a nightmare, maybe she would wake up in the morning and everything would be all right.

"Herman, that nurse keeps motioning at me, I guess I have to talk to her." Her head throbbed, she rubbed her forehead.

"Sit down, Kris, you don't have to do anything right now," Herman said.

"I hate whoever did this. I want my husband and my life back. I want to wake up and these two days never happened." Tears streamed down her pale face. "I'm so tired and confused, I can't think anymore."

"Stay here. I'll talk to the nurse." Herman dug in his pocket trying to find his handkerchief then grabbed a handful of tissues from the side table and handed them to Kris. "They need to know about a funeral home. What about Sparkman Hillcrest where your dad is? Will that be all right?"

Kris nodded and Herman went to the nurse's station muttering, "Damn it, Josh, your daughter needs you. If you're alive, get yourself home."

Kris moved the chair closer to Jeff and stared at his face, she tried to memorize every feature. Visions of their wedding passed before her, she could see Jeff smiling at her when she walked down the aisle. She loved him so much; there was no way she could go on without him. Sophie would miss all the fun times with her daddy, no more piggy back rides, no more playing chase or hide and seek. Sophie would never get to really know him; she was so young she might not even remember him. Kris's stomach churned at the thought and her head throbbed.

The constant mumblings running through her head made no sense and Kris was getting more and more anxious. It had to be Laurie and she wasn't making any sense. "It's too much, Lord. Help me, I can't even think. This can't be real."

She stood up and walked over to the window and stared out. *Maybe Jeff will open his eyes when I turn around,* she thought. *Maybe...*

Nothing changed, Jeff hadn't moved. It was impossible to let go, no one should ever have to do that. She picked up his hand and ran her fingers over his wedding ring, "I promise you, we'll get the people who did this. One way or other, they are not going to get away with it. I'm so sorry, my love."

She tried to tell him she and Sophie would be all right, but she didn't really believe it. She had never felt so scared and alone and lost. She leaned down and kissed her husband's lips, they were already cold and unresponsive—she almost fainted. Kris grabbed hold of the bed railing until the dizziness went away then she gently wiped her tears off his face with a shaking hand.

She couldn't say goodbye, the words would not even form in her mouth. She slipped his ring off his finger and held it tightly. She could never say goodbye. Through blurry eyes, she looked at her love one last time and whispered "Goodnight."

Lost in a maze of pain and hanging on to his ring, Kris turned away from her husband. She was very, very wrong when she thought kidnapping was the worst thing that could happen.

It wasn't.

HERMAN TALKED WITH THE nurse then filled out the paperwork for Kris. When he finished, he sat down at an empty desk and called the precinct. He thought he had heard just about everything, but he was way off base. Chief Sanders told him General Thurman of Army G-2, INSCOM, had called. The chief paused and exhaled, "Davenport is on his way to Texas. He has commandeered you for the duration of his stay."

"How on earth…so Davenport is alive. Is his wife with him?"

"I don't have a clue," answered the chief. "No one is explaining anything. All I know is that for however long Davenport wants you, he's got you."

"When will he get here?"

"Davenport told the general he would be in Texas before dark and would get in touch with you at your home."

"I guess that means I take Kris and go back there and wait."

"That's my best guess. Keep me in the loop, Wilkens."

"I'll do my best, Chief. I know how hard it is to be in the dark, that's where I've been living this past year."

Good luck, Wilkens. Find those bastards that killed Joey Parrino and Jeffrey Williams."

"I will, Chief, I'll do everything in my power. I want them off the face of the earth. There are two young women with babies who are now widows because of them."

KRIS LEANED AGAINST THE edge of the door until she quit shaking. She turned and looked at Jeff one last time. She had to get away from the sounds and smells of the intensive care area and she stumbled out of the room and down the hall. When she came to the waiting area, she collapsed in a chair sobbing. It seemed like she had cried constantly since yesterday morning. She wiped her eyes. What really needed to stop was the craziness going on in her head, but if it was coming from Laurie she didn't want to block her. She had to find her sister.

Drawing her chair closer to the window, she closed her eyes and tried to talk to her. *Laurie, please be quiet a minute, you're not making any sense. I want you to listen to me. I'm your sister, I'm Kris. Are you hurt?*

All she heard was more of the same jumbled words except for an occasional, *I hear you, I'm here.*

Kris was getting a definite feeling that Laurie didn't know who she was, and, worse than that, Laurie didn't know who Laurie was. *I'm your twin sister, my name is Kris. Is your name Laurie?*

I don't know, but I know I have a baby. I want my baby.

Chapter 9

THE PASSENGERS IN THE twin-engine Sikorsky helicopter watched the terrain as the huge chopper lifted higher and higher in the mountains above the small village of Engelberg. This conference was unprecedented; Chairman Houser had called an emergency meeting of the *Brotherhood*. An unplanned gathering spelled trouble and the men were tense.

The six men were part of the ruling body of the group which was comprised of thirteen of the world's most powerful men, five men from the United States, four from the British Isles, and four from Europe. It started in the early 1950s when three separate and powerful groups, the Illuminati from the United States, the Inner Circle from the British Isles, and the Alliance from Europe combined forces and organized a controlling nucleus known as the *Brotherhood*. With the unification of these groups their power became almost unlimited.

The chopper zoomed over the treetops and dropped onto a landing pad fast enough to keep ahead of the swirling snowstorm. When it settled, the men emerged and looked around the area. The *Brotherhood* had met here last February for the group's annual meeting so the men were familiar with the location. Everything was the same as it had been earlier in the year. They cautiously navigated the slippery path to the isolated chalet. The dark-timbered structure was balanced on the edge of a rocky precipice high in the Swiss mountains with Mt. Pilatus looming over it like a sentinel. The rumble of the rotors revving up for takeoff stopped conversation and the chopper lifted off to pick up six more men waiting in the town below. The drone of the blades gradually faded as the men climbed the steps to the entrance.

Chairman Houser's assistant Hans was waiting at the door, "Welcome, gentlemen. I trust your journey went smoothly. You will occupy the same rooms you did in February. If you require anything, please ring and it will be attended to. The meeting will begin promptly at 1100 hours in the conference room at the end of the hall."

The men were solemn when they climbed the curved staircase to the second floor. Apprehension clouded their minds. The unscheduled meeting could mean only one thing; something had gone wrong with their plans.

YEARS OF EXPERIENCE HAD taught Hans to make last-minute inspections of whatever facility the group gathered in. The chairman tolerated no mistakes. The bedrooms were in readiness as was the dining room. The chef already had dinner underway. The last place Hans checked was the conference room. All areas of the room had to be accessible for Chairman Houser's motorized wheelchair. His place was at the head of the large oval table where ample space had been left for the wheelchair to maneuver between the table and credenza. Within reach was a silver tray holding brandy, Evian water, and crystal goblets. A slight deviation today, the chairman had ordered an extra bottle of brandy. A gold gavel lay beside a leather notebook and pen at the chairman's place.

Hans walked around making slight adjustments to the placement of matching notebooks around the table. He had started a fire in the enormous rock fireplace early in the morning and the room was quite comfortable. He looked around the room and nodded.

This was his favorite location for the meetings, he loved the mountains. They called out to Hans. He went over to the ceiling high windows and looked up at Mt. Pilatus' almost seven thousand foot elevation. The magnificent view never failed to move him. He wondered if any of the men ever noticed it, he doubted they paid any attention to it.

Security was of prime importance to the thirteen men attending the meeting. One armed guard stood at attention at the entrance to this room and another on the balcony outside the windows. Other guards were placed strategically around the perimeter of the property.

Hans stirred the fire to a higher blaze. All was ready. He heard the sounds of the helicopter arriving and he rushed out to greet the last six men.

THE MEETING CONVENED ON time. Dr. Claude Houser, chairman of the *Brotherhood,* looked around the room and felt the tension of the assembled men. The men were nervous and so they should be. This was the first time he had ever called an impromptu meeting, however, circumstances demanded it. Their glorious plan to build a new world order under the sole control of the *Brotherhood* was progressing according to schedule. However, there was one critical problem, Davenport had to be stopped. If he wasn't, all could be lost. Anger spread over the chairman's countenance. That man, that deceiver, that traitor had to be eradicated. He shifted his position in his chair attempting to calm down. Thus far, the man had proved elusive and escaped their best efforts. There could be no more excuses, no more mistakes. Davenport was a mere man, he wasn't invincible, even if he did have a way of appearing and disappearing when they least expected it.

The chairman shook with anger. If he could just get out of this damned chair and do the job himself it would already be done. His frustration with incompetent men almost overpowered him. Leaning back he took deep calming breaths. This is our destiny. It is our calling to make this a better world. We cannot let this man destroy us.

He rolled around the room then paused before the glowing fire. The warmth of the burning logs was soothing and his thoughts strayed to the past.

He had carefully selected each man to join in this endeavor. His subordinates had to feel as strongly as he did, he demanded total commitment, and he would accept no less. Together they had the power and means to unite this divided world into one government under their sole control. It would be their gift to all the ignorant people of the world, to all mankind. But that blasted Davenport had to be stopped. He could not endure any more failures to eliminate the man.

His blood pressure skyrocketed. He closed his eyes and settled back in his chair repeating his mantra. *I am the chosen one. I am leader of the new world order. I will succeed.*

The chairman reached in the side pocket of his chair and pulled out a pointed spear, the *Spear of Destiny*. His eyes feasted on it. He had waited so long for it and its mystical powers, Charlemagne carried it into battle, and now it was his. He fondled the spear running his fingers up and down the smooth blade feeling the power flow into him, ecstasy spread over his face. *Oh, yes, the power is mine. I will not be stopped by that madman. He will be exterminated this time.*

Calm at last, he took a deep breath and relaxed his shoulders. Rolling back to the head of the table he watched the men entering. He waited until all were settled then asked the man on his right to pour brandy and pass it around. *I will make them understand.* He picked up the gold gavel and rapped on the table.

"Gentlemen, I have good news. Although the time is not ripe yet, it is in sight. America is filled with monomaniacs, simple-minded people whose values are unsettled, whose only thoughts are on their puny lives. They focus solely on what is in front of them at the moment. They do not see the big picture as you and I do, their eyes are blinded to the future. American society is reaching a place where somebody who is absolutely sure of his position can step in and carry the day. That, my brothers, will be our time, the time of the *Brotherhood,* and we will reign."

His words brought a roar of excitement. Applause exploded all around the room as twelve of the world's most powerful men jumped to their feet. Gratification and excitement filled their faces, their day was coming. The news was good and their anxiety evaporated.

Chairman Houser rolled his motorized wheelchair around the ornately paneled room. He watched and waited until the men settled back in their seats. Very good, the men were with him.

He raised his hands for silence then began to speak. "Thank you, gentlemen, it is only a matter of time until we wipe out the capitalist system. Khrushchev warned long ago we could not expect the gullible Americans to fly from capitalism to communism instantly. They are too embedded in doing only what they want. Thus far, our mission has been to assist the leaders in giving the sleeping Americans small doses of socialism. Our strategy has been to destroy capitalism from within by gradually removing all control from the hands of the people and eliminating the Constitution. We'll keep weakening the economy and making the people dependent on the government for their every need until America falls like overripe fruit into our hands. On that day, they will wake up to find they are fully enmeshed in communism with us in charge."

The room exploded in excitement again.

He let the excitement run its course. "Two major phases are actually ahead of schedule. America's financial institutions along with many other global ones will be fully under our control within two or three years. This will enable us to be in command of the interest rates and, therefore, the economy of America and all other nations. The continual diversions we have created are keeping the naive Americans from focusing on the banking takeovers. The savings and loans are already in our hands. We have made great strides in orchestrating what the newspapers, television and radio programs show and tell. Now that television is under our leadership, we can manipulate most people through subliminal messages."

The men rose again and called out, "Let us raise our glasses to the emergence of the *Brotherhood*."

All turned and saluted the chairman repeating, "To our glorious future."

"It's a chess game, gentlemen, and we are winning. The stock market takeover comes during the 1990s, control of food by 1998, gas and oil by 2000, the airlines by 2002, and electricity by 2005. After that, with our man in the White House the military forces and medical community will belong to us. That means total power, gentlemen, we will smite our enemies and take our rightful place as leaders of the world. The future is indeed ours."

The men rose to their feet once more with thunderous applause. Another round of brandy was poured and glasses lifted again in a toast to the chairman. Houser bowed his head and crossed his hands over his chest in acceptance of the acclamation that was rightfully his.

The chairman watched as the men settled back in their seats sipping their brandy and visualizing the future. They were fully with him and faces were flushed with excitement. Now was the time to rally them to the cause.

"Glorious as that is, we are at an impasse; one that could destroy us," said Chairman Houser. He struggled to his feet, his face reddened with the effort. "It is Joshua Davenport, the man who became a part of our elite assembly, the man who betrayed us. He is jeopardizing our plans. He is wrecking years of careful placement of our people and is systematically removing them from key positions." He grabbed hold of the marble table and rocked back and forth bellowing in rage. "That traitor has now caused another one of our own to perish. It is crucial he be found and stopped. As long as Davenport lives, our plans are in jeopardy. What is the current status, Fleicher?"

The man waiting at the far end of the room stepped forward. "Davenport is like a ghost. We get him in our sights and he disappears. Yesterday brought even more complications, Mr. Chairman. We had

Davenport's two daughters and two grandchildren in custody. We were almost to the private airport when a car driven by the husband of one of the women crashed into us. He jumped out and attacked us yelling for the women to run. The two women with the children took off in opposite directions. One managed to get away with her child; she disappeared in traffic while we were dealing with the husband. The man is no longer a problem, he was eliminated." A glow of pride crossed the speaker's face. "We caught the other daughter, but in the struggle for the child, she backed up and fell off the bridge into the traffic below, twenty, maybe thirty feet. As difficult as it is to believe, she survived that fall and is in a coma in a Fort Worth hospital."

Otto Fleicher, the Enforcer, stopped talking and looked around the room; his lips slowly widened across his face in a smile that never reached his dead eyes. "All is not lost, gentlemen." The menacing man peered intently into the face of each man until he made them squirm then he laughed out loud.

He turned to face the chairman and the grating voice continued, "All is not lost, Chairman Houser. We now have leverage. I have observed the woman who fell off the bridge and she is in a coma near death. I left her alive as bait. I will keep watch on her; however, one way or another she will die when we don't need her anymore." He stopped and looked at the men. "As insurance, I have Davenport's grandson. Davenport will come after the boy."

The men around the table visibly shivered. Fleicher laughed again and announced, "Davenport now belongs to me."

Chapter 10

Monday Night
October 24, 1983
SCOTLAND TO TEXAS

THE LEARJET SLICED THROUGH the sky toward Texas. "I love this plane," Jack Harrell said with a grin. "It was a good choice, particularly if we do very many overseas flights. The extra fuel tank makes a huge difference; we can fly a greater distance without refueling."

Davenport looked up from the map he was studying. "After all the problems Jennie had getting to London last spring, we had to have it. I can't depend on the president to step in and lend me his plane every time I need transport." Davenport's voice roughened as he thought about Kris and Laurie's husbands. Two young men loved by his daughters were murdered, two young men he would never know. "I sure didn't expect to be using it this soon, certainly not to go after my daughters."

"That cursed *Brotherhood*," he muttered. He had no doubt they were responsible. He had no clue how they found out he was alive, but he was damned well going to find out. There had to be a traitor somewhere in G-2.

Davenport watched Harrell at the controls and was grateful this plane was one thing he never had to worry about. Harrell loved flying. He could fly anything that had wings or blades. He had been with him for several years now. It was a wise decision to bring him on board.

Getting Harrell out of that Russian prison had been quite a feat. Davenport smiled and glanced at his friend. That undertaking had given him a trusted friend and pilot. A young man named Gabriel had been in the prison cell with Harrell. There was a lost look in the boy's eyes that struck a chord in Davenport and Harrell and they took him with them.

He had to admit that he and Harrell might not have made it over the wall without Gabriel's help. Gabriel had shown them a place in the wall where the guards could not see them. In return, they helped Gabriel get new identity papers and a job in London. He was doing well in his new life and the three of them had shared some pleasant evenings together.

It had been a roller coaster kind of year. Jennie was with him now and his team was enlarging. Owen Blakely's recovery from the *Brotherhood's* attempt to kill him had been slow and difficult, however, in another month he would be back in action. Dr. Colin Fitzgerald had been a real surprise and a good one. He was a crotchety and unpredictable old Irish doctor who bossed all of them. He had invited himself along with his nurse to join the team and live at the castle. Doc Fitz didn't trust anyone to take care of his patients. "I've saved the lives of both you and Blakely and somebody has to stay around to keep you alive," he told them in no uncertain terms when he announced he and Scully were staying at the castle. Scully didn't say much, but she was a tyrant when it came to her patients. She even bossed Doc. They seemed to function as one, she appeared to read Doc's mind.

Davenport looked back at his wife. "It's been a smooth ride. Jennie seems comfortable back there; she's been asleep for the past hour. How much longer till we get to Hensley Field?"

"About an hour or so, we've made good time," Harrell said.

"Have you flown into Hensley?"

"No, never have. I've flown in and out of Carswell Air Force Base in Fort Worth many times. Air control tells me it's raining again in Texas, but I don't expect any problems."

"Weather report said it's been raining for days and there's some flooding around low-lying areas in Dallas. I know the Trinity River asserts itself every few years." Davenport stood up, stretched, and put the map and several papers on his seat. "I'm going to wake Jennie. She needs to eat and I should tell her our plans. I'll come back shortly and you can take a break. I want you fresh for the landing."

The galley was well stocked; Harrell always took care of it. Josh poured half and half in a cup and filled it with coffee the way Jennie liked, then picked up a sandwich along with a couple of napkins for her and sat down in the adjoining chair. She looked soft and vulnerable, so different from the fiery woman who irritated him earlier. He never understood Jennie's intuition about their daughters, but she had been spot on this morning. He was grateful for it, how ever the thing worked. She did her job of alerting him, now his job was to get their daughters back safe and sound. He had already decided his daughters had to go back to Scotland with them. They would be safe there.

Smiling, he touched Jennie's shoulder and brushed hair off her face. "Time to wake up, we're about an hour from landing in Dallas. I thought you'd want some time to eat and have coffee."

She woke slowly, somewhat confused. "Oh, my, I guess I did go to sleep. I didn't think I'd be able to. Umm, coffee, it smells so good."

Josh handed the cup to her and put the sandwich on the console beside her chair. "This is chicken, but there are ham sandwiches if you'd rather have that. You didn't eat anything earlier and you'll feel better if you do."

She stood up and stretched then sat back down and sipped her coffee. "Thank you for always remembering the cream, it's so good. Chicken is fine, thanks. Where will we land?"

"Hensley Field in Grand Prairie, it's halfway between Dallas and Ft. Worth. It's a naval air station."

"I remember. We used to go to the air shows at Mountain Creek Lake when the girls were little. Remember? We'd drive out there and park by the lake. The girls always wanted to sit on the hood of the car. They thought that was so wonderful.

"I remember, the girls would get excited when we told them where we were going."

Jennie's smile faded away and concern took over. "Josh, I just remembered I didn't get my passport, it's at the castle. What will we do about that?"

"Don't worry about it; I'll take care of it. I'm sorry about this morning, Jennie. I shouldn't have reacted so strongly, it was only because I can't stand the thought of anything happening to you or the girls. I admit to paranoia when it comes to your safety."

It was chilly in the plane and she wrapped her hands around the warm cup as she sipped the coffee. "I knew what you meant this morning, Josh, but I had to come. You know that."

"Understood, but now you have to listen to me. This is important. I don't know what we are going to encounter in Texas. If the *Brotherhood* took the girls, and I feel sure they did, they haven't gone away. I will do everything I can to keep you all safe, but I have to know you will do exactly what I say in an emergency. So, if I say 'hit the floor,' do it instantly. There may not be time for explanations."

"Yes sir, you just want me to be obedient. I'll be the most dutiful little wife you could ever want," Jennie said with a slight smile.

Josh grinned.

"Seriously, Josh, I get what you're saying. General Thurman made a lot of things very clear to me when I was in Atlanta and you've explained even more. I promise to do what you say. You know how worried I have been about our daughters. I have to see them and Sophie and Nicky. So, what's the plan?"

"A car will be waiting for us when we land at Hensley and we'll go directly to Herman's house. The general said Kris and Sophie will be there. I hope by the time we arrive Herman will know about Laurie and Nicky. What we do next depends on what we find out, one step at a time. Right now, you should eat that sandwich. There are some cookies in the service area. I'm going to relieve Jack and give him a coffee break."

"Whoa," Jennie caught his arm and held on to him. "Not so fast, sir, when did you learn to fly?"

"Several years ago, by necessity and under fire, after that I took lessons and got my pilot's license. I've actually learned quite a number of things during the past six years. You might be surprised." His face clouded. There was so much he couldn't explain to her. He could never tell her about the Farm and how he became a non-official covert operative for the Army, a NOC. He couldn't tell her about learning to deceive, to psychologically assess people, and to kill with a variety of weapons or none at all. No, he would not inflict that burden on Jennie.

The last few years weighed heavily on him, particularly the things he'd seen and the skills he wished he'd never learned. Sometimes his mind replayed the past in his sleep and he'd wake up in a cold sweat. What he wanted was to turn the calendar back to earlier times and not know the things he had learned during the past six years. What he wanted deep inside him was to go home again, but that was a dream. He sighed and closed his eyes. He could never go home again. All he could do now was protect his family.

"I probably would be surprised," Jennie reached over and touched his somber face with her fingertips. "I saw a man I didn't know this morning." She pulled him against her and kissed him. "Don't slip away from me, Josh, not again. I'm not ever leaving you and I want the real you with me."

Willing him back to her, she tightened her arms around him for a minute then she leaned back and looked him in the eyes. "Now, go fly this thing, but don't do any fancy rolls or I'll throw up on your pretty airplane."

With tears filling her eyes she watched the man she loved, the man who could turn into a stranger in the blink of an eye, and she knew her fight to bring him back was beginning again.

HARRELL DID HIS USUAL good job, the plane held steady on touchdown and rolled to a stop in a torrential rain storm. Rain hit Davenport in the face when he opened the cabin door. He quickly closed it and turned a wet face back to Jennie. "Better put your raincoat on, Jennie, rain's coming down hard. Someone is bringing the car out to the plane so we won't have to go very far, but we're going to get wet."

Josh went back to the cockpit when Harrell stood up and stretched. "Good landing, Jack. I assume they'll get you into a hangar sometime tonight. I have no idea what's ahead of us, we may have to leave at moment's notice so keep the plane ready. There will be more of us when we head home, we'll be taking Kris and Sophie for sure. I don't have any news on Laurie yet, I should know more tomorrow. No one seems to know where Laurie's son is. When I get this sorted out, I'll let you know. Get some rest and a good meal while you can, and don't stay up all night polishing this plane."

Seeing headlights come along side the plane, Josh motioned to Jennie. "The car's here, it just pulled up beside the door." He helped Jennie into her coat and picked up two bags. "Okay, let's see if we can get to the car before we drown." He opened the door and rushed down the steps with Jennie following. They splashed through puddles to the waiting car.

THE DALLAS SKYLINE WAS welcoming. Jennie could see Pegasus, the flying red horse, on top of the Magnolia building. It was home and it looked like home. She had missed familiar sights and she watched the signs as they drove toward Dallas. There was comfort being where she recognized street names and buildings. However her heart was heavy, it was thudding in her chest as she thought about her daughters and what they had gone through. She should never have left them. She'd been torn between finding Josh or staying with Kris and Laurie. Would it have made any difference if she had stayed? Would their husbands still be alive? She would never know.

"Josh, do you think the woman who fell off the bridge was Laurie?"

"The general thinks so. We should find out more when we get to Herman's."

"I'm so afraid Kris and Laurie are going to hate us."

"They won't hate you. You've been with them all these years. Now me, well, that's a different story, I wouldn't blame them if they did. No matter how they feel, we have to be strong or we can't help them. That's our job. That's what I tried to do six years ago when I left. They will need you now more than ever."

"I know, that's what I tell myself. I'm just scared of what's ahead of us. Slow down," Jennie said pointing. "That's the house on the left with the porch light on."

Holding hands, they ran through the rain to the front porch. The door opened before they could ring the doorbell and Herman and Molly drew them into the warm house.

Jennie looked past her friends, her eyes went straight to her daughter's face and she gasped. Kris' lovely face was ravaged and streaked with tears. She couldn't speak, she just opened her arms and Kris ran into them crying, "Oh, Mom, I'm so glad you're here."

It was all right, they would be okay. She tightened her arms around her daughter and just held her for a minute before she whispered, "Kris, honey, daddy's here."

Kris looked behind her mother. He was there? She couldn't breathe or move, her dad was alive? Back from the dead and standing right in front of her? No, he couldn't be—his body was in the casket at the funeral home. She watched it go down into the ground and heard the dirt land on top of it. Kris closed her eyes still holding her breath, she was hallucinating. The past few days had shattered her, she had no strength left and she clung to her mother. The room darkened and, for the first time in her life, Kris crumpled to the floor in a dead faint.

Jennie went down with Kris and gathered her in her arms. Everyone in the room froze for a second then Molly ran to the kitchen and came back with a wet towel.

"She's just been hanging on by a thread," Molly whispered. "I haven't been able to get her to eat anything all day. She hasn't eaten since yesterday and she's very shaky. Should I call a doctor?"

"I don't think so; let's see how she is when she wakes up. She thought Josh was dead and seeing him alive is shocking. Maybe a little brandy when she wakes. You're right, Molly, she needs food. Some soup, chicken noodle if you have it. I'll see if I can get her to eat in a little while," Jennie answered as she wiped Kris' face and neck with the cool cloth. "Just give her a few minutes."

Molly rushed to the kitchen leaving Herman and Josh talking. Jennie heard Herman's angry voice rise, "Where the hell have you been all these years? Your family has needed you."

"Not where I should have been, Herman. Anything you can say to me I've already said to myself. I wish it could have been different, but that treacherous *Brotherhood* would have hurt my family years ago if they had known I was alive. I was caught in a no-win situation and the faked death appeared to be the only way to keep my family safe. I know that was horrible and wrong and I'm sorry for all the pain it has caused. Yes, you are right. I should have been here protecting my family."

Herman's tense face relaxed a little and he calmed down as Josh agreed with him. Jennie watched the two old friends and football buddies come to an understanding. Josh always had a way of smoothing out stressful situations.

Jennie pushed Kris' hair away from her face and whispered, "Kris, try to open your eyes. Daddy and I are both here now and we are not going away again. You're not alone. We're going to find Laurie and Nicky."

Kris stirred murmuring, "Mom…"

"Josh, come down here, Kris is waking up. She needs to see you are really here."

Josh sat on the floor beside Kris and looked in the face of the beautiful woman his daughter had become, his little girl was gone. His mind reeled at how much she had changed. He took her hand in both of his, "Krissie, I didn't mean to scare you. I'm sorry I had to go away but I'm back now. I'm not leaving you again."

Kris blinked several times then stared at him. She raised her hand and touched him. "You're real, I thought I was hallucinating," she said struggling to sit up. "Mom, did I faint? I've never fainted before."

"You did, but you're all right. Take some deep breaths and then sip a little of this. It's brandy. It'll make you feel better, just small sips. When you feel like getting up, we'll move to the sofa."

Josh grinned and stood up. He leaned down and picked Kris up, "You're not so grown up that I can't carry you." Kris laughed and the tension broke. She threw her arms around her dad, "I'm so glad you're here, Daddy. I thought I'd gone crazy."

"I'm glad I'm here, too, Krissie." He put her on the sofa and sat beside her. "What's this I hear about you not eating?" Jennie smiled, slipped out of her wet raincoat, and went in the kitchen with Molly. Josh and Kris needed some time alone.

"Soup's ready," called Molly when she and Jennie came back in carrying food. "Herman, would you push the coffee table closer to Kris so I can put this on it?"

"You've been trying to make me eat all day. Oh, that's chicken noodle, it looks good." Kris crumbled a couple of crackers into it and took a bite. "Thank you, Molly." She looked around then jumped up, "Where's Sophie?"

"She's sleeping, Kris," Molly said. "Remember, you put her in bed a little while ago.

"Sorry," she said, sitting back down, "I get scared when I don't see her." She looked at her dad with a grin surprisingly like her dad's grin. "Daddy, you are a grandfather, did you know that?

"What are you doing, trying to make me old before my time?" Josh responded.

Kris laughed and took another bite of soup, color was returning to her face.

HERMAN LOOKED AT HIS old friends. "Welcome home, both of you. I'm a lousy host, what can I get you? Would you like coffee, tea, wine, or something stronger? Are you hungry? How about a sandwich? I can make you a ham and cheese.

"I've had quite enough coffee today, but I would love a glass of wine, red or white, whatever you have." Jennie stood up, went over and hugged Herman. She pulled back and looked him in the eyes. "I owe you an apology. I'm very sorry I left without telling you anything, I didn't have a choice. I've told Josh what a good friend you've been to all of us."

Josh grinned and walked over to the bar and picked up an empty glass, "Thanks, old friend, you've always had my back and I'm grateful. I'll take bourbon and seven, if you have it."

"I should have remembered that, you always liked bourbon, Josh." Herman turned to his wife, "What would you like, Molly, white or red wine?"

"I'll get the wine, you get Josh's drink," Molly answered.

When they were all seated and Kris had eaten, Jennie spoke up. "Herman, have you heard anything about Laurie? Do you know where and how she is?"

"We think she's at John Peter Smith Hospital in Fort Worth. The young woman who fell off a bridge is there and her description matches Laurie. I haven't been over yet, but the chief had the Fort Worth police post a guard on her room. She's in intensive care and it's pretty hard to get in there unnoticed so I believe she's safe."

"Her condition?" asked Josh.

"The last report said she is in a coma, but stable. She either fell or was pushed off an overpass to the highway below. Report said it's almost unbelievable she survived. She landed in a truck carrying a load of hay and it cushioned the fall. She has a concussion, a broken arm and rib, and is unresponsive. The doctor is cautiously optimistic."

"I don't like the word 'cautiously' optimistic," Jennie said with a frown on her face.

Kris looked at her. "She may not be talking out loud, Mom, but I'm getting all kinds of crazy mumblings from her. She's very confused and I don't think she knows who she is. If I can get next to her, I can help her remember."

"That means her mind is working, alive is good, the rest we can deal with. I want to go now," Jennie said standing up. "I don't think you should, Kris. You've had more than enough for one day and you should stay here with Sophie."

"I'm going, mom. I can talk to Laurie in ways you can't and maybe I'll hear something that will help."

Kris stood up beside Jennie and Josh knew he was in trouble. The determined look on his daughter's face reminded him of Jennie a few hours ago when she announced she was going to see her daughters. Yes, he was definitely in trouble.

"Kris, I'm telling you what I told your mother earlier, I'm expecting trouble," Davenport's voice hardened and his eyes went cold and unyielding. "I don't know when or where the *Brotherhood* will show up, but they will. If I let you go with us, I want your promise you will do exactly as I say the instant I say it. I mean it, Kris, if I tell you to run, you better take off. Is that understood? I want all of us to come out of this alive. We've already lost too much."

Kris looked at her dad for a long minute as tears ran unchecked down her cheeks again. He had changed. There were lines in his face, an intensity she didn't recognize, and his eyes made her uneasy. This man was very different from the daddy she remembered, this man scared her.

"Yes, Daddy, we've lost enough. I'll do what you say."

She turned to Molly. "Will you look after my daughter?"

Chapter 11

AL LINDBERG'S FEET HAD barely touched the ground in Washington, D.C. when General Thurman ordered him to board a commercial flight to Dallas, Texas. It was raining in D.C. and Lindberg splashed through puddles getting to the plane. The G-2 agent sat in wet clothes and the woman next to him never stopped talking about her grandchildren. He hated flying commercial, particularly in coach. He had no idea why he had to fly it. The general said it was the quickest way to get him to Texas. *What difference would an hour or so make*, he fumed.

Jet-lagged, worn out, hungry, rain-soaked, and angry, Lindberg landed at the Dallas-Fort Worth airport in a thunderstorm. He stomped through the airport parking lot trying to find the car that was supposed to be waiting for him. His orders were to go straight to John Peter Smith Hospital in Fort Worth as fast as possible.

"Damn weather," he muttered as he drove through the pouring rain, "Raining in Washington and now here." He was clueless what he could do when he got to the hospital. He'd never met Davenport's daughter so he couldn't identify her and, if she was in a coma, she couldn't tell him anything.

"So why the hell am I going there?" he muttered as he circled up the entrance ramp to the Dallas/Fort Worth turnpike. Visibility was appalling with all the cars and trucks speeding by, and his foul mood wasn't getting any better. He had to find a phone, he needed a secure line but that wasn't going to happen. Finally, he exited the turnpike and made his way through the streets of Fort Worth to the hospital parking lot. The only place he found to park was about as far from the entrance as was possible, he was going to get wetter. He slammed the car door hard.

Running across the parking lot and giving vent to all the expletives he could think of, he plowed through the revolving door. The information desk was not manned. "That figures," he exploded. "How the hell do I find what room she's in?"

He searched until he found a public phone. It was as safe a phone as he was going to find here and he punched in a number. "I'm on location at John Peter Smith Hospital in Fort Worth, Texas. I've been sent here by General Thurman to provide security for Davenport's daughter. What are my orders?"

As Lindberg listened his scowl deepened. "Yes, sir, I'll meet him in the lounge outside the intensive care unit. We'll make it happen. I understand the woman's in a coma, what kind of transport do we have? Yes, sir, I'll let you know when we get there."

He looked down the long hallway and spotted the elevators. He punched the up button and checked the directory to see what floor ICU was on. Glaring at the elevator and willing it to hurry, he straightened his wet jacket and tie then ran his fingers through his dripping hair trying to look more professional.

"Not much I can do," he muttered. "I'm soaked to the bone." The elevator door slid open and Lindberg entered.

BETWEEN DALLAS AND FORT WORTH

THERE WAS VERY LITTLE traffic on the Dallas/Fort Worth turnpike and Davenport pushed way past the legal speed. Kris watched her parents and it felt like her dad had never been gone. There were so many questions she wanted to ask him, but they would have to wait. There would be time for that later. Right now Laurie was screaming and she couldn't concentrate.

"Mom, something's happening to Laurie. I can't make any sense of what she's saying. She's screaming and her words are all jumbled. She's scared, Mom." Kris leaned forward and rubbed her temples. "My head is pounding."

"Hurry, Josh. Something is happening to Laurie. We've got to get to the hospital fast."

"Doing my best, honey, I'm going eighty-five." He shoved the accelerator to the floor.

Kris lay down in the back seat holding her head. Every time the car swerved, she felt like she was going to throw up.

The car came to a screeching halt at John Peter Smith Hospital under the emergency overhang just behind an ambulance. They all jumped out and Davenport led the way. "Herman said ICU is on the fifth floor," he said as he punched the button.

"Laurie's quit talking and screaming, Mom. Could she be asleep?"

"I don't know, but we need to get up there and find out."

Exiting the elevator, they started toward the double doors of intensive care when Josh stopped, "Jennie, Kris, go in the restroom and wait till I come for you. I'm going to see what's happening."

"No…" Jennie started to protest. Josh's face turned hard as he pointed at the restroom. She nodded and pulled the protesting Kris inside with her.

Davenport pressed the button on the wall and the ICU doors opened. Activity looked routine, the only people he saw were nurses or aides. The curtained cubicles were in a horseshoe around the nurses' work station. Several nurses sat at the desks working on papers. Others were going in and out of the small rooms where the patients were.

"I'm here to check on the woman who fell from the bridge yesterday," Davenport said. "I have someone with me who can identify her."

"I've been hoping some of the family would come. May I ask who are you, sir?"

"Joshua Davenport, Army Special Forces." He showed the nurse his identification.

"I'm sorry, sir, but they've already picked up the young woman."

"Who picked her up?"

"Two men, one man showed me a badge that said Army Special Forces."

"What was his name?"

"Hmm," she stopped and thought a second. "I can't remember what he said, let me get the paperwork he signed." The nurse went over to the cart and pulled a folder out. "Here it is. Oh my, he signed John Peter Smith. That can't be right."

"How long ago?"

"They just left. They were probably going down when you were coming up."

"What did the man look like?"

"He wasn't as tall as you, maybe a little under six feet, slim with brown hair, and very grumpy. He said he was moving her to a hospital near her family. She was so pretty."

"Wait here a minute. I need to get someone," Davenport said as he ran out of ICU.

Pounding on the restroom door, he called, "Come quickly, we've got problems." Jennie and Kris hurried to keep up with Josh as he went back to the nurses' station.

"Did the woman who fell off the bridge look anything like her?" Josh asked the nurse as he pushed Kris up to the desk.

Startled, the nurse stared at Kris and stammered, "I, uh, yes, I think she did. Hair color was a little darker, but the face is the same. Yes, they could be sisters, maybe even twins."

"Oh, Lord, what's happening to Laurie?" Kris cried. "Where is she?"

Davenport looked at the nurse. "What else can you tell me? Think a second, anything at all could help. The man who took her had no authorization. You said another man was with him?"

"Yes, the man who talked to me was wearing a dark suit. He was very wet and looked like he'd been out in the rain for a long time. He acted tired and was extremely rude. There was a huge man with him. I assumed he was a paramedic because he was wearing scrubs. He didn't say anything, he just glared at me. He was quite strong; he lifted the young woman on to the stretcher as if she were a little child. They took her to the elevator that goes down to the emergency entrance."

"Where's the guard the Fort Worth police posted to watch the woman?"

"The Army man dismissed him and sent him away. I don't know his name."

"Thank you, you've been helpful." Davenport turned to leave but the nurse stopped him.

"That young woman is severely injured and could be hurt more if handled roughly. I'm worried about her; she shouldn't have been moved. If I can help her in any way, please call me," she said handing her card to him. "I know she's in a coma, but I think she can hear us. There were times when I felt she was trying to respond to me. I know I shouldn't say it, but I didn't like those men who took her."

Davenport stared at the nurse while his mind ran through what might be needed, "I may be calling you when we find her." He looked at her card then shoved it in his pocket and rushed toward the exit. Jennie and Kris had to run again to keep up with him.

He had parked at the emergency entrance and an ambulance was there when they arrived. He didn't wait for the elevator, but went to the stairs calling out to Jennie and Kris he would meet them by the car.

Attempting to find out who took Laurie had taken too long. He made the five floors down in record time jumping the last few steps of every floor. When he got down the last flight of stairs and out the door the ambulance was gone. Several people were standing around. He asked if they had seen the ambulance that was there a few minutes ago. A couple of people answered they had.

Davenport flashed his identification and asked what they had seen.

"A paramedic rolled a patient out and pushed the stretcher in the back."

"It was a young woman with lots of dark blonde hair," another woman said. "She was asleep,"

"Was anyone with the paramedic?" Davenport asked.

"Yes, probably the doctor, he looked stressed and tired. His clothes were rumpled and wet. He was yelling at the paramedic to hurry. This must have been some type of emergency."

"Which way did they go?" asked Davenport.

"The ambulance drove out the south exit and turned right. It pulled away very fast. I remember thinking they're bouncing that poor patient around."

"Did any of you see the license plate?"

"Nope, I didn't pay any attention to it. It was just an ambulance."

"Thank you both for your help."

Davenport turned to Jennie and Kris who were waiting by the car. "Get in and sit down. I have some calls to make, I won't be long."

Chapter 12

GENERAL THURMAN SLAMMED THE phone down and hollered for his aide. He stood up and stormed out of his office. Every time Davenport called the man dropped another mess on him. How far, he wondered, and how deep would all these traitors go. "If Silverman hadn't killed himself, I'd have the man up in front of a firing squad," he murmured.

"Complications, Reaves. Davenport said from the nurse's description Al Lindberg took his daughter out of the hospital. That means we have another traitor in our midst; that means we sent a traitor out to Texas. Damnation, man, when is this mess going to end? Issue an order to have him picked up. Reaves, I want Lindberg here in my office. I want to confront him personally. That damned *Brotherhood* has got to be stopped, no matter what it takes."

The general thundered around the room. "Davenport said he was going after his daughter and he wouldn't be reporting in until all the traitors are found." He hit the desk with his fist. "There's no telling what that man will do." Looking straight at Reaves, he sighed and muttered, "We've got a black op officer off the reservation and out of control."

He stopped pacing and sat down in his chair. "Get me the files on all the G-2 agents and hurry up. I need to see if I can figure out who else may have turned traitor. If you have any ideas, you better tell me."

He slumped down in his chair and put his head in his hands. "All I ask for is one day, just one day when no disaster happens. Just one day."

Chapter 13

Late Monday night
October 24, 1983
FORT WORTH, TEXAS

THERE'S NO PLACE DARKER than the mind and Davenport was lost in his. He was crawling inside the head of Lindberg to find where he was taking Laurie. *You should know better, Lindberg, that's my daughter. I will find you and when I do, you aren't going to like it.* He sifted through his memory for all the possible places where the *Brotherhood* might hide Laurie.

Racing back into the hospital, Davenport punched the elevator button repeatedly. He'd been distracted by Jennie and Kris and hadn't checked out the room in ICU. Lack of focus, this could destroy all of them.

He was losing valuable time. He ran out of the elevator before it finished opening and raced down the hall toward the intensive care unit. Pulling the nurse's card from his pocket, he looked quickly around for her. Spotting her he called, "Miss Coleson, which room was the young woman in?"

"The third room on the left, what can I do to help?" She pointed and followed him in the room.

"Has it been cleaned yet," he asked when he entered.

"No, we haven't had time yet."

"Well, thank you for lack of time," he muttered. Davenport walked around the room looking at the floor; he wanted something, anything that could give him a clue. The floor was clean. He found nothing, not even a scrap of paper. Only a small radio and a glass with chipped ice were on the table beside the bed. The drawer was empty. The bed was rumpled; he threw back the sheet then lifted the pillow. Eureka! A piece of paper. Picking it up by the edge, his face hardened as he read it.

He put the paper in his coat pocket. "If you are serious about helping, Miss Coleson, I'll call you when I find the young woman. Experienced help will be needed in caring for her in a coma."

"I'm serious. I was very drawn to her. I think she can hear us. Please, if you find her, be very careful how you move her. She has a broken arm and a cracked rib; moving will be painful for her. She's not gone, sir, I felt she was trying to talk to me. I believe her mind is active and she can come out of this."

"Thank you. I'll be in touch."

JENNIE AND KRIS WERE getting more and more anxious waiting in the car. "I'm going to find dad," Kris said. She couldn't sit there any longer, she had to do something. Kris got out of the car and ran toward the entrance before Jennie could stop her.

"Whoa there, where are you going?" Davenport grabbed her by the arm as she flew past him and spun her around to face him.

"I was going to find you, we can't just sit here. We have to find Laurie."

"That's what I'm doing, Kris, I'm making plans. You can't barrel around in the dark when you have no idea where they are taking her." He turned her around and pushed her toward the car. "Get in the car and we'll talk."

When they got in, he turned an angry face toward his daughter. "First, Kris, you've already disobeyed me, I told you to wait in the car until I got back. If you won't follow orders to the letter, you'll have to go back and stay with Herman. I've already lost time because I was distracted by the two of you, I lost focus and that's dangerous. I know you don't understand, but the only way you can stay with me is to follow my orders without argument and without hesitation. I can't function and be continually worried about your safety. This isn't a movie or television show where the good guy always wins, this is real life and good guys lose sometimes. Sooner or later we'll encounter men from the *Brotherhood* or the Illuminati and it will not be pretty. They don't use blanks in their guns, ask your mother about that."

Davenport stopped and stared into his daughter's eyes for a full minute. "Do you understand me?"

The atmosphere in the car changed, it became menacing. Kris studied his face for the dad she knew and he was not there. This was the face of a stranger, a man she didn't recognize, and one she didn't want to know. She looked over at her mom, "I don't know what they have done with my dad, but this man is not him."

"We're in a different world now," Jennie said putting her hand on her husband's arm to stop him from responding. "When we have time, Kris, I'll explain, but right now trust us and do exactly what your dad says. This is your dad and he knows what he's talking about."

"I'll try, Mom, for you, but not for him, and only because we have to find Laurie. She's mumbling again and she's scared." Kris glared at her dad trying to figure out what had happened and who this man was.

"Do you understand me, Kris," Davenport asked again.

"Yes, sir, I do, sir, I'll do what you say, sir." No matter what her mother said she didn't like this man and she wasn't sure she could trust him.

"Kris, I've no time for sarcasm nor do I have the patience for it."

Davenport looked at Jennie and his manner softened. Bottom line, Kris could hate him, but he had to know they were both safe. So he would do whatever it took to keep them safe. He started the car and whipped out of the hospital parking lot heading for I-30 going west. There was a private airstrip near Weatherford and he was guessing that was where they took Laurie. He was sure they were already off the ground, but he needed to find out where they were going. There were three or four locations where they could be taking her.

"Here's the plan. Herman will stay with Sophie. He won't be going in to work so she's safe. We're on the way to check out a private airstrip near Weatherford. I suspect that's where they were taking you and your sister when the accident happened. This is probably where they took Laurie. I checked the ICU room where Laurie was and found a note under her pillow. It said, *If you want your daughter, come get her. I'm waiting for you.*"

Jennie gasped and grabbed Josh by the arm. "What …?"

"I'm going after her, but first I have to talk to whoever is at the airstrip. It belongs to the Illuminati and they function as the strong-arm of the *Brotherhood*. I have a fair idea where they are taking Laurie, but it's a guess. I need confirmation." Josh slowed the car and turned on I-30.

On the west side of Fort Worth, Davenport switched to I-20. Twenty minutes later, he pulled off the highway on a side road and parked in a clump of trees. "Across that field is a private airstrip and I'm going over there. Stay in the car, doors locked and windows up. I won't be long. If anyone approaches, sit on the horn and don't let go. I'll come running."

Dawn was breaking and there was just enough light for Jennie and Kris to watch him run across the field. There was a small prefab building on the far side of the airstrip and he was heading toward it.

"What's with his attitude, Mom. He never used to be mean."

"Calm down and listen to me, Kris. Your dad had to fake his death six years ago so the *Brotherhood* wouldn't come after us. I didn't know he was alive when I married Nathan and I sure didn't know Nathan was working for the *Brotherhood*. He wasn't supposed to marry me, just keep tabs on me to see if I made contact with Josh. When Josh found out he came after me. It's a long involved story so I'm just giving you highlights. The *Brotherhood* found me when I was on my way to Josh, and I had to change all the plans your dad made for me. Josh has a partner named Owen Blakely who helped me. When Nathan found

Owen guarding the train compartment I was in, he tried to kill him by shoving him off the speeding train."

"Nathan tried to kill someone—oh, Mom, that's crazy, he wouldn't do that…"

"Yes, he did, he fooled us all and he's a traitor. When I arrived in Atlanta Nathan was following me and Army G-2 took him into custody. Josh says he's being held at Fort Leavenworth waiting court-martial. It should have ended there, but Nathan had already alerted the *Brotherhood* your dad was alive so they are after him again."

"I don't understand what Nathan and daddy have to do with them, Mom."

"That's way too long a story to get into now. I don't think we have that much time."

"Well, how did you find daddy?"

"Another long story and one filled with lots of problems. On the last leg of the journey, I took a train to a small town west of London where Josh was to pick me up. Owen went by another route and was supposed to meet me there, but he didn't show up or so I thought. When your dad got there, a man stepped out of the bushes pointing a gun at Josh. I threw myself in front of Josh and was injured."

"You mean you got shot, Mom? Was it Nathan?"

"No, Nathan didn't shoot me. A man from the *Brotherhood* shot me in the shoulder. Owen had arrived before me and the *Brotherhood's* man shot him in the chest. He hid Owen in the bushes and left him for dead. When Owen came to, he crawled out just in time to see the man shoot me. He was barely conscious and bleeding profusely, but Owen was still able to shoot that man. He saved our lives." Jennie paused. "Josh got both of us into a helicopter and to a private hospital. Owen almost died. He's a strong young man and he survived, but he hasn't been able to return to work yet. When we left the hospital, Josh took us to a safe place. I'll tell you about it when we have more time, it's a castle and you'll love it."

Jennie looked across the field and saw Josh coming back. Closing her eyes, she took a deep breath and wiped tears off her face before continuing. "There's so much more I need to tell you, but we're out of time, I see your dad coming. You have to understand he never wanted to leave us. He did the only thing he could to keep us alive. Your dad is still there and I know he's difficult, Kris. Just give him a chance. It will be better if you do exactly what he says. Believe me, he knows what he is doing and he loves you. He will find Laurie."

Jennie unlocked the car door right before Josh got there.

"The mechanic didn't know very much, but he heard one of the men say something about Arizona," Davenport said as he started the car. He pulled back on the road and turned toward Dallas.

"That's all I need. I know exactly where they are going."

Chapter 14

THE DRIVE BACK TO Dallas and Herman's house seemed to take forever. As soon as Kris got in the house she ran to find Sophie. When she had her daughter safe in her arms she felt better. Sophie was one person she felt comfortable with.

Davenport brought Herman up to date and then said, "I'm going after Laurie, but we have some things to work out before I leave. Is it possible the *Brotherhood* or Illuminati know where you live?"

Images of dark blue cars following him this past year flashed before Herman's eyes. "After all that's happened, Josh, I'd say it's a definite possibility. Last spring someone followed me all the time, but it stopped in August. It started again a few days ago and they have tailed me ever since. They aren't even attempting to be invisible, it's like they want me to know."

"Just because you didn't see them doesn't mean they weren't there. I don't want to scare Molly, but you, Molly, and my family have to move. Do you know of a safe place that has no connection with you or anyone you know?" Davenport looked at Herman. "I've been away too long, does anywhere come to mind?"

"Are you serious? I can have this house secure within the hour."

"That's not good enough, Herman, trust me on this."

"All right, but before I scare Molly, there are a few things I have to know. Such as how the hell did you get involved in all this?"

"It's a long story, and we don't have that much time."

Herman glared at Josh, then sat down and settled back in a chair. "Well, we're not going anywhere until you explain so start talking. I've been in the dark this entire year and I'm not moving until I know what we're dealing with."

Josh groaned and pulled a chair close to Herman. His old football buddy had dug in his heels; Herman could be damn stubborn sometimes. He glanced at Jennie and Kris. They were asleep on the sofa and he hoped they would stay that way.

He thought a moment before he started. "It's a long convoluted story and we only have time for the main points. Listen up cause I'm going to talk fast. It all started when I was a G-2 in the Army and stationed at the clearing house for military information. I had access to top-secret files and part of my job was to keep classified data from being released to the public. I came across some very suspicious activities within various departments of the government and I began to follow the trail to see where it went. It went almost all the way to the top of every department of our government. You know me, I couldn't leave it alone. I had to find out more. Well, it led me right into the middle of a covert plan to take over our government. I was just beginning to put it all together when one of the moles in this clandestine group realized what I was unearthing. Fast forward, I was mustered out of the military four months early."

"No one gets out early, someone powerful wanted rid of you," muttered Herman.

"You got it. Jennie and I moved back to Dallas and several years passed, we had two daughters and moved into a new home. That's when G-2 reactivated me. I was an asset living across the street from a known member of the *Brotherhood*. They wanted eyes on the man and, after a couple of months, they had me make contact. Time passed and I was accepted. I was able to gain access to the top echelon. I learned their plans, the immediate ones as well as the long-term goals. When my cover was blown, decisions had to be made about the safety of not just Jennie and my daughters, but all of my extended family. The only solution we found was for me to die. There was no other way to keep the *Brotherhood* from going after my family. Just disappearing wouldn't protect them. They wouldn't hesitate to use them to get to me, and that's what they're trying to do now. I had too much knowledge in my head by that time so I did what I had to do. Think about it, Herman, would I ever let Jennie think I was dead if it wasn't absolutely necessary."

"Damn it, man. I had no idea. No wonder Kris kept saying that the man in the casket didn't look like her dad. This explains a lot, it has to be why I was ordered by the Dallas PD to go to the funeral home to provide security. There were a number of official-looking men watching everybody and I wondered who the heck they were. They hung around for two full days. For the next three months after that, I was assigned to shadow your home and I never knew why." Herman picked up their glasses and refilled their drinks. "Tell me about the *Brotherhood*."

"It is a power-hungry group of the world's wealthiest men. They operate globally and their goal is world domination with the United States as the first takeover. The enforcing arm of the *Brotherhood* is the Illuminati. They are a formidable force and never hesitate to remove anyone who gets in their way."

"That's what I've heard, I have enough knowledge of those two groups to know what you're saying is real. So what happened next?"

"You're testing my patience, buddy." Struggling to remain calm, Josh knew Herman wasn't going to be satisfied with less than the whole story. He took a long drink of his bourbon and seven and looked at his sleeping family again.

"At first I was secreted away in the bowels of Little Washington outside of Denton and I didn't see daylight for a couple of months. The Army wanted to make sure the *Brotherhood* accepted my death. Fast forward again, I was moved around a lot and sent on undercover assignments in Europe. On one of my assignments, I found out that the *Brotherhood* had corrupted Mason Silverman, the head of NSA. He was selling crucial intelligence to them. Here's the problem, the NSA doesn't answer to any governing authority other than the president. Silverman was also an old and trusted friend of the president. The traitor was only telling the president what he wanted him to know. It was apparent the president didn't know about Silverman." Davenport paused trying to decide how much to tell Herman.

"A bit of background so you'll understand my situation in this, before World War II intelligence operations were conducted by independent agents. They knew one another, traded information, and even split fees at times. After the war, bureaucracy took over. Instead of a dozen or so agents in the field, about a thousand were gathering information and feeding it into computers. So many restrictions were placed on the old-timers that they disbanded. The bureaucracy was not and is not good at sharing information. All departments operate on a "Don't tell the others anything" pact.

"This is where I came into the picture. The president had to know about Silverman and there was no one I could trust to tell him. After a while an opportunity opened up for me to talk to him, and here's where it spiraled out of control. It's difficult to say no to the president of the United States. I became the president's eyes and ears, not even General Thurman of Army G-2 knew what I was doing. I was trapped and there was no way I could get out."

"What do you mean, trapped…"

Davenport stopped Herman in mid-sentence. "No time for that story, Herman. Someday when time isn't crucial, I'll fill in all the details." He stood up and walked around.

"When I found out Jennie had married Nathan Scott, I almost lost it. I knew him and his connection with Silverman and the *Brotherhood*.

"You mean Scott's part of the *Brotherhood?*"

"Not that I could prove at that time. The group had enough on him to control him and he followed their orders. Bottom line, I had to get Jennie away from him and, in doing that, my partner and I killed a member of that group. Scott was taken into custody, but not fast enough. He had time to inform the *Brotherhood* I was alive, so they have another contract out on me and my family."

Davenport kept pacing around the room. "The bastards killed my daughters' husbands and are holding Laurie and my grandson. Believe me, Herman, there's not a chance in hell that they don't know you are involved so I'm asking again, do you know a safe place where you can move?"

"I might. There was a minister who helped Kris when she escaped. He and his wife live in Burleson and they might know a place we could stay. He's unconnected with this or anyone I know, I believe he'll help us. I didn't tell the chief about him or where Kris was."

"Good, call him."

JENNIE HAD BEEN AWAKE for some time and was surprised at Josh's patience with Herman. She peeped through half-closed eyes at her husband. She had learned in the past months that he was not reachable when he was in this dark mode. What she saw now frightened her more than the *Brotherhood*. He was slipping away from her again. She looked at Kris and willed her to stay asleep, then closed her eyes and listened.

HERMAN SPOKE ON THE phone for some minutes before turning back to Josh. "Pastor Crane will help us. The church has a house they keep for the use of visiting missionaries. It's empty now and he says we can stay there as long as we need to. When do you want us to leave?"

"Two hours ago. Pack a few things and get out of here as fast as you can." Josh handed Herman a piece of paper saying, "Get settled in that house then call this number and give my partner, Owen Blakely, the address and phone number. He will be our contact. You can leave messages for me with him. I try to check in every few hours. My plan is to join you there with Laurie and Nicky."

Josh made sure Jennie was still sleeping. He lowered his voice and continued. "If you don't hear from me in three days, call Blakely and he'll give you instructions about where to board my private plane. Don't wait a minute longer. I'm depending on you to get everyone out of the country as fast as you can. My pilot's name is Jack Harrell and he knows where to take you. It's a place where everyone will be safe. Jennie knows Jack and my partner, Owen Blakely. She'll be resistant, but tell her I'll be there as soon as I can."

"Good heavens, man. Is all that necessary?"

"The *Brotherhood* is not playing games, Herman. They won't hesitate to take the rest of you hostage or worse, think about my daughters' husbands. You're the only chance I have to keep what's left of my family safe. Promise me you will get everyone out of here so I can go after Laurie and Nicky." Davenport watched his friend nod his head. "Herman, don't tell anyone the location of the safe house, not even your chief. We have no idea where all the traitors are embedded."

Herman answered softly then he left the room to wake Molly.

Josh leaned over his sleeping wife and whispered, "Wake up, Jennie. I'm going after our daughter and grandson. You need to stay here with Herman and take care of Kris and Sophie. Please, don't argue with me now. I love you."

He leaned down and kissed her and was gone before she could get off the couch.

Chapter 15

DAVENPORT DROVE THROUGH THE familiar Dallas streets to Hensley Air Force Base in Grand Prairie and parked his car near the hangar where his plane was housed. The wet runway glistened in the meager sun that was struggling to break through the clouds. Slipping his keys in his coat pocket, he scooted out of the car and was immediately boxed in by six men who came out of nowhere. He could see the slight bulge of shoulder holsters under the jackets of the men. *Uh-oh, this can't be good....*

"Joshua Davenport, Mr. Parrino extends his invitation for you to visit him. Please follow me," said the man in front of him.

Parrino—that was Laurie's last name, her husband was Joey Parrino. Parrino, Italian name, Mafia maybe... Brotherhood, doubtful, not their style... Davenport looked toward the hangar wondering if Harrell was watching. *Six to one—bad odds even with Harrell...*

"Lead the way, gentlemen. I accept Mr. Parrino's cordial invitation."

The men never cracked a smile. They led him to a waiting limousine, opened the back door and motioned him to get in. Davenport slid in and the men joined him. He filtered through names of the men in the *Brotherhood* and the Illuminati. There was not a Parrino among them. The connection had to be his daughter.

Leaving the air force base, they traveled north passing DFW airport through Irving and into the Las Colinas area. The car entered a gated community and made several turns before rolling through another gate to stop in front of a secluded house at the top of a wooded hill. Surrounded by the black-suited men, he was escorted inside and down a long hall to a richly furnished study. The room was large with a desk at the far end near French doors. Two wingback chairs flanked the fireplace and an elderly, gray-haired man sat waiting in one of them. He was leaning toward the burning fire. He straightened up and studied Davenport as he entered the room.

"Welcome to my home, Joshua Davenport. Thank you for coming." The man did not stand, he gestured for him to sit opposite him. The six men remained standing at attention around the room.

Davenport observed his host for minute before responding, "It was an invitation I couldn't refuse."

Parrino nodded. "How was your flight here? The weather was not favorable."

Hmmm, it would be interesting to know where Parrino got his information. "It was smooth for the most part, we encountered some minor turbulence."

Parrino watched Davenport for a minute then picked up a glass from the coffee table and handed it to him. "Bourbon and seven, I understand. If you prefer coffee, it is available. We had a little trouble finding you."

"Bourbon is fine, Mr. Parrino. I suspect you had more than a little trouble finding me," Davenport said with a smile. He raised his glass and took a sip of his drink. *Yet you found me where many others have not. You know about my plane, you picked me up near the hangar so it's a fair bet you know about my pilot.*

"Our meeting has been long delayed and it is time we talk. We have a mutual problem." The man paused, his breathing raspy and loud. "Joey Parrino was my grandson and your son-in-law."

Ah, there's the connection. Jennie thought Joey's family was Mafia, but Laurie wouldn't confirm it. He looked straight in the eyes of the man who was obviously head of the family, "I am very sorry about your grandson, Mr. Parrino. It is difficult to lose a loved one, even more so when they are young. I regret that our meeting is under these circumstances."

Parrino nodded. "Family is important to us. I assume it is to you because of the drastic measures you employed years ago when you faked your death to protect your family. It now appears the ghost of Joshua Davenport has returned from the dead to find his daughters and grandchildren. Is my assumption correct, Mr. Davenport?"

"Yes, my family is of utmost importance to me, I have returned to find my daughters and grandchildren. I am curious how you found me." *Interesting, he doesn't know Kris and Sophie are safe.*

"We have our ways, just as you do." Parrino leaned forward and set his glass on the table never breaking eye contact with Davenport. "We feel you may know who murdered Joey. Understand me, this is highly personal, Joey was my grandson. We want to know who the assassin was and what you know about him."

"It is highly personal for me as well; he was my daughter's husband." He studied the elderly man's face before continuing. "I arrived last evening and have not had time to ascertain all the facts. However, an educated guess is the assassin is a man named Otto Fleicher. He is a brutal, sadistic, ruthless killer, and totally without conscience. He is the hit man for the *Brotherhood* and has strong connections to the Illuminati."

"Thank you, we will find him, nobody hits our family and gets away with it. We take care of family, Mr. Davenport, as you have endeavored to do." Parrino's hand shook betraying emotion his voice did not when he picked up his glass from the table. "Now, Mr. Davenport, where do you think Joey's wife and my great-grandson are?"

Davenport sipped his drink then sat it down. *He doesn't know as much as I thought and his interest is in Laurie and Nicky. Maybe I can get out of this, I only have to tell enough to appease....*

"There are a number of locations where they could have concealed my daughter and grandson. I was on my way to determining this when the invitation to visit you interrupted me. I have to say time is of the essence, my daughter is in a coma and her life is in danger if she's not cared for properly." Davenport locked eyes with Parrino. "Her life as well as my grandson's life is my priority. Time, Mr. Parrino, is not in our favor." He picked up his drink.

"I understand." Parrino stared into the man's eyes. "Time is a problem. We have a proposition for you, Mr. Davenport. From our investigation, you are an honorable man and you care for your family as we do. This we respect," Parrino said nodding his head. "You by virtue of my grandson and your daughter's marriage are now family. I am proposing we join forces, a temporary alliance you understand. We will help you get your family back if you help us find Joey's killer."

Davenport got to his feet and went to the French doors. He stood looking out with his hands behind his back. The grounds were extensive and surrounded by a high brick wall. Guards were in sight and stationed around the property. *If I don't agree, it's possible I won't leave here alive even if Parrino did call me family. If I agree, I'll have a powerful backup, something I've never had in any of my past situations, albeit a very dangerous one.*

The question being, will he honor his word? The Mafia seldom allows outsiders in. This might be a chance not only to find Laurie and Nicky, but to make a substantial dent in the *Brotherhood's* plans. If, and it was a big *if*, if the Mafia took out Fleicher, he would have a much better chance of getting Laurie and Nicky back. All he had to do was stay alive long enough to get them to safety and back to Jennie. If today was a forecast of things to come, staying alive was going to be tricky. On the other hand, Nicky was Parrino's great-grandson and that gave him a little edge.

"So, Mr. Davenport, do you agree?"

Davenport turned his back to the French doors and went over to the fireplace. He remained standing. "As I said, my family is the most important thing in the world to me. I will do whatever it takes to get them to safety. Although I had no opportunity to know Joey, he was my son-in-law and that makes him my family as well. Exactly what are you proposing, Mr. Parrino?"

"We have a mutual friend from days long past when you were alive and enjoying life in Dallas. His name is Tony Falco. Do you remember him?"

"Oh yes, we played a few chess games back in the day. We also enjoyed many fine dinners at the Chateaubriand in Dallas where he introduced me to some of his friends. Yes, Mr. Parrino, I remember Tony well."

"We are familiar with the *Brotherhood* and the groups attached to them and have not found them honorable men. We are well aware of the power they wield; your knowledge in this instance is valuable to us. Tony will accompany you and provide whatever assistance you require. And, if needed, additional manpower will be available to him."

Davenport stared deep into Parrino's eyes wishing he could read the man's thoughts. His face was etched with his many years, but it betrayed no emotion. The men stationed around the room were watching intently. He had no other choice and no way out right now. Davenport nodded in agreement.

Parrino rose and joined Davenport at the fireplace. He motioned for the tray waiting on the console to be brought to him.

"Now, Mr. Davenport, we will seal our alliance with a cognac."

Chapter 16

BY THE TIME JENNIE got off the sofa and opened the front door, Josh was backing out of the driveway. He knew better, he knew she would not be left behind. Jennie had told him many times it was never going to happen again. She stormed around the room, her mind working at a furious pace. He might not admit it, but he needed her. She couldn't let him go back to that dark place where he had been before she joined him; she wanted her husband and their life back. He wasn't having as many nightmares as he did when she first arrived at the Cameron Compound in Scotland. She knew he reached over and touched her during those times.

Her anger and frustration settled down when she decided what to do. He needed her and she was going where he was. Where that was she didn't know, but she would find out. She dialed the number of the phone in the airplane and hoped Jack was there. She waited tapping her fingernails on the table through six long rings.

"Jack, it's Jennie, I know Josh is planning to leave, but I was half sleep when he told me the plans and I'm confused. I have to get to the plane on my own this evening so I need to know where the plane is, what time we're leaving, and where we're going."

"Josh didn't say anything about you going to Phoenix with us. We're parked in hangar three at Hensley and leaving about eight tonight or earlier if Josh gets here. He said to stand ready. The plane's checked out and food is on board, but I better grab half and half for your coffee."

"Thanks, I appreciate you thinking of that. Where are we landing in Phoenix?"

"It's a small private airstrip Josh knows about. We'll be off the grid and flying low under the radar. No flight plan turned in."

"I thought you had to file one."

"Yeah, we're supposed to, but we've done this before when we need to slip in somewhere quietly. I know the route, so no problems there."

"Thanks, Jack, see you later. I'll get there as quick as I can."

She bent over her sleeping daughter wishing she didn't have to wake her. She had been through so much and needed to rest. "Wake up, Kris. I'm sorry to wake you, but we need to get ready to go."

Kris stirred and looked up at her mother's face. "What time is it? Go where, Mom?"

"It's late afternoon. I want to tell you what is going on then you need to pack up whatever you have here, a sack will do."

"Where's dad, Mom?"

Taking Kris' hand she led her to the kitchen. Jennie opened several cabinet doors looking for coffee cups. "We can talk better in here; I don't want to disturb Herman and Molly. Do you want some coffee?" Kris shook her head and picked up a banana. Jennie poured what was left in the pot and splashed a little milk in her cup.

"Josh left a little while ago and I've been making plans. He wants us to move somewhere safer, somewhere the *Brotherhood* doesn't know about. Herman has made arrangements with Pastor Crane for everyone to stay in a house he has for visiting missionaries."

"All of us, including Herman and Molly?"

"Yes, that's Josh's plan. He feels the *Brotherhood* knows about Herman. All he said when he woke me up was he was going after Laurie and Nicky. I've been stewing about what to do. He is not going to leave me behind again, I have told him that many times. I've made plans that I need to tell you about."

"You're not going without me, Mom, I'm not being left behind either," Kris blurted out staring at her mother. "He needs me to hear

Laurie. She's mumbling again, but I still can't understand anything she says. So, what are we doing?"

"If Laurie is mumbling it tells us she's alive. I've been in touch with Jack at our plane and they're leaving for Phoenix when Josh gets there. I don't know where they are landing; they are not filing a flight plan. We have to leave as soon as we can and get to the plane. If we miss them, my alternate plan is to fly to Phoenix on a commercial plane. I've made reservations for tonight under the name of Jennie Cameron and Kris Williams. As soon as we get there we can start searching for Laurie, I'm hoping she will say something you understand and it will give us a clue about where she is. We'll figure it out from there. We can do this, Kris."

"Yes, we can, Mom. I guess daddy has a reason to think she is in Phoenix?"

"He does. He didn't explain, but remember at the airfield he said the man told him Arizona. I called our pilot and he said they are going straight to Phoenix. And that's also what Josh told Herman.

"I'll get my things. What about Sophie? I hate leaving her, but we can't take her with us."

"I've left a note for Molly and Herman. They'll take good care of Sophie at the safe house in Burleson; they will be safe there. Be very quiet, Kris. Let's try to get out of here without them seeing us. Herman will try to stop us.

HERMAN LOOKED AROUND THE living room then followed soft voices into the kitchen. Kris and Jennie stopped talking the minute they saw him and Jennie sipped her coffee. She was quiet, too quiet for his comfort. Something was going on. The last time he saw that look on her face she had disappeared.

"Have you told Kris the plans, Jennie?" Herman asked.

"Yes, I was just telling her you talked with Pastor Crane and he is going to help us."

"He was very nice and seemed happy to help. We'll be leaving soon so gather up whatever you need, Kris. Molly will show you the children's clothes we have. Take anything you can use for Sophie. While you're in the kitchen, you might grab a few snacks for her. Check the pantry for them. Molly put out a small suitcase for you, be sure to put some toys and books in it for Sophie," Herman added smiling. He loved children and Sophie was warming up to him.

"I have to pack my stuff so I better get moving," he said. Stopping at the kitchen door, he turned around and looked at Jennie. "Please, don't do anything foolish."

Jennie waited until Herman was out of sight before continuing. "Hurry and get Sophie's things ready, Kris. I'll find some snacks for you to put in the suitcase. I've already called a taxi and it's on the way. I told them not to honk and to park next door, I'd be watching. Hurry, Kris, it will be here in a few minutes."

Chapter 17

SWEAT WAS ROLLING DOWN Davenport's face and back when he slid into the cold car. Adrenaline was still pumping through him. He watched the black limousine turn around and drive away. Parrino's men had not uttered a word on the tense drive back to Hensley Air Force Base. His emotions had run from calm to fear and back to calm. Fear was what kept him alive in many situations in the past; controlled fear focused his mind on what he had to do. With both the Mafia and the *Brotherhood* in the mix, this could become an explosive combination in a nanosecond.

He was a realist. Years ago when he agreed to help the president fight the *Brotherhood*, he accepted the fact he might not come out alive. The subversive group had gone too far this time by attacking his family. No matter what happened to him, he had to get Laurie and Nicky back to Jennie. He had promised her and that was a promise he intended to keep.

A chilling drizzle had settled in the air. He turned the motor and heater on hoping it would take the chill out of the car. He needed time to think before he joined Harrell. Tony Falco, he had almost forgotten his old friend. That time period felt like another life, maybe it was. Years ago they both played in a small band at a local nightclub in Dallas. It was something he had done to relax from the gravity of his situation. Between sets, he and Falco had played chess. Many evenings they slipped out to dinner at the Chateaubriand Restaurant. Falco had told him it was a major meeting place for the local Mafia. One evening Falco took him downstairs to their private dining room and introduced him to some of the men. He and Falco had joined them for dinner. Yeah, he remembered Falco.

A tapping on the car window startled Davenport out of his reverie. He turned and looked straight into Falco's face. He rolled the window down.

"Unlock the door and let me in, old pal, it's cold and wet out here," Falco said grinning and jiggling the door handle.

There was no mistaking that grin. Davenport reached over and unlocked the passenger door. The past was back.

Falco slid in shivering, "I never get used to cold weather. Fortunately, we don't have a lot of it here in Texas." He took a long look at Davenport before continuing. "You look pretty good for a dead man. You haven't gone to fat like a lot of the guys in our little band."

"Neither have you, my friend. Do you still get together with them?"

"Occasionally, I don't have as much free time as I used to, it's always fun when I manage to join them. Any time away from responsibilities is a good thing, you know about that. So tell me, Davenport, what's going on and why you're back."

"Parrino didn't tell you?"

"He told me you were a friend and needed help. So here I am waiting to hear why you've come back from the dead, what you've been doing, and what kind of help you need."

Davenport studied Falco looking for the laughing pal he used to know. This man was different; he was more serious and had a tougher look about him. "It's a long story, Falco, no need to go into all the past. I'm sure Parrino told you about his grandson Joey being killed."

"Of course I know, we all know about Joey. Parrino didn't tell me, he didn't have to."

"I just got back from meeting with Parrino. He proposed I help find Joey's killer and, in return, he would help me find my daughter and grandson. You know Joey was married to my daughter, Laurie."

"I do. Do you know who killed Joey?"

"Best guess is a man named Otto Fleicher. He's the hit man for the *Brotherhood* with strong ties to the Illuminati."

"So how are you connected with these groups?"

"It's involved, Falco. The important part is the *Brotherhood* has a contract out on me, but I suspect you already know this." Davenport's voice became soft, wrapped in an icy, unyielding monotone. "They are the ones who kidnapped my daughters and grandchildren. From what I've learned, Joey was killed trying to save his wife and son."

Falco shivered and looked at Davenport in the fading light, his old friend was not the man he remembered. His hair had turned gray and his face had aged, but he looked fit enough. There was a cold-blooded look and intensity about him that he didn't remember. His eyes were disconcerting and pierced into him making him uncomfortable. There was power here he had not had before, no, this was not the same man he used to kid around with. This was a man who had encountered evil. "You're traveling in some deep waters, Davenport, why the contract?"

"I have a history with them and know too much. As long as I'm alive, I threaten their plans and they threaten my family." Davenport had no intentions of revealing his connection with the president or Army G-2. It would not help his cause with the Mafia. However, he would not be surprised if Parrino and Falco both knew.

"Details, Davenport, if I'm going after this man who killed Joey, I have to know what I'm getting into."

"Are you telling me you are the one the Mafia is sending to kill the man who murdered Joey?"

"You know better than to ask questions like that, or have you forgotten?" Falco reached over and turned the blower up on the heater. "Let's just stick to the facts. What are you doing getting mixed up in all this? You were always straight."

"That was another life, another time and place, another man, Falco. We've both changed in the past six years."

"You got that right," Falco chuckled. "So what's the deal?"

Davenport studied his friend wondering how far the old friendship would go. He wished he knew if Falco was sent to terminate Fleicher or was just the intermediary. Falco was always close-mouthed when it came to talking about what he did in the Mafia. The nightclub had been different; Falco was popular with the women and never short of companions. He actually played a great five-string guitar, not just strumming it, he could really play. That was a big attraction plus it didn't hurt that he looked like Adonis. The years had aged him in a good way.

"Are you married, Falco, do you have children?"

"No, I've never had the time. Got close once, but she didn't like my lifestyle. No children I know of. My sister has two little kids and to them I'm Uncle Tony, bearer of all things fun. What does this have to do with what you're doing?"

"Humor me, my friend, one more question. How far would you go to protect them?"

"All the way, they are family. You know how important family is to me."

"I do. I'm just reminding you because that's what I'm doing now. Long story made short, I tried to protect my family by faking my death, however the bad guys still found out I'm alive. The bastards took my daughters and grandchildren, and I'm here to get them back."

"I got it. You just said daughters and grandchildren, earlier you said a daughter and grandson?"

"One daughter with her baby daughter escaped when the car wrecked on the bridge where Joey was killed. You knew all this already, didn't you?"

"Of course, you don't think I'd come into this blind. I had to know if you arc shooting straight with me." The sideways grin crossed Falco's face again. "You asked a question earlier about my job. All you need to know is I'm here to find the assassin and help you get your family back. They are also Parrino's family, his great-grandson and his grandson's wife. Even though Joey is dead, they are family and important to him." Falco paused and looked intently at Davenport before continuing. "We're not old Chicago anymore, my friend. We have sophisticated people on the payroll now for the more questionable situations. By the time we're done, no one will know what happened."

The two men's eyes met and they nodded as the sun dropped behind a cloud and darkness descended on the car. A cautious understanding had been reached. Lightening flashed and both men shivered.

Davenport turned off the motor and pulled his raincoat around him, "Time for you to meet my pilot." They left the car and hurried toward the hangar.

"YOU DID WHAT? YOU told Jennie where we're going. Damn it, Harrell, what were you thinking? You should know better."

Davenport looked over at Falco. "You might remember my wife; she's short with blonde hair. She came to the club a lot and always sat at a corner table. She was rather quiet and reserved, but that has changed." He sighed, "She's developed a strong mind of her own now which sometimes makes me crazy."

Falco grinned, "Good for her."

"Not so good for me."

Davenport turned to Harrell, "It's time to go. Get us out of this hangar and in the air, we need to leave before Jennie gets here. I want her to stay with Herman at the safe house."

Davenport went to his small office and called the airlines, he found a flight leaving for Phoenix in an hour. He dialed Herman as he muttered to Harrell, "Want to bet me she also has reservations on this plane, she may actually beat us to Phoenix."

"Herman, where's Jennie?"

"Gone, I should have suspected she was planning something. I didn't think she and Kris would sneak away. I'm guessing they are joining you."

"Not if I can help it, we are pulling out of the hangar now. Get out to DFW Airport, Terminal C, as fast as you can. There's a flight leaving for Phoenix at eight tonight, and I bet she and Kris have reservations on it. You've got to stop them; it's too dangerous for them in Phoenix. We're going into one of the *Brotherhood's* secret locations. Stop them, Herman, arrest them, do whatever it takes, just stop her. She'll come here first then to the airport so I'm hoping you can stop her."

"I'll do my best, Josh. I'll leave now and be waiting when she gets there. I'll let Blakely know when we get to the safe house."

"Thanks, tell Blakely about Jennie and where she is. I owe you, pal."

"You better believe it. I'm planning to collect someday," said Herman.

Davenport pulled a handkerchief out of his pocket and wiped the sweat off his face. He wondered how he could get so angry at someone he loved so much.

The plane was out of the hangar and taxiing to the airstrip. "Harrell, I need to make a call from my office. Let me know when the phone is available."

"We're flying low and quiet, off the radar. You can call as soon as we get in the air."

Davenport turned back to Falco. "Tony Falco, meet my friend and pilot, Jack Harrell. Jack plays a pretty good guitar, too. I bet it's here somewhere; he has to do something while waiting on me besides polishing this plane.

Harrell motioned at the copilot's seat where his guitar stood and welcomed Falco aboard as he maneuvered the plane into position for takeoff.

"Sit down and buckle up, gentlemen."

The engines revved, the jet aircraft raced down the runway and with a thump jumped off the ground into the air.

The hunt had begun.

Chapter 18

JENNIE AND KRIS ARRIVED at the air force base in Grand Prairie just as a plane lifted off the runway and soared into the sky. Jennie jumped out of the taxi and watched it, she was almost sure it was their Learjet.

"We missed Josh," she said sliding in the car and pointing at the sky. "That was our plane that just took off. I was afraid this would happen. I knew Josh would try to leave without us. That's why I made reservations on American."

"DFW airport, driver, as fast as you can," she ordered in frustration. "We have an eight o'clock flight to catch. Can you get us there?"

"It'll be close. I'll do my best," said the driver.

He spun the taxi around and drove off the base then turned toward the airport. He picked up speed when he reached the highway.

Between Dallas and Phoenix, Arizona

As soon as the plane leveled off, Davenport went to his office, if you could call an area the size of a closet an office. There was only enough space for a chair and a built-in shelf which served as a narrow desk. However, there was a secure phone line.

Stopping in the doorway, he turned back to Falco and pointed to the galley. "Get something to drink if you want, feel free to look through the cabinets. There's usually some sandwiches in the fridge, take whatever you want."

Davenport closed the door to his tiny office and picked up the phone. He was grateful this room was soundproof.

"Mr. President, I apologize for keeping you out of the loop. Things have moved rapidly and I haven't had access to a secure phone until now. I know you've been hearing lots of stories…"

"I have. Are you back in the states?" interrupted the president.

"Yes, sir, I'm here and traveling in my plane. My daughters and grandchildren were abducted by the *Brotherhood*. Kris and her daughter escaped and are safe. They still have Laurie and Nicky, and are using them as bait to lure me out…"

The president interrupted again asking how he was handling this.

"I'm worried, sir, but I'm okay. Thank you for asking. We just left Hensley Field in Grand Prairie. We're heading west and are not filing a flight plan. There are too many ways the *Brotherhood* could get that information. From now on, we will be flying under the radar and using small private air strips wherever we go…"

"What do you know about your missing daughter?" the president asked.

"Very little, Mr. President, all I know is Laurie was pushed or fell off a bridge and was in a coma at a Fort Worth hospital, but the *Brotherhood* moved her before I got there. Another G-2 agent, Al Lindberg, was involved so I won't be making contact with General Thurman until we find out if anyone else in G-2 has sold out. I have to get my daughter and grandson back to Jennie. Some unexpected help has shown up. Laurie's husband was Tony Parrino, grandson of the powerful Parrino Mafia family. Parrino had me picked up and taken to his home for a visit. He knew everything about me, he even knew about my private plane." Davenport paused considering how best to tell the president. "He made me a deal. He said I was now family and offered his help if I pointed out the killer of his grandson. There was no way to refuse…"

"You know that alliance is volatile. Have you told General Thurman?"

"No, sir, I haven't told him. I'm hesitant do so, I don't know what other traitors could be lurking in G-2. I'm hoping you can keep him calm and from issuing orders to bring me in. I have no illusions about this, sir, any which way I turn could go bad. I'll keep you informed when I can. If I make it through and get my family back, I'll turn myself in to the general. You're likely to hear more stories, sir, but I wanted you to hear it from me first. With the Mafia behind me, I may be able to slow the *Brotherhood* down, at least for a while."

"Davenport, listen to me, you don't have to do this. Who knows what could happen. This could precipitate a war between the Mafia and the *Brotherhood* like we haven't seen since years ago in Chicago. Tell me where your family is and we'll pick them up. Tell me where you're landing and we'll extract you and move you all to Little Washington in Denton. Everyone will be safe there."

The president was silent for several seconds before he began slowly, "Josh, my friend, I understand this is your family and I know what you're capable of. In spite of that, your judgment is clouded; you don't operate on your own family. Let me help."

"No way, sir, I am not involving you or deserting my family again. I wanted you to know the truth in case this goes bad. I'll call you when I can."

WASHINGTON, D.C.

THE PHONE LINE WENT dead, the president stood motionless for a minute before he put the phone down. He wandered aimlessly around the room. Davenport was not listening, the man was in a no-win situation and there was no way to stop him. The only thing he could do now was what he did not do well. He had to wait for the next phone call and watch the news. The president stared blindly out the window.

"He said he was going west," the president muttered knowing full well what *west* meant. "The man's lost it."

Feeling helpless, he paced back and forth pounding his fist in his hand. The president knew exactly what Davenport had in his mind, he was going straight into the *Brotherhood's* nest somewhere deep in the Superstition Mountains near Phoenix.

"Damn, this is their headquarters. Going there is insanity, and there's nothing I can do about it except wait."

DFW Airport, Irving, Texas

Jennie breathed a sigh of relief when the flight attendant shut the door of the airplane and asked the passengers to buckle their seatbelts. She leaned back and tried to relax.

Poor Herman, there was no way he could have stopped them short of physically restraining them from boarding the plane. He tried hard to reason with them and everything he said made sense. She knew all the reasons she shouldn't go better than Herman did, but she also knew she had to go. As she walked away from him, he told her to call him if he could help.

Jennie and Kris sat near the back of the plane studying an Arizona map. The Phoenix insert showed the main airport, but not the private ones. She'd pick up a new city map at the car rental in Phoenix and see if it showed any of the smaller airstrips. However, she had a feeling the place where Josh was landing would not be on any map.

"How are we going to find daddy?" asked Kris.

"We won't have to. I'm sure he knows by now we're on our way. He'll find us and he won't be happy. When he does, just listen and please, Kris, don't talk back. He may try to send us away, but I won't go."

Jennie watched a range of emotions crossing her daughter's weary face and wondered how in the world she was holding up. She remembered how impossible it was to keep going when they told her Josh was dead. Kris was dealing with more than just her husband's death. Her twin daughters were linked in ways that defied logic and Laurie was missing. Either one of these happenings was devastating. She picked up Kris' hand and held it, "We'll manage."

"He really is different, isn't he, Mom?"

"He is, but the daddy who loves you is still there. He's been through some awful things in the past years and has had to deal with circumstances you and I cannot even imagine. He froze off his emotions to survive and he still suffers nightmares. Deep inside his mind, he'll be glad we are there. Just be patient, he's better than he was when I first found him and he will find his way back to us."

Kris pretended to study the map while watching tears slip from her mother's eyes.

Chapter 19

GEORGE REAVES' SHOULDERS DROOPED when he hung up the phone. General Thurman had ordered him to find Davenport and that was not happening. He checked all the known contacts and no one had a clue where the man was. Slapping the desk and muttering, he twisted around and stared out the window at the raging storm. Only a few lights were visible in the D.C. skyline. Thunder cracked and he shivered, it was not a night to be out and about. He decided not to go back to his quarters; he would rather stay here and bed down on the couch. He'd done that many times before.

The general's aide wondered if Lindberg ever dried out. The man was already rain-soaked when the general ordered him to fly out to Texas. There was no time for him to change clothes before boarding a commercial flight. He was furious and left in a huff slamming the office door. Reaves smiled, he enjoyed giving Lindberg those orders. He'd never liked the man; he was always talking down to him and now Reaves knew why. Davenport told the president that Lindberg had sold out to the *Brotherhood* just like Nathan Scott did. Well, he was going to end up in the brig with Scott. A big smile spread across Reaves' face.

Reaves picked up the phone and tried again to find Herman Wilkens. The police officer in Dallas had not shown up at the precinct and no one answered at his home. Wilkens was his last hope of finding Davenport. One of these days Davenport was going to cause the general to have a stroke. Reaves almost called the paramedics when Davenport told the general he would not be checking in again. Now, he was going to have to tell him that Davenport and Wilkens were nowhere to be found.

Sighing, Reaves poured a scotch and handed it to the general before he spoke.

"Hmm, news that bad, eh…" The general reached for the glass of amber liquid. He listened to Reaves then tossed back the drink and roared, "I want Davenport brought in."

"But, the president …"

"Issue that order. I want that undisciplined rogue in here. End of discussion."

"General, the president said…"

"I don't care what the president said," the general roared. "The man is under my authority, issue the damn order. Not another word, Reaves."

Reaves backed away and left the room without speaking. General Thurman was really riled up this time and wasn't about to listen to reason. He understood the general's frustration, the man hated being out of control and left in the dark. Reaves had no choice, he had to issue the order; however, he could postdate it and give Davenport a few more days to find his daughter.

Between Dallas and Phoenix

THE PLANE SOARED LOW beneath the clouds and just above the tree tops. Davenport poured a coffee and sat down across the aisle from Falco who appeared to be dozing.

What in the world was Jennie thinking? He closed his eyes. *She knows what I do is dangerous; she's already taken one bullet meant for me. Coming out here is not only foolish but, well, I don't want to say stupid, but it is, and she's not stupid. She knows worrying about her hampers me, I can't help it. Not only that, it doubles the risk in getting Laurie back.*

He could think of only one reason why she was doing this. She was afraid he would slip back into his survival mode, that robotic state without feelings. He'd felt himself closing off his emotions the last few days. He hated the way Kris' eyes welled up with tears when he cut her off. He felt Jennie watching him and he knew what she was thinking. She understood him so well it made him angry. He'd almost gone over the edge when she was shot last spring. Davenport cradled his head in his hands in prayer or despair. He wasn't sure which it was or how he was going to go forward. The problem was he didn't know if he could do what he had to if Jennie was there.

FALCO WATCHED HIS OLD friend through almost closed eyelids. The man was visibly shaken, how bad he couldn't tell. It had been too many years since they shared confidences. He could envision to a small degree what it would be like if his niece was abducted and his sister insisted on going with him to get her back. Could he carry out his orders with her along and watching? It was one thing to do his work when he was alone, but…? Interesting question…

HARRELL LOOKED BACK EVERY now and then checking on his passengers. Davenport came out of the office looking like the world just ended. Whatever the call was about, it wasn't good. The only time he had seen his friend look like this was when Jennie got shot. That was a really bad time. Davenport lost focus for a while and that was dangerous for everyone involved.

His eyes moved over to Falco. The man looked like he was asleep, but he was watching Davenport through almost closed eyes. *Hmmm,* Harrell muttered aloud. He wished he knew who the man was and why he was on the plane. More than that, he wanted to know why he was watching Davenport. *Maybe he's the cause of the tension.* Davenport had never mentioned him.

Well, his job was to fly the plane and keep under the radar. However, something was going on so he'd watch the man and time would tell.

WHEN HE WAS BEING logical Davenport knew why Jennie was coming. She loved him as he loved her. A faint smile crossed his face, but, damn it, she made him crazy sometimes. She'd told him repeatedly during the past six months that she'd never be left behind again. He understood that. He had let her think he was dead for six years and he knew how painful that had been for Jennie and his daughters. This new woman she'd turned into was much more capable than the woman she was years ago. The past few months he'd spent a lot of time teaching her defense tactics, simple ones, but effective ones she could manage. She could execute the moves, whether she'd use any of them remained to be seen. She had not been tested in real life situations and that was very different from practice sessions. From what Blakely told him, she did well defending herself last spring. However, the memory of when she was shot haunted him, he would never get that image out of his head.

He was the reason that happened. Jennie didn't deserve it, and his daughters did not deserve what was happening now. Two young men he never met, two young men his daughters loved were dead and all because of him. How did a father live with that? Could his daughters ever forgive him?

Turmoil clouded his mind. Davenport knew he couldn't function like this. He reminded himself that the only way out of a bad situation was to control his mind and do what had to be done. He had conquered personal issues before and he could do that again. His daughter and grandson were all that was important and it didn't matter who was watching. *I will not let the Brotherhood win this battle. I will get my family back.*

He asked himself the question he had asked six years ago. *How far am I willing to go to save my family?* The answer was the same as it had been back then. There could only be one answer, *All the way.*

Eyes closed, head bowed, Davenport cleared his mind of all the "what ifs" and went deep inside himself to that place where nothing existed except what he had to do. He had to seal his emotions off and not let anybody sidetrack him. When he raised his head and looked around the plane, he knew what he had to do. He'd come full circle, he was back in control.

He would put Jennie and Kris in a hotel, or better yet, leave them on the plane with Harrell. That might be best; they would be there if he needed to leave in a hurry. Either way, he would do whatever was necessary to get Laurie and Nicky back, no matter who was watching.

As always, the only real answer was to stop the *Brotherhood.* They would never leave him or his family alone. He had to stop them or die, and he did not want to die. Now that Jennie was with him again, he desperately wanted to live. This time they would be a family, their daughters and grandchildren would be with them.

He got up and went to the bathroom and splashed water in his face. The fog in his mind lifted and his mind was finally clear, his armor was in place.

When he came back and sat in his chair, both Falco and Harrell knew Davenport had grounded himself.

The man the *Brotherhood* called the *Ghost* was back.

Chapter 20

Tuesday Evening
October 25, 1983
DALLAS, TEXAS

HERMAN WILKENS DROVE LIKE a man possessed when he left the airport. His frustration level was off the scale, however, that was nothing new. The past year had been a continuous series of maddening events. He wasn't going to think about all those now. He had plenty of other problems to deal with today. Jennie and Kris had been more than enough.

There was no way he could have kept them from boarding that plane short of handcuffing them to a post and he chose not to do that. Maybe he should have, but they presented very convincing arguments. They could recognize Nicky while Davenport could not. Coupling that with Kris' ability to hear Laurie, he knew they'd have a better chance of finding her. He also figured that even if he took them to the safe house in Burleson they would make a run for it the minute his back was turned. He had no doubt about that.

"Well, the deed is done. Davenport will just have to handle it this time, I've been dealing with them all year long," he muttered aloud. "It's his turn now and I wish him luck. He's going to need it."

His main concern now was to get Molly and Sophie to the safe house in Burleson without being followed. He picked up his car phone and called Molly, he wanted her packed and ready to leave the minute he got there. After a year of not knowing what the hell was going on, he finally had the whole picture. Davenport's story had convinced him of the urgency to move his family.

He could not get Josh's parting words out of his mind, *"I'm sorry, old friend, but I'm afraid the life you were living yesterday is over."* It kept echoing in his head along with what would they do when this was over? Would they be able to live in their home if the *Brotherhood* knew about him? Would he still have a job? "Damn," he muttered and his foot pressed harder on the accelerator.

A few blocks from his house, Wilkens spotted someone tailing him. He detoured and went the opposite direction. After several fast reverses, the car was still following him. Playing with a couple of options, he settled on going home and then creating a diversion so Molly could get away without being followed. Pulling in the driveway, he hurried into the house.

Molly was on the sofa trying to put Sophie's shoes on her. Herman couldn't help laughing as Sophie kept wiggling her feet. "What are you doing, Sophie?" he asked the child. She just giggled and wiggled more.

"Good, you're packed and ready to go," Herman said when he saw the suitcases sitting beside them. "It was a useless trip. I missed Jennie and Kris at the air force base and had to go to the airport. There was no way I could talk them out of going to Phoenix so I conceded defeat nicely, you'd have been proud of me." Herman smiled, "Davenport will have to look after his wife and daughter. I've done it long enough; it's time for him to take over."

He sat down beside them and Sophie crawled into his lap. He held her feet still so Molly could get her shoes on her.

"Molly, my love, plans have changed slightly. The chief called me to come in so I need you and Sophie to go on to Burleson now. Take my bag with you, it's packed and in the bedroom. Here's Pastor Crane's address, it's about forty-five minutes there. He and his wife will take you to the house where we'll be staying and help you settle in. You'll like them, they are very kind."

"I thought you were on leave from the precinct."

"I am. I just have to finish up some paperwork. I'm hoping it won't take long. I'll load the suitcases and whatever else you need in your car before I go. It's in the garage, isn't it?"

"Yes, of course. I always park in the garage, you know that."

Herman smiled at Molly. He loaded the suitcases in the car along with a couple of boxes of food that she had packed. "You're ready now, everything is in the car. I checked the gas and you have a full tank. Call me at the precinct as soon as you get there and give me the address of the house where you are staying. I'll come as soon as I can."

He handed a piece of paper to her. "Hang on to this number, Molly. When you get to the safe house in Burleson, call it and leave the address with the man who answers. His name is Blakely. It's a contact number where Josh leaves messages. This way Josh can get the address and will join us there, hopefully with all his family. Here's what we're going to do. I'm going to leave first, and I want you to wait five or ten minutes before you open the garage door. Go straight to I-20 and take the exit to Burleson. It's an easy drive, I jotted the directions down."

Herman picked up Sophie and tossed her in the air. She was giggling when he sat her down. He kissed Molly and left before she could question why he wanted her to wait for a few minutes.

She really didn't need to ask him why. She had lived with a police officer way too long to be fooled. She knew someone was tailing him again and he was leading them away from her and Sophie. Molly looked at her watch and slipped the paper in her pocket.

She sat down and started playing patty cake with Sophie.

Chapter 21

ELEVEN HUNDRED MILES WEST of Dallas, Texas, a small plane made a rough landing in a remote field in the foothills of the Superstition Mountains in Arizona. Two men climbed out and walked around in utter silence as they waited for an ambulance to pick up their passenger. The pilot followed the men down the steps and stretched. Flying the plane was easy, but the landing was a bad one. "Sorry about the bumpy landing, this is not much of an airfield. I'm going to scout around and see if there's a place to take off with a few less potholes."

Al Lindberg was miserable and exhausted and rehashed his day. The way it was going, he was lucky the plane didn't crash. It had rained the entire time he was in Russia; he had put his jacket in the overhead bin hoping it would dry during the long flight from Moscow. It didn't. The jacket was damp and wrinkled when he landed in D.C. and the general didn't give him time to change out of his wet clothes. Upon landing at DFW, he drove straight to the Fort Worth hospital where Davenport's daughter was. He should have checked in with the *Brotherhood* hours before he did. When he reached the chairman, he was reprimanded and given more orders. He was to pick up Davenport's comatose daughter and accompany her on the *Brotherhood's* plane to Phoenix. Another plane ride, his mood didn't get any better.

It was a tense ride from Dallas to Phoenix and Lindberg was not happy. On top of everything else, he was saddled with Otto Fleicher, a man known as the *Brotherhood's* enforcer. He had encountered Fleicher several times in the past and the man was a certified lunatic. You could not turn your back on him, not safely anyway.

"Well, the idiocy ends now. I want a hotel room, hot food, a shower, dry clothes, and a bed," Lindberg muttered to himself as he paced around the potholes. The place was desolate; all he could see was low-growing shrubs, cactus, and a few scrawny trees near the end of the runway. Beyond that was a jagged rock mountain with heavy clouds looming overhead.

"Damn, damn, damn," he grumbled. It was going to rain here if they had to wait very long.

Otto Fleicher stood stock-still with a poker face watching him. Lindberg couldn't read him, the man never blinked. He just stared, it wasn't natural. He was devoid of normal feelings for his self or anyone else; even worse, he was sadistic and enjoyed torturing people. Lindberg had seen him take down several men for no reason at all with that razor blade he carried; it was not a pretty sight. Lindberg shivered as gusts of wind blew over him. At last, he spotted the headlights of an ambulance coming toward the plane.

"The woman's inside," Lindberg told the two attendants. They hauled a stretcher up the ramp and moved the unconscious woman to it, then carefully carried her down to the ambulance.

"Where are the doctor's orders?" the smaller attendant asked.

"The doctor didn't send written instructions, the woman's in a coma. She was in an accident, has multiple injuries, and not expected to live. I'm to tell you she's a high security risk so there will be no name, you can call her Jane. Verbal orders are to keep her in isolation with a guard at her door around the clock until further notice. No one except a nurse or doctor is to be allowed in her room. Further instructions will be sent."

The two paramedics shook their heads in confusion and started asking questions.

Fleicher's rasping voice filled the night, "It's time to leave. You have all the instructions you need, get her out of here." The enforcer started toward them. The attendants backed away as fast as they could and looked over at Lindberg who motioned for them to leave. They jumped in the ambulance and took off.

Another car was supposed to pick up the two men. Lindberg sat down on the ramp steps to wait. It was too cold to sit still and he got up and walked around. "Where's the child being held?" he asked looking at Fleicher.

"He's at another place. He's not your problem, just the woman."

Lindberg flinched at the growl coming at him. Suddenly, he knew he had to get away right now and he changed his plans. He climbed up the ramp and stood in the door of the plane to put some distance between him and Fleicher. He turned and looked down at the man.

"Tell your boss the trap is set. I have to get back to Dallas and wipe my trail clean before G-2 finds out about me. You can also tell him I'm through doing his dirty work. This was the last job; my debt is paid in full."

Lindberg turned to face the pilot, "Start the engine, I need to get back to Dallas fast." Without warning, he was yanked backwards out of the plane and down the ramp. His body crashed into every step.

"You're not going back to Dallas; your orders are to stay in Phoenix until you're told otherwise. No one leaves the *Brotherhood* alive, you know that. Do you still want to go back?"

"Damn right, I do," he yelled fighting his way to his feet only to be flattened again. Crawling to the stairs, he pulled himself upright and was starting up the steps again when something exploded against the back of his head. Everything went black.

A dark limousine came to a stop beside Fleicher. The man took one last look at the body on the ground and the blood forming a puddle underneath Lindberg's head. He smiled and got in the car.

At the sound of the gunshot, the steps to the plane were rapidly pulled up and the door slammed shut. The pilot moved fast, he'd been around Fleicher before and didn't trust him. The engine started after a couple of tries then the plane taxied down the field and turned around.

The small plane powered up, hit the potholes hard, and was off the field before the limousine pulled back on to the highway.

BETWEEN DALLAS AND PHOENIX

DAVENPORT LEANED BACK IN the seat watching as ominous sky grew dim. It would be dark and probably raining before they landed, that was not going to make his search easier. Harrell had the coordinates of the *Brotherhood's* private airfield and would do a flyby before landing. It would be a bonus if the *Brotherhood's* plane was still there, but he doubted it.

"What's the plan?" asked Falco.

"We're headed for a small airfield east of Phoenix near the Superstition Mountains where I've landed in the past with the *Brotherhood.* I'm guessing this is where they're heading. It's as close as you can get to their headquarters by plane. The bastards have baited the trap with my daughter and grandson and they'll be waiting for me, they know I'll come. The chairman is fanatical. I've been a thorn in his side for years now, and he'll want to be in on the kill."

"Attacking your family, that's major. There's no honor in that. We honor families."

"I know, Falco, these people have no consciences or loyalty except to the *Brotherhood.* I infiltrated the organization years ago and I know too much. I was there long enough to learn all their plans and the names of the people involved. Fear is the most potent motivator, and what the *Brotherhood* fears is what's in my head." His eyes went dark and cold, "They will never rest until I am eliminated or I eliminate them."

Unable to sit still, Davenport got coffee and went back to his office and stood there for several minutes. Then he leaned over and pressed a spot under the shelf releasing a panel that slid sideways. Reaching into the cavity he pulled out a small notebook wrapped in plastic. When his hand touched it, years of memories flashed before his eyes. Places he had been with the *Brotherhood*, the things he had heard and seen, and the men, always the power-hungry men. He would never forget them and their monstrous plans for taking control of United States. Breathing deeply, he sat down and focused on the book. Scanning the coded pages, he refreshed his memory of all the places where the *Brotherhood* had connections and the locations where they might take his daughter and grandson. There was only one place where they would have taken his grandson and that one he knew without looking. The unknown was where they would take a woman in a coma. That was what he had to figure out. He sat very still and scanned each page several times then put the book back in its hiding place. With the locations firmly planted in his photographic mind, he took his coffee and went to his seat behind Harrell.

He turned toward Falco, "This isn't your regular ballgame. My daughter's in a coma and requires special care and handling. This limits the places they can take her, there are three possibilities.

"I'm about to do the flyby," Jack Harrell called from the pilot's seat. "It's almost dark and the wind has picked up."

Strong winds sweeping off the nearby Superstition Mountains bounced the plane around. The field appeared empty except for something stretched out on the ground, it looked like a body. "Loop around, Harrell, I want to see if that's a body and if there are any other men down there."

Harrell pulled up and circled the field again then Davenport gave him the go ahead to set down. It was a rough landing when the plane hit the potholes. Falco grabbed the arms of his chair; he wasn't used to small aircraft. Harrell swung the plane about and came to a jarring stop near the body. Davenport had the door open and was shoving the steps down before it had fully stopped. Cold rain pelted the men when they stepped on the hard-packed desert airstrip. Gusts of wind coming off the mountains made it difficult to stand upright.

Bending over the man on the ground Davenport checked the pulse in the man's neck. "He's alive." Looking up at Falco he continued, "It's

Al Lindberg, he's the one who took my daughter from the hospital in Fort Worth."

He dragged the unconscious man over to the plane and propped him against the stairs. He shook him until his head tossed back and forth on the metal steps, "Wake up, you bastard, where's my daughter?"

Lindberg blinked trying to clear his vision then scowled when his eyes focused on Davenport. "Well, well, look who came back from the dead." He leaned away from the steps and rubbed the back of his head, his hand came away bloody.

"Where's my daughter?" asked Davenport.

Lindberg wiped at the blood running down his neck and back, "I need help, can't you see I'm injured? My head is bleeding."

"You're not hurt bad, it's just a surface wound. That's not all that will be bloody if you don't answer me. I'll ask one more time, where is my daughter?"

"You're not calling the shots, Davenport. I'm not taking orders from you anymore."

Falco leaned forward and plunged his knife in the ground between Lindberg's legs, "You will show some respect. The next time I won't be aiming at the ground. I suggest you think before you answer. Where is the woman?"

"I don't know," Lindberg yelled as he twisted away from the knife. "I don't know. I was going to leave with the plane, but Fleicher yanked me down the stairs. The last thing I remember was fighting with him."

Lindberg watched with horror as the knife struck closer to his body.

"Last chance, where's the woman?" ordered Falco. He grabbed and held the knife up.

"They put her in an ambulance. I don't know where they took her, I didn't even see it drive off," he screamed as he tried to back up the steps of the plane.

"Who are they?" Davenport jerked him down and slammed him hard against the metal steps.

"I don't know," his voice elevated to a higher pitch when he saw Falco step toward him again. "I don't know who they were, I don't know."

"One more time, who were the men?" Falco came closer brandishing the knife. This time the knife sliced through Lindberg's trousers grazing his upper leg.

"Two guys in paramedic uniforms put her in an ambulance and I climbed back into the plane," he screamed as he tried again to back up the steps. "Fleicher yanked me down the steps. The last thing I remember before everything went black was fighting with the bastard. The next person I saw was Davenport, that's all I know. I don't know anything else."

Falco turned and smiled at Davenport. "That's probably all we're going to get from him. Does this give you any ideas?"

"A few ideas and a few questions, "What color was the ambulance, Lindberg?"

"It won't do you any good, Davenport. The big guys are watching; you'll never get to her now."

Davenport put out his arm and stopped Falco from moving in. "Tell me the color of the ambulance and everything else you know or I'll let him at you again. You think Fleicher is a mean bastard, you better not aggravate my friend and his knife."

Pulling himself up a step, Lindberg faced Davenport. "It was Army green, a military ambulance. Now you know all I do."

"Why, Lindberg, why did you do this?"

"My freedom, man, I made a mistake. I had to do what they told me or they would have turned me in."

"You got greedy, didn't you? You always were." Davenport laughed. "Well, your freedom is history now, you should have known better than to cross me. Keep him here, Falco, I'm calling the military police to pick him up."

Davenport climbed over Lindberg and went inside the plane. He called the general then dialed another number. "I need transportation, here's my location."

When Davenport came down the stairs, he jerked Lindberg to his feet. "Jack, move the plane over near those boulders and bushes so it won't be so visible then I'll handcuff Lindberg to the steps. Military police are on their way to pick him up. After they pick him up him, move the plane to the other airstrip we talked about. It has a hangar so you will be out of the weather. There's also a café within walking distance. I'm hoping to bring Jennie and Kris out to stay in the plane with you. I have no idea how long this will take so fuel the plane and be ready to leave on a moment's notice."

The plane taxied over and Davenport handcuffed a loudly protesting Lindberg to the staircase railing. It wasn't long before two black sedans rolled up. A man got out and shook hands with Davenport as he passed car keys to him then he got in the other car and left in a matter of minutes.

"I'll be in touch as soon as I can," Davenport said tossing the handcuff key to Harrell. "Get some food and rest up."

Harrell grinned and gave him a thumbs-up when he closed the door to the plane.

"You can't leave me hooked up out in the rain," yelled Lindberg shaking water and blood off. "I'm injured and bleeding…"

Davenport nodded at Falco and they got in the black sedan. As they drove away, thunder cracked, the sky opened up, and torrents of rain poured down on the air field.

WASHINGTON, D.C.

GENERAL THURMAN WAS SILENT when he hung up the phone. Davenport made him furious, the man was impossible; he didn't give him a chance to say a word. He picked up the paper he'd dropped when Davenport's call came in and read the memo again.

"Reaves, get Davenport back on the line."

The phone rang and rang. "He's not answering, sir."

"Have you issued the orders to pick him up?"

Reaves turned away and walked back to his desk. "I'm almost finished with the paperwork."

"Cancel the orders, but keep trying to reach Davenport; I have to talk to him. For a change, there are things I know that he doesn't. Get the president on the line; he may talk to Davenport before I do. I have to get word to him some way. Any news on that cop in Dallas?"

Reaves shook his head, "No, sir. I haven't been able to reach him either."

The general dropped down in his chair with a thud. He stared at the paper again and shook his head. The whole world was going insane. Davenport and that cop had to know about this. He leaned back in his chair and sat motionless for a while. He felt sick at his stomach.

"Keep trying to reach one of them, Reaves," he said. "It's urgent."

Chapter 22

CLAUDE HOUSER WATCHED THE sun sink below the mountaintops; darkness fell fast in the deep canyon. The 5,000-foot Superstition Mountains loomed high above him. Sheer-sided, jagged rock ridges protected his hidden sanctuary on all sides. This was home, the one place he felt safe and secure. There was only one narrow hazardous road leading to where he and Jacob had built their fortress. The rocky overhangs made it impossible for anyone to get in other than by the one road and a heavy iron gate bolted into the rock wall guarded the entrance. The gate could only be opened with an access code.

His brother had traveled to the United States ahead of him to search for the perfect location for their headquarters. When Jacob found the place, he'd joined him and together they built a small cabin near a small fresh water spring. Digging deep into the mountain at the back of the cabin, they created a secret hiding place for the gold they had accumulated. All went well until a landslide buried him under a ton of rock. Jacob dug him out and patched him up as well as he could, but the damage to his legs was done.

They planned and built the fortress to resemble the ones in their homeland of Hungary. Pain crossed Houser's face as memories invaded his mind. He had to stop thinking about his brother. Jacob had died a year ago. Swiping at his face, he turned his back on the view and rolled to his desk. He picked up the Spear of Destiny and let himself feel the power. *Oh, yes Jacob, I will carry out all our plans.*

The chairman immersed himself in the latest reports from the *Brotherhood.* They were getting close to total domination, it was working exactly like Khrushchev predicted. *Just feed the unsuspecting Americans small doses of socialism until the takeover is complete.* One major threat still existed, but that would be eliminated in the next few days.

"If all goes according to plan, Davenport will be in my hands tonight," Houser gloated. He was still smiling when Hans brought in a silver tray covered with a cloth. He sat the chairman's dinner on the table near the fireplace and stirred the fire to a brighter glow. "Otto is here, Mr. Chairman. I put him in the front study."

"See if he wants food, Hans, tell him I'll be with him within the hour. You may open the wine now."

Hans was his first successful experiment in mind control. The young man now functioned as his legs. His brother had found the boy wandering lost in the mountains and offered him a home. He and Jacob remembered the Fuhrer's experiments in brainwashing children's minds and it intrigued them. Hans had been a perfect subject. This test case led to the creation of a school for children, a school where they could train assassins.

He picked up the large crystal goblet and swished the red wine around enjoying its subtle aroma. He nodded at his brother's picture on the mantel and raised his glass in a silent toast before cutting into his steak.

In exactly one hour the chairman rolled into the front study. Fleicher was just finishing his meal. "You have news about Davenport?"

"Yes, Mr. Chairman, he is on his way here."

"I was expecting Lindberg to be with you. Where is he?"

"He refused to come."

"Elaborate, I want the whole story."

"He said to tell you he had paid his debt to you and was through doing your dirty work. He tried to leave, but I stopped him. We fought and I won," Fleicher growled with satisfaction. "He will not be a problem ever again."

"Are you sure?"

The muscled man grimaced and dropped his eyes. "I am sure," he answered through gritted teeth.

"Where is Davenport's daughter?"

"She has been put in the infirmary under guard just as you ordered."

"Davenport, where is he?"

"Lindberg said he would be flying in tonight."

"Very good, Otto, I knew he would come for his daughter. When he does, you'll be waiting. Bring him straight to me. The woman will no longer matter, she's just the bait. Do whatever you want with her. She's of no further use once we have Davenport in our hands."

You're mine now, Davenport, Houser gloated. It paid to have friends everywhere, even in the military. The child was well hidden. He had very definite plans for that boy, plans that Davenport would not be happy about. He grew excited at the thought of watching the man's face when he told him about his plan to brainwash his grandson. After all the trouble and delays Davenport had caused him, it would be a pleasure to watch him realize he could not prevent it.

The chairman looked deep into Fleicher's empty eyes, the man had no soul. The little bit of humanity he once possessed was destroyed when he and Jacob attempted their first brainwashing experiment. However, it made him a most useful tool.

"Make sure you don't let Davenport disappear again. He's not a ghost; the man is flesh and blood. You've lost him several times and disappointed me."

The chairman held up a black cylinder and put his thumb on a button. "You know what will happen to you if you lose him again. Do you understand me?"

When the pain started Fleicher felt the blood drain from his face, sweat poured down his face. He stammered nervously.

"Do you understand me?"

"Yes, master, I understand you, I will not fail again." Digging his fingers into his legs, Fleicher glared at Houser. "I will bring Davenport to you."

"That's good, Otto. I want to see his face when he hears my plans for his grandson and realizes he has no way out."

Chapter 23

*H*ELP... *THE EVIL IS BACK. Help me...i'm so scared.*
The young woman tried as hard as she could to move, she couldn't even wiggle her little finger. She listened to the sounds around her and her fear grew. She didn't know what was happening, she tried to scream. Once again, no sound came out of her mouth. That other voice, the one in her head, confused her. Her head pounded, she felt like she was going to throw up.

Is anybody here? Please, somebody, help me....I'm alive. Help...

JENNIE AND KRIS LANDED at Glendale Airport in Phoenix. Jennie was headed for the nearest car rental when Kris stumbled and dropped her purse and suitcase. She bent over holding her head.

Jenny grabbed her daughter to keep her from falling. "What's wrong, honey?"

"My head is hurting so bad, I can barely see." Tears ran down Kris' face and she leaned against her mom.

Jennie guided her to a seat. "It's Laurie, Mom. She's scared and yelling for help. I don't know what's happening to her." Kris sat and held her head as she rocked back and forth. Jennie grabbed their bags and put them beside Kris.

"Sit still, Kris, I'll be right back. I'm going to get a wet towel. Try to get Laurie to calm down."

Kris was still rocking when she returned and Jennie wiped her daughter's pale face then sat down beside her. "Are you hearing anything else?"

"Not much, Mom. Laurie's scared and confused; she doesn't know where she is. She keeps saying the evil is back. I think her fear is making me sick."

Jennie dug in her purse and gave Kris a peppermint hoping it would ease her nausea. "Ask Laurie where she is."

"She thinks she was in an airplane and then a car, but that's all she knows. She doesn't know where she is. Oh, Mom, she doesn't know me. She's asking who I am," Kris sobbed. "We have to find her soon, something is horribly wrong."

"We will. Can you sit here for a few minutes by yourself? The car rental is just across the hall. It's not crowded so it shouldn't take me very long to arrange for a car then we can leave and check the hospitals."

As she ran to the car rental, Jennie kept looking back at Kris and praying she wouldn't faint and fall off the chair. When her daughters were little and one of them got hurt or sick, the other one felt the pain and suffered the same symptoms. The connection they shared was bewildering and quite often frustrating. Jennie was usually aware when something was wrong with them although she never had the bond they did. By the way Kris was reacting, she knew Laurie's head was hurting really bad. Jennie was hoping Kris could tell if they got close to Laurie when they drove around. It was time to find out just how good her extrasensory perception was.

She had no idea where Josh was or even where to look for him. She knew he would be searching for Laurie and she intended to be there when he found her. Kris would be able to communicate with Laurie and keep her calm.

Kris was still having trouble focusing when the rental car arrived. Jennie took her to the car then went back for their bags. Rain peppered the windshield as they drove away from the airport. The clerk at the car rental had circled the locations of the Phoenix hospitals and it wasn't far to the first one, St. Josephs Hospital. Ten minutes later, Jennie parked under a portico and hurried inside.

"I'm looking for a young woman who was brought in earlier today. I think she might be my daughter. She was in an accident and has a head injury, they told me she's in a coma. Could you check and see if anyone is here in that condition?" Jennie asked the woman at the information desk.

"I haven't heard of anyone in a coma. Are you sure it's this hospital?"

"No, I'm not. I don't know where they took her. I just know it was a hospital."

"If you don't mind waiting, I'll call the other hospitals and see if she's in one of them. What is her name?"

"It's Laurie Parrino, but I don't think they know her name."

"Let me make a few calls." The receptionist pointed to the far side of the room, "There's coffee over on that table, please help yourself."

Jennie paced around the room. Coffee might help Kris, she thought. She poured a cup and added sugar and cream. Looking across the room at the receptionist, she called out, "I'll be right back."

Kris was getting out of the car when Jennie opened the door. "I can't wait out here, Mom. I'm coming in with you, I can see better now."

Jennie handed Kris the coffee as they went back in. "We won't have to go to all the hospitals; the receptionist is checking them for us."

Kris sat down and sipped her coffee and Jennie poured another one for herself. It had been a long time since she ate that chicken sandwich on the plane. "We have to eat something when we leave here, Kris. I'm getting hungry."

The receptionist walked over to them shaking her head. "No one has been admitted to any of the Phoenix hospitals in that condition. Maybe it wasn't right in Phoenix; there are several small towns around here. Do you know where she was injured?"

Jennie closed her eyes and took a deep breath. It was in Fort Worth, but that won't help, she thought. "No, I don't know any details."

"I'm so sorry. I wish I could help more," said the woman.

Jennie drove west. When they came to a group of hotels and places to eat, she stopped at a small café that had several cars parked around it.

"We need to eat, Kris, and I want to look at the city map. Afterwards, we'll drive around and you can listen, maybe we'll find a place where Laurie's voice is stronger."

DAVENPORT WAS HEADING FOR Luke Air Force Base on the west side of Phoenix. The chairman had connections there and Lindberg described a military ambulance. Doctors and nurses would be available to take care of her there. He was betting this was where they took Laurie. Jennie was landing at the Glendale Airport not far from the base so maybe he would get lucky and find her. He had to get his wife and daughter safely stashed in a hotel or in the airplane with Harrell. He knew it was unlikely they would stay put, but he had to try.

Falco kept bugging him for food, and it sounded like the man was not going to shut up until he got it. Davenport grumbled and pulled in the parking lot of the next café he saw. When they stepped inside the door, Davenport's eyes landed on his wife and daughter. He stopped and pointed them out to Falco.

Davenport went straight to Jennie and Kris and leaned on the table staring at them. "Not that you have ever paid much attention to what I've told you to do, but what do you think you're doing here?"

Falco followed and slid into the booth directly behind Jennie. He picked up the menu and motioned to the waitress.

Jennie looked up at the dark scowl covering her husband's face and a smile lit up her features, she was relieved to see him. "I knew you'd find us, but I didn't think it would be this quick. I told you I wasn't going to be left behind again, you know that."

"I do, but you also know I don't agree." Shifting his angry eyes to his daughter his voice softened a little when he saw her, "Kris, you're pale, are you feeling all right?"

"No, not very good, Daddy, Laurie's scared. It's making me sick and mom is trying to make me eat again." She looked at her mother, "I'm not hungry." She rested her aching head on her hands for a second then looked back up when she felt her dad staring at her. "Well, are you going to sit down or just stand there glaring at me?"

Josh slid into the seat beside Jennie. "Tell me what you know."

"Laurie's been crying for help ever since we landed, I think she's close by. I don't have to strain to hear her, it's like the sound's been turned up. We checked St. Joseph Hospital and she wasn't there. The receptionist called the other Phoenix hospitals and no one in a coma has been admitted to any of them. She said there are a lot of small towns around the area. Laurie could be in one of their hospitals, and we're wasting all this time eating," Kris fussed.

The waitress put a grilled cheese sandwich and a chocolate milkshake down in front of Kris. She looked at it and her stomach growled. "It does look good, Mom."

"Then you better eat, Krissie, you know your mother," Davenport said.

The waitress sat Jennie's bowl of soup and sandwich down and asked Josh if he wanted anything.

"A cup of coffee will be enough."

"Hey, Falco, look who beat us here, my wife and daughter." He turned to Jennie, "Remember Tony Falco? You met him years ago when I was playing the drums in the band on Friday nights. We've sort of joined forces in finding Laurie."

"I remember him. It's been a long time, Tony, I'm glad you're here."

"Now back to business, my dear wife, just what were you going to do if you found Laurie?"

"I don't know exactly, I just know I have to find her. I'll get her home somehow."

"The people who took her don't play by the rules, Jennie. They are not going to let you have her, they won't respond to a mother's tears either. Did you rent a car?"

"Yes, it's out front, the small silver Mercury."

"I want you and Kris to check into the hotel next door. You know I need to know you are safe, Jennie."

"No, I'm not staying behind. You can take the car away, but I'll just rent another one."

He sighed heavily. "Remember what you and Kris agreed to in Dallas, you promised to do what I said. It's the only way I can keep everyone safe."

"No one's after us now, Daddy. I can still hear Laurie and I can talk to her."

"I know you can, Kris, and the time may come when I need you to do that for me. But right now, please listen to me. Here's what's going to happen. You and Jennie can either sit here in the restaurant or go to the hotel next door while Falco and I check the air force base. It's possible she's been taken there. Neither of you can go on the base, you don't have clearance. I told you once before, I can't do my job while taking care of you."

Seeing Jennie's tired face, Davenport's voice softened. "You're exhausted, you need to rest and Kris is almost sick. She's pale and her hands are shaking. You both need to trust me to take care of this. Remember, Laurie and Nicky are what's important."

"Do you really think Laurie is at the base, Josh?" asked Jennie.

"It's one possibility. There are a couple of places they could have taken her where someone would be available to take care of her."

"What will you do if you find her?"

"I'll make arrangements for her to be transferred to my plane and Harrell will fly her back to Hensley Field in Grand Prairie. You and Kris will have to go with her. We can't send her alone, not in a coma. Kris, it would be better if you're with her, you can reassure her."

"What then, Josh? What about Nicky?

"I'll have Herman meet you at Hensley Field and he will take you to the safe house in Burleson. That's where you were, Kris. Molly and Herman are already there with Sophie. I've arranged for a nurse at that end to take care of Laurie. If Laurie's at the base, we'll stop here and pick you both up in the ambulance. If she's not, I'll let you know."

"You'll let me know? What does that mean? Sounds like you're going somewhere else. What about Nicky?"

"Jennie, no more questions. I will find Laurie and I'm pretty sure I know where Nicky is. I will find him. Don't cause me to fail worrying about you." He paused and looked at Kris, "I have a feeling when I find Laurie Kris will know about it before I can call you. Just sit here and eat now. If we're gone more than an hour, you should go to the hotel and check in until you hear from me."

"You don't have the phone number…"

Josh stood up. "A phone number, really, Jennie. Kris, if you can, tell Laurie I'm coming to get her and I'll take her home."

He pulled out a small notebook and wrote a number on it then ripped the page out and handed it to Jennie. "This will reach Blakely. I don't expect to have trouble, but if anything goes awry, this is where we leave messages for each other. Falco and I ate on the plane and only came in for coffee. Let's go, Falco."

Falco didn't move. "Speak for yourself, I ordered a hamburger and fries. I've learned not to pass up food when I have the opportunity."

"Outvoted, I see," grumbled Davenport. "He motioned to the waitress and asked what kind of pie they had. Falco's hamburger and Davenport's pie arrived at the same time and they ate quickly.

"Jennie, I really think you should finish eating and check in the hotel to wait for my call. There's no need to sit here for an hour or so, you both need rest. Take the car over there, we may want it later." He swallowed the last bite of his coconut cream pie and got up.

"Let's move, Falco."

Kris and Jennie watched the two men leave. "Well, now we don't have to worry about finding Josh," Jennie mumbled. "It'll be all right, Kris. You need to eat your sandwich." Jennie stirred her soup before taking a spoonful. "My soup is already cool."

DAVENPORT PULLED UP TO the gate at the base, rolled down his window, and handed the guard his identification. "We have orders to pick up a young accident victim who was admitted to the infirmary earlier today."

"You're cleared, sir, but who is the other man?" asked the guard. "I need to see his papers."

"He's the paramedic assigned to take care of the young woman."

"His identification, sir, or he will have to wait out here."

Davenport turned to Falco saying, "You heard the man, you'll have to wait out here. I'll check the infirmary. If she's there, they will have people who can move her to the car for me. If not, I can carry her."

He turned his face away from the guard and lowered his voice, "If anything goes wrong and I don't come out in about thirty minutes, come find me."

A slow grin crossed Falco's face, "What makes you think I can get in?"

"I haven't forgotten some of the skills you had years ago. I doubt you would have a problem."

Falco gave him a thumbs up and grinned. "It would be a pleasure, all this sitting around is boring." Falco slipped out of the car and walked over to the gatehouse and started talking to the guard.

Davenport's black sedan drove deep inside Luke Air Force Base and stopped when he located the infirmary.

JENNIE PAID THE CASHIER and they went to the car. "Kris, are you hearing anything now?"

"Nothing that makes sense, Laurie's still screaming and my head is pounding again." She closed her eyes and massaged her temples.

Pulling in a parking space near the side entrance to the hotel, Jennie turned the motor off and leaned back in her seat. "I'm really tired, Kris. Your dad's right, we do need to rest. I've been on the go ever since a nightmare woke me up back in Scotland. I guess that was yesterday but I've lost track of time."

They checked in, signed the hotel register, and started toward the elevator when Kris stopped and grabbed Jennie's arm.

"Something has happened, Mom. Laurie's not making a sound. She's not answering me either, she's not even mumbling."

Chapter 24

HERMAN WILKENS' FACE WAS grim when he put the car in gear and pulled away from his house. The street was empty except for a black sedan parked down the block. He drove slowly watching the rear view mirror and was turning the corner before the sedan started moving. He speeded up trying to draw him away from Molly. The sedan caught up with him at a red light, the guy wasn't even trying to hide the fact he was tailing him.

Watching the time, Wilkens relaxed when five minutes passed and the car was still with him. Molly and Sophie had left the house and were on the way to Burleson and away from all this mess. He drove straight to police headquarters making no evasive moves in hopes the guy following him would think he was going on duty.

Davenport's words had made an impact. He pulled in the parking lot and just sat in the car, he couldn't help wondering what kind of future they would have when all this was finished. Would they be safe in Dallas? Would he even have a job? If so, what would he do, his police career was most likely ended. His shoulders drooped like a man carrying a heavy load when he left the car and went inside the building. It was like he was seeing it for the first time, or maybe the last time. Wilkins loved his job and he was good at it, all he ever wanted to be was a police officer.

Opening his desk drawer, he picked up a notebook and wrote the contact number Josh had given him on the inside of the cover then dropped it in the bottom drawer. Just a precaution, who knows, he might need to have someone call Blakely. It never hurt to have a backup plan or a couple of them. Next, he wrote a short note to Chief Sanders saying if he didn't call by midnight he should call the number in the note and talk to a man named Blakely. *Tell Blakely I've picked up a tail and was going to try to lose him before joining Molly and Sophie at the safe house. If I haven't reported in, tell him I've probably been picked up. I'm guessing my tail is the people who took Davenport's family.*

Wilkens tossed the note on his desk and paced back and forth waiting for Molly's call. He'd feel better when he knew she was at the safe house. Looking out a window, he spotted a dark car parked in the next block; it looked like the black sedan that was tailing him. He could only make out one person in the car. *You're right, Davenport, they are sill with me.* Sighing, he turned back to his desk and put the note in an envelope with Chief Sanders name on it. Wilkens' frown deepened when he walked down the hall and knocked on the chief's door.

The chief looked up from his desk then back at his watch. "I'm assuming you met with Davenport. What are his plans?"

"He arrived a few hours ago but didn't stay very long. There's not much I can tell you, Chief. All he told me was he's going after his daughter and grandson; he didn't say where he was going. He wants me to stay with his family at a safe house he arranged, that's where I sent Molly and Davenport's granddaughter." Wilkens went to the window and looked down the block at the car then turned back to the chief.

"I'm being tailed so I came directly here trying to draw the guy away from Molly. There's a car parked in the next block with one man in it. I'm guessing he's waiting for me to leave."

"You said Molly and Davenport's granddaughter, what about his wife and daughter? Where are they?"

"He wanted them to stay at the safe house but they refused. Both women are pretty headstrong and they boarded a plane for Phoenix so he'll have to deal with them when they get there." He checked his watch. "I'm hoping Molly and Sophie get to the safe house without incident, they haven't had time to get there yet."

"You said Phoenix? If his wife went there, that's where Davenport is." The chief reached for a notepad and wrote a few words on it. "So where's the safe house and what's the plan?"

Wilkens ignored the chief's question about the safe house and stood staring at the envelope in his hands. Something was disturbing him and he wasn't sure what it was. Davenport didn't say he couldn't give the number to the chief, but he was uneasy about it. *However, I'm being tailed so I better have a backup plan.*

Wilkens handed the envelope to the chief, "This is a contact number where messages can be left for Davenport. I'll wait here until I know Molly and Sophie are okay then I'll try to lose the tail so I can join them. Davenport wants me there for extra security. If I don't call you by midnight, call that number and tell the man who answers I'm missing."

"Who do you think is tailing you?"

"I'm not sure. I'm guessing it's the people who snatched Davenport's family and they are hoping I'll lead them to the daughter who got away. If I can't lose them by midnight, I'll let them follow me back here."

"Are you saying you think they might try to pick you up?"

"I don't know what they are up to. I'm being extra cautious."

"Well, this is a mess. I knew when General Thurman told me Davenport was alive, we had problems." The chief fiddled with the envelope for a minute then put it in his desk and closed the drawer. "Go, do what you have to, Wilkens."

Wilkens was almost out the door when the chief called him back. "There are phones everywhere. Keep me in the loop."

Yes, sir. I'll let you know when I leave."

Wilkens counted the tiles in the hall floor as he started pacing again waiting for his phone to ring. A very long hour later, Molly called and Wilkens relaxed. She and Sophie got to the house without any problems. Pastor Crane and his wife had been very kind and helped

The Davenport Daughters

131

them get their things in a house located next door to the parsonage. Mrs. Crane even left a casserole and cookies in the kitchen for them.

"That makes me feel better, Molly. I'll come as soon as I can so save some dinner for me and don't worry. The chief stacked a lot of papers on my desk; it will take a while to go through them." He tried not to worry Molly any more than he had to. She knew when he evaded telling her the truth, she always did. He could never fool her.

Wilkens looked out his window one more time; the dark car was still there. He closed his eyes and rubbed his temples. It was going to be a long evening.

WASHINGTON, D. C.

GENERAL THURMAN SNATCHED UP the phone the instant it rang, "Yes, Mr. President, thank you for calling back so promptly. It's about Davenport, I can't reach him and I'm hoping you can…"

"I have no way to get hold of him right now. He checks in with me at midnight when he can. What do you need, General?"

"Here's the situation. We're still uncovering dirty recruits of Mason Silverman, the traitor who sold out to the *Brotherhood*. Several of his recruits are embedded in high places in the government. I don't have all their names yet, but I will, and I will take care of them. However, we have a more urgent problem tonight. I found out this evening there's a spy in the Dallas police department. We've been trying to reach Davenport and Wilkens, the police officer in Dallas, and we can't locate either man. They have to know about this, this is a game-changer, Mr. President. The spy is the interim chief of police in Dallas. The real chief had a heart attack last month and a man named Ralph Sanders has taken over his job. I just found out he's one of Silverman's recruits."

"Blast that man. The trouble Silverman has caused just won't quit."

"Well, there's more, we found out a lot from Nathan Scott during interrogation. The man's angry and wants to take everyone down with him. He told us CIA has sent a death squad after Davenport."

"What? That's insane, Davenport's loyalty has been proven time and again. What do you mean, a death squad in CIA?"

"Scott said the man orchestrating this is a very dirty and powerful analyst inside CIA. We haven't been able to discover his name; we're still working on it." The general paused. "Mr. President, it is urgent Davenport be warned. He's been set up to look like he's gone rogue and totally out of control, that's what I thought until I heard this. Orders are to stop him, no matter what it takes, that's why the death squad. Can you get word to Davenport? Wilkens needs to know, too. If he's sharing information with the acting chief of police in Dallas, it could compromise everything."

"You're right. This could put Davenport in the *Brotherhood's* hands. I have one number I can try. It may not reach him, but I can leave him a message. Other than that, I have to wait for him to call me. As soon as I hear from him, I'll let you know. I've no idea how to reach Wilkens except to call the police department, so you'll have to work that out. Stay in touch with me, General. Let me know who the other traitors are inside CIA. I want names."

"So do I, Mr. President, so do I."

Chapter 25

"**D**ARN ELEVATOR IS STOPPING on every floor," mumbled Jennie as she punched the button repeatedly. When they got to their hotel room, Jennie went straight to a bed and sat down. She could barely keep her eyes open. Josh was right, she was exhausted. She'd been moving nonstop since the nightmare woke her up, oh, so many hours ago, she was too tired to figure it out. Her eyes closed and her shoulders drooped and she rubbed her eyes. Kris wasn't any better, she was pale and tense, and had lived her own nightmare for two days now. Jennie knew only too well how it felt to lose your husband and she grieved for her. Besides losing her husband, her twin daughters shared an unfathomable connection and that was weighing heavy on Kris.

"Has Laurie said anything?" Jennie asked quietly.

"Not really, Mom. She's just mumbling, more groaning than words."

Jennie scowled and leaned back on the pillow. "Maybe she's sleeping."

"I thought about that. I know you're about to fall asleep, Mom, but you should take your clothes off and get comfortable. While you're doing that, listen to me, I want to try something with Laurie. I'm thinking I might have a way to help jog her memory. Laurie and I have a special place we go to, not a real place, a fantasy place in our minds. If I can get her there, it might help her remember. What do you think?"

"You and Laurie have never mentioned this to me. Tell me about it."

"I know, we've never shared it with anyone. You remember when we were little we were always fascinated with that metal file box filled with pictures of the castle you and daddy wanted to build someday. Well, Laurie and I made up this place in our minds. It's a castle on a hill overlooking a pond. We pretended to go there when we were sick or scared or lonely. Sometimes we'd just go there for fun and pretend to ride the little ponies that daddy talked about. Other times we played in the maze. What do you think, Mom, should I try this?"

"I don't understand how you can do this, but I know you communicate with each other. I used to watch when you were babies. You would have the same expression on your little faces. You'd look at each other intently like you were talking."

Jennie stood up and took her raincoat off, pulled the covers back on the bed and propped the two pillows together. "I wondered back then if you were communicating in some way. I don't think it could hurt her, it's worth a try. If you could get any idea about where she is, it would definitely help."

"Get some rest, Mom. I'm going to push that big chair over to the window and see if I can reach Laurie. It's just make-believe, but it might help her remember. I have to do something."

"I know you do, honey, but you need to rest as much as I do. You've been through so much."

"I can't rest when Laurie keeps mumbling, Mom. I want to see if this will break through to her."

Jennie nodded and hugged her daughter. She slipped out of her clothes and crawled under the covers. The bed felt so good and she gave way to exhaustion. She was asleep before her head hit the pillow.

Kris turned the lights off and shoved the overstuffed chair to the window. It was big and comfortable and she wiggled down in it. Propping her feet on the edge of the window sill, she rested her head on the back of the chair. Mom was right, she was worn out. Maybe a short nap would help before she tried to talk to Laurie.

She tried to relax and closed her eyes, but the second she did she saw her husband's face. She was instantly transported back to the hospital room where Jeff died. Tears slipped down her cheeks as she remembered she had promised Jeff she'd find his killer.

"Oh, Jeff, I will keep that promise, but first I have to find Laurie," Kris whispered. "She's still alive. I think the same people who took you away from me have her." Wiping furiously at the tears, she told herself she would think about Jeff later. She drew a deep breath and forced her thoughts to her twin sister, Laurie had to answer.

"Laurie, remember our special place, the one where we go together. I want us to go there now. Picture it, sis, there's a castle on a hill and down in the valley is a beautiful pond where you and I pretend to swim. Let's go to the castle now, meet me at the top of the tower where we can look down at our special world. Remember our castle, Laurie, tell me you remember."

"I hear you. Are you the one who keeps talking to me?"

"Yes, I'm Kris, your sister. Your name is Laurie."

"Laurie, Laurie. I don't remember that name, but I have a baby, a little boy. I want my son. Help me, help me…" her voice faded into incoherent whimpering.

"Don't cry, Laurie, listen to me. Think about our castle, remember the pictures in mom and dad's little file box. The castle has turrets and spiral staircases we like to climb, you always raced me to the top then you'd giggle and call me a slowpoke. Look out over the countryside, Laurie. See the tops of the green trees, feel the soft breezes blowing your hair around your face. It's so quiet and beautiful here, remember, it's our special place. You and I are the only ones who can go there. No one can find us, we're safe there."

"I remember feeling safe, I liked that. I want to feel safe again, but I'm so scared. I can't move or talk out loud, something is wrong with me. Are you really my sister?

"Yes, we're even more than sisters; we're twins. That's why we can talk like this. Can you tell me where you are?"

"I don't know. Someone keeps moving me and I can't open my eyes. They won't open, help me, help me…" she screamed.

"I'm trying to help you, but you have to quit screaming and talk to me. Is anyone hurting you?"

"No, not now, but the evil man will be back. He scares me. He tells me I'm dead, I'm not dead, I'm not…"

Stop it, you are not dead. You're alive and talking to me. Think about mom and daddy. Daddy's alive and he is trying to find you to bring you home."

"Daddy, my daddy's dead. He died years ago."

Kris jerked her legs off the window sill and looked over at her mother, Laurie was starting to remember and she wanted to tell Jennie, but her mom was sound asleep. Kris was wide awake now. She reached over and pulled the bedspread off the empty bed and wrapped it around her. She had to keep Laurie talking. She settled back in the chair tucking the cover around her cold legs.

"Very good, Laurie, I'm thrilled you remember daddy. I need to tell you about our daddy, we thought he died but he didn't. I've seen him and talked to him. He's on his way to bring you home, would you like to come home with daddy?"

"Someone's coming. I hear footsteps, heavy footsteps. It's the evil man," Laurie cried. "I'm scared, help me, help…"

"It might be daddy. If it is, he'll tell you who he is."

"No one is talking, no voices except yours. Are you here with me?"

"No, Laurie. I don't know where you are, but I want to come to you. I need you to help me find you. Tell me what you hear."

"Someone is pulling me up. I'm in a chair now and it's moving. My head is bouncing all around, it hurts so much. I can't hold my head still. Don't let me fall," Laurie cried. "I'm being lifted into something. A door slammed, it's a car. It's moving, are you in here with me? Please, somebody help me find my baby…"

LUKE AIR FORCE BASE, PHOENIX, ARIZONA

A MAN DRESSED IN hospital scrubs pushed a wheelchair down a long incline. The woman in the chair slumped forward, head bouncing up and down on her chest. Long blonde hair hid her face. Through half closed eyes, the intern peered at a military guard he passed. His hands shook and he gripped the wheelchair. So far, no one had questioned him and he pushed her faster. It was only a little further to the exit and he was anxious to get her to the ambulance. If anyone found him taking her without authorization, he'd be in the brig for sure. He started running. The unconscious woman was flung back and forth precariously.

URGENCY WAS DRIVING DAVENPORT when he reached the infirmary at Luke Air Force Base and he grabbed the first person he saw. "Where's the comatose woman who was brought in today?"

"Who are you, sir?" asked the nurse pulling away from him.

"I'm here to pick her up," he said flashing his identification.

The woman looked at it then went to the desk and shuffled through some papers. "She is on the second floor, third room on your left, sir."

Running up the stairs two at a time, he got to the room in time to see a nurse straightening the bed. "Where's the young woman who was here?"

"I'm not sure, sir. She could be down in the x-ray room."

"Where is that located?"

"Downstairs in the basement, take that elevator," she said pointing right.

He arrived at the x-ray department only to find another empty room. "Damn, too late again. I shouldn't have stayed so long at the restaurant. I know better."

Running back to the first floor, Davenport asked where the ambulance area was. The nurse turned her face toward a ramp. He ran down it and out the door in time to see a man in white scrubs close the door of a van. He grabbed him by his arm and whirled him around. "Who did you put in the van? Open that door."

The man pulled away from him and slapped the back of the van twice. It took off fast.

He shook the man. "Damn it, man, you should not have done that. Was it a young blonde woman?"

"I don't pay any attention to who comes and goes, I just load them."

Davenport's hand went to the man's throat, "Don't smart off with me. You saw. Was it a young woman?"

The choking man sputtered, "Yeah, but it won't do you any good."

"Where are they taking her?"

"How should I know…."

Davenport's hand tightened the grip on the throat of the struggling man. "You know. Talk to me."

"Can't… talk…" his voice faded out. Davenport released his grip on the man's throat and shook him until his eyes opened.

"Where are they taking her?"

"Don't know. Can't tell you what I don't know."

"Listen carefully and you might live. You're going to give the chairman a message from me, don't even pretend you don't know him. Tell the bastard if he releases my daughter and grandson right now and returns them to me, I'll drop my search and give him the notebook. If he doesn't, I will find him and he won't like it. I have acquired quite an arsenal of skills over the past years, skills that make me a nightmare for a man in a wheelchair. Tell him I will find him, and I will kill him, slowly and painfully. Tell him I know all his secret locations and I'm coming after him. Tell him the only reason you are alive is I needed you to deliver this message to him."

Davenport slammed the man into the side of the building bouncing his head against the brick wall. "Tell him the Ghost is back and I'm on my way."

He threw the man down on the concrete drive and left.

Phoenix, Arizona

"I KNOW, LAURIE, I KNOW YOU want your son. We will find him. Try to remember me; I'm your sister Kris. You and your son Nicky, and my daughter Sophie and I were all kidnapped and taken away in a van," Kris said.

"I remember, I remember…I want Nicky…"

"Sophie and I escaped and you fell off a bridge. You got hurt and you're in a coma, but you can think and you're talking to me. When you wake up, you'll be okay. Please, Laurie, calm down and listen to me. We're hunting for you, daddy and I will find you and we'll take you home. But right now, I need you to help us, tell me what you hear and feel."

"I can hear an engine. I must be in a car or van. It's moving,"

"What else?"

"Traffic, I hear cars. The car is speeding up, it's swerving around. I'm falling," Laurie screamed. "Oh, that hurts, something heavy fell on me. It's on top of me, it hurting my head…"

"Laurie, listen to me, you have to stay calm. Daddy is alive and he's trying to find you. Keep telling me what you hear."

Laurie didn't respond. All Kris could hear were her own thoughts. Something bad had happened to her sister again.

"Laurie, please answer me…"

Chapter 26

DAVENPORT WAS SO ANGRY he couldn't think. He was responsible for what had happened to his family, and now the chairman was playing games with him and enjoying every minute of it. He kept seeing his little girl crying out for help and fury exploded in his mind. He made his way back to the car wondering if his life would always be like this. Part of him said it would, another saner part of him said only if he allowed it to continue.

"No more," he ranted. "I'm through with secrets and deceptions, lurking in the shadows, inflicting pain, and being dead inside." He knew what he had to do, but he also knew this was what Jennie was afraid of. She feared who he turned into when he choked off all emotions.

"The bastards hurt my daughters and took my grandchildren. They crossed the line. They should not have touched my family." He had no choice this time. There was no other way when it involved the *Brotherhood*. He stormed through the parking lot to his car, his temper building with each step.

Winding around buildings, Davenport drove through the base as fast as he could. When he reached the gate he slowed the car, but kept rolling while Falco chased the car and struggled to get in.

"What's going on?" Falco yelled slamming the car door. Davenport hit the gas hard and roared away from the base. Falco stared at Davenport's face then checked the back seat. "Sorry, my friend, that's tough. What now?"

Davenport's fist pounded the steering wheel and he floored the accelerator. Anger etched his features and radiated from him, the car swerved all over the road.

"Slow down, Davenport, slow down. We'll find your daughter. We can get her back if you don't wreck us first. I can help if you let me— that's what I'm here for. Talk to me." Falco grabbed hold of the steering wheel and held the car steady. "Damn it, man, slow down."

Davenport let up a little on the pedal. "I was too late again, she was gone." He drove for a few miles holding the car on the road.

"Sorry, Falco, it's hard to be in my head right now, much less talk," he said breathing irregularly.

"I've learned a lot these past years," said Falco. "You and I both know there are two worlds, one public and one hidden. Today, I'm learning there are more than two worlds living in the shadows. Listen to me, old friend, I can help you deal with this. It's what I do, I deal with the unthinkable. It's all about control."

Falco stopped and watched Davenport's expression. "Listen to me, we can find your daughter, but you have to rein in your emotions and get control of yourself. It's time for a real talk and we need a plan. Now slow this car down."

Davenport gradually slowed down to the speed limit and looked sideways at Falco wondering what he meant, he deals with the unthinkable. *Well, the unthinkable is exactly what I've been dealing with for six years. Falco is right. I lost control and that's unacceptable. That will not get Laurie back.*

Disgusted with his actions, he turned the car into a shopping center and looked for a place to get a drink. Falco was probably ready for one, too. If he remembered right, Falco drank straight scotch. Maybe he'd have that instead of bourbon and seven.

"Over there, that place on the corner looks like a bar," Falco said pointing to the left.

He looked at Falco. Yeah, the man was ready for a drink. The place was open and they found an empty table in the back corner. Both men chose seats with their backs to the wall looking toward the front entrance. Falco ordered scotch on the rocks.

"At least my memory hasn't gone to pot," muttered Davenport. "You're right, Falco. It's time to talk and make a plan. I'm a little out of practice working with anyone, I've always worked alone."

"I understand loners. A lot of jobs are that way, mine in particular." Falco paused and watched Davenport down his drink. "You never knew what I did, did you?" he asked in a soft voice.

"No, I didn't. I doubt I would have approved of it, that's why I never asked. You told me you were in the Mafia and I knew better than to ask questions. But now, this is a different time and place."

Falco leaned back in his chair and chuckled, "You're right, you were a different man back then from the one I'm getting acquainted with tonight. You've changed, old friend, we both have." He tossed back his scotch and motioned at the waiter for refills. "Time to talk, what exactly are you into and how did you get there."

Davenport hesitated to tell him he worked directly for the president. Maybe he would just go with G-2 and the general. That should be enough. He gave Falco an abbreviated version of what he had told Herman.

"What's happening now is the *Brotherhood* found out I'm alive and they have put a contract out on me. The bastards kidnapped my family and are using them as bait to get me. The complication is Jennie and Kris, they cloud my senses. It's dangerous for them here, but I can't seem to stop them. I want them back in Texas in the safe house with Herman Wilkens on guard, that's where my granddaughter Sophie is."

"Why do you do this, Davenport? You had a sweet life back then."

"It's complicated, Falco, it wasn't intentional. G-2 called me back in to do one mission for the military then that job led to another and another, and there has never been a time I could get out. The United

States has been snoozing for a century and now it's on a downward spiral. It's racing toward an ending none of us who have lived in a free country are going to like. It's a new world order where citizens become mere pawns on a chess board. Socialism sounds great in speech and it looks really good on paper, but I've seen how it affects the people in other countries. It's not pretty. In practice, socialism corrodes not only the economy, but the human spirit itself. Look at those socialist countries and you'll know I'm telling the truth."

"So that's what the *Brotherhood* is trying to do, take over control of the United States."

"Not only the U.S., but the world; they have plans for a one-world government. Once you give power to the government it's nearly impossible to get it back, and you can bet on it, that power will be used in ways you would never expect. There's a world of difference between capitalism and socialism. Basically, it's the difference between freedom and slavery. It is capitalism that brought billions of people out of poverty in the twentieth century. Socialism enslaves and impoverishes people because a society that relies too heavily on redistributing wealth eventually runs out of wealth to redistribute. It's all in the history books, you can read about it. Socialism is not about the people, Falco. It's about control, and that's in the hands of the ones who have power and money."

"What's your job in all this?"

"It all began way back in the 1950s when I chanced upon what was happening. I made a few waves and the military discharged me early. In other words, someone very powerful wanted rid of me, I evidently stumbled on something too close to him. The *Brotherhood* already had spies in prominent positions so they were able to control my actions back then. I didn't have the whole picture until years later when I infiltrated that secret group of power hungry men. I learned all about that organization, their long-range plans and the names of all the members. It's what I have in my head that they want to destroy. As long as I'm alive, I'm a threat to their plans. I've managed to sabotage some of their activities and unearth enough of their spies in government to slow them down and cause problems. Here's the catch, I get rid of one traitor and another pops up to take his place."

Falco stared at Davenport. This was definitely not the same guy that used to play in the band with him. "So, what are their plans?"

"Huge question begs a long answer, Falco, and we don't have all night to talk about it. So, shortened version, three things are happening today. First is the destruction of the U.S. monetary system. They want people to believe they have to have help from the government. The *Brotherhood* is well on their way to accomplishing this. Second is the destruction of nationalism and patriotism, which shows itself in fear of neighbors and lack of loyalty to the U.S. End result is to increase people's dependence on the government and not their own abilities. And third, destruction of the Christian faith and values that has held our country together in troubled times. It is simply that old adage put into play. Divide and conquer, and it works very well."

"Oh, man, I didn't see this coming. Why hasn't someone or the media figured this out?"

"Most people don't have a clue there are bastards like that out there. They sit innocently in front of their televisions watching a reality that doesn't exist. They are mostly interested in what affects them personally, that's just human nature, Falco. The media promotes whatever makes the most sensational story and benefits their program the best. Besides that, the major newspapers, television and radio stations are almost all controlled or owned by powerful covert groups promoting the one-world government agenda, so they can't be trusted. Then you get into the intelligence community and you find nothing is ever what it looks like. There's a hidden agenda with a shadow government controlling nearly everything. My objective is to stop the *Brotherhood* and expose the truth, but all I've been able to do is slow them down."

"And I was talking about a couple of hidden worlds," Falco grimaced. "On a personal level, don't you ever get lonely or tired living away from home?"

"Trust me. I'm always trying to get home. But the longer this goes on, the further away the road to going back gets."

So who gives you the assignments and what is your job?"

"I report to a couple of men in high positions. My job is to be invisible. The mandate is I live in the shadows and expose the ones I can, upset their plans, and generally create havoc for the *Brotherhood*. At times, I'm sent on specific missions no one else wants to do. Not pretty, Falco."

"No it's not. My job isn't pretty either. It's mostly containment and whatever else needs done. However, I'm here with you because of Parrino's grandson, Joey, and my past connection with you. We have a common interest."

Davenport stood up and stretched. He studied Falco's face wondering how far the common interest would go, how much loyalty he could expect from Falco. He was so tired of not trusting, it was a miserable way to live. He sighed and checked his watch. Midnight, the time had rolled around fast, he looked for a phone.

"Order me another drink. I need to make a call."

FALCO WATCHED HIS OLD friend walk away and wondered who this call was going to, his wife or someone else, probably both.

Some honesty, he thought, *same as me, just so much honesty can be voiced.* So far as Davenport went, he told the truth about the *Brotherhood.* The Mafia had been aware of and keeping tabs on them for years. The man has changed; he's not the same laughing guy who used to play in the band. *Well, I'm not the same either, we've both seen too much. I think he might be okay in a showdown, I believe I can depend on him. For now, we're on the same side.*

Davenport's steps were decisive when he came back to the table and picked up his drink. "Okay, it's time to make plans. I have to add one more complication. I was just told an informant let slip that another group has sent their death squad after me. I doubt they know I'm in Arizona, but I wouldn't make bets on that."

Death squad, interesting term, thought Falco. "So, what else is new? We're already watching for the *Brotherhood,* another group after you won't make much difference."

"I talked to Jennie and told her nothing would happen tonight and to get some sleep. She seemed okay with that, at least I hope she stays put. My daughter Kris had some new things to tell me. You might remember my daughters are twins. They have this twin thing where they can talk to each other in their minds, not that I understand it, but I have seen them do it. Kris has been talking with Laurie and gotten her to remember a little. That's encouraging because we don't know how severe her injuries are. Here's the problem, she was at the infirmary at the base and someone took her away. She told Kris she was in a car or van driving fast and swerving around. It made her fall and she was injured again."

Anger flew over Davenport and his voice roughened. "I don't know any more than that. I told Kris to keep trying and I would be in touch with her in case Laurie can give her any idea where she is. Laurie is in a coma and can't open her eyes; however, she can hear what's going on around her. Her mind seems to be functioning."

"Do you have any idea where they're taking her?"

"There are several possibilities. The first place we are going is a school where I believe they have taken my grandson. I don't want him there very long; it's a dangerous place. It's also a hospital staffed with doctors and nurses who could take care of a comatose patient. Laurie could be there."

Davenport finished his drink and stood up. There was another problem he was not ready to disclose; the president told him the acting chief of police in Dallas was a recruit of the *Brotherhood*. Lord, help us, when will this stop? Silverman was reaching out from the grave to cause problems. It sounded like Herman Wilkens was in trouble; no one had been able to find him. The president had already called Blakely and told him about the police chief in case he heard from Wilkens.

Falco stood up and stretched, twisting his shoulders back and forth. "Sat too long, got a little stiff. Well, I'm ready, best we go before daylight. Darkness can help conceal us."

Chapter 27

THE CITY WAS QUIET in the middle of the night; very few cars were on the streets. Storm clouds hung low and the moon was hiding. Earlier in the night, Herman Wilkens drove his regular route and made his usual stops checking with officers on duty. For the last hour, he'd made several attempts to lose his tail. During his years as an undercover officer, he'd learned many evasive tactics, but none of them were working tonight. The guy following him was experienced, it was evident he wasn't going to lose him.

"Damn," muttered Wilkens. "The guy's good, it's as if he has a tracker on my car." Could be, he supposed. He didn't know when it could have happened, however, it wasn't impossible. Switching vehicles was the next ploy he was planning. He pulled into the precinct lot and drove around looking for his partner's car; it was in the far back corner. Good spot, if he borrowed John's car he could slip out the back gate. He drove to the front entrance and parked his vehicle where it could be seen from the street. Next, he wanted to talk to his partner and check in with the chief.

Nodding to a couple of officers he passed in the hall, he went straight to his desk and picked up the phone. Wilkens dialed the number Davenport had given him and was hoping the contact had heard from him. Davenport was probably mad about Jennie going to Phoenix. Well, he'd done all he could to stop her and he wasn't going to worry about it, he had more pressing problems now. The contact needed to know he was being tailed so Davenport would have some clue what happened to him if he didn't check in again.

Blakely answered before the first ring finished and before Wilkens could utter a word said, "This number is compromised. Give me a number where I can call you back." Wilkens told him the precinct number and the phone disconnected. The phone rang almost as soon as he cradled the receiver. Grabbing it back up, he answered and listened.

"Yes, I gave Chief Sanders the number. What do you mean the chief is corrupt? I need an explanation." Disbelief spread over face as he listened, anger building with every word. "Are you sure? No, I haven't told him location of the safe house...yes, I hear you. I understand." Wilkens had to slow Blakely down while he grabbed a pencil and scribbled the new number down.

"Yes, I'll check in when I get to the safe house. Someone is following me and I have to lose them before I go there. If I don't call in again, tell Davenport I've probably been picked up. I'm guessing the *Brotherhood* is tailing me."

Plopping down in his chair, he thought about what Blakely told him and wondered how and why Chief Sanders was betraying his men. The man had been on the force for many years and they had worked cases together, so how long ago did he turn? Damn, the man was acting chief while Dallas' chief of police was recovering from a heart attack. Herman's mind took a leap forward and he wondered what had happened to the real chief of police, was it a heart attack or something more sinister? This thing is like an octopus, it has tentacles everywhere. *I bet my car does have a tracker and the chief knows I'm here. I need to get away without letting him know I know about him.*

He checked the room, everybody was busy and he went straight to the supply room. The officer on duty wasn't there and Herman filled his coat pockets with ammunition. He started to leave then turned back and picked up another gun along with several items and shoved it all in his pockets. "Good thing I wore a raincoat tonight," he muttered patting the mini arsenal in his bulging coat.

His mind was going at warp speed considering all the implications. *I can't fathom Sanders betraying us. This puts the entire department at risk. Okay, Davenport, point made, I've got it now. I understand what you told me, you're right, my life here is over.* Wilkens sighed and shook his head. *What will my family do when this ends? Will Molly and I even be able to live in our home?*

He made it back to his desk without running into anybody. He looked around the small workspace wondering when or if he would ever see it again. He rifled through his desk and shoved more items in the already overstuffed pockets of his coat before leaving. He didn't want to talk to anyone, definitely not the chief. He had nothing to say to him, he didn't even want to look at the man.

Wilkens managed to get to the back door without talking to anyone as he rushed out of the building. No one was in the dark parking lot; he ran to his partner's car and slid in the driver's seat. If he could get out of the police lot without the tail spotting him, he could go somewhere and dump the patrol car then he could disappear.

He knew how to do that, it was something he learned long ago.

PHOENIX, ARIZONA

"HERE'S THE PLAN, FALCO. We are going to break in a school that the *Brotherhood* runs and there are things you need to know about it before we go in. First, it's usually well guarded and getting in and out might take some doing. Second, it's a very dangerous place where nothing is what it seems. It looks like a small clinic or hospital, but sinister stuff goes on there."

Falco looked at Davenport and grinned, "You're telling the story of my world."

"I'm not joking, Falco, I'm dead serious about this place." Davenport was reminded of Falco's sense of humor and how he used to try to make light of any situation. "If we screw up, we're dead and my grandson will be left to the horrors of this school."

He looked to see if Falco was paying attention. "Here's the background. Chairman Houser of the *Brotherhood* started it years ago. He patterned it after a British institute whose prophet was Sigmund Freud. The British institute claims it's concerned with behavior, both group and organizational, but actually it's a brainwashing facility."

"You mean they mess with people's minds?"

"Oh, yeah, much more than mess, they destroy memory and replace it with their programmed agenda. The chairman took the institute's ideas and coupled them with Hitler's brainwashing techniques. His first experiment was that bastard Otto Fleicher who murdered Joey. In many ways it was not successful; it completely erased all human emotions except for Fleicher's love of inflicting pain. However, it created a powerful tool for the chairman. The chairman has used him for many years to dispose of people who have opposed the *Brotherhood*. There is nothing human about Fleicher and the chairman controls every move he makes. This is the man you are after, Falco, the man known as the enforcer."

"I was expecting bad, Mr. Parrino told me what you said about him."

"It is far worse than I described. When a man exists only for the enjoyment of pain, it changes the whole ballgame. We have to be very careful and very vigilant." Davenport paused and drove for a while without talking. "Here's where the rubber meets the road, Falco. I believe this is what the chairman is planning for my grandson. He would think it the supreme irony to make an assassin out of my grandson. No matter what I have to do, I cannot leave Nicky in that man's evil hands."

Falco stared into the dark night trying to absorb what he had just heard. The Mafia had known for a long time that the *Brotherhood* was not honorable, but they never comprehended the depravity or how large a threat this group really was.

Angry storm clouds blotted out the moon as they drove east toward the Superstition Mountains. The clouds hung low over the distant mountains. Time was on their side, dawn would not break for several hours.

They drove in silence.

Chapter 28

THE PERSISTENT RINGING GRADUALLY penetrated the chairman's sleep. Claude Houser rolled over and fumbled for the phone knocking it to the floor. "Blasted phone," he muttered as he pulled the handset up by the cord.

"This better be important. I told you never to disturb me except in an emergency, what time is it?"

"It's past midnight, sir, and it is an emergency. The man you sent to pick up the woman is on the phone and he's in a panic."

"Always problems; connect us, Hans." The man struggled to a sitting position. He was not pleased, he did not like his sleep or his plans disrupted. He had ordered the woman moved to the fortress where the trap for Davenport would be under his control.

"Slow down, you are not making sense. Slow down and tell me what's going on?" the chairman demanded when he heard the man's frantic voice.

"I took the woman to the ambulance you sent…her condition hasn't changed…nurse says there are no signs of awakening from the coma…there was a complication before the transport could leave the base…Davenport showed up…" the man blurted out in one breath.

"I've already told you once, slow down, you're incoherent," roared the chairman.

The chairman listened to the man struggle for breath as he tried to calm down before continuing. "Davenport showed up and I signaled the driver to leave and he took off fast. She's on her way to you. Davenport was furious and sent you a message. He said to tell you the Ghost is back, that he knows all your secret places, and he's on his way."

"He's coming here?"

"That's what he yelled at me." The man stopped and took several deep breaths before continuing. "He said if you release his daughter and grandson now, he'll drop his search and give you the notebook. If you don't, he'll find you and you won't like it. He said to tell you he's learned a lot of things that will make him a nightmare for a man in a wheelchair. Davenport said to tell you, he'll find you and kill you slowly. He also said to tell you the only reason he let me live is because he needed me to give you this message."

The chairman sat straight up in bed and slammed the phone down. He yanked the nightstand drawer open and pulled out a 9mm Luger pistol. He made sure it was loaded then he pushed his pillows up behind him and leaned back. His gaze swept the room stopping at the open window; he wondered how many other windows were open downstairs. He shouted for Hans through his clenched jaw.

"Enter," he bellowed when he heard Hans knock on his door. "Get my clothes and move that wheelchair closer to me. I've told you time and again it has to be within my reach. Can't you do anything right? Close and lock that window over there."

Furious at his inability to walk, he tugged on clothes then wiggled into the wheelchair. "Make sure all downstairs doors and windows are locked and secure. Tell the guards an intruder is coming," he said as he rolled out of his bedroom.

He was not going to face Davenport in bed. He might not be able to stand very well, but that didn't mean he would be a sitting target or an easy one. He'd learned a few tricks in the past years, too. He had to get downstairs to his study.

"Quit standing there staring at me, you idiot." He glared at Hans, "Open the blasted elevator door so I can get in." He rolled in and punched at the controls. Hans ran down the stairs and was waiting when the chairman emerged and wheeled to his study.

"Are you going to check the doors and windows like I told you? I should activate the remote and remind you who's in charge. Make sure everything is locked up then get me coffee and a sandwich, I need food. Stop wasting time, go outside and alert the guards."

Hans turned without a word and checked the downstairs windows and doors. He heard the chairman bellowing, "Alert the guards now. How many times do I have to tell you what to do?"

HANS' FACE WAS RIGID as he made the rounds of the house and talked to the guards. He was not sure how long he could keep obeying. All he knew was what the chairman had programmed into him years ago. He didn't know where or how to live somewhere else, but he had to get away before the chairman killed him with that remote. The remote was his biggest problem. If he could get his hands on it he'd destroy it. It was always in the chairman's pocket.

A couple of memories had begun to creep into his mind the last few days. Enough had surfaced that he knew there was someone who loved him once. He could almost see his mother's face and he could hear a soft voice whispering she loved him, she wouldn't yell at him or call him an idiot. Anger rolled over the young man. He'd had another life and a family before the chairman destroyed his mind.

He wasn't a robot like Otto, he had feelings. Oh, how he hated that man, Otto had beat and hurt him so many times through the years and then he'd stand there and laugh like a maniac. He tried hard to stay out of Otto's way. He was not like that madman; he didn't enjoy seeing people suffer.

He went back to the chairman's study and stood outside the door listening. Something was happening; his plans must have gone wrong. Hans frowned when he heard the chairman give orders to Otto to pick up Davenport's wife. He liked Davenport; the man was nice to him and treated him like a real person.

Hans wondered if Davenport's wife was pretty and if she had a soft voice like his mother. It wasn't right to give that order to Otto; he would hurt or kill her. He turned and went in the kitchen and stood staring at the can of coffee sitting there. After a couple of minutes, he added water to the percolator then spooned coffee into it. A sick feeling flowed over the young man when he started to plug in the pot and he froze.

He had to do something, it wasn't right to tell Otto to take Mr. Davenport's wife. All of a sudden, he knew he couldn't live like this any longer. If the chairman killed him with that remote, he would just have to die. He'd rather do that; at least it would be over. Someone else would have to make coffee and sandwiches for the chairman. There were plenty of other people in the fortress; they could be his slave. "No more," he said aloud. He dropped the percolator in the sink.

Hans grabbed a jacket and car keys and slipped out the back door. The young man stood still and looked around. No guards were in sight and he ran across the narrow lawn and through the gate to the cover of the trees. He knew the way in the dark. He had traveled it many times, he knew every rock and bush and all the slippery spots. Without looking back, he made his way up the treacherous trail over the mountain and to the school.

BETWEEN PHOENIX AND SUPERSTITION MOUNTAINS, ARIZONA

DAVENPORT WAS MAKING GOOD time. The storm clouds had dropped rain on them a few miles back and he was grateful it had stopped. It would be hard enough to get to the school without rain peppering down on them and making the ground slippery.

"We're getting close to the mountains, Falco. We can drive another ten miles then we'll have to hike the rest of the way, about a mile. The school only has one road in and it is guarded and gated."

"Describe it to me. I don't like to go in cold."

"It was originally part of a large ranch and the terrain is rugged. The land surrounding the building hasn't been cleared in years. Horse nettle, bear grass, and cactus cover the ground. There are granite boulders that look like patrols on guard duty. A person could come upon the place and mistake it for an abandoned building. This is intentional camouflage to discourage hikers from exploring."

"Is there a path or do we just make our way through the brush?"

"The paths are guarded so we go through the brush, I've done it before. The chairman bought the property years ago and turned it into an experimental laboratory he calls a school. I don't know what is going on in there right now; it's been several years since the chairman showed me around. As I mentioned earlier, Falco, when I heard the *Brotherhood* kidnapped my daughter and grandson I knew instantly what the chairman had in that insane mind of his. I'm trying not to think about what they might have done to my grandson already. There is no way I can leave him here as long as I'm alive."

"How the hell does he do that brainwashing, Davenport?"

"I don't know the how, I have only seen the end product and it's not pretty. I understand a chip is inserted somewhere around the person's shoulder blade and the chairman uses that to control the person. He has a remote control he uses to signal the man by causing it to vibrate. He can also cause pain if they don't obey. I'm assuming the pain can get extreme because it controls Fleicher."

"That's nasty business. Do you think Fleicher will be there?"

"It's possible. I know he hates the place. It's where his mind was wiped and reprogrammed. I've also heard he hates and fears the chairman; that might be something we can use. He has a hideout somewhere in these mountains. There are a lot of abandoned gold mines, cabins, and a few ghost towns scattered throughout the mountains. It's quite possible he uses one of those. He'll be the one who comes after me and that will be your chance, Falco."

Davenport drove in silence for a few miles then he looked over at his old friend. "Whatever you do about Fleicher is up to you. I'll not stand in judgment."

"Describe him to me," Falco said.

"He's a little over six-foot tall, stocky, built like a sumo wrestler. He works out with weights so his arms and legs are massive and strong. He has light skin, dark hair and odd pale-colored eyes. He didn't have facial hair when I saw him last, but who knows now. His voice is deep and grating, and when he smiles it never reaches his eyes. He moves fast and wears rubber-soled shoes that don't make a sound."

"In other words, he could slip up on you from behind."

"Yes, you'd never hear him. One more thing, his favorite weapon is a razor blade mounted in a holder which he carries in his right pocket. I've seen him pull it out and use it." Davenport shuddered at the memory. "It's not a sight I want to see again."

The thought of Laurie in the control of the enforcer unnerved him. He shoved the accelerator to the floor.

Chapter 29

THE ROOM WAS DARK when Jennie rolled over and reached for Josh. By the time she got her eyes open, the events of the last few days flooded her mind and she realized where she was. She sat up and looked around the room for her daughter. Kris was curled up and sleeping in a chair facing the window. A soft light was breaking through the slit where the drapes didn't pull together.

Jennie stood up and stretched her weary body. She washed her face and gasped when she looked in the mirror. The mirror wasn't her friend, it reflected how stressed she felt and she rubbed her aching head. She needed her bag from the car so she could shower and change her clothes, but not bad enough to go downstairs and out to the parking lot. They should have brought their bags in last night. However, she needed coffee even more than she wanted to change clothes. She poured water into the small coffeemaker and watched it drip into the container. Frowning at the packet of powdered creamer, she shook it then dumped it into a cup and poured the coffee over it. A quick stir with the wooden stick made it lumpy and caramel colored.

"This is not going be good," she mumbled quietly as she went back and sat on the side of the bed sipping the coffee. It was bad, but she swallowed another mouthful and wondered how much longer it would be before Josh called. Forcing herself to finish the awful stuff, Jennie leaned back against the headboard and waited for the caffeine to clear the fog out of her brain. Even awful coffee should have some caffeine in it. Staring at the phone wasn't making it ring any sooner, but she couldn't keep from it. Her eyes were on the phone when it rang and she grabbed it before the first ring finished. "Josh?"

"I have a message from Davenport," the muffled voice said. "He said to tell you to come downstairs and meet him at the side parking lot. He has your grandson."

"You mean Josh wants me to come downstairs now?"

"Yes, he can't wait long."

"Tell him I'll be right down."

Jennie looked at her daughter and decided not to wake her, Kris had gone through so much and she needed the sleep. "I'll go get Nicky and it'll be a wonderful surprise when she wakes up."

Jennie grabbed her raincoat and room key and slipped out of the room without making a sound. The elevator door was opening and she hurried to get in.

The elevator stopped at each floor. Her anxiety grew each time the door opened and hitting the down button didn't help. The elevator finally got to the main level and she ran out the door the instant it started opening.

SUPERSTITION MOUNTAINS, ARIZONA

THE MOUNTAINS BLOCKED WHAT little light there was when Davenport pulled off the road and drove into a narrow gorge. He wedged the car among some scrubby trees and bushes. Thick storm clouds obscured the moon and the two men climbed uphill using only a small penlight. It was slow going through the thick underbrush and cactus. Crickets announced their tedious ascent.

"Slow down," said Falco. "You may be used to this type of thing, but I'm a city boy. I can't see where I'm stepping."

Without stopping, Davenport reached back and handed a penlight to Falco. He continued the grueling climb for another fifteen minutes.

"Wait up. You've made your point, you're in better shape than me," Falco said through gritted teeth.

Davenport looked back and grinned. Falco was now in his world, not the paved city streets. He kept going a few more feet until he came to a small clearing where he waited for Falco to catch up. He could use a rest too, but he wasn't about to tell his old friend. He didn't remember needing to rest when he came here several years ago. Time and stress were taking a toll on him, however, he wasn't as winded as Falco who was bending over and gasping for air. "Maybe it's not so much the age, but the mileage on both of us," he muttered under his breath as he sat down on the rocky ground. It would feel good to rest for a few minutes. He had lived through some rough times since the last time he was here.

Falco got to the clearing and plopped down near him. "What did you say, I couldn't hear you?" He pulled up his pants leg and rubbed his shin.

"Nothing important, just remembering this hill was easier a few years ago."

"Climbing uphill would be enough to deal with, but that blasted cactus is eating my legs up," Falco complained picking needles out of his pants leg. "Isn't there a cleared trail we could use?"

"No, the trails are guarded. We're through the hard part; we're almost at the back of the place. If memory serves me right, there's an entry into the basement there."

Hearing leaves crunch, Davenport twisted his head around in every direction. He couldn't see anyone and the sounds had stopped. "Don't talk," he mouthed at Falco.

Adrenaline surged through him and his other self, the one they called the Ghost, took over. He motioned at Falco to stay put. Ignoring the cactus and horse nettle, he belly crawled uphill for several feet before stopping. There was a guard a few feet in front of him; Davenport slid back into the bushes. Good thing he stopped to rest or he might have barreled into the man. He had reached the school faster than he thought.

The guard paused and looked around the area. After a couple of minutes, he cupped his hand to his face and lit a cigarette. The man leaned back against the building smoking. Davenport watched the glow of the cigarette as the guard's hand went up to his mouth then down to his side, and up and down again and again.

There was just enough light for Davenport to see the low door to the basement, it was where he remembered. Finally, the guard tossed the burning cigarette away and smashed it with his foot before continuing his walk around the building. When he rounded the corner, Davenport motioned for Falco to follow him and they ran across the cleared area to the door.

Without a word, Falco pulled out a tool and opened the locked door in a second. The two men stepped inside and closed the door behind them then eased down squeaky steps into the basement. "Not much of a lock," he said in a low voice. "Not going to keep anyone out."

A dim light was on in the basement, probably a ten-watt bulb, but enough for Davenport to find his way around. He went straight to the staircase and started up the steps halting at every creak to listen. When he reached the top, he turned the doorknob and peeked through a small slit. The kitchen was dark except for a nightlight on the stove which provided a view of the room. Davenport couldn't see anyone. The two men slipped in pressing against the wall.

"The patient rooms are beyond that door at the far end of the kitchen," Davenport whispered to Falco. "If my grandson is here, that's where he will be. There's a nurse's station a short distance down the hall. Wait here while I check the rooms."

Falco bristled and grabbed Davenport by the shoulder whispering, "I'm not waiting. I didn't trudge through that damned cactus to be left twiddling my thumbs in a kitchen."

"Then stay behind me and be quiet. Watch your back, Fleicher could be here."

Davenport opened the door to the patient wing, it was total darkness. Enough light came from the kitchen door to see that the nurses' station was unmanned. Feeling his way along the wall, he checked each room. They were dark and empty except for the last one, a faint light was sliding under the door. He pointed at the light and motioned for Falco to be ready.

He cracked the door a slit. The room was unoccupied and he opened the door enough to step in. The glow was near the floor next to the bed, it was a nightlight reflecting off a paper on the floor. He cast his penlight around the room one more time to make sure no one was hiding in the shadows or under the bed. The room was empty. Turning his light back to the paper, he picked it up. It was an envelope with his name on it. He ripped it open then shoved it in his pocket.

Muttering under his breath, Davenport took off running not bothering to be quiet this time. It had been way too easy to get in; he had only seen one guard. They knew he was coming and had emptied the place. It didn't take much to figure out who anticipated his arrival at the school; he had told the chairman he was on his way. This was the price he paid for losing his temper, his grandson had been moved.

"Damn," he muttered. He had hoped Fleicher was waiting for him. That would have solved Falco's problem and made it easier to get Laurie and Nicky back. There was always a price to pay when you lost control in this business. He knew that well. Davenport plunged out of the building and down the hill at a breakneck speed.

FALCO KEPT UP WITH him, cursing every bush and cactus. The downhill trek was fast. Davenport never slowed; he ran fast vaulting over bushes and boulders. Falco had to ignore the cactus to keep up with the man. He had no choice; he didn't know the way to the car. Huffing and puffing, he fell into the car and started picking cactus spines out of his legs again and rubbing the stinging welts from the horse nettle.

It wasn't until they were in the car that Davenport handed Falco the paper he had picked up. The only thing written on it was a phone number, no name or message. Falco looked over at his old friend's grim face and decided not to ask questions, he doubted Davenport would even hear him. Davenport backed up the steep ravine to the road then burned off sending a shower of gravel into the air.

Chapter 30

"BE STILL, I DON'T WANT to hurt you, you're making this harder than it has to be," the man told the struggling woman as he pulled her toward the car. "We can do this the easy way or the hard way, but either way you're coming with me." The man's forearm pressed against Jennie Davenport's throat.

"Where's Josh and Nicky? You said they would be here," she asked hoarsely. "Who are you?"

Not waiting for his answer, she yelled as loud as she could and jerked at his arm. She stomped on his foot, grabbed his hair and pulled as she twisted away from the man.

He almost lost hold of her. She was all hands flailing at him and he wrapped his arms around her. "Be quiet, I'm trying to help you." The man looked around the parking lot, it was empty.

She wiggled and stomped on his foot again and he lost hold. He quickly struck both his hands into the woman's shoulder blades where the tendons merge with the neck muscles. The yelling stopped and she crumpled to the ground in a heap.

"I'm so sorry, I didn't want to hurt you, I asked you to cooperate. Now, I have to carry you," he said trying to pick up the woman. He half carried her as he dragged her to the car. Balancing her on his knee he yanked open the back door of the car, backed in and pulled the unconscious woman across the seat. He slid out the opposite door.

"You're going to have a headache when you wake up. I warned you, we could do this the easy way or the hard way. I didn't want to hurt you," the man muttered.

He tied her hands behind her and then to the door before he climbed in the driver's seat and drove away from the hotel. He could hear her moaning in the back seat. He grimaced and pounded the steering wheel. "You should have cooperated with me. I tried to tell you, I'm better than the alternative."

DALLAS, TEXAS

"FIRST DRY MORNING WE'VE had in a while." Herman Wilkens looked at the sky, the clouds lifted as the sun rose over the city. It would be a beautiful day if the rain didn't start again. Wilkens' patrol car splashed through Dallas streets that were flooded in low areas. He hoped the rain had stopped for a while, the city needed to dry out. It had rained so long and hard that the storm drains were full and running over. Wilkens watched the water pooling in the street. Much more and cars would hydroplane.

He'd been driving for the past few hours and listening to the two-way radio in case his partner tried to contact him. He'd left John a quick message saying he would explain why he took his car later. So far so good, he thought.

The enigma was the chief. Wilkens wished he had paid attention to the uncomfortable feeling he got when he had talked to him, but a dirty chief of police never entered his mind. It was obvious now that Davenport knew what he was talking about. However, it was hard to stomach a traitor in his own precinct, his hands tightened on the steering wheel.

Wilkens had not spotted a tail, it looked like he was in the clear and he headed for the Dallas-Fort Worth Airport. Exiting Hwy 183, he turned in the main airport entrance and down the road that led between the terminals. He checked out the parking garages at several of the airlines. Some were almost empty and he went back to the busiest one at American Airlines. He drove in the covered area and parked in the middle of group of cars. Fifteen minutes passed as he sat in the car watching and waiting, no other cars came in.

"All clear," he said. "That took long enough." Wilkens hurried inside the busy terminal.

He'd walk around for a while. If he didn't spot anyone suspicious, he could be on his way to the safe house. He was anxious about Molly, she worried about him when he was late and he was way past late. He didn't like worrying her.

Wilkens walked the concourse to the far end before he found a gift shop. He looked around for a few minutes then bought a small travel bag and a couple of magazines. A lot of people were in the terminal, but he saw no one that worried him as he retraced his route. His next stop was the bathroom where he unloaded his coat pockets into the travel bag. Bulging pockets attract attention and he felt better when he left the room with empty pockets. No one followed him in or out and he went to the nearest car rental kiosk.

"How about a black Chevy sedan," Herman said to the young woman behind the counter. He handed her an alternate identification the department provided for undercover officers. Leaning on the counter and smiling he said, "I really like black cars."

While he was waiting for the car, he found a pay phone and called the new number Blakely had given him. "I'm at DFW airport. As soon as my rental car arrives, I'll be on my way to the safe house. I should get there before noon, any word from Davenport?"

"Yes, he called last night at midnight. He found Jennie and Kris if that's what you're wondering," Blakely laughed. "He said he wasn't surprised."

"Thanks, I'm glad they are with him, any other news?"

"Not yet, let me know when you get to the safe house."

Wilkens stood inside the terminal and watched for the arrival of the car.

PHOENIX, ARIZONA

KRIS WOKE WITH A START. Ten o'clock…that can't be right. She'd slept in the chair all night, her legs were folded under her and they didn't want to work. She stood up slowly, wiggled her shoulders, rubbed her stiff neck, and waited for circulation to come back to her legs before trying to walk. Laurie was talking again, but she wasn't making any sense. Kris yawned and drew open the drapes. The sun was almost blinding, she closed her eyes and let the warmth flow over her.

Jennie's bed was empty and she looked around the room then checked the bathroom. Jennie wasn't there. She hoped her mom had gone down to get their bags out of the car or maybe some food.

"Oh my," she groaned when she saw herself in the mirror. Her eyes were swollen and red and makeup had long since been washed off by tears. She needed to shower, wash her face and comb her messy hair. What she needed most was shoes, Molly's had been too large for her, she was still wearing sandals. She guessed they were better than barefoot, but not much. Hunting for her purse, she found it hidden under the bedspread she had tossed there when she got out of the chair. Kris looked longingly at the bed, it was tempting. Sleeping in a chair was not as comfortable.

"Well, maybe for a little while," she murmured as she sat down. She leaned back on the pillow sighing, "It feels so good."

I'll just rest until mom gets back. I can't change clothes anyway without my bag. Molly had packed a couple of shirts along with some other necessities and she needed those before she bathed. She turned on her side and snuggled under the cover and was sound asleep when an insistent ringing woke her up.

Bleary-eyed and groggy, she fumbled for the phone.

"Put your mom on the phone, Kris," the curt voice said.

Kris looked around the room for her mom thinking it would be nice if he said hello to his daughter then she saw the clock.

"Good grief, it's after twelve, I slept two hours."

"Put your mother on the phone, please."

"Wait a minute, daddy, she must be in the bathroom. Let me check." Kris opened the bathroom door, Jennie wasn't there.

"She's not here, daddy, I don't know where she is."

"When did you see her last?"

"Last night when we checked in. Mom was really tired and she went straight to bed when we got to the room. I pulled a big chair over to the window and sat there trying to talk with Laurie. When I woke up earlier this morning, mom wasn't here. I thought she'd gone down to get our bags out of the car."

"What time was that?"

"Two hours ago."

"And you haven't seen or talked to her since last night?"

Kris sat down on the bed, "Wait a minute, I remember mom and I talked to you about midnight. She got up after that saying she needed aspirin then she went back to bed. I was still trying to get Laurie to make sense."

"Would she have gone off on her own without talking to you?"

"I don't think so, daddy. I bet she's gone downstairs to get food or our bags out of the car. She probably decided not to wake me."

"Go down and check, see if the car is in the parking lot. I'll call back in ten minutes." The phone clicked and the dial tone returned.

"You could at least say goodbye," Kris fumed. He looked like her dad, but it stopped there. She didn't like this man, he was rude and unfeeling and he hung up on her. Ten minutes, that was not long enough to get downstairs and back up here.

She jumped up. Her mom's purse was on the dresser and the room key was gone. Kris grabbed the car keys and ran. She could get their bags out of the car while she was downstairs.

Jennie was probably in the café drinking coffee and she went straight there, but her mom wasn't in sight. The gift shop in the hotel was small and she could see from across the lobby that Jennie wasn't there either. The parking lot, daddy said to see if the car is there. It had to be, she had the car keys in her hand. She went outside anyway.

The car was there; both bags were still on the back seat where they had put them last night. Where could mom have gone, she couldn't go far without the car. Maybe she was walking around to get some exercise or at the café where they had eaten last night.

I have to find her. I can't get back in the room without the key, she thought.

Cars were parked on all sides of the building and Kris ran down one side and looked in the back before going across the parking lot to the restaurant. Jennie wasn't there and she started to feel scared.

She ran over to the far side of the hotel, her mom wasn't there either. Daddy would be calling in a couple of minutes and her stomach churned. That was barely enough time to get upstairs and she had to go to the front desk for a room key. Kris ran to the side of the building and pulled the door. It started to open then jammed, she tried to squeeze through the narrow space, but she couldn't make it.

Now was the time to panic, she could still see her dad's angry face when he found she got out of the car at the hospital. She jerked at the door with all her strength, it wouldn't budge. She had to get it open. She looked down and something was stuck under the bottom. Wiggling the door back and forth, she worked a piece of plastic out from under it. She yelled when she saw it was a hotel key with her room number on it, it had to be her mom's key.

"Oh, Mom, where are you?" she cried looking all around the parking lot.

The door opened and she flew down the hall to the elevators. She had to get to the room and talk to her dad. The phone was ringing when she ran in.

"Mom's not here, Daddy, the car is where we left it last night and our bags are still in it. Yes, I checked the restaurant where we ate, she's not there either. I looked around the building, all four sides." She started crying, "I'm scared, Daddy, I don't know where mom is. I found her room key; it was jammed under the side door."

The line went dead.

"Daddy…" she cried as the dial tone returned. She slammed the phone down.

Kris looked around the empty room and tried not to panic.

Chapter 31

PAIN SHOT THROUGH DAVENPORT'S head and he hung up on Kris. *Where the hell was Jennie?* He knew something would happen if she came out here.

All of a sudden he realized what the number on the note was about. The bastards had his wife. He dialed the number on the note and waited through five long rings before the phone was answered. "Unable to come to the phone right now, please call back in an hour" was the message. He slammed the receiver against the wall of the phone booth then turned and yanked the door open at the exact instant a gunshot rang out. A bullet blew the telephone apart.

Davenport dropped to the ground. He looked at the shattered pieces of what had been a phone. If he had been talking, it would have nailed him.

More gunshots, he crawled away from the booth.

Gunfire continued to break the silence.

When he got under cover of shrubbery, he turned in the direction the shot had come from. Falco was racing down the street and shooting at a vehicle that was speeding away.

Davenport jumped up and ran toward the car yelling, "Did you get the license number?"

"No, no plates," Falco called. "It was a Ford sedan, black or navy, hard to tell for sure. Two men were inside, a driver and a shooter. *Brotherhood* or death squad?"

"Has to be the death squad, that's how they handle it. The *Brotherhood* would send Fleicher and he works alone."

"It sounds like you know who's behind this."

"I do, Falco. The death squad I told you about earlier, it's a dissident faction within the CIA. Someone planted the word I've gone rogue and issued orders to remove me. I told you, the *Brotherhood* has people everywhere."

"Even in the CIA?" Falco opened the passenger door of their car.

"Oh, yeah, nothing is out of reach for them."

"Follow them," Falco ordered sliding into the car. "I got the two back tires and maybe the gas tank, either way they aren't going very far. I want to make sure it's not Fleicher."

Davenport spun the car around and floored the accelerator. They were speeding down the empty street when an explosion lit up the road in front of them. Davenport slammed on the brakes and skidded to a stop a few feet away from the burning vehicle.

The shooters' car had swerved out of control and hit a brick wall. The impact crumpled the front end, flames and black smoke billowed toward the sky. Eyes glued to the scene, they had to wait until the flames lowered before they could get close enough to see if anyone survived. The heat was fierce. They got the doors open and tried to get the men out, but it was too late. The men were already dead. The windshield had imploded shooting shards of glass into them.

"I've got the driver's ID, check that man's pockets for identification and bring it with you. We need to get out of here before the police come or we'll be tied up for hours." Davenport backed away from the fiery vehicle and wiped the sweat off his face.

The car was smoldering as they drove away, sirens were echoing in the distance and getting louder every second. They drove several miles before pulling in the parking lot of a busy diner. Davenport parked in the middle of a group of cars and switched off the motor. "Let's see who the men are."

Falco opened a bloody billfold. "This one says James Harcourt. Who do you have?"

"Miles Turnball, he and Harcourt were CIA. I didn't know them, but I know the names. I have to call this in and try the other number again."

Davenport looked around and found a phone at the end of the diner. It was not likely there was second shooter, but he didn't relish going in another phone booth. It made him an easy target. He dialed the general and gave him the location and names of the two dead men.

Surprisingly, the general was not yelling, he was calm and controlled. "Turnball and Harcourt are two of the names we got from Scott along with some other double agents in the CIA. They must have already been on their way to Phoenix when we picked up the other three," said the general. He was silent for a minute before continuing. "The president briefed me on your situation. I'm in the loop now and know what you're up against, Davenport. I wish you had told me a long time ago, I'll do what I can to help. All I'm going to say is try not to make too many messes for us to clean up."

Davenport never thought he'd hear those words from the general. "Thank you, sir, I wanted to tell you, but it wasn't my place to do so. We're not out of this yet, my wife is now among the missing. I can't promise anything."

"Understood, I hope you find her, Davenport. Let me know if I can help." The general plopped down in his chair when he broke the connection.

Davenport tried the number on the slip of paper again and got the same message, "Call back in an hour." He could not quit worrying about the nasty news that awaited him when that damned phone was answered. With eyes closed, he stood very still before going back to the car. Any time it involved Jennie, he was in trouble.

Falco watched Davenport slide under the steering wheel and turn the motor on. "There's a question bothering me. Why doesn't the government send in troops and take down the *Brotherhood*?"

"Nothing can be proven in a court of law, there's no hard evidence. The *Brotherhood* has infiltrated every branch of the government making it impossible to even find out who all of them are. They send me to do what I can to sabotage their plans and slow them down. Legally, I don't exist. It's a workaround for political expediency."

"Well that stinks, what happens to your life?"

"What life?" Davenport laughed bitterly. "I gave that up six years ago, Falco. You only stopped two of the *Brotherhood's* minions. The catch-22 is when you cut off one head the *Brotherhood* grows another and sometimes even more than one. I can't kill the thing, it keeps reproducing. The urgency now is to find my wife, daughter, and grandson and get them to a safe place."

"It still stinks. What do you mean, find your wife?" asked Falco.

"Jennie's missing." He closed his eyes. "I haven't had a chance to tell you that. When I talked with my daughter she told me Jennie had disappeared. When Kris woke up this morning her mother was gone. She doesn't know what time Jennie left or where she is."

Davenport backed away from the café. "We're going to the hotel where we left them. I know what that number is on the paper now; it belongs to the person who snatched Jennie."

"Have you called it?"

"Twice, both times an answering machine said to *call back in an hour*.

Chapter 32

KRIS STARED BLINDLY OUT the window as tears streamed down her face. She was lost, broken in ways she didn't think could ever heal. Her husband dead, her twin sister missing and talking gibberish, and now, her mother had disappeared again without telling her. Her dad, who came back from the dead yesterday, was a stranger who bossed her around with ice in his voice, and hung up on her without even saying goodbye.

Her world had become frightening and hostile. She felt trapped, it was crushing her and she couldn't get away from it. She couldn't stay here in Phoenix, she wanted to go home. But, where was home? Jeffrey was gone, he'd never come home again. She gasped for air and started coughing. Her stomach churned and threatened to erupt. She collapsed on the floor as great heaving sobs wracked her body. She curled into the fetal position and cried until she had no more tears.

Wiping away tears she remembered she still had her daughter. Sophie needed her and she needed Sophie. The coughing slowed down and, when the nausea subsided, she raised her head. "That's what I'll do. I'll go to my daughter."

Kris worked her way to a sitting position and rubbed her eyes. Sophie was with Molly and Herman at the safe house. She had no idea where it was, she only knew it was in Burleson. She had followed Pastor Crane across a field. Her temper rose in a heat of passion and adrenaline surged through her.

"Enough, I've had enough, I have to get up and quit crying. The house is in Burleson and his name is Pastor Crane, I can find the address. Daddy can go back where he's been all these years. I survived without him for a long time and I can darn well do it again."

"I'm on my own now and I have to find my daughter." She stood up and looked out the window then she turned and yelled at the empty room. "I will find Sophie."

Kris grabbed the room key and raced down to the car to get the overnight bag Molly had given her. Clothes rumpled, hair uncombed, face red and streaked with tears, she ran through the hotel lobby and out to the car. She unlocked the door, grabbed both bags, and ran back inside the hotel and up to her room.

Kris filled the tub with hot water and sighed in relief as the steamy water washed over her. She closed her eyes and started making plans. She tried to remember the last time she ate. It must have been yesterday when her mom made her eat that sandwich. Okay, first things first, bathe, get dressed, then go down and eat. She might quit shaking and think clearer when she had some food in her.

It was amazing how much better a bath and clean clothes made her feel. It helped to look presentable and have a plan, even one as simple as bathing and eating. Molly did great; she had filled the bag with clothes, deodorant, toothbrush, toothpaste, comb and a lipstick. Kris found what she needed except for shoes. She could check the gift shop.

"That's another plan," she said.

Searching through her mom's purse she found money and a credit card, exactly what she needed. She took the purse and went down to the coffee shop. She was back in control of her life for the first time in several days and it felt good.

While she was waiting for her lunch, she found a small notebook in her mom's purse and started making a list. Eat, look for shoes, check the gas in the car, and drive around. She had to find a place where she could hear Laurie's voice better. The little she was hearing today was faint and muddled; if she could get closer to Laurie, she might be able to understand her.

Digging deeper in her mom's purse she found a slip of paper with a phone number written on it, it had to be the number daddy gave her. Kris closed her eyes and tried to remember exactly what he had said. *I think he told mom if he didn't come back to call that number and whoever answered would help. This was a contact where they leave messages.*

She might be able to get the address of the safe house from him then she could go and stay with Sophie. Molly and Herman would help her as would the pastor and his wife. They had been kind to her. She could do this; she wasn't as lost as she was when she ran away from the kidnappers. This time she had a car and her mother's purse with money, credit card, tissues, and mints. This was what she needed the other day.

"Oh, Lord, has it only been three days?"

Kris was so deep in thought she almost yelled when the waitress set a plate of food and coffee down in front of her. Her nerves were raw and she swatted at a stray tear rolling down her face. "No more tears," she muttered. "I'm not doing that anymore."

She sipped the coffee realizing she had not even had a cup of coffee today, no wonder she felt horrible. Plans made, she picked up her fork and started eating. *Mom always wants me to eat even if I'm not hungry.*

WASHINGTON, D. C.

GENERAL THURMAN LOOKED LONG and hard at George Reaves while the man worked at his desk. It was a lousy day when a person had to question the loyalty of everyone he came in contact with, particularly his aide who had been with him over ten years. Nathan Scott had given them the names of a dozen men who were recruited by Silverman and had turned traitor. It was beyond any reason he could comprehend for a man to betray his country. What happened to loyalty?

"Reaves, what would it take for you to sell me out?"

Reaves dropped the papers he was holding and looked up at the general. "I'm sorry, sir, I don't think I heard you correctly."

"You heard right, son, what would it take for you to sell me out?" The general paced around the room, he was too troubled to stand still. "A higher paying job, a promise of power, a million dollars, what would it take?"

"I wouldn't, sir, I couldn't, I love my country and my job. Of course, there are times when days are hectic and I don't enjoy it, but that's part of any job." He pushed his chair away from the desk and watched the general pace up and down.

"I'm thinking about the police chief in Dallas and the men in the CIA we just took into custody. Why did they do it? Was it the money, the thrill of the chase and the danger? They have to know every moment becomes dangerous when they sell out to the enemy. Maybe there's a high associated with danger they become addicted to. I understand the motivation behind someone like Davenport who got caught in a situation, but the man chose our country. He chose to stay loyal to America even to the detriment of himself. That's loyalty, I get that. What I don't understand is what's happening in our country now. What happened to loyalty?"

"I don't know, sir. I know Silverman, who sold out to the Illuminati and *Brotherhood*, always looked down on everyone. He thought he was better because of his position as head of NSA. He loved to exert his power and he did it all the time even when it wasn't necessary. From what I've observed, it seems to be those with an attitude of *I'm better than you*. They evidently feel they don't have to play by the rules and they deserve more than everyone else. I know that's how Nathan Scott felt. He once told me rules were for others, not for him."

"You may be right, Reaves, that makes sense in a warped sort of way. Davenport called a few minutes ago and reported that the two men we haven't apprehended were in Phoenix and tried to kill him. Turnball and Harcourt died in a car wreck so we don't have to worry about them. You can cross them off the list. We still need to see what we can learn from the others, we may get more names. I'd sure like to get my hands on the instigator who planned all this. We've had encounters with the Illuminati and the *Brotherhood* before, and we both know it's next to impossible to find out who controls either group. The president is pressuring Davenport to find out who is orchestrating the *Brotherhood*."

The general stopped pacing and sighed heavily. He started back to his office then turned to face Reaves. "If you hear from Davenport, tell him we have the Dallas police chief in custody now. I'm praying no one else in that precinct has defected."

PHOENIX, ARIZONA

DAVENPORT AND FALCO PULLED in the hotel parking lot and parked by the side door. "Here's the drill, Falco. This is the door where Kris found Jennie's key. I doubt there's anything helpful here, but I want to look around. Jennie wouldn't have gone without a struggle, she could have dropped something. I taught her some defense moves and she would have fought. Then we'll go inside, I have to try that number again, the bastard has to answer sometime. I also want to check with my daughter and see if she has heard from Jennie."

Davenport got out of the car and walked around staring at the ground. When he got near the side door, he picked up an earring and a key. The earring was familiar, it could be Jennie's. The single key, he had no clue if it was important or not. He studied them then he pocketed both.

A DARK SCOWL COVERED Falco's face face as he followed Davenport into the building. He did not pussyfoot around when he did a job; he took charge and took care of business. Following Davenport made his head ache and his nerves raw. He felt like a babysitter trailing after him from place to place and he resented it. He was here to do a job and that wasn't happening, it did not sit well that he had nothing to tell Mr. Parrino. The man wouldn't be happy and that was never good. Parrino wanted retribution for his grandson, not excuses, and he wanted it now. He would be calling in favors from the Mafia in Phoenix if he had to wait much longer. Falco hated reporting when he had nothing to tell. He stopped at the first phone he came to and gave the operator a number and waited again. Waiting was not his long suit, something had to break soon.

DAVENPORT CHECKED TO SEE if Falco was with him. The man had stopped at the line of phones in the hotel lobby. He knew Falco was impatient to do the job he had been sent to do, however, there was no way to find Fleicher. The killer would find them and probably when they least expected it. He motioned he was going to the hotel restaurant. Falco nodded.

Kris was sitting at a table in the far corner by the window and he went straight there, "I'm sorry I was sharp with you earlier. I realized that the minute I hung up. I know I get a little crazy worrying about your mother. Are we okay?"

Kris looked up at her dad and her emotions were all over the place. He looked and sounded like him, maybe her mother was right. Maybe he was in there somewhere, but she wasn't sure she could trust him and she sure didn't like him.

"No, we are not. Everything I held dear vanished in a matter of a few days. I'm hurt and scared and all alone. You need to understand, my husband just died. My sister is missing and talking gibberish, my mother has disappeared again, and I don't know where my daughter is. The man who says he is my dad is a stranger. You look like my dad, but the man I knew is not there."

Kris glared at him. "I believe you could say we are definitely not okay. I'm very lost right now. I've made a plan, but I'm guessing you are here to wreck it."

Davenport flinched like he'd been hit and his shoulders drooped. "Krissie, I'm here because I love you, you're my daughter and I do realize all that. That's what driving me, along with finding Jennie and Laurie and Nicky. The reason I let you think I was dead was because it was the only way I could keep everyone safe from the *Brotherhood*, but that didn't work. So I'm back."

Davenport looked over at the door where Falco had just entered and waved him off. Falco turned and went back to the lobby.

When Davenport sat down in the seat next to Kris he could feel the animosity. For the first time, he saw her as a grown woman with a strong mind. His little girl had grown up while he was gone.

"I'm so sorry for everything, the kidnapping, your husband, being away while you were growing up, and for all the pain and heartache. I understand that doesn't change anything, but I want you to know how truly sorry I am. I never wanted to go away, and I never quit loving you."

He hesitated for a second as he watched Kris' frozen face. "I know I've changed. I had to block out emotions in order to survive and to do the work I had to do, but feelings are coming back. Your mom understands this. I'm trying not to let them overwhelm and disable me from doing what I have to do to find Laurie and Nicky and Jennie. Please believe me, I never wanted to leave or hurt you. I never wanted to miss my daughters' growing up years and your weddings. I did not want to miss knowing the men you both fell in love with, or the births of my grandchildren. All I have ever wanted and thought about was getting back to you, Laurie and Jennie."

He reached over and tried to take her hand but she pulled away. "Give me a chance, Kris, and a little time. Will you at least try to believe me?"

Kris looked deep into his eyes with eyes that were cold and penetrating and so much like his. Neither one backed down. "I want so much for all that to be true, but I don't recognize you anymore. I don't even know if I can trust you. I'll have to see how this plays out. Right now, I want to go to my daughter. Do you know where Sophie and Molly are?" Her eyes never wavered.

"Yes, if that's what you want, I'll take you to the plane and Jack will fly you there today. If you want to call and talk with Molly, you can do that now."

He stopped and watched her reaction. Her pretty face showed signs of recent crying and it stabbed him in the gut. Memories of rocking and singing to her when she was a baby flashed through his mind. He remembered the little stories he used to make up and tell his girls. Did they remember any of them?

He coughed and cleared his throat before continuing. "Since you're here and can communicate with Laurie, I'd like you to stay and help me find your sister, but it's your choice. I will do whatever you decide."

"Is Sophie all right?"

"I haven't talked with them since they got to the safe house. Blakely told me he heard from them and they were safe and comfortable. Molly told him the people there were very nice."

"Can I talk with Molly?"

"Yes, as soon as you finish eating."

Kris gave her dad a weak smile and took a bite of her scrambled eggs. She was not hungry, but she needed food and she was going to eat it all because that was her plan. Maybe, just maybe, daddy was back. If she could talk with Molly and hear Sophie's little voice then she would think about staying, she needed to find her mom and Laurie.

"I have to make a call, Kris. As soon as you finish eating, come out to the phones in the lobby and you can call Sophie and Molly."

Davenport stood up then leaned over and kissed Kris on her forehead. Startled, her eyes filled with tears as she watched her dad leave the restaurant. More than ever before, she needed the dad she knew and loved.

"SORRY FOR WAVING YOU off, Falco, I had to talk with my daughter alone. I keep forgetting she is grown woman. I missed the last six years of her life and, in my mind, she's a young teenager. I didn't even know she was married until Jennie joined me. Her husband was murdered a few days ago and her mother and sister are missing. Kris is really hurting and struggling hard to hang on."

The thought flew through Falco's mind that he was glad he never married and had kids. He had enough to contend with. Parrino was getting very impatient and that was never good.

"When do you think we'll be able to find Fleicher? Mr. Parrino is not happy and that means trouble. If he decides I'm not getting the job done, he will send in reinforcements."

"You know there's no way to find Fleicher, we've talked about this. We've never been able to find where he hides out. I was hoping he would be at the school waiting for me. All I can do is let him find me, and he will, Falco, that's definite, he has orders to eliminate me. I suspect he'll show up when we least expect him."

"All I've done so far is stand around. I don't wait well, Davenport, and neither does Parrino."

"I hear you, but this is a waiting game. The only thing I can do is stay in Fleicher's path and let him find me. In the meantime, you can tell Mr. Parrino that if Fleicher doesn't show up by tomorrow, we will breach the *Brotherhood's* headquarters. Maybe that will appease him for a day or two. Right now, I need to call that number again."

Both Davenport and Falco picked up phones and dialed.

Davenport looked over at Falco. "This could be Fleicher's number. I don't know who else would leave a message for me at the school. You can tell Parrino a meeting will take place in the next twenty-four hours."

Chapter 33

IT TOOK THE MAN longer than he thought it should to get to his place. Or maybe it just seemed like it, driving in Phoenix always made him anxious. He was grateful he was out of the city. The lonely road stretched out as far as he could see and he accelerated. He passed several small, isolated huts along the route before he reached the small settlement of Cave Creek. It was higher up in the foothills of Black Mountain than Phoenix and it felt like the old western towns of long ago he had read about. He loved Cave Creek; it always made him feel safe when he got here. He was careful to obey the speed limit driving through the little town. With no license or identification, he could not afford for the police to stop him with a woman tied up in his back seat.

"We're almost there. Keep still a little longer and I'll explain what's going on."

The woman lying on the back seat wiggled and tried to talk, but she could only mumble. She shook her head trying to get the gag out of her mouth.

"Please quit struggling, you'll make the binding more uncomfortable. I'll loosen it and remove the gag as soon as we get there and we can talk. I promise you, I'm not going to hurt you."

The young man watched the woman in the rear view mirror, she reminded him of the faint memories he had of his mother. He remembered her soft voice singing to him and saying she loved him. He treasured the feeling someone loved and cared about him once. Was this woman caring like that? She came running when he said he had her grandson so she must care about him. He wondered if she told him she loved him. Did she sing to her grandson?

After he passed through Cave Creek, he accelerated and drove a couple of miles before turning up an unpaved bumpy road. Jennie bounced around the back seat; it was difficult to stay still with her hands tied behind her back. He drove to the side of an old stucco hut and parked between two huge boulders. It was surrounded by scrawny sycamore and cottonwood trees. Getting out of the car, the man stretched and looked around the secluded area. The low growing trees, bushes, and boulders hid his place from the main road. Unless you drove back in, you couldn't see the little hut. He looked at it and smiled, it was his and it made him feel good. It was his safe place whenever he could slip away from the chairman.

"We're here," he said opening the back door of the car. "I'll help you out, but you have to walk to the house. There's no where to go so don't try running away. We're in the desert and there's no water out there so you better come with me." He untied her from the door handle, but left her hands tied behind her back.

The woman scooted over to the door and swung her legs around. It was difficult to get up with her hands behind her and the man helped her out. He had told her the truth, all she could see was desert, scrawny bushes, trees, boulders, and beyond that were mountains with low-hanging clouds. She couldn't even see a road. The sandy ground around the house was neat and swept clean of debris. There were a couple of uncomfortable-looking chairs on a porch with a low hanging roof.

The man held the end of the rope that tied her hands and pulled her toward the house. "When we get inside, I'll get you some aspirin and water. I know your head is hurting and I'm sorry."

He led her to the porch and dug in his pockets for his key. He was sure he had taken it with him, he always did. It probably fell out in the car; he hoped he hadn't lost it in the scuffle. "I've got to look in the car and see if my key fell out there. Can I trust you to sit down in that chair for a minute or do I need to tie you to the post?"

Jennie looked all around and there was nowhere to run. There were no houses or buildings or highways, only the dirt trail the car had driven on. There was nothing but a small hut and the desert. She nodded and sat down in the chair.

The man's words, "I'm better than the alternative," kept running through her mind. She wasn't sure what that meant. He didn't seem to want to hurt her and he sounded sorry her head was aching. Jennie knew she couldn't get very far with her hands tied behind her and she really wanted those aspirin. All things considered, she would wait until he untied her. Josh had told her if she ever got in trouble to make a plan then be patient and choose her time to run.

The man looked all around and she could tell he couldn't find his key. He went to the side of the porch and climbed in a window. Opening the front door, he motioned for her to come in. He really didn't need to lock it if a window was that easy to get in. There was only one room with a single bed in the corner which was neatly made up with a pillow and a tan blanket. The only other furniture was a small table with two chairs and a chest with a little hot plate. If this was where he lived, he was very poor. It was clean and neat, but then there was nothing to clutter up the place. It was obvious he needed money so maybe he had taken her for ransom, but he knew about her grandson.

He removed the gag and untied her hands then told her to sit down in the chair by the table. He tied the rope around her waist to the chair and one hand to the arm of the chair leaving one of her hands free. He sat a glass of water on the table beside her hand and shook a couple of aspirin out of the bottle and dropped them beside the glass.

"I know your head is hurting, Mrs. Davenport. I didn't want to hurt you, but you kept fighting me."

Jennie studied the man. He was younger than she thought he was when she fought with him in the parking lot.

"Why are you doing this, do you want money?" Jennie put the aspirin in her mouth and reached for the water on the table.

"I met your husband, Mr. Davenport, several times. He was nice to me; no one else has ever been nice. I need his help."

"Well, this is not the way to get it. He's not going to like you kidnapping me, he will be very, very angry."

The young man flinched. "I know. But when I heard him ordering Otto to take you, I thought it over and decided there was no other way. Otto would hurt you so I had to get you away before he came after you. I'm not going to hurt you. I want you to make Mr. Davenport listen to me."

"You want me to help you after you did this to me," she said rubbing her forehead. Jennie wiggled and tried to get comfortable on the hard, straight back chair then stared at him. "Who are you? How do you know my husband and how do you want him to help you?"

"My name is Hans. If he agrees to help me, I can help him find your daughter."

Jennie's head jerked up, "You know where Laurie is?"

"Is Laurie your daughter's name? I know who has her and I know the places he would have taken her. I can take Mr. Davenport there."

"Yes, my daughter's name is Laurie. Is she all right?"

"I don't know. I haven't seen her, I just heard them talking."

"I don't understand, tell me how you know my husband? *Them*— who are you calling *them*, Hans? Who ordered Otto to get me?"

"Mr. Davenport used to come to the meetings with the group. It's the chairman and Otto. I heard the chairman ordering Otto to pick you up. I couldn't let Otto do that, he would hurt you. Mr. Davenport was nice to me so I couldn't let him hurt you."

Jennie searched her memory. Josh had talked about the chairman; he was head of the *Brotherhood* who wanted him killed. Otto was evidently his henchman or something like that, but Josh had used another name. If she remembered right, he was the one who was trying to kill Josh. She never heard Josh mention anyone named Hans. This young man talked like he was a lot younger than he looked.

"What do you want my husband to do?"

"I want him to help me get away from the chairman."

"You're away from him now. If you can go into Phoenix to get me, why don't you just leave and go where he can't find you?"

"I can't, he controls me. Your husband knows all about it. I heard the chairman tell him about his school where he did bad things to me. I need Mr. Davenport's help to get away."

"What do you want my husband to do?"

A wave of emotions spread over Han's face; fear, hate, pain, Jennie wasn't exactly sure what she was seeing. Whatever it was, she felt the young man was afraid, very afraid of something. He better be afraid of Josh, she thought.

"So what do we do now?"

"We wait. I sent a message to Mr. Davenport with a phone number for him to call." He looked over at the phone. "I have a phone and as soon as he calls, we'll meet and talk."

"When he calls, you better let me talk to him. He's not going to be happy and he'll want to know I'm not hurt."

Hans nodded. "That's what I plan to do. You can tell him I haven't hurt you."

Jennie stared at him. He was tall, slim, pleasant-looking, and definitely younger than she first thought. Probably younger than her daughters, she doubted he was even twenty years old. The boy was terrified, his hands were shaking. She had never met anyone so scared. She asked him for more water then said, "Tell me more about yourself and this little house."

"Do you think Mr. Davenport will call?" he asked with a quiver in his voice.

"Oh, yes, he'll call as soon as he realizes I'm missing and he gets your message."

Hans looked at the pretty woman and wondered if his mother had blonde hair. He had no memory of how she looked, just her voice and how it made him feel. That was all that had come into his mind lately. He didn't know how to answer her, what could he tell about himself? He didn't know anything to tell her.

"I have some cookies and I can make tea if you like that."

"That would be good. I haven't eaten anything today."

The young man jumped up. "It's after lunch, you're hungry. I'm sorry, cookies are all I have." He poured water from a gallon jug into a pan and sat it on the hot plate. He opened the small chest and got two cups, a box of cookies, napkins, and a sugar bowl and placed them on the table. "It won't take long for the water to heat," he said putting tea bags beside the cups. He opened the cookies and sat the box in front of her.

Jennie picked up a cookie and took a bite. It had sugar and that was energy, it would help. The teacups looked like Dresden, now where in the world did he get Dresden teacups? They were as out of place here as the imported cookies and Hedley tea. From the looks of this place he couldn't afford to buy specialty items.

Hans poured boiling water over the teabags. He looked at her with apology written all over his face. "I don't have any milk or lemon, just sugar."

"That's all right, Hans, sugar is enough. Thank you for the cookies and tea." Jennie let the tea brew for a few minutes before pulling the teabag out and dropping it on the saucer. She sipped the fragrant black tea and ate another cookie. "This is very good, Hans. It will help my headache. Now, tell me about yourself and what you want my husband to do."

"I don't know where to start, but I need help. I've been held captive for the past ten years and I have to get away."

"What do you mean captive? I don't understand, you've got a car and a house and are driving around Phoenix."

"I know, but he can summon me back at any time and I won't have a choice. I'll have to go back."

"Back where, Hans?"

"If I don't go back to the fortress where the chairman is, he'll cause me pain. If he gets mad enough, he could make me die."

Jennie stared at the boy, that's all he really was. What in the world had happened to him?

The phone rang loudly and Hans jumped up and answered it. His face paled as he listened. "She's not hurt. She's drinking tea and eating cookies. Please listen to me then you can talk with her."

Hans' face was full of fear as he looked at Jennie. "He won't listen to me until he talks with you."

The boy's hands were shaking when he handed the phone to Jennie.

"Josh? Yes, I'm fine. I'm not hurt. I want you to listen to this young man. He needs our help. No, Josh, he does not have a gun. I'm saying this of my own free will...."

"Calm down, Josh, let me talk. I can't explain if you keep asking me questions. I am all right, I'm sitting here drinking tea and eating cookies. Please, listen to him and do what he says...."

"Yes, I told you, I'm okay. He is not pointing a gun at me, he doesn't have one. Just listen to him, Josh." She handed the phone back to Hans.

"Mr. Davenport, you know me as Hans, the chairman's servant. If you help me, I can help you find your daughter. Will you meet and talk with me?"

"Yes, sir, I'll bring your wife. I give you my word, sir, I won't hurt her. She's hungry and all I have is cookies so we need to get some food for her."

"Yes, sir, there's a diner on Highway 60 in Mesa. We'll meet you there in an hour. Yes, sir, it just says *Diner* on the sign, no other name. One hour, sir."

Chapter 34

DAVENPORT HUNG UP THE phone and stared at his watch. "We're on the move, Falco. Jennie is in Mesa. We're meeting her in an hour so there's no time to waste," he said turning around and going toward the hotel restaurant.

"Kris, your mom is out in Mesa and we're going to get her. If you come now, there's time for you to call Sophie before we leave."

Davenport picked up her bill and went to the cashier. Kris swallowed the rest of her coffee then jumped up from the table and ran after her dad. "Did you talk with mom?"

"Yes, just now. We are meeting her in an hour."

"Where's Mesa? Is she all right?"

"Mesa is east of here near the mountains. She said she was okay and her voice sounded normal. Actually, she was giving me orders and telling me what to do. You know how she is when she does that." Davenport grinned at Kris. "I think she's safe, but I want to get out there and make sure. You have a few minutes to talk to Sophie."

Davenport pocketed his change and started to the phones with Kris running to keep up. "We'll leave as soon as you finish your call." He punched in the number and handed the receiver to Kris. "I'm going to see if the hotel has a map."

"Falco, I talked with the man who took Jennie. Hans is the chairman's main servant and another one of the chairman's brainwashing victims. We're meeting him in an hour out in Mesa. Jennie said he wants my help. He functions almost normally except he has no past memory. However, he knows everything that goes on around the chairman and he said he can help me find my daughter. If he can do that, he may know where Fleicher is."

Davenport looked to see if Kris was still talking then turned back to Falco. "This could be exactly what Hans said, or it could be a trap and Fleicher is waiting."

Davenport watched Kris talking on the phone. When he saw her smile, he figured she was talking to Sophie and hoped it would relieve some of her anxiety.

He went to the reception desk and asked the clerk for information about Mesa. The man pulled a handful of brochures from under the counter and selected several on the Superstition Mountains. "There should be something in one of these about the town of Mesa, sir. It's less than an hour's drive out there."

Davenport looked through the colorful folders and stuck a couple in his pocket then went back to Kris as she was hanging up the phone. "Did you talk with Sophie and Molly?"

"Yes, and I feel better. They both sounded fine. Sophie was playing with Herman, she was laughing and telling me all about riding on Herman's back."

"Do you still want to fly home today?"

"I don't know, Daddy, I want to see mom first."

Davenport nodded and put his arm around his daughter, "Okay, let's go get her." He motioned to Falco and started for the car.

MESA, ARIZONA

IT TOOK ABOUT THIRTY minutes to drive to Mesa and the diner was where Hans said it would be. "Stay in the car, Kris. I'll go in first in case there's trouble."

Davenport slid out of the car and Falco followed him.

Kris sat still and watched them. She waited in the car until Falco opened the café door and motioned for her to come. Her dad was standing beside her mom and a young man at a table in the back of the cafe. Her mother looked tired, but she seemed okay. Kris was relieved and ran back there.

"Next time you leave the hotel room, Mom, you better tell me," she fussed. "You really scared me."

"I'm sorry, Kris, Hans didn't give me a chance to let you know."

Kris glared at Hans and started to say something, but Jennie interrupted her. "Sit down, Kris. Tell the waitress what you'd like. I've already eaten a sandwich and soup." She looked up at the waitress and ordered pecan pie and coffee.

Kris asked the waitress for a cup of coffee.

When Davenport sat down in a chair, his hand gripped the back of Han's neck and applied pressure. The young man flinched and tried to pull away. "Sit still, Hans. Kidnapping my wife was a damn fool thing to do; you better have a good explanation. The only reason you're sitting at this table is because Jennie wants me to listen to you, so talk."

Fear crossed Hans' face as he tried again to pull away from the pain of Davenport's fingers. He stammered nervously looking at Jennie. She put her hand on her husband's arm, "Let go of Hans, you're hurting him. It's all right, Hans, take a deep breath and tell him your story like you told me."

Hans looked at Davenport's unyielding face and stammered, "I'm sorry, sir. I know this was wrong. I didn't have time to think about what to do when I heard the chairman order Otto to pick up Mrs. Davenport. I knew what he would do to her. I didn't want him to hurt her like he hurts me so I decided I had to get her first and take her somewhere he couldn't find her and then talk to you," he said all in one breath.

"Go on," Davenport said.

"I know the *Brotherhood* has a contract out on you, sir, and that's wrong. You're not like the others, they were mean. You were always kind to me. You aren't really one of them. You know what the chairman did to me, but I'm not like Otto, I care about people. I had to get Mrs. Davenport somewhere Otto couldn't find her, he would have hurt her," Hans blurted out.

He closed his eyes for a second before looking up at Davenport. "Please, sir, I need you to help me get away from the chairman. If I don't get away from him now, he'll kill me for doing this."

Davenport released the pressure, but kept his hand on the back of Hans' neck. "I know he destroyed your memory as well as Fleicher's memory. You're away from him now, just don't go back. So why did you do this?"

"I thought you knew, sir. The chairman put a chip in Otto's and my back and he controls us through it. He uses it as a signal to call us to come to him. If we don't do what he wants, he causes pain. It can get really bad if we are slow, it has even knocked me down. He says it can kill us if we don't obey him."

Jennie looked over at Josh, "If it's like the chip the Army implanted in me when you were in the military, it's easy to remove. It only took a few minutes and a very small incision."

"That's what I need you to do, sir, get that thing out of me," Hans said. "But that's not all. I still won't have any memory of who I am and I don't know what to do or where to go. I don't even know my real name so I'm begging you to help me. I'm not like Otto."

Davenport sat down and stared into the boy's teary eyes, "How old are you, Hans?"

"I guess I'm eighteen, sir. The chairman said I was about eight when he found me and I've been his servant for ten years."

"Did you go to school, can you read?"

"I didn't go to school like regular kids. He hired tutors to come to the fortress and teach me. I only know this area and Phoenix. I've never lived anywhere else that I can remember. A few memories have come in my mind lately, actually more feelings of a woman singing softly to me. I like to think it was my mother and she loved me."

Jennie put her hand over Hans' hand and squeezed it. "You really have no memory at all?"

"No, only a few feelings. I do know I can't go back now that I've done this. The chairman will be furious because I disobeyed orders and picked you up before Otto could get you. He'll make me die." Hans looked down at Jennie's hand on his and tears formed in his eyes. He continued slowly, "He's been threatening to kill me lately. I think he knows I'm beginning to remember some things. He'll make the chip kill me or have Otto do it. Otto would enjoy killing me; he's always trying to find me alone so he can hurt me. He's jealous because I live in the chairman's house, but the chairman doesn't trust him and won't let him stay in the fortress."

Jennie caught her breath and looked straight at Josh. "We have to help him get away. How did you get that little house you took me to, Hans?"

"I've done the grocery shopping for years and I manage to keep a little money. I bought the little hut for less than a hundred dollars. It doesn't have running water or electricity or anything and it took all the money I'd saved, but it's mine. It already had the phone and I pay for it every month, but I don't know anybody to call. I go there and pretend I'm a real person."

"Oh, Hans, you are a real person," Jennie said with tears in her eyes. "Josh, please let go of him, you're hurting him."

Davenport removed his hand from the boy's neck and reached in his pocket. He laid a key on the table and stared at Hans.

"That looks like my key. I lost the key to my house this morning."

Davenport watched his expression then looked at Jennie who nodded. "All right, Hans, we will help you, but you have to help us. You said you can find my daughter."

Hans rubbed his neck. His shoulders relaxed and some of the strain went out of his face. "Yes, sir, Otto took her away from the air force hospital where the chairman had hidden her. He was supposed to take her to the fortress where there's a nurse to take care of her. The chairman wanted her there so he could get you in his trap, but Otto didn't do it. He took her to one of his hideouts."

"Why do you think he did that?"

"He's mean and angry and he wants to get away from the chairman, too. I'm guessing he's planning to use your daughter as leverage. I also know he likes blonde women, there's no telling what he might do to her. There's not a nurse at Otto's hideout, it's not even clean, and there isn't anyone to take care of her." Hans paused and frowned. "The thing is, sir, leverage won't work. No one can make deals with the chairman, he will kill Otto. I've seen him kill people who tried to make deals."

"Do you know where Otto's hideouts are?"

"Yes, sir, he has three of them. There's one he favors and I think he took her there. When I heard the chairman tell Otto to pick up Mrs. Davenport I got worried, I knew Otto would keep her, too. I left right then and went to the school and left that message for you. I thought you'd go there first looking for your grandson, but he's not there. The chairman has him hidden in the fortress."

Hans grimaced and looked straight at Davenport, "I can't go back, sir." His face clouded in pain when his shoulders jerked. "We have to get the chip out of me soon or I'll die."

"How does he activate the chip?" asked Davenport.

"When I'm away or in another part of the fortress, he presses a remote controller and I feel it. If I don't respond quickly, he holds the button down and it hurts. The longer he does that, the stronger the pain gets. He says if he continues to hold it down, I'll die. He's been pressing it for the past hour and holding it down longer each time. If he holds it much longer it will knock me down and I won't be able to get up for a long time. He's done that before."

"Where do you feel it?"

"In my back, it's right below my shoulder blade just under the skin. I've tried to dig it out with a kitchen knife, but I couldn't. All it did was make my back bleed. That's what I want you to do, cut it out. Real soon, sir, he is holding the button down longer each time."

Davenport's thoughts were racing. He reached over and rubbed his hand across Hans' back. "Tell me if I go across where it hurts."

"That's it, you just touched the spot."

Davenport rubbed a little harder. "I feel a tiny bump under the skin. We might be able to do this, but we have to find some place other than a restaurant. I could take you to the Army hospital, but that's an hour away. Do we have that long, Hans?"

"I don't think so, sir, he's been activating it for over an hour now and it gets stronger each time. The last time was bad; it came close to knocking me down."

"Could you call and tell him you came in to get groceries and have a flat tire?"

"It would infuriate him; he didn't give me permission to leave. I don't think it would help."

"Then let's find a doctor here in Mesa."

Falco stood up and felt the chip in Hans back. "I can take it out, I'm a paramedic. I've removed bullets and stitched people up lots of times. We need to get some antiseptic and bandages and go some where no one will see us." He looked straight at Hans, "If I do that, do you promise to help us find Laurie and Fleicher?"

"Oh, yes, sir, I will," Hans said looking up at Falco with admiring eyes.

"We won't have any real pain killers, but there's an over-the-counter spray that will help a little. It will hurt, can you tolerate me cutting it out."

"Oh yes, it can't be worse that the shocks I'm getting now."

Jennie stood pulling Hans' up with her. "Let's go. We have to get what Falco needs and get that thing out. This young man is in pain."

Kris was struggling to listen to two conversations, the one in front of her and another one in her head. She was trying to tell Laurie that daddy knew where she was and he was coming to get her, but Laurie kept screaming for help. Kris' head started throbbing as she followed her mom and dad out of the restaurant.

The Fortress, Superstition Mountains, Arizona

CHAIRMAN HOUSER REARRANGED HIS study positioning one chair in front of his desk and near the fireplace. If Davenport showed up and sat there, he would be trapped. He rolled to the other side of the desk and checked the cache of loaded guns he kept in the side drawer. He picked up the spear; it never failed to energize him.

"The Spear of Destiny," he murmured as he rubbed it. "He can't touch me as long as I have it." He slipped it in the side pocket of his motorized chair and punched the remote signaling Hans.

"Where is my coffee," he yelled as he rolled to the kitchen. There was no coffee and no Hans, the boy had been disappearing for hours at a time. "This is the last time I put up with his disobedience; I've warned him several times what would happen if he continued to disobey me. Well, it's happened too many times, he's outlived his usefulness," he mumbled.

He pushed the button on the remote and held it down for thirty seconds. "That should shock him hard enough to get back here. I'll give him fifteen minutes to get here. If he's not back by then, well, he won't be a problem ever again."

He turned to the cook and ordered her to get him coffee and a ham sandwich.

The cook shrugged and reached for the discarded percolator. She rinsed it before setting it to perk then she got meat and cheese out of the refrigerator for a sandwich.

"Hurry up with my food, I'm hungry," he yelled as he went back to his study. The chairman could hear the phone ringing and he wheeled as fast as he could to answer it. "What is it," he shouted at the phone.

"We've had intruders. Two men came to the school and entered through the basement door and looked around. They didn't disturb anything, but I thought you'd want to know," said the guard.

"What did they do?"

"They just walked around looking at the kitchen and patient rooms then they slipped out and left."

"Get over here and coordinate with the other guards. They will tell you what to do."

The chairman slammed the phone down then picked it up and dialed a number.

"Quick update, Davenport is back and he's on his way here. This is my chance to get rid of him for good. One way or another, he'll be in a body bag by sundown…

Yes, sir, I'll let you know when he's eliminated." The dial tone returned and the chairman slammed the phone down.

He rolled through all the downstairs rooms checking the locks on the windows and doors. He wasn't sure if Hans had done that before disappearing. The chairman wasn't happy, the house felt empty without the boy. He had used him for his every need for ten years. He could train another helper, but it would take time. In the meantime, he was without help. His face turned red and his finger pressed the button on the remote. This time he didn't release it for several minutes.

"Well, wherever you are, boy, you are dead. It's your fault, you knew the rules."

He opened the front door and yelled for the guards. There were a couple of young men he'd been watching lately. The brainwashing would take a month or so. This time he decided, he would train two helpers so he would always have a backup.

He reached in the side pocket of his chair and ran his hand over the Spear of Destiny letting its strength flow through him.

Chapter 35

HANS DID NOT UTTER a sound when Falco made a small cut in his back and dug the chip out. Falco put the bloody chip on a piece of gauze and handed it to Davenport. He pulled the incision together with surgical tape, covered it with iodine ointment, and bandaged it pressing the tape securely against Hans' back.

"This should be okay in a few days. You need to add a little of this ointment and change the bandage daily so it won't get infected. It'll be sore for a day or two and it may seep a little blood, but it won't be much, not enough to worry about." He handed the ointment, gauze and tape to Hans who was looking at Falco like he was his savior or king.

Davenport watched the procedure. It took less than five minutes to free Hans from the chairman. Falco knew what he was doing; his actions were deliberate and without hesitation. All of a sudden, Davenport felt the chip move in his hand. It vibrated for a long time, but he felt no pain with it. "Look at this. It's been shaking over a minute, it doesn't hurt my hand."

Hans shuddered as he stared at the chip. It was going way too long.

"You're only feeling the vibration," Falco said. "It was embedded in a cluster of nerves in his back near the spine where it could work on the nervous system. Someone knew what they were doing when they implanted it."

"Fascinating piece of technology, I'm wondering what to do with it?" It continued to vibrate in Davenport's hand. "If we destroy it, the chairman might know Hans has removed it. Maybe I should just drop it in the trunk of the car. It can't do any harm there."

"Do you think the chairman can track its location like the one G-2 had in me? Jennie asked looking at Hans.

"I don't know, he never told me." Hans couldn't quit watching it. "I don't think so. He doesn't know about my little house. I don't feel anything now." He turned to Falco with a broad smile on his face, "Thank you, Mr. Falco, I don't know how to thank you. I'd be dead now if you hadn't taken it out of me. I'll do anything you want me to, sir, just tell me."

Falco laughed and patted him on his back, "You've had a bad break, son, but you're free now. What do you want to do?"

"I have no idea. I don't know anything except the fortress and a few stores where the chairman sent me to shop in Phoenix."

Falco laughed again and put his arm around the young man. "Well, we're going to have fun introducing you to the world."

Jennie watched the excitement in Hans' eyes, the boy was free. Now, if they could just find her daughter and grandson she could relax. "Hans, I know you're excited, but remember, you agreed to help us find my daughter."

"Oh, yes, ma'am, I will." He turned to Davenport, "There's a dirt road about fifteen miles from here that goes up in the mountains and then into a canyon. You can drive most of the way, the last half mile we'll have to walk. This is Otto's favorite hideout; it's larger than his others and more isolated. I'm guessing this is where we should look first."

"How did you find out about these places?" Davenport asked.

"I followed him, hid my car in the bushes and went on foot through the rocks and brush. I wanted to see where he went when he disappeared. He has a couple of other hideouts out there, but they're only caves in the mountains. This one is what's left of an old mining town. There are a few buildings still standing and he has a bed in one of the rooms in the old hotel."

"Fifteen miles, that won't take long. Let's get going." Davenport turned to leave and his eyes met Jennie's eyes. Damn, he'd forgotten she and Kris were there. There was no way they could crawl through the brush and cactus on the mountain terrain and he wasn't taking them. This motel was as safe as anywhere to leave them.

"Kris, are you hearing anything from Laurie?"

"Not much. I've been telling her you are coming to get her and take her home."

Josh turned to face Jennie and started to talk, but she interrupted him. "I know, Josh, you want us to stay here. It's all right." Jennie put a hand out to stop Kris from interfering. "Go get our daughter and bring her back to me."

Davenport face darkened as he hurried out of the room with Hans and Falco following. That was too easy; he hoped Jennie wouldn't do anything foolish. He threw the chip in the trunk of the car and slammed the lid. If the thing was transmitting location, he would lead the chairman away from his wife.

Falco got in the car moaning, "I knew it, you're not going to let me stay here and watch television with the ladies, are you? I knew there would be more cactus somewhere and you're gonna make me walk through it."

Davenport laughed. It felt really good to laugh.

Kris and Jennie watched as the car pulled away from the motel. Faces downcast, they turned and went into the empty room. Jennie flipped the lock on the door and plopped down in the nearest chair. Waiting, that was all she was doing. They stared at each other a minute then both women started talking.

"You first, Kris," Jennie said.

"I haven't had a chance to tell you I talked to Sophie and Molly before we met you. Daddy called them for me. Sophie was laughing and riding on Herman's back saying "Giddy up, horsey."

"That's a relief. Sophie sounds like she's doing fine. Did Molly say everything was okay there?"

"She said it was. The house is next door to Pastor Crane and Cathy's house. They've been very kind; Cathy took them some food and cookies."

"That's great, I know they appreciate it. I guess Herman can go to store and get whatever they need. They'll take good care of Sophie."

"I know, Mom, but I should be there. Sophie was crying when we hung up and it breaks my heart. Daddy said he would fly me back if I want to go." Kris' eyes filled with tears, "It's so hard to hear Sophie crying. I don't know what I should do. I want to help find my sister, but I really need to hold my daughter." She paced around the small room.

Jennie pulled Kris down on the bed and hugged her. "I know. I'm not sure I can sit here and do nothing."

Kris wiped the tears away. No more tears, she reminded herself. She turned and faced her mother. "I'm hearing Laurie better than I did in Phoenix. Her voice is coming through much stronger, I think we're close to her. She is finally making sense and, at times, she seems to know who I am."

Jennie was elated Laurie was remembering. She also felt sick at her stomach, Laurie was her baby and she was badly hurt. She tried not to think about how serious her injuries were or what that man might have done to her. She leaned over holding her stomach and prayed it would settle down.

Would the men be able to find Laurie? Jennie looked in Kris' teary eyes then out the window at Hans' car parked out front. Kris could find her sister, she could follow her voice. If Laurie was conscious, she would be so frightened. Jennie's heart beat faster and her mind went into high gear. It would be dark soon.

Kris followed her mother's eyes to the waiting car outside, "Mom, are you thinking what I'm thinking…?"

Chapter 36

THE DRY DESERT DIRT caused the man to cough even with a heavy cloth over his nose and mouth. Otto Fleicher paused and leaned on the shovel for a minute before pulling a rag out of his pocket. He wiped the sweat off his forehead. A faint breeze stirred the leaves and a forlorn bird chirped in the distance. His eyes narrowed as he scoured the surrounding area, nothing unusual attracted his attention.

Fleicher looked at the buildings in the fading light. An old wagon stood in front of the rundown hotel, it had a large room downstairs and six small rooms upstairs. The balconies were crumbling and part of the railings had broken off. Three small shacks stood a short distance away, all were weather-beaten and falling apart. It was doubtful any of them had ever seen paint. He'd heard it was a lively little town back in 1892, however, that had changed when the vein faulted and the grade of ore dropped. The town had died a slow painful death. It belonged to him now; this was the only home he could remember.

Lately, thoughts of another place had been slipping into his mind. It was happening more and more often. He'd think it was a dream except it happened when he was awake. There was a woman with a little boy and pain enveloped him when this thought came. Not physical pain, but something else inside him. He couldn't figure out what it meant and it confused him. He understood pain in his body, but this made him hurt in a different way.

He shook his head hard and wiped the sweat off his face again. The hole was almost filled; a few more shovelfuls should do it. The muscles in his back rippled as he scooped up the loose dirt. There were several things he needed to do before he could leave. He'd already set two traps and he wanted a couple more around the edges of the hole. His plan was coming together easier than he thought it would. With a little luck, the damned ghost would not be a problem any longer and he could finish up things at the fortress.

After that, all he had left to do was pick up the boy and he could be on his way. A smile crossed his face, but his eyes remained lifeless. He shoveled faster.

THE BLACK CAR CREPT up a narrow dirt road barely fitting between brush, boulders, and a sharp drop off. The so-called road was only a couple of ruts winding its way along the edges of a deep ravine. Davenport's foot never left the brake. At times, the rut was so close to the edge he could hear the ground crumble under the tires. Falco white-knuckled the door handle as he stared at the road. He yelled every time the car got close to the edge. Night was coming fast and the car's headlights were like a beacon signaling their arrival. Davenport turned them off and stopped the car to let his eyes adjust to the fading light. Night fell fast in the mountains. It was already pitch-dark on the far side of this mountain.

"How much further do we have to go, Hans? It'll be too dark to see in a few minutes."

"We're close, sir. There's a small clearing up ahead where we can leave the car. We'll have to walk from there."

"I'm assuming there will be room enough to turn this car around. I'd hate to back all the way down."

"Yes, sir, I've turned around several times. It can be done with some maneuvering. There's the clearing, pull to your left and stop."

"Does Fleicher have a car? Obviously, this isn't where he parks."

"Yes, he has a car the chairman gave him. He uses another road that goes closer to the little town. I figured he might be parked there. I don't think this road is used any more."

"I'm sure it isn't," Davenport muttered. He loosened his grip on the steering wheel and turned off the motor, it had been a nerve-racking drive. He wasn't ready to think about driving out and Falco certainly wasn't, he was still hanging on to the door handle.

Leaving the car and going over to where Hans was waiting, Davenport and Falco stared down a steep incline then looked at Hans. "It looks worse than it is," Hans laughed. "Here's how you do it." He grabbed hold of the nearest bush and started down the deep gorge hanging on to the closest bush or tree. "You have to take it slow and hang on tight. It's steep and the ground is uneven and rocky so watch where you step."

"No joke, Hans, are you sure this is the only way down?" asked Falco. "Those bushes don't look strong enough to hold us."

"Yes, sir, the only other way is where Otto parks. Just hold on tight and don't hurry. The bushes and trees are stronger than they look, the roots are embedded in the rocks and they'll hold you."

Falco mumbled a few words and Davenport grinned. The man might be in the Mafia, but he was way out of his element here.

Davenport looked at the scrawny bushes and hoped they wouldn't pull out of the ground. He was a lot heavier than the young man. He took a deep breath and started down testing each bush before putting his full weight on it. It was a long way to the bottom. When he felt solid ground under his feet, he relaxed his tense shoulders and looked up to see how Falco was doing. The moon was beginning to rise and he could see somewhat better than he could on the road.

Falco grumbled when he saw Davenport and Hans waiting at the bottom, "I assume we have to climb up the other side?"

"Yes, sir, we do. Don't rush it. You're almost down, just hang on tight."

The men were silent as they hauled their way up the far side of the ravine. The small shrubs and trees bent almost double with their weight. Davenport said a silent prayer of thanks that the shrubs were tough and the ground was so dry and hard that the roots held.

Hans stood at the top watching the older men wrestle their way up the steep embankment. Davenport's arms were aching by the time he got to the top of the ravine. He reached down and helped Falco up and over the edge. Falco had quit complaining some time back, it was all he could do to breathe and keep up.

Falco's legs collapsed under him when he tried to stand. "I don't think my legs will carry me any further."

"Sit down and rest for a few minutes." Davenport knew exactly how Falco was feeling and he dropped down on the ground. Hans was walking around. Youth definitely had its advantages. He and Falco were both massaging their aching arms.

It had been a long stressful day and it wasn't over yet. The possibility of Laurie being here was a powerful incentive and that kept him going. How he'd get his daughter down the mountain would be a major problem, but he'd figure that out later. One step at a time, first he had to find her.

"Stay alert, Falco, I've no idea what's ahead of us. Fleicher could be here." Davenport checked his shoulder holster for his gun. It would not do to lose it. The two men stood up, stretched, and followed Hans.

A memory hit Davenport hard and fast sending him back in time to another mountain, one he didn't like to remember…

It had been snowing for hours and was close to a whiteout. He'd been running a long time when he hit an icy patch and slid off a ledge. He tumbled down several feet and the abrupt landing dislodged his gun. He watched it fly away and finally disappear in the snow. By the time he reached the bottom of the mountain, his gun was long gone and he was in trouble. The two men chasing him were getting closer by the minute. They had him in their sights and were firing at him. One of their bullets caught him in the back knocking him down. He could feel blood running down his back as he fought to keep going. He managed to get to where Harrell was waiting with the helicopter before he passed out.

The bloody trail Davenport left in the snow made it easy for the two killers to follow him. Harrell heard the gunshots and shoved Davenport into the chopper. They lifted off just as the men chasing him reached the clearing. The chopper took several hits before it was out of range. The flight was a blur and his first conscious memory was of an old man ordering him to be still. It was his introduction to the irascible Doc Fitz, a grumpy and obstinate old Irish doctor, who ignored everything Davenport demanded and did what needed to be done. He'd lost several pints of blood and it had taken him close to a year to regain his strength. He almost smiled at the memory of Doc Fitz ordering him around. That was one of the few good memories from that long convalescence…

HANS STOPPED ABRUPTLY AND signaled for silence. Lost in his thoughts, Davenport ran into Hans almost knocking him down. Davenport shook his head and looked around—he was back on the mountain in Arizona.

"We're close to Otto's place so be very quiet." Hans stared at Davenport for a second then turned to Falco. "The ground is level from here to the ghost town."

The flat ground was easy to walk on as Hans led the men through the brush. Hans could hear Falco cursing the cactus and mumbling about ghost towns. He wished could help his new friend.

LAURIE'S BODY JERKED AND her eyes popped open, they were gritty and burning. She blinked, closed her eyes then blinked again. It didn't help. Not a glimmer of light, it must be night. Her eyes closed and her head throbbed, she moaned and fell back to sleep.

Sometime later she woke for a second time, it was still dark. She reached up to rub her eyes and her hand hit something solid above her head. She felt all around her, she was walled in. There wasn't room to sit up and she could only move her legs a few inches. She was inside something. It felt like a box—or a coffin, she panicked and screamed.

She had to get out. She beat on the wood just inches above her face.

No one answered.

She screamed, again and again.

The more she struggled the more her body hurt. Her back sent waves of pain through her. She was lying on bare wood and she ached all over. She needed to turn on her side, but there wasn't enough room. Her face contorted with fear and confusion.

"Help me," she cried as loud as she could.

She couldn't hear anything except her own breathing; she held her breath and listened until her ears started popping. She coughed then choked when she sucked in air.

Kris and I were in a van, they made us sit on the floor, it had carpet on it. This doesn't feel like the van. Where am I? The van wrecked, Joey yelled for us to get out of van. Oh, dear Lord, Joey was shot. Where is my son?

"Nicky," she yelled, she felt all around her body. "Where are you?"

Her heart raced and she pounded on the walls.

"Kris, are you here? Where's Nicky? Kris? Talk to me, please, somebody answer me…"

Laurie listened, but nobody answered. She struggled to breathe and started coughing again. Tears rolled down her face and she broke out in a cold clammy sweat.

Chapter 37

DAVENPORT FROWNED AS HE WATCHED Falco pick his way through cactus and shrubs complaining loudly every step of the way. Hans stopped and motioned for them to be quiet. "We're almost at the town. Wait here. I'll see if Otto's car is there."

Falco plopped down on the ground and turned angry eyes on Davenport. "I've had enough of these mountains. This isn't what I bargained for. Mr. Parrino never mentioned it would be an expedition into the wilderness."

"Damn it, Falco, grumbling doesn't help anything. I didn't ask you or Parrino to come along, you invited yourselves. I go where the job takes me and it has taken me lots of miserable places I didn't want to go. I'm only going to say this one time, so listen up. There's more at stake here than a little cactus and your personal vendetta against it. It's the lives of my daughter and grandson. And, if that's not enough, there is the little matter of national security. If you don't like it, go home, but quit gripping and slowing me down." Davenport's face was immobile, his eyes hard and cold. "This is not negotiable."

Startled, Falco glared back at him and rubbed the knot in his neck. The man had developed a temper along with some guts since the old days.

"Go back and wait in the car if you want. This is my problem and I'll deal with it, I did not ask for the Mafia's help."

The two men heard Hans call *All clear* from ahead of them. Davenport turned his back on Falco and left without another word.

The place was deserted, only the ghostly remains of what had once been a town still stood. He headed straight for the most likely structure, a two-story clapboard building with a faded hotel sign swinging in the breeze. Laurie could be there.

"Hang on," Falco said running to catch up with Davenport. "I don't often find myself in situations where I feel so totally out of control. I'm city boy. I've never seen this kind of terrain and it's thrown me, but I heard what you said. I'm here to do a job, too, so how can I help?"

Davenport studied the man's face. "All right, we have to check out the buildings. Hans, where would Otto have put my daughter if she's here?"

"Probably in the hotel on the second floor, he has a bed up there," answered Hans pointing at the dilapidated building.

The decaying porch leading to the hotel entrance looked like it might collapse under his weight and Davenport stepped around the worst of the rotting boards as he crossed to the entrance. Stopping in the doorway, he checked the interior of the abandoned building before entering. On the left wall was a long bar with a cracked mirror above it and several broken barstools. A few dusty bottles still sat on the bar. A collapsing staircase angled up the right wall.

"I'm going upstairs if it doesn't fall down when I step on it. Falco, check out the downstairs. There could be another room or two in the back," he said pointing at a couple of doors.

Some of the staircase steps were missing as well as the hand rail. The existing steps were shaky and Davenport hugged the wall. The staircase was in the shadows; he pulled a flashlight out of his pocket and flashed it up the steps. He examined each one before putting his weight on it. He was almost at the top when something dark flew past his head. He ducked and fell back several steps yelling, "What the hell was that?"

"Probably a bat, sir," Hans pointed at the ceiling "The last time I was here they were roosting in the upstairs hallway."

Davenport grimaced and continued up the steps with his eyes glued on the ceiling. It was moving; the bats were rousing. A pungent odor hit him when he reached the top and he clamped his hand over his nose and mouth. Bats were hanging from the hall ceiling, hundreds of them. The smell was oppressive and he held his breath. The bats were restless and squeaking, the light must be disturbing them and he aimed it at the filthy floor. He sure didn't need them all flying at once, one had been enough.

"Otto's room is on the left at the end of the hall, sir," Hans called from the foot of the stairs.

Davenport opened the door and ran his light around the small space and the ceiling; there were no bats. He stepped into the room and took a deep breath. The window was closed and the air was musty, but it was better than the hall. His daughter wasn't here; the only thing in the room was a cot with a rumpled blanket and dirty pillow. Backing out of the small room, he left the door open hoping the bats would invade Otto's space. The other rooms were empty. A window at the far end of the hall had several panes broken out; he guessed that was where the bats were coming in. Holding his breath again, he dashed down the hall and hugged the wall as he crept down the wobbly staircase.

"Did you find anything, Falco?"

"Not a thing, just the remains of a kitchen and a storage room filled with decayed food."

"Nothing upstairs either unless you count the stinking bats," Davenport said. "Let's get out of here and leave it to them." It was almost dark when he stepped outside. He inhaled the fresh air and went toward the smaller buildings.

"The bats will be leaving soon, sir, Hans said. "They fly in the early evening."

The first shack yielded even less than the hotel, a few old tools and an ancient forge with several horseshoes beside it. The next shack had a makeshift worktable and Davenport pointed his flashlight at it.

He saw some small round objects and rusty tools scattered over it. He looked closer and gasped, "Oh, hell, landmines..."

Falco and Hans were out there walking around. Davenport ran to the door yelling as loud as he could. "Stop where you are, don't move. The sadistic bastard has been messing with landmines. He probably set traps in the ground out there." He took a breath and looked around. "Hans, you've been here before, do you see any signs of recent digging or raking?"

Hans looked all around the area, "The ground where I'm standing is hard and crusty, there's not enough light to see very well."

"Either of you have a flashlight?" asked Davenport.

"Yes, sir, I have a penlight," Hans said. He pulled it out of his pocket and handed it to Falco. They examined the ground all around them.

"Watch where you step; be sure you can see the ground," Davenport said. "Don't step on leaves or piles of dirt. Try to walk on the hard-packed areas. Watch out for anything sticking out of the ground. We haven't had a problem so far, but that doesn't mean we won't. They could be anywhere, the mines are small and they will be difficult to spot. Something will be sticking up, probably thin and small like a piece of wire or a nail."

"KEEP GOING, MOM, LAURIE'S voice is stronger, I think she's nearby."

"I can't see very well, it's almost dark. Wonder where this road ends, hopefully somewhere I can turn the car around," said Jennie.

"I think I see a wide spot ahead. Slow down, Mom."

"I can't go any slower, we're crawling now." She frowned trying to see the where she was going. "Yes, there's a clearing." She pulled into it and rolled to a stop.

"Kris, there's a house or building. Look straight in front of us where the headlights are hitting," she said turning the motor off. "This is as far as we can go; the road ends here. Maybe Laurie is in there, is she saying anything, Kris?"

"She's talking, Mom, but she doesn't know where she is. She doesn't sound good; it sounds like she's having trouble breathing." Kris got out of the car and started toward the building.

"Trouble breathing…oh, Lord, help my daughter." Jennie jumped out and followed Kris when all of a sudden a loud voice came out of the dark, "Stop where you are. Don't move."

It was Josh. He was shouting and Jennie ran straight toward his voice. She had to get to him and find Laurie.

"Laurie's here, Josh, she's having trouble breathing," she yelled.

DAVENPORT DUCKED DOWN WHEN car lights hit the hotel, Fleicher was here. He was signaling Falco and Hans to get down when he heard a woman's voice. It was his wife; he spotted her running toward him. "Stop," he yelled. "Stand still, Jennie, don't move. There are landmines here."

Davenport left the shed and retraced his path to the hotel. "I'm coming after you, do not move." He aimed his flashlight in her direction. Kris was already at the edge of the porch, Jennie a few feet behind her, the headlights illuminating her.

"How did you get here?"

"Laurie was crying about that man she calls evil. Then she started screaming, we had to do something. We drove all around the area while Kris was trying to find where Laurie's voice was the strongest. Her voice got louder when we came to the foot of this mountain so we stopped at a gas station and asked if there were any houses in the area. An old man told us that there was an abandoned town further up the road, but nobody lived there anymore. Kris was hearing Laurie's voice clearly so we followed the road up here. She says Laurie's here and she's having trouble breathing. Josh, we have to find her soon."

"We've already checked and she's not in these buildings. We looked in all of them. She's not here, Jennie."

Jennie gripped her husband's arm, "Listen to me, Josh. Kris said Laurie is here and she's having trouble breathing."

He looked around the small town. "The only place we haven't looked is behind the old hotel, maybe there's another shack there." He started toward the back of the building.

"Wait up, Davenport. I looked back there when I checked the kitchen, there's nothing but trees and cactus." Falco voice softened and he continued slowly, "There might be another place to look." He joined them by the hotel porch. "If she's having trouble breathing that bastard may have buried her."

"Buried…" Jennie cried, her face drained of color.

Falco looked straight at Davenport. "Several years ago I encountered a man who was buried. Fleicher may have set a trap for you and baited it with your daughter. Find where he planted the landmines, Davenport. That's where she'll be."

Kris turned to Jennie and put her arm around her mother. "Daddy, I can find Laurie. I'm hearing her and I can follow her voice. She's talking to me, but she's struggling to breathe. She's very close to us."

"I hear you, Kris," Davenport said. "Falco may be right, that's something that sick bastard would do. But where, she could be anywhere." He looked around the grounds surrounding the buildings.

He turned to his wife and daughter. "Both of you listen to me. Stay on the porch or next to the steps, this area is safe, we've walked all over it."

Kris and Jennie stepped on the porch and Davenport took a deep breath. "You scared me. You both could have been killed."

Jennie interrupted him, "Don't fuss at me, Josh, you can do that later. You and Kris need to find Laurie right now, she can't breathe."

"Tell me more, Falco, what makes you think he could have buried Laurie?"

"When I dug the man up the air was almost gone inside the coffin. He was wheezing and trying to breathe. If Fleicher didn't put an air vent in it, the air will run out. She may not have long,"

"Kris, you're sure Laurie is here?"

"Yes, she's here. Daddy, she says she's in a box."

"Oh, damn, you're right, Falco. Tell me where to go, Kris. I'll go in front of you, you follow right behind me," Davenport said. "There's no way to know where the landmines are."

"I'll go first, sir, I owe you. Which way should I go?" said Hans stepping in front of Davenport.

Kris pointed, "Go right, her voice is coming from over there."

Hans copied Davenport and picked up a stick. The two men scraped away the leaves and debris and tested the ground to see if it was hard or soft before taking a step.

Kris followed keeping her hand on her dad's shoulder. *Keep talking to me, Laurie. Daddy and I are almost to you.*

They went a couple of yards before Kris said, "Stop, this is the place." She pointed at the ground on her dad's right side.

The ground had been disturbed, Davenport poked at several places where Kris pointed. It was mushy and the stick dug in without resistance.

"This could be the spot, the ground is soft. Kris, turn around and go back exactly like we came. Get on the porch with your mother. We'll have to dig her out."

"Yes, sir," she went back and stood beside her mom. Jennie put her arm around Kris and watched Josh test the area in front of him.

"Is Laurie talking?"

"Not much, Mom, it's harder for her to talk now. I told her to quit trying to talk and just breathe. I told her daddy is almost there and will get her in a few minutes."

Falco had searched the sheds while they were trying to finding Laurie and he thrust a rusty shovel at Davenport.

Hans dropped to his knees and started scraping leaves and loose dirt aside. His hand brushed across something sharp sticking out of the ground. He jerked his arm back, but it was too late. A landmine exploded sending dirt, leaves and shrapnel flying. Hans flew backwards.

Davenport grabbed him and pulled him over to where Jennie and Kris were standing.

"I'm okay, I'm okay…" Hans said. "I'm okay."

Falco knelt and checked him. Hans was dazed and his face was covered with dirt. The only injury he found was on Hans' arm and it was bleeding, something was embedded in it. He didn't have time to help him now; he pulled his belt off and wrapped it around Hans' arm to stop the bleeding. Looking at Jennie he said, "Can you keep a little pressure on this? Be careful, there's something sticking out of the wound, it looks like a nail. Just put enough pressure to slow the bleeding down if you can. Hans, this isn't bad. I'll patch you up later. I need to help get Laurie out of that hole before the air runs out."

Hans nodded. "I'm okay, sir, I'm okay."

Standing back as far as the shovels would reach the two men raked the leaves and dirt away then examined the ground before digging.

"I doubt he dug any deeper than he had to, it's grueling work," Falco said looking at Davenport's strained face. "We'll get to her."

"You're right, Falco, the soil is loose and dry like powder. I've hit something solid about six inches down, he didn't dig deep. I'm guessing more landmines are hidden around here. Be careful brushing stuff away."

The sound of the shovels tossing dirt away from the grave was deafening as Jennie watched Kris breathe irregularly. Both her daughters were in trouble, she'd seen it happen to them before. She kept a slight pressure on Hans' arm and watched the shovels scooping up dirt and pitching it aside.

"I'm okay now, Mrs. Davenport," Hans sat up straighter and took hold of the makeshift tourniquet. "I can do this now."

Jennie couldn't restrain the tears back any longer. "Is Laurie saying anything, Kris?"

"No, not a word," Kris sat down on the step coughing. "It's getting harder to breathe. Laurie is barely breathing, Mom."

Jennie turned pale listening to Kris struggling for air. She prayed and drew her daughter close when she sat down on the wooden step.

All of a sudden a whirring noise filled the air and the lingering rays of light were blotted out.

The bats had taken flight.

Chapter 38

CHAIRMAN HOUSER STARED OUT the open door at the craggy mountains. He marveled once again at the sheer mass of rock walls surrounding his fortress. The rugged mountain terrain made it almost impossible for anyone to get to the fortress. He assumed a very experienced rock climber might rappel in; however, it would be one hell of a vertical drop. Even if a climber managed to scale the boulders, he'd be in plain sight of the guards stationed around the fortress. As far as he knew, this was not one of Davenport's skills. The man was too old for such activity; he was too old for lots of things now. The chairman turned away from the door with a smile on his face. It had been a long time coming, but Davenport was now his. The trap was set.

The man leaned back in his chair and closed his eyes while he massaged his forehead. A headache had plagued him for hours and wouldn't go away. His life was much harder without Hans. He had trained the boy well; he had been his feet for ten years. He could be replaced; the problem was it would take time and lots of effort. He rubbed his temples. Coffee, where was his coffee? He yelled for the cook. This would be a long night.

He looked at his watch again. He had put off returning the phone call as long as he could. The blasted call must be made, his face darkened and his head pounded. Houser governed the *Brotherhood* alone. It was easy to forget he had a superior who demanded a report every other day. He had good reason to forget, he was the one who had put all the plans into action. He alone had done all the work. He was the one in charge, the only one the men knew. They looked to him for guidance, they were loyal to him and not to an invisible man they had never met or even heard about.

This whole day had been one problem after another. Slamming and locking the door, he rolled to his desk and picked up the phone. The chancellor would not be pleased with tonight's account. His hand shook as he listened to the phone ring. In spite of all their attempts, Davenport was still alive. He wasn't sure what he was going to say to the chancellor, he had to word it so the man would understand the situation.

Otto had turned into a major problem. He committed an unpardonable offense; he had disobeyed orders two times. The chairman didn't know where Otto had taken the comatose daughter; he had not brought her to the fortress as ordered. Last night Otto disobeyed instructions again. The man should have brought Davenport's wife to the fortress and that hadn't happened either. Otto had become unmanageable, but he couldn't get rid of him like he did Hans until he had the wife and daughter under his control, or until he knew where they were.

After many rings a raspy voice came on the line, the chairman cringed and his hand tightened on the phone. "Good evening, Mr. Chancellor, this is Claude Houser," he waited for the man to answer; all he heard was labored breathing. "I'm pleased to report tonight that our plans are going according to schedule, some are even ahead of schedule. There are no major problems on the horizon. As of now, we've created significant ideological unrest all around the country, the divide and conquer is happening fast in America. All the planned protests and political opposition in congress has worked as we hoped. The members of congress are fighting among themselves. People are now distrusting the president, congress, government agencies, the media, and even their neighbors. We have our people ready to take control at a moment's notice in every section of the government."

The chairman pulled the phone away from his ear. "No, sir, I'm not avoiding the subject. I wanted to bring you up-to-date with where we are today. Yes, sir, we are in agreement, Joshua Davenport is still a problem. Up to now, he has evaded all our efforts to terminate him. However, I have a foolproof plan in place. The man will be in a body bag within twenty-four hours. This time I will see to it myself."

There was no response, only a bout of coughing. The chairman could feel the chancellor's wrath radiating through the phone line when suddenly the dial tone returned.

Houser hung up the phone with a trembling hand. He resented the fact the chancellor made him so nervous his hands shook. He rolled around the room in a burst of temper. It infuriated him when the man hung up on him. All he did was make demands, never a word of praise for all his hard work. The man could not do anything to him; he could only make threats. He had never been to the fortress. If he did come, he couldn't get in the locked gate and he certainly wouldn't let him inside.

It hung over him like a dark cloud that he had not met the Chancellor in person, or if he had, he didn't know it. He didn't know what the chancellor looked like, what his name was, or even where the man lived. For all he knew, he could live in Phoenix. All the chairman knew for certain was what happened to those who disobeyed the chancellor. It wasn't pretty. It brought back memories of the Gestapo and what Hitler did to the prisoners in World War II. He rocked his chair back and forth.

He tugged at his collar then dug in the side pocket of his chair for the Spear of Destiny. Holding the spear with both hands, he rested his head on it and gradually calmed down. Relaxing his shoulders and straightening up, he continued circling the room while he made plans. What he had to do now was get Otto in the fortress and find out where the two women were. He wanted the wife and daughter under lock and key in the safe room. The child was not a problem; he was already secure in the back section of the building with an attendant. The boy was probably enough leverage even without the women. After all, they were merely extra insurance, what man would not want his grandson?

"Where the hell is my coffee?" he yelled. "I want it now."

He picked up the remote controller and signaled Otto. He held the button down for several minutes, long enough to knock the rebellious man out and down on the ground, but not long enough to kill him. Otto had to understand he meant business. Next time, well, he would hold it down for five minutes. Houser smiled thinking it would be a relief to not have to worry about Otto anymore, and good riddance. He never trusted him to stay overnight inside the fortress anyway. He didn't trust him enough to be in the same room without the remote controller in his hand and a guard nearby.

Houser called all the guards inside and told them to be on high alert all night, intruders were expected. He instructed them to watch for anyone rappelling down the rock walls. There would be no time to loiter tonight or to leave their appointed stations, absolutely no coffee breaks.

Everything was in place. He had done all he could to prepare for his reunion with Davenport. He was ready.

Now, it was just a matter of waiting.

Chapter 39

A COLD WIND BLEW through the deserted town. Davenport and Falco flinched when lightning cracked and zigzagged across the sky, it sounded like another landmine. Deep rumbles of thunder rolled around the mountains and drops of rain peppered the ground making patterns in the dust. The men dug faster.

Shovelful by shovelful, the top of a crudely built pine box became visible. The instant the dirt was cleared away, Falco reached down to pull the top off the coffin.

Davenport's hand shot out and stopped him. "It could be booby-trapped."

"We have to get air to her fast," Falco said.

"I know, but it won't help to blow us all up." He examined the ground then belly crawled around all four sides running his hand along the edges of the coffin, the muscles in his jaw clenched tight.

"I don't feel any wires or obstruction around the opening. The bastard could still have a pressure bomb under Laurie, don't be too fast to move anything. It could go off with any change in the weight."

"Damn it, man, what kind of sick mind thinks up things like this," Falco asked.

Hans ran over to the grave and pulled Falco back a step, "It's exactly what Otto would do, sir. He likes to hurt people."

Davenport double checked the top then checked it a third time. He sat up and sucked in air. "We can't lift the lid all the way off. We have to keep weight on the box. I'll slide it down an inch and see if she's there, that'll give her air."

Jennie started off the porch, but Kris grabbed her. "Stay here, Mom. If there's a bomb under Laurie and it goes off…please, Mom, I can't lose everybody." Tears streaked down her face.

Jennie stopped and wrapped her arms around her daughter. "It will be all right, Josh knows what he's doing."

"I don't know. That man who buried Laurie must be insane, who knows what he's rigged up underneath her?"

Jennie stood still holding on to Kris and watching the men.

Hans aimed his flashlight at the box while Davenport eased the lid an inch. Blonde hair, she was there. Davenport visibly shook. "It's Laurie. If you've ever prayed, pray now. If she's still alive, she has air to breathe."

Jennie shivered when she heard Josh's words, *If she's alive…pray.* The wind blew harder sending leaves and dust all over them. She fell to her knees pulling a swaying Kris down with her. She didn't think Kris' face could get any paler, but it did, and she was holding her breath. Jennie shook her daughter, "Breathe, Kris, open your eyes and breathe."

Kris started coughing then nodded her head, "I'm okay, Mom, Laurie is breathing now, just a little."

Davenport moved the lid another inch; he could see part of his daughter's face. Her eyes were closed. "Get some rocks. I have to put enough weight on each end and all around Laurie so the pressure doesn't change before we can remove the top."

Hans ran around gathering up rocks with his good arm and piling them where the men could reach them. Davenport placed the rocks, first on one end and then the other end. Finally, after removing dirt from the side, he pushed the top over a couple of inches and slipped rocks along each side of Laurie. It took time, beads of sweat glistened on his forehead when he straightened up. He arched his back and neck trying to relieve the pressure, his heart was thumping in his ears.

"It's as ready as I know how to make it. We have to get both ends off at the same time." He turned to Falco. "When we lift it, go toward the hotel fast."

Davenport looked straight in the man's eyes, "No guarantees, Falco, it could blow." He stood still and watched him.

"Are you ready?"

Falco looked down at the blonde hair and thought about his little niece. He nodded, "Let's do it."

"Okay. On the count of three, we lift the top off together." Davenport bent down and took hold of one end. He watched Falco squat down and grab hold of other end.

He started counting…

One…

Two…

Three…

They jerked the top off throwing themselves sideways as fast as they could.

No explosion, the top was off. They were alive.

Sweat poured off Davenport and Falco as they stared down at the young woman in the coffin.

Laurie wasn't moving and he couldn't see her breathing. His daughter was so thin and fragile looking, her hair tangled and matted. The right side of her face was swollen and purple. She wasn't breathing— his daughter was dead.

Davenport's world shook more than it ever had, his heart raced, sweat drenched his clothes. All control was torn away and he fell to his knees, this was his baby and he'd failed her. The emotions he'd frozen off so long ago burst open and engulfed him. Tears streaked through the dust on his face.

Kris stood up, eyes closed, willing her sister to take a breath. *Breathe, Laurie, I'm here with you, mom and dad are here, too, we're going home. Take a deep breath, Laurie, we're going home…*

Jennie watched her daughter and was about to shake her again when Kris' eyes popped open. She took a breath and called out, "Laurie's breathing, Daddy. I know she is, I can breathe better now."

Hans went down on his knees and touched her wrist. "I feel a faint pulse, sir, she's alive." Hans looked up at Davenport and said louder, "Your daughter is alive."

Little by little the words *your daughter is alive* penetrated his anguish. He stared at his baby girl. Maybe, just maybe, if she was alive, he could go home again.

His voice was faint when he choked out the words, "We have to get Laurie out of there, but we have to add more weight. Hans, Falco, I need rocks or anything heavy, things I can slip beside her in the coffin. We have to try to equalize her weight."

Hans flashed his light about the ghost town. Forgetting to watch for landmines, Hans and Falco ran around gathering up rocks and anything that would fit in the coffin. They stacked it where Davenport could reach it.

Davenport laid the objects along the side of his daughter. Each time he added one, he prayed a bomb wouldn't go off.

Thunder boomed and lightning lit up the night again. He could see Laurie's face and he thought he saw her chest rise, it energized him. He looked over at Jennie and Kris and nodded. He wanted to tell them it was all right, but it wasn't yet. He and Falco still had to get her out of that coffin.

Davenport stood up. "I think there's enough weight, but there's only one way to find out." He breathed deeply and looked at Falco. "It's time to see if we can get her out. Falco, take her legs, I'll lift her shoulders. When we pick her up, run like crazy toward the hotel."

Jennie and Kris held their breath and each other.

Clouds obscured what little light there was, hot streaks of lightning split the sky again, thunder came seconds behind unleashing torrents of water.

The wind drove the rain sideways into the men when they knelt to pick up Laurie.

Chapter 40

OTTO FLEICHER WAS ALMOST happy and that was something he couldn't remember feeling. Maybe, he thought, being in control of his own destiny was what made a person feel this way. Whatever it was, he liked the feeling.

Everything was falling in place. If he had figured the timing correctly, Davenport would be a dead man by the time he got to the fortress. His only regret was he couldn't stay to watch the man die, that would have been the ultimate pleasure. He had thought the matter through; it was possible Davenport wouldn't get to the ghost town until later tonight. The timing was the unpredictable part. *Well, my plans are made and I can't wait around, I have a plane to catch.*

Lightning slashed across the sky, thunder boomed, and rain hammered the windshield obscuring his view. Fleicher fumbled around the unfamiliar car in the dark searching for the windshield wipers. He had borrowed this car from a café parking lot. He'd stash it at the fortress and take one of the chairman's cars when he left. The man wouldn't need them anymore after tonight. There would be no way for anyone to track him.

He had tried many times to remove the chip from his back, but it was impossible to get to it. His back was lined with scars from the knife he'd wielded. Pain was not the problem; pain told him he was alive, he just could not dig the thing out. He had two options left, destroy the remote that controlled the chip in his back or do away with the chairman. He had decided to do both.

He accelerated making a quick turn onto the highway heading for the fortress. The ghost town had been a safe hideout for a long time; it was the only place he could remember that belonged to him. It would now be the graveyard for Davenport and his daughter, his lips widened in a smile of pleasure at the thought. If everything goes according to plan, he and his son would soon have a new life.

He was feeling relaxed when the pain started. He howled in agony, the chairman was holding the button down too long. It was way too long.

"Damn you," he screamed as the pain intensified.

His head snapped backwards, his eyes rolled up in their sockets, and his hands flew off the steering wheel. The car careened off the road picking up speed as it raced down a steep hill toward a huge boulder.

The impact flipped the car up and over.

It came to an abrupt stop upside down.

Lightening flashed across the sky and rain pelted the car's tires spinning in the air. The man was not moving.

Chapter 41

DAVENPORT AND FALCO LEANED into sheets of rain as they ran with Laurie toward the hotel porch. Suddenly, a series of blinding flashes lit up the night. Glowing balls of fire and smoke exploded out of the grave and billowed up and out. The force of the blast hurled the men and Laurie down on the muddy ground.

A long low scream pierced the battering racket of the rain and explosion. Kris collapsed pulling Jennie down with her as she fell to the rotting porch floor. Jennie couldn't tell who screamed, it seemed to come from all around her.

"Look at me," Jennie yelled shaking her daughter. "Wake up, look at me." There was no response. She shook her daughter's head until she heard her moan, Kris was breathing. Jennie eased her head down on the floor and looked around for the others. She couldn't see anybody.

"Josh, Falco, Hans?" she yelled as she jumped off the porch into the rain. Sloshing through the mud and dodging fiery smoke and sparks shooting out of the grave, she searched for the men. The darkness was broken only by flickering flames. She found Josh, Laurie, and Falco crumpled in the mud a few feet from the grave. Hans was on the far side of the grave. Nobody was moving and fear enveloped her.

The explosion had shot up and all around. A pillar of fiery smoke was boiling up from the coffin where Laurie had been. The rain was beginning to put out the fire, Jennie could hear sputtering.

Jennie went down on her knees in the mud beside Josh and Laurie. Josh stirred and twisted to his side. "I'm all right," he said hoarsely. When he saw her face, he reached over and took her hand, "I'm okay."

Jennie stood up pulling him with her. Davenport was unsteady and held on to her, "That was a huge blast. It was intended to kill us."

He stared at the smoke and sparks still shooting out of the grave. The sides of the grave were beginning to cave in and mud was smothering the burning coffin. "We can thank the rain we're still alive."

He was alive. Jennie let the fear go, the others would be okay, too. She went down on her knees again beside Laurie. "Her pulse is weak, Josh, we have to get her out of the rain. I don't know how much more her body can stand. Can you help me lift her?"

"I'm steady now. I can carry her back to the porch," Davenport bent down and picked up his daughter. He cradled her in his arms and eased her down beside Kris who was rubbing her forehead and trying to sit up. "What happened, Mom?"

"There was a bomb under Laurie. When they moved her, it exploded and the blast blew everyone down. It knocked Josh and Falco out and they dropped Laurie. I think that's when you screamed and passed out. I'm guessing you felt Laurie's pain; it must have been bad. Her pulse is weak, but she's breathing."

Davenport listened to what Jennie told Kris. The connection between his twin daughters had always amazed and baffled him. If Kris was awake now, he hoped it was a good sign that Laurie might be all right, or at least not much worse.

He looked back at Falco and Hans lying on the ground in the rain and stepped off the porch. "Jennie, stay here with Kris and Laurie. I'll go help Falco and Hans."

Davenport limped across what was fast becoming a giant mud puddle to where Falco lay facedown in the mud. He took hold of Falco's shoulders and rolled him over. The rain began washing the mud from his face and the man opened his eyes. He coughed and pushed up on an elbow, "What the hell happened?"

"The bastard had a bomb not only under the coffin, but under Laurie. It exploded when we picked her up and the impact knocked us out. I need to see to Hans."

Falco sat up and tried to wipe the mud out of his eyes and mouth. He struggled to his feet and followed Davenport on shaky legs. "Is he okay?"

"He's starting to wake up. Let's get him over to the porch and see what kind of injuries we all have." The men pulled Hans across the ground and up the rickety steps out of the rain. "Are you injured, Falco?"

"No, nothing is bleeding. Can't get all the mud out of my eyes, but I'm in one piece." He couldn't quit staring at the grave. "Sparks are still shooting out of that hole. I know a little about bombs, enough to know he planted something really big."

"Yeah, he did. It was large, but amateurish. It was big enough to kill me and anyone with me except it didn't go off quick enough. He didn't plan on the rain, that's what saved us. The mud washed in on top of the bomb and stopped some of the shrapnel from flying. More mud flew than anything else. It was the force of the explosion that knocked us down."

Hans sat up looking dazed.

"Are you hurt, Hans?" Falco asked the young man.

"My arm is throbbing. I think I must have fallen on it when the blast went off."

Falco bent down, "Let's have a look at it, son. The nail is gone, and your arm is bleeding again. We'll have to take care of that when we get off this mountain." He looked over at Laurie and Jennie, "How is Laurie, do you think she's worse?"

Jennie was sitting beside Laurie and wiping mud off her face. "She's still not conscious, but her pulse is getting stronger. Kris says she's not talking."

She looked up at Josh, "Can you get us out of here?"

"We can't go back the way we came, that's for sure. There are six of us so we'll have to crowd in the car you and Kris came in. If you and Kris hold Laurie in the back seat, we'll get in the front seat. How bad was the drive up here?"

"Not too bad, the road was a little narrow in places. I didn't have a bad problem." She pushed Laurie's hair away from her face then looked up at Josh. "We're all wet and it's getting cold. We need to get Laurie out of this weather and somewhere warm and dry. We've got the motel room in Mesa, it'll be warm there. She can't get any wetter than she already is so there's no use waiting until the rain stops. We need to leave now."

Josh picked up Laurie and led the way to the car. Kris and Jennie got in the back seat and Josh put Laurie in with her head in Jennie's lap. The men squeezed in the front seat of the small car.

"What about the other car? Falco asked.

"I'll call my contact later and give him the location; someone will come get it when the rain stops. I don't think any of us want to drive it down that road in the rain anyway," Davenport answered.

"Well, that's the best news I've heard today," Falco said. "I definitely don't want to climb down this mountain and I don't ever want to come to this place again. I've had my fill of ghost towns and mountains. I'll take the city anytime."

It crossed Davenport's mind that without Falco they might not have found Laurie. It had not occurred to him that Fleicher might bury his daughter. He owed Falco now. The man had earned his keep so he could complain all he wanted. He glanced at him with a slight grin and nodded.

The car was parked in a narrow clearing. Davenport started the motor and rocked the car back and forth until he got it turned around. When they drove away from the ghost town, everyone relaxed a little.

They were all alive—and for now, that was enough.

Chapter 42

THE OCCUPANTS OF THE car were wet, cold, muddy, and exhausted. It seemed like they were never going to get to the motel in Mesa. Davenport's left leg was throbbing and a wave of frustration flew through him. He'd felt something hit it when the explosion happened, but he'd ignored it until now. It was bad timing, he shook his head shaking off the pain and emotions.

No one was talking, Falco wasn't even complaining. Hans was asleep and his head was bobbing back and forth. He checked the rear view mirror when he heard stirring in the backseat. They were all right, just changing positions.

The dirt road was fast becoming a mud-covered slippery trail as it twisted and turned between the desert trees and boulders. He was focused on driving and trying to miss the potholes when right in the middle of the road was a huge pile of tree limbs…he hit the brakes throwing everybody forward.

"What the hell…" yelled Falco when his head hit the front window. A chorus of other voices yelled out.

"The road's blocked, tree limbs have washed across the road. There's no way around them, we have to move them." Davenport said getting out of the car. "Stay in the car, Hans, we'll get this."

He and Falco tugged and pulled enough of the limbs and debris off the road to get the car through.

Back in the car, Falco looked over at Davenport, "Well, the good thing is we couldn't get any wetter than we already were. Actually, that little outing may have washed off some of the mud."

"That wouldn't hurt, the stuff is caked on my face," answered Davenport as he started the car. "We're all grubby, we need to get dry clothes and clean up. I'm hoping there's a store in Mesa where we can get something to wear. Hans, are you awake?"

"Yes, sir, there's a general store. The sun will be up before long and it usually opens early. I doubt there's anything for the ladies, it has jeans and overalls and sweat shirts. It doesn't have much else."

"Jeans and sweat shirts sound good. A man's size small will work if they don't have women's sizes." Jennie said. "We'll be happy to have anything dry and clean."

"You were limping back there, Davenport. Did you get hurt in the blast?" Falco asked.

"Yeah, something hit my left leg."

"We'll take a look when we get to the motel."

"Are you making yourself official doctor now?"

"Someone's got to do it, this group keeps getting in trouble," Falco laughed.

"Well, doctor, heal thyself. You've got a goose egg on your forehead."

Falco rubbed his aching head. "No blood, no problem."

The car crawled down the mountain accompanied by the moans and groans of the passengers. At last, the deplorable trail ended at a two-lane highway. Davenport turned on the road and pressed on the gas.

"Not much further now. Road's paved so it won't be bumpy. We'll be at the motel in a few minutes," Davenport said looking in the rearview mirror at his wife. She nodded and smiled at him, exhaustion spread across her face. They were all tired; he couldn't remember the last time he slept. No other cars were on the road and he drove faster. The dark was broken by a few faint lights in the distance, it was Mesa.

Ten minutes later, Davenport turned into the motel parking lot. The light above the office door was on, but the office was dark. He parked in front of their unit. Two black cars pulled up on either side of them as he and Falco were getting out of the car.

"What now," Davenport muttered. He leaned back in telling Jennie and Kris to stay in the car.

When he straightened up a man blocked his way. Falco and two more men came around the car to where he was. Falco turned to Davenport and spoke quietly, "Stay by the car for a minute. I need to speak with these men."

The three walked a few feet away as they talked in low voices. Davenport stood still and listened, he caught just enough words to figure out the men were local Mafia. After a few uncomfortable minutes of standing in the rain, Falco came back.

"Parrino asked friends in Phoenix to see if we need help."

"Who are these men?" Davenport asked.

"You don't need to know names. All you have to do is be respectful. *Capisce?*"

"Yes. What are you telling them?"

"I told them the situation is under control and the problem will be concluded in a day or two. You need to understand, Davenport, time is running out on Parrino's patience. He won't wait much longer, he'll send in a lot more than these three and they will take charge."

"I understand, Falco, but Parrino needs to understand who we are dealing with. As you're finding out, there's no way to find Fleicher in these mountains. We have to let him find us. He has no pattern and we've just come from his home base. What he does is unpredictable because his mind isn't normal. I guarantee he will find me when he realizes I wasn't killed in the explosion. Until then, all we can do is put ourselves in his path and that's what I'm doing. Our next stop will be the chairman's fortress."

Davenport opened the car door. "I'm taking my family in the motel and I better not be stopped. They are wet and cold and they should be inside where it's warm."

He leaned in the car and smiled at Jennie and Kris. "You can get out now. Let's go inside where it's warm."

He helped Kris out then picked up Laurie as gently as he could and started toward the room. Jennie ran ahead and unlocked the door with Kris and Hans following. He put Laurie on the bed and Kris sat down beside her sister and started whispering to her. Davenport sat down beside his daughters. "How is Laurie?"

"She is talking again and she knows who I am. Her side and head are hurting bad and I told her we'd get her some help. I also told her you and mom are here and she doesn't have to be afraid anymore. I think she understands."

Jennie came out of the bathroom with towels and a wet washcloth and started washing mud off Laurie's face and hair. "Who are those men, Josh?"

"They're friends of Falco's family, nothing to worry about. Just dry off and get warm. Do what you can to make Laurie comfortable. Hans says the general store is across the street from here, we'll get dry clothes as soon as it opens."

Davenport went outside. Falco and the two older men had moved out of the rain and were still talking. Falco was frowning and looking uneasy. The third Mafia man was watching from a distance.

A pay phone hung on the wall outside the office door. Davenport wondered if the Mafia men would stop him from making a call. There was some equipment he needed before going to the chairman's fortress and he had a few favors he could call in. He stepped back inside the room.

"Kris, have you decided what you want to do?"

"Laurie's still scared, she's afraid the bad man will come back. I told her I won't leave her. I don't know what to do, Daddy, I really need to be with Sophie."

"Then that's what you're going to do. I want you and Laurie to go to the safe house in Burleson. I can't send her alone, someone has to go with her and you can communicate with her. The nurse at the hospital in Fort Worth said she would come help Laurie if we call her and I think it's a good idea. I have her number and that's one of the calls I plan to make. I'll arrange transportation for you to the airplane and Jack can fly you back. A car will be waiting when you land to take you and Laurie to Burleson. You can be with Sophie in a few hours."

Some of the tension left his daughter's face and she visibly relaxed. "What about mom? I don't want to leave her."

"Don't worry about me, Kris. I'll feel better when you two are safe. I'm not leaving until we have Nicky and we all go back, your dad knows that. Besides Nicky knows me and it'll be better if I stay to take care of him. You need to go with Laurie, tell her I'll bring Nicky to her later. Kris, this is a good plan."

Davenport looked at his wife. "I didn't think you'd leave so here's what we're doing. I'll make several calls and get this arranged. I'm guessing it may be a couple of hours before a car can get here to take Kris and Laurie to the plane. After they are on their way, I'll go after Nicky."

"That sounds like you know where Nicky is," Jennie said.

"I do, so quit worrying about it. When the store opens, Falco and I'll get food and clothes. In the meantime, clean up as best you can, try to get comfortable and rest a little."

Davenport left the room and made his first call. As he talked, he watched Falco's face when the conversation heated up between the men.

DAVENPORT HAD WASHED HIS face and was dozing in a straight back chair by the door when Falco came in the room. He stood up and pulled Falco outside, "What was that about?"

"Parrino isn't happy, but crisis averted for twenty-four hours. That's all the time Parrino will give us to finish up. I saw you making calls so what's happening here?

"We're waiting for the store and café to open so we can get clothes and food. A car is on the way to pick up Laurie and Kris and take them to the plane; I want them far away from here and back in Texas. I also have some supplies coming, things we need before breaking into the fortress."

"What do you mean by supplies?"

"We have to be armed when we go there."

Falco nodded, "Gotcha, what time does the store open?"

"About six," Davenport looked down at his watch. "Thirty minutes from now. Hans says he can take us to the fortress the back way so we won't have to rappel down the mountainside."

"You're kidding, like I'd ever do that."

"Not kidding, my friend," Davenport laughed and it relieved the tension. "Just wait until you see this place. Hans saved you this time."

Falco glared at him a minute before grinning. "Let's go in and take a look at your leg and Hans' arm."

"Hans, where are the medical supplies I gave you?" Falco asked.

"I left them on the dresser."

"Okay, the doctor's taking calls, who's first?"

"Check Hans arm," Davenport said.

The young man's arm was red and swollen, but whatever stuck in it at the first explosion had been knocked out when the second blast hit him. Falco cleaned the wound and put antibiotic ointment on it then bandaged it and checked his back. "Your arm is pretty agitated; you're going to need antibiotic by mouth. For now, I'll watch it. Your back is fine, no problem there. Have you ever had a tetanus shot? If not, you better get one. That thing stuck in your arm looked like a rusty nail."

"Okay, Davenport, your turn."

He rolled up his torn pant leg and Jennie cringed. There was a huge gash on the side of his leg above the knee with blood encrusted all around it. "Did that happen when the bomb exploded?" Jennie asked.

"Yes, I knew something hit me and it was bleeding. It's not as bad as it looks."

Falco frowned as he cleaned and pulled the wound together with a several butterfly bandages. "It's not good either, it needs stitches and you need antibiotics. It'll probably heal without the stitches, but it'll make a ragged scar. Is your tetanus up-to-date?"

"Thanks, Falco, tetanus shot last year. It'll do for now, Doc Fitz will take care of it when we get home." He smiled at Jennie, "You know Doc will want something to fix and fuss at me about."

Jennie laughed, "All too true. You would enjoy meeting him, Falco. He is quite a character, he bosses everyone including Josh."

Davenport looked out the window and saw lights on across the street in a couple of small buildings. "Looks like the store and café are opening. Who wants to go with me and get clothes and food?"

Kris' head popped up, "Daddy, see if they have any size six tennis shoes, I don't care what color. Anything will be better than what I've been wearing. If the office is open, we need more towels, there were only two."

Chapter 43

"**T**OTAL INCOMPETENCE," EXPLODED REAVES. "Major breach of protocol, you should have notified General Thurman immediately." He slammed the phone down and massaged his forehead, his head was pounding.

Nathan Scott had escaped from prison twenty-four hours ago. "Unbelievable, we can't do our job if we are not informed." Monitoring all activities involving treason, espionage and sabotage fell to INSCOM. It was their job.

Scott had been in the maximum security prison at Fort Leavenworth where he was being held for treason and the attempted murder of Army G-2 agent, Owen Blakely. The general's aide could not grasp how the man managed to escape. This was a nasty problem, the man had a whole day's head start and the implications spread far and wide. The president and Davenport were involved plus Davenport's wife since Scott had married her. She chose to return to Davenport so there was no telling what Scott might do if he found her with him.

Then there was Davenport, a G-2 agent already out of control and on the general's bad side. Reaves closed his eyes, he wasn't going to think about that now.

Furthermore, he was sure Scott couldn't have escaped without inside help, the ramifications were mind-boggling. The general would see this as a huge failure; he might actually have a stroke.

During interrogation, Scott had revealed the names of a number of men Silverman had recruited for the *Brotherhood*. They were scattered in different branches of the government, however, Scott never said anything about a spy stationed at Fort Leavenworth. The man had left himself a way out in case he was ever sent there.

"Damn," muttered Reaves, "There's no way this could get worse. Scott only gave us the expendable ones, so how many others hasn't he told us about and where are they lurking? This means the *Brotherhood* has one or more of their men hidden in the prison at Fort Leavenworth. Heads are going to roll."

A wave of dizziness hit Reaves and he plopped down in his chair. He stared at the papers on his desk; he couldn't remember what he was working on when the phone rang. It paled in light of Scott's escape and he shoved all the papers on his desk to the far side. The general had to know without delay, Reaves jumped up and ran down the hall.

He was going to interrupt the general's meeting. This was an emergency.

Chapter 44

"WHAT HAPPENED TO YOUR shoes?" Davenport asked looking at his daughter's feet.

"I had these on when those men grabbed me," Kris said. "Molly's shoes were too large and the hotel gift shop didn't have any. I haven't had a chance to go anywhere else. I really need shoes. Socks would also be good, it's so cold."

"I'll do my best." His wife's shoes looked okay, but she needed socks too. "Glad you mentioned socks, I wouldn't have thought about them. Need anything else?"

"Just get what you can, Josh, anything clean, dry, and warm will be fine. We are all about the same size and you know my size," Jennie said. "Don't forget coffee."

"Not a chance," Davenport smiled as he left the room.

"I'VE SEEN MOVIES WITH stores like this, but I didn't know they really existed," Falco said. It felt like he and Davenport had stepped into the past when they entered the white clapboard building. As Falco's eyes adjusted to the dim light, a grin spread across his face. He saw a meat counter with cheese stacked on top and fresh produce in bins next to it. Distinct aromas of aged cheese, pickles, kerosene, leather and tobacco assaulted him as he walked around. Scattered over the countertops and shelves were beans, canned goods, and basic staples. On the other side of the store was a mixture of all kinds of things, cooking utensils, cleaning supplies, guns, knives, and small farm implements. Next to those were fabric, sewing items, toys, dolls, and medicines. Everything was mixed up and stacked on the shelves in no apparent order.

"It's typical of general stores in small towns. The towns don't have enough residents to support a lot of stores so it stocks a bit of everything," Davenport said as he dug through stacks of overalls, khaki pants, jeans, cotton shirts, and sweat suits.

"I bet if you looked hard enough you could find anything here," said Falco. "There's a sign saying feed and hay are outside in the shed."

Laughing, he pointed at an enclosed booth with a barred window in the back section of the store and headed there. "It's a post office, a funny little post office."

"I hate to disturb your small town education, but you should quit gawking and pick out some clean clothes for you and Hans." Davenport said while he hunted for jeans small enough to fit Jennie and his daughters. Sweatshirts were easy to find, and he went to the front with an armful of clothes.

"Do you have women's tennis shoes and socks?" Davenport asked dumping the clothes on the counter. The man raised his eyes from his newspaper and pointed.

Near the back of the store in a corner, Davenport found plain white tennis shoes for Kris. He picked up a bunch of socks, they all needed dry feet. As he zigzagged around the barrels and tables to the checkout counter, he grabbed some cookies and cold drinks.

Falco added jeans and sweatshirts to the pile of clothes on the counter. "We'll blend in with the locals now. The guys back in Dallas won't believe me when I tell them about this place."

Their next stop was the café. Davenport sat down at a red-checked vinyl-covered table. "Wait until you see the big breakfasts these little places serve."

Davenport ordered five breakfasts, a lot of coffees, and sweet rolls to go. Falco walked around looking at the pictures of local people and baseball teams that lined the walls.

Arms loaded with packages, Davenport knocked on the motel door with his foot and laughed at Jennie and Kris' expressions. Falco dropped sacks of clothes and towels on the unused bed and Davenport passed out the food. "Better eat while it's hot, it looks really good. You can clean up afterward."

Davenport sat down beside Laurie and picked up her hand. "Jennie, I'm sure they were feeding Laurie intravenously. It's been about a long time since she was in the hospital, she has to have liquid or she'll dehydrate."

"I know, Josh," Jennie said. "Kris and I have been talking to her. We've been moistening her lips and putting small drops of sugar water in her mouth. Laurie tries to open her mouth when we tell her and her fingers moved a little. A few minutes ago, she opened her eyes and looked at us. I asked if she knew me and she blinked. When I asked if she knew what happened to her she moved her head back and forth just a little. Kris asked her if she was thirsty and she blinked again. She's awake, Josh, she will get well. We just need to get her home. Doc Fitz and Scully can take care of her."

Davenport smiled at Jennie calling the castle in Scotland home. "Yes, they can, but first we have to get her back to Texas." He leaned over and kissed Laurie on the forehead. "If yanking her out of that grave and throwing her in the mud didn't kill her, she's strong and she'll come out of this." Leaning close to his daughter, he whispered to her.

He got up and opened his breakfast. "I have to make another call after I eat. I want a nurse on the plane with her; she needs glucose on the way to Dallas. The only thing you can do now is keep putting drops of water in her mouth. It's not enough, but maybe it will help."

Kris went through the bags of clothes and hollered when she found the tennis shoes. "Thank you, daddy," she yelled and gave him a hug.

"If I had known a five dollar pair of tennis shoes would get that response, I'd have found them sooner." He hugged his daughter. "Kris, the car will be here in the next hour to take you and Laurie to the plane so you better change clothes."

"You don't know how sore and cold my feet are," Kris said grabbing clean clothes. "I'm going to shower. If I have time, I'll eat after that. If I don't, I'll take it and a sweet roll and eat in the car."

"That'll work, Kris." Davenport wolfed down his eggs and bacon. "Jennie, see if you can get dry clothes on Laurie. It'll make her feel better."

With a coffee in his hand he turned toward the door, "I have to make that call. I don't think a nurse will be a problem, she can come straight back on the plane with Jack. I've already arranged for another nurse to be at the safe house in Burleson."

DAVENPORT GROANED ON HIS way to the payphone. He rolled his shoulders and arms around trying to loosen up and work the knots out. A hot shower and dry clothes would help if he got the chance. A bed and a good night's sleep would help more, but that wasn't going to happen anytime soon.

He tried not to limp in front of Jennie; it was getting harder not to give in to the pain. The cut on his leg was probably infected, it throbbed all the time. There was nothing he could do about it now. The thought flew through his mind he might be too old for all this. It wasn't that he wanted to keep working; he simply hated to give up before he stopped the *Brotherhood*. If there was any justice left in the world, he'd stop those bastards someday. Maybe Jennie was right; maybe it was time to turn this job over to Blakely. Doc Fitz had Blakely on a strenuous exercise program to rebuild his strength and his partner was about ready to resume working.

His first call was to General Thurman asking if he'd arrange for an Army nurse or aide to fly from Phoenix to Dallas with his daughter. It would be a same day round trip for the person. His comatose daughter needed glucose to keep her from dehydrating. He kept the conversation short and on the subject. He had one more call to make and it would be a long one. The car to pick up his daughters should arrive soon and he needed to talk with Kris again.

"Mr. President, I'm sorry to keep you in the dark, phones are scarce out here in the mountains. Good news, my wife and daughters are with me now." He told the president what had occurred and that both daughters would be in a safe house in the Dallas area by evening.

"Yes, sir, I'll make sure Wilkens knows the police chief in Dallas is in custody. I'm anxious for the general to find out more names from Scott so he can get the rest of the traitors out of G-2, NSA, and CIA. I'll breathe easier when those traitors are in custody…"

"What? Scott escaped? Davenport slammed his fist into the wall. "How the devil did he get out of Leavenworth?"

He rocked back and forth clenching and unclenching his fist.

"I'm listening, sir. I'll tell Wilkens about Scott. Yes, sir, I know he may try to find Jennie and my daughters."

"Thank you, Mr. President. I'm relieved my daughters and wife are safe. As soon as my daughters are on their way home, I'm going to the chairman's fortress in the Superstition Mountains. That's where my grandson is and I expect to find Fleicher there…" The president broke in again asking questions.

Yes, sir, Falco is still with me. The Mafia is making some not-so-subtle threats about the delay. They are impatient, they wanted revenge yesterday. Parrino sent the local Mafia to check on the situation, they are probably watching me as we talk."

"I hear you, Mr. President. I know this could be a trap, but I have to get my grandson out of there. Yes, sir, you may tell the general."

Davenport tried to focus on what the president was saying, but he was running out of time and he spoke up, "I'm sorry to interrupt you, sir. An ambulance will be here any minute to pick up my daughters and I need your help with something else. If I don't call you back by midnight three days from now, call Blakely and tell him. He knows what to do; he will send you a package containing full disclosure on the *Brotherhood* and Illuminati plus my notebook with names, locations, and plans…."

"No, sir, I don't expect to die, this is my leverage to get out of there alive. One more thing I have to tell you, I've recorded the entire story about what is happening in the United States and the world including names and locations. Blakely will send this to all newspapers, radio and television stations. I expect it will cause a major media explosion throughout the world. I don't think the *Brotherhood* will let it happen even if it means letting me live a little longer. It's my insurance, sir."

Davenport rocked back and forth while he listened. "Yes, sir, it's all about who has the power. It would definitely create a major frenzy in the news, and I believe the *Brotherhood* will back off, at least for a while. Their work depends on staying in the shadows and keeping the people of the United States in the dark about their real agenda, which you and I know is a Communist society under a one-world government…"

"Yes, sir, I know. I have two goals now, getting my grandson out of the hands of the *Brotherhood* and finding out the name of the person behind Chairman Houser…" Davenport shifted his weight to the uninjured leg as he listened.

"Yes, Mr. President. There is another person, he's the missing link. I can't go after him until I know who he is. The instant I find who it is, I'll call you."

A car drove by at a snail's pace catching Davenport's attention. He stopped talking and watched it park across the way, Falco's friends were keeping an eye on him. He turned his back to the car and continued, "When I find my grandson, I'll take my family and the Wilkens family out of the United States to my safe place. You can call me there or on the plane as usual."

"Use your discretion about what and how much to tell the general, but it should go no further than you and the general. If traitors are at Fort Leavenworth, they could be anywhere."

He hung up the phone and leaned against the wall to take the pressure off his leg as he watched the black car across the street. When he stepped away from the phone, his leg threatened to give way and he grabbed at the wall to keep from going down. He stood still then tested his leg before hobbling back to the room.

"LAURIE, WE HAVE TO get these wet clothes off you then get you into some dry ones," Jennie said bending over her daughter. "Blink once if you understand me."

When Laurie blinked Kris cried out, "She hears and knows us, Mom, Laurie's better. She keeps asking for Nicky. I told her he isn't here, but daddy would find him and bring him to her. I explained we would leave soon and fly back to Texas."

Kris held up a blue sweatshirt, "How about this one?" Laurie blinked again and followed Kris with her eyes.

Jennie and Kris washed the mud off Laurie and wrestled her into jeans and a sweatshirt. It was difficult; she was limp as a rag doll. She had lost so much weight and the clothes were way too large for her, however, they were clean, dry, and warm so that made up for being too big. Jennie brushed her hair and got most of the mud out. It was an exhausting task, and they rested on the bed beside her.

After a few minutes, Jennie opened the door and told Falco it was his turn to clean up. He picked up clean clothes and headed for the shower.

Fatigue lined Davenport's face when he limped inside. He'd aged in the last couple of days and Jennie reached out her arms to hug him. They were both still muddy and he tried to wipe the mud off her face.

"It's hopeless, Josh, I'll clean up later. You're next in the bathroom."

DAVENPORT TURNED TO KRIS. She'd cleaned up and, as beautiful as this young woman was, all he could see was his little girl. "We have a few minutes before the car arrives for you and Laurie. Come, sit beside me, I want to talk to you."

What now, Kris wondered. She sat down near her dad.

"Kris, I know you've had a terrible time and you're angry with me. I realize I've been preoccupied and haven't made it easy for you. I'm sorry for that," Davenport watched her eyes, but her expression didn't change. "You are and will always be my little girl, my Krissie. I love you and I'm so sorry for everything you've gone through."

Kris studied his face trying to read behind his words.

"I regret I never got to meet the man you loved. If you loved him, I'm sure he was a good man and I would have cared about him, too." He watched a range of emotions cross his daughter's face as tears formed and she fought to keep from crying. He wrapped his hands around hers and looked into her eyes. "I have a job to do. I have to get the man who killed your husband and Joey. I give you my solemn promise, he will come to justice. I'm asking you to trust me to do this for you. Will you try?"

Kris studied her dad's face for a few seconds. "I'm trying, Daddy. I realize none of this has been easy for you either and you are struggling. I've watched you limp around here and not say a word; I know your leg hurts." She looked at her sister. "You knew what you were doing when you were getting Laurie out of that grave; you knew the bomb could explode anytime." Kris' voice broke as she watched Laurie. "Thank you for saving my sister, she's a part of me, you know. We're bound by the twin thing."

She dropped her eyes and stared at the floor before continuing, "There are times I can't find my dad. You look like him, but I don't feel a connection with you. You turn into someone I don't know, you become someone I don't even like."

"I know and I'm sorry, your mother tells me that, too. It's a survival mode I had to adopt to make it through these past years. I wish we had talked in Dallas, but we didn't have time. Even though I don't seem the same, I never stopped loving you and Laurie, not even for a minute."

He looked at Laurie then back at Kris. "You can talk to your sister in ways I can't understand. I've watched it take place all your lives and I don't know how you do it. Maybe you could try to think of my other self like that. It doesn't mean I don't love you. Feelings are just tamped down so I can do my job, sort of like when you close your mom and me out and talk with Laurie in your mind. Just remember, I'm still here."

"It's so easy for me to talk like that with Laurie, it just happens. We've always talked in our heads and I never think about it. I know other people can't do it, but it's natural for us." She looked at Davenport, "I guess this stranger you become could be something similar, I'll try to think about it like that, Daddy," Kris said with a slight smile.

"Have you decided if you are going home?"

"I've thought of nothing else. I told you I would go back with Laurie and I will. I need to see her safe with Molly and Herman and the nurse. I'll feel better when I see and hold Sophie, you'll like my Sophie."

Kris pulled her hands from his and leaned away and stared at him. "But, hear me, Daddy, if you haven't found the man who killed Jeffrey, I will come back. While I was at the hospital, I told my husband I would see his killer brought to justice and I can't rest until he's caught."

Kris stood up and did not stop the tears that ran down her face. "I have to. I promised."

"I understand promises. I made a promise, too, I promised the President of the United States I would help rid our country of the *Brotherhood* and bring them to justice. That's what I've been trying to do these past years."

Davenport stood up and pulled his daughter close to him. "I will get the man who killed your husband, that's a promise, Kris. Maybe then you can rest." He leaned down and kissed her on the forehead.

They heard a car pull up near their room and went to the window. The ambulance door opened and two people got out and came toward them. It was time to go.

Kris looked at Laurie and told her they were going home then she wiped tears off her face and picked up a sack of muddy clothes.

She wanted to rest. She really hoped she could someday, but now was not the time. She still had to bury her husband.

Chapter 45

JENNIE AND KRIS WATCHED the attendants push the stretcher with Laurie into the back of the ambulance. Kris hugged her mom and said, "We'll be fine, call me tonight." She climbed into the ambulance and sat down beside her sister.

Tears rolled down Jennie's face as she nodded and waved at her daughters. It was hard not to go with them.

Davenport leaned down and gave the driver directions to the airfield where the plane was waiting. When the ambulance started to pull away, two black cars blocked the way.

Falco signaled Davenport to stay where he was as he went over to the man in charge. "What's the problem now?"

"We have orders to stay with the mother of Parrino's grandson. Where are you taking her?"

"Back to Dallas," Falco told the man. "She's being moved there so she can have better medical help. We're staying here to find Parrino's grandson."

"You can't take her anywhere without Parrino's approval."

"All right, all right, hang on a minute. I'm calling Parrino," Falco said as he went to the pay phone.

"No, sir, Davenport is not trying to hide his daughter from you. He's sending her back to Dallas where she'll be safer and have better care. As soon as the ambulance leaves with her, we're going after the man who shot Joey." Falco looked around for Davenport. "Yes, Mr. Parrino, I'll ask him." He gave the phone to the man standing beside him and motioned at Davenport.

"It's all right, but Parrino wants to know where you are taking her."

"That isn't going to happen right now, there are too many ways for the *Brotherhood* to get to her. I'm not telling anyone where the safe house is, not even my superior. Parrino will have to wait until this is over," Davenport's voice was uncompromising.

"That's a major problem. He wants to talk to you, you have to or nobody is going anywhere."

The man at the phone handed the receiver to Davenport.

"Yes, Mr. Parrino," Davenport listened for a minute. "No, sir, I'm not trying to hide my daughter from you, I'm just moving her out of the line of fire. I want her away from here and in a safe place in the Dallas area where she can get expert medical help. She's beginning to come out of the coma, but she can't speak or move yet. I can't get my grandson, who is also your great-grandson, away from the *Brotherhood* if I have to worry about them getting their hands on her again. Furthermore, I can't find Joey's killer if I'm taking care of my daughter…"

"No, Mr. Parrino, I have no battle with the Mafia, my battle is with the *Brotherhood*." Davenport lowered his voice. "They want their man in the White House and my job is to stop them. Yes, sir, they are the real menace to our security and our country…yes, I know this from many years of personal experience."

"I understand your position, but you must understand mine if you want me to find the man who killed your grandson…Yes, I will be let you know when I have Nicky and find the man who killed Joey."

Davenport gave the phone to the waiting man and went back to Falco grimacing when he put weight on the injured leg. "Parrino said we have twenty-four hours to complete the assignment. After that the local Mafia will move in."

"I'm surprised he gave us that long, he's used to getting results within a few hours of the crisis. What did you say?" It crossed Falco's mind that Parrino may have met his match.

"I told him the truth. You know by now that it's never simple dealing with the *Brotherhood*. The main problem is finding them or Fletcher, that's always the challenge. Parrino seemed to have background knowledge of the situation, but that's no surprise. He has knowledge of lots of things."

The man on the phone gestured to the other men to back off. They moved their cars out of the way of the ambulance and it pulled away. Jennie waved at her daughters as the ambulance turned toward Phoenix. She leaned back against the door, grateful they were on the way to Dallas.

"We need to talk," Davenport said taking Jennie's arm and drawing her inside the room leaving Falco and Hans outside.

"As soon as my supplies arrive, Falco and I are leaving," he said checking his watch. "They should be here any minute now. We have to take care of some things at the chairman's fortress and get Nicky."

"I'm going with you, Nicky knows me and he won't be scared."

"You can't go with me this time, you would be more of a hindrance than a help."

"I have told you…"

"Don't fight me on this, Jennie, not this time. It's a treacherous place to get to. I can't look after you and do my job."

Davenport walked back and forth in the small room. He interrupted her when she started to oppose him. "No arguments, Jennie, no compromise. Not this time. I need you to listen to me, we don't have long to talk."

He pulled out a pen and paper and wrote a number down. "This is Blakely's number, memorize it. Put the paper in your purse and don't lose it. Kris has the number in case she needs to get a message to me."

Jennie glared at her husband and answered through gritted teeth, "All right, Josh, but I don't like it. What do you expect me to do, just sit here and wait?"

"Yes, sitting is good. It would also be a good idea for you to clean up," he said hoping she would listen to him and quit arguing.

"I'm not laughing, Josh. You can't tease your way out of this."

"I'm not teasing. I have a job for you to do, so listen carefully. If Falco and I are delayed and don't make back by tomorrow morning, call Blakely and give him this motel address. He will send a car to take you to the plane, Jack will be back in Phoenix by then and he'll fly you to Dallas where another car will take you to the house in Burleson."

"You're scaring me, Josh. What exactly are you going to do?"

"I'm sorry. I don't mean to scare you. We have to take care of some problems at the fortress and pick up Nicky." He watched her. "Please pay attention, Jennie, I need a backup plan and you are it. Timing is crucial. As soon as you get to Burleson, have everyone get ready to leave, this includes Herman and Molly. Then take them to the plane, Jack will fly everybody to the compound in Scotland and you can help them get settled in our castle."

Jennie stood up. The stubborn look was back on her face. "I am not leaving without you, you know that."

Davenport took hold of her arms, "I know your feelings, Jennie, but you have to put them aside this time. Your job is to get everyone to Scotland because all hell is going to break loose in the United States in three days. Blakely is sending all my notes and papers about the *Brotherhood* to the president and to the media. Their plans will be exposed to the world and I want you all far away from here and safe in Scotland when that happens. The *Brotherhood* and the Illuminati will be desperate to get their hands on any of my family. If they can get hold of any of you, they'll control me. You don't want that, do you?"

"Where will you be? Are you telling me you'll be dead?"

"No, absolutely not, this is my leverage to get away from the *Brotherhood* alive. When the chairman knows what I've planned to do, he'll have to let me go. Then he'll be after you and our daughters. He can't afford for the world to know his plans. It won't stop the *Brotherhood*, but it will create publicity they don't want and it will bring their plans to a halt for a while."

"Do you really think he'll let you leave?" Fear and anger poured out of her and she turned her back on him. "I can't lose you again, Josh," she said softly as tears formed in her eyes.

He turned her around and touched her cheek, but she pulled back watching his face.

"It will be all right, I promise. I'll deal with the man who killed our daughters' husbands. Then I'll pick up Nicky and join you in Scotland."

He drew Jennie into his arms, closed his eyes and held her tight. "I need to know you'll do this for me, that you'll take everyone to Scotland where they'll be safe. You are my backup plan."

Chapter 46

DAYLIGHT GRADUALLY ILLUMINATED THE interior of an overturned car. Otto Fleicher stirred, drifting in and out of consciousness. Pain shot through his body when he tried to move and his face contorted. The bloody taste in his mouth was sickening. A vague feeling of the car careening down a hill slithered through his mind as he slipped back into oblivion. His head rolled sideways.

Rain stopped with the break of dawn. It unleashed a cold wind that blew across the injured man's face forcing him awake. He turned his head toward the wind, the windshield was broken and glass was everywhere.

For a few minutes he couldn't think where he was then he remembered, he was on his way to pick up his son. He rubbed his throbbing head, his shaking hand came away bloody. His face hurt and his nose felt like raw meat. Hanging above him was the steering wheel, the damned car had flipped.

He moved his arms and legs. They hurt like hell, but they moved so nothing was broken. He had to get out of the wrecked car. He pushed on the door nearest to him; it was jammed against a tree. Wiggling to the other side, he caught his breath as a sharp pain in his side took him unaware, a rib was probably broken. He yelled in frustration as he tried to force the other door open, it wouldn't budge.

The man gritted his teeth, drew his legs to his chest and shoved them at the stuck door. It gave way and he pushed it open enough to squeeze out. Screaming against the pain, he crawled out of the crumpled mass of metal and fell to the ground. He lay there waiting for the pain to subside. Rolling to all fours, he grabbed hold of a small tree and hauled himself up. Hanging on to the tree and holding his side he bent over and spit out the coppery-tasting blood that was pooling in his mouth. Sweat rolled down his face.

Waiting for his legs to quit shaking, he tried to remember why he wrecked. It was night and rain was pounding the windshield. He remembered hunting for the wipers, but he got them on so that wasn't the problem. As memories surfaced Fleicher groaned, the chairman had tried to kill him. When the pain came it was severe, and it didn't let up. He must have blacked out and lost control of the car. It had left the road crashing into that boulder and flipping over.

In spite of the pain he smiled. He shouldn't be alive, but he was. He shouted at the chairman, "I'm alive, you've done your worst and you couldn't kill me." He'd survived that damned remote. Nothing could stop him now, not the chip in his back or the chairman, he laughed out loud. He started up the hill hanging on to whatever bush was nearest.

He looked toward the mountains where the chairman lived. Pain vanished with the thought of revenge. He fingered the razor in his pocket and laughed again. He had a score to settle.

MESA, ARIZONA

"COME WITH ME, FALCO, the supplies are here."

Davenport and Falco met the man at the door and followed him to the back of a car. The man opened the trunk.

"Whoa, there's an arsenal in there," Falco said as he stared in the trunk. He was puzzled and full of questions. "You must have some powerful friends."

"Yes, I do, particularly in the Phoenix area." Davenport said. "Take whatever you need." Davenport bent over, took the lid off a small wooden chest, and picked out several electronic devices.

"What's that gadget?

"It blocks surveillance cameras, might come in handy at the chairman's fortress."

The men dug through the trunk and made their choices. Arms full, Davenport stepped away and nodded at the driver.

"Good luck, Davenport." The driver got back in the car and left without a word or exchange of money.

"Well, I have to say, that was impressive," Falco said watching the car disappear in the distance. "I've never seen that kind of service."

Davenport laughed at Falco's astonished face. "Maybe you don't travel in the right circles." He put three bullet-proof vests along with guns, ammunition, and other items in the front seat of their car.

"That looked like military equipment, is that who brought it?"

"As you are fond of telling me, don't ask. All you need to know is it's a source I use. *Capise?*"

"Understood, and very impressive," Falco said with a grin. "So when do we leave?"

"In a few minutes," Davenport said going over to where Hans was waiting.

Hans started talking before Davenport had a chance to say a word. "I want to go with you. I can take you in the back way." He waited a second then said, "I need to see the chairman one more time, I want to ask him some questions."

"I'm planning on you taking us in the back way, Hans. I figured you might want to question him about your name. It would help to find your family if we knew your real name."

Davenport grinned and turned to Falco, "I don't think Falco wants to fast-rope in any more than he wants to rappel down the rock face of the mountain."

"What the hell is fast-rope?"

"It's dropping to the ground from a hovering helicopter. A rope hangs from the open door of the chopper and you just slide right on down to the ground. When you fast-rope down, you're not attached to the rope like you are when you rappel down a mountain. You just hang on tight."

"You really enjoy goading me, don't you? Well, you got that one right, I'm sure not doing that. I've had about enough of these mountains."

"You can thank Hans you don't have to do either one of those," Davenport said. "He knows a back way in. We'll hope it isn't as bad as the last time he showed us the way."

Falco glared at him, "And the torture continues."

Davenport laughed, but stopped the instant he saw Jennie standing in the door. She was shivering as a biting wind blew her hair all over her head. She had a look on her face he hated seeing and his shoulders drooped. He went over and pulled her to him, she was cold and shaking.

"It's time, we're going after Nicky. I have to do this, you know that. I promised you I would find Nicky and bring him to you."

Jennie nodded. "I know you have to go, but I hate it. I feel so useless."

"Never useless, you have a job to do. Remember what I told you and don't lose Blakely's phone number. If you need it, he'll send a car to pick you up and take you to the plane. Jack knows where to go and what to do."

Tears formed in Jennie's eyes as she reached up and hugged her husband. "Be safe, I can't lose you again."

"I'll be fine, I promise, I'm not alone this time. I have Hans and Falco to help plus the Mafia." His hand lingered on her shoulder. He'd left her too many times, it never got any easier. "Go inside out of the cold wind."

Fear took over as she watched her husband limp to the car. His leg was bad and that worried her, it would slow him down. She understood more than Falco did about what they were going into at the fortress.

Josh had told her about that place and the rock formations surrounding it and about the chairman.

Davenport followed Falco to the car. He turned and looked at his wife once more. "Tomorrow morning, Jennie, remember what you have to do."

She nodded. She would do what he said because she had no choice, her daughters would need her. She wrapped her arms around her cold body. She was so afraid this was the last time she'd see her husband, tears slipped down her face.

Jennie stood shivering in the doorway long after the car was out of sight.

SUPERSTITION MOUNTAINS

OTTO FLEICHER REACHED THE top of the hill and looked down the deserted road willing a car to come. He needed wheels to get to the fortress; it was too far to walk. He took a deep breath and pain shot through his side. He rubbed his side then pulled his jacket tight around him. His legs were unsteady, and he sat down on a small boulder by the side of the highway.

"You'll pay for this, Mr. Chairman. You'll pay for every bit of my pain and for my lost son. You'll pay for everything you've done to me."

He checked his watch; he only had two hours until his flight time. Well, if he missed it, he could arrange another. He shifted positions trying to lessen the pain. "Oh, yes, the chairman was going to suffer, he fingered the razor in his pocket."

A distant sound caused him to raise his head. Finally, a car was coming; he stood at the side of the road and waited. He waved his hands in the air as the car drew closer.

The car slowed to a stop. A man rolled a window down when he saw Fleicher's bloody face, "Looks like you need help. Accident?"

"Yes, lost control of my car in the rain and slid off the road. I need a doctor. Can you give me a ride?"

"Sure, get in. There's a town about five miles down the road, it has a doctor." The man reached over and unlocked the passenger door.

Fleicher opened the door, leaned in and grabbed hold of the man. He yanked him out of the car and threw him down the hill. He slid in the car, gunned the motor and burned off.

The man jumped up yelling and ran after his car. When it disappeared in the distance, he gave up and started walking.

"Five miles," he muttered, anger building with every step he took.

Chapter 47

"**Y**ES SIR, I'M READY to come home now," said the man standing in a phone booth in Dallas.

"You disobeyed me. If you had listened to me and done what I told you several years ago, you wouldn't be in this mess now. Why should I help you?"

Anger masked the rasping voice on the other end of the line and the man in Dallas visibly cringed. Instantly transported to childhood, he shook with the memory of how furious his father got in the past when he disobeyed. Pulling the phone away from his ear, he took several deep breaths trying to calm down. He'd grovel if he had to; he had nowhere else to turn.

"Because I'm your son and you raised me to think for myself." He checked to see if anyone was nearby and listening to him. "I'm blood kin, you always told me that was more important than anything else. Will you help me?"

The old man's sneer came through the phone, "You screwed up big time; you ignored what I told you to do. You married that woman. What were you thinking?"

"Not what I should have been thinking, I admit I messed up, I won't do that again, Father. I'm sorry I caused you trouble, I'll do whatever you say." He hated begging, but the old man loved him and begging had worked in the past.

"Here are my terms. I do not tolerate failure from anyone, not even my son. You fail me one more time and you can say goodbye to any inheritance that is coming your way."

The man in the phone booth relaxed his tight shoulders as some of his tension dissolved. A smile spread across his face, he was not disinherited. By the sound of the old man's voice and coughing his health was worse. It was time to do what his father wanted.

"I'll do whatever you say, Father. You and I have a common enemy; he stands between me and my wife. I lost track of that last year, it won't happen anymore. I won't fail you again."

"Wife," the old man sneered. "She was never your wife, someone had already married her. I told you and you didn't listen. That woman was your undoing."

The line went silent. For a moment he thought his father had hung up then he heard labored breathing. Years of experience had taught him to wait and see what the old man was cooking up, he shifted his feet impatiently.

"HERE ARE MY TERMS, son. Forget her and you can come home. I want to look you in the eyes before I decide what to do about you and that woman."

All the old man ever wanted was for him to forget his wife. Well, for now, that's what he would do. "As you wish, Father, I'll forget about her if you help me. I need money and transportation."

"You said you're in Dallas. I'll think about sending my plane to Love Field to pick you up. If I do, it will take three or four hours. You know where I land…" Spasms of coughing stopped him from speaking.

"Don't talk, Father, it makes your cough worse. Take some deep breaths and don't worry about me. I know what to do and where the plane lands at Love Field. I'll go there now and wait."

He knew what the old man wanted. He wanted him to crawl a little more. Well, he'd give him what he wanted—this time. He kept his voice soft and gentle as he said, "I got lost for a while, but I'm back and I love you, Father. I'm really sorry for all my past mistakes and for upsetting you. I'll do whatever you want from now on. Please take your medicine and rest. Send the plane and I'll be with you tonight. I'll help you and take care of you."

"All right, but do not… fail me… again," the old man squeezed out between coughs.

The man in Dallas hung the phone up and laughed. Maybe the old man would cough himself to death before he got home. It wouldn't be a tragedy; it would be the best thing for both of them. He'd inherit everything and he could take over. He was smarter than his father ever was. He'd be in charge of the family business and he would get his wife back. He knew exactly what to do first; he would rid the world of Davenport. That would solve all his problems. Life was finally going his way. He'd learned from the best and no one would ever stop him again or keep him from his wife.

"You taught me well, old man," he murmured. Nathan Scott laughed out loud as he walked away.

Chapter 48

"**I**T'S TIME TO CLEAR the air, old friend, we've pussyfooted around long enough," Falco said. "I know you work for the government. Parrino told me you are the president's hit man, but I didn't believe him. I couldn't reconcile that with the man who played in the band with me in Dallas so I've watched and waited. After seeing the car loaded with ammo that just left, I'm thinking it could be true."

The sky was overcast and drops of rain spattered against the windows. Davenport turned the wipers on. "I was hoping the rain had stopped for good, but it looks like we'll have to deal with it."

"You heard what I said, Davenport, no more evasion."

Davenport's hands tightened on the steering wheel. He glanced at Hans sleeping in the back seat then he turned cold, steely eyes on Falco, his voice dropped low and menacing. "What else did Parrino tell you?"

Whoops, he'd hit a nerve, he knew that look. Falco leaned away, if he was a fearful man he'd get out of the car. He was dealing with a man who'd seen too much, a man you never wanted to cross. Now he knew.

He watched Davenport a minute before answering softly. "Parrino told me G-2 was your cover and you report only to the president as his hit man."

"What makes you think this is true?"

"It shows in the eyes, they don't lie."

"Who told Parrino this?"

"As we are fond of saying, don't ask. All you need to know is Parrino knows. I want the truth, Davenport."

Davenport's voice deepened becoming fierce and intimidating again. "Truth, what's that? Our world is not exactly crowded with truth or saints, is it? How about what you do, old friend? What kind of saint are you?"

"You're evading again. You know I'm no saint, and from what I've observed you aren't either. The arsenal in the trunk of the car told me you have major clout with someone. What you gathered up told me you are well trained. It also tells me that we are going into a highly guarded fortress. I'm not judging you, but I have to know where I stand before we get there. When trouble comes, and I have a feeling it will, I want to know I can count on you." Not backing down, he stared straight at Davenport.

Davenport drove a few miles in silence. "There's a great deal I'm not at liberty to discuss. Yes, I work undercover, and I do special assignments for the president. It's a workaround for political expediency."

Davenport pulled the car to the side of the road and faced Falco. "Listen well, friend. We will only have this conversation once. I'm no saint, but I am not a hit man, never have been, never will be. That's not what I signed on to do. I'm an outrider. However, if it becomes necessary, I will do whatever it takes to defend myself and my family. I told you once before that the threats to the U.S. are constant with shadow governments trying to take control. My orders and my only orders are to prevent this from happening. In the beginning, G-2 called me back to active service to infiltrate the *Brotherhood* and to do what I could to thwart their plans. When my cover was blown, the only way we could find to protect my family was for me to die. So, I've been dead for the past six years. I suspect you know all about this, Parrino did."

"I know most of it. Outrider…?"

"Works alone without help, just what it sounds like. If I get caught, no one comes to save me—governmental deniability. As I told Parrino, I have no quarrel with the Mafia."

"How much does your wife know?"

"Most everything, she found out when the *Brotherhood* went after her. She's stronger than she looks. She's a survivor and she will defend herself."

Davenport hit the accelerator and pulled back on the highway. "Do I need to tell you this conversation never happened?"

"That's understood. What you told me in the bar in Phoenix a couple of nights ago, was all that true?"

"Yes, as far as it went." Davenport and Falco's eyes met, and they nodded. For the time being, the two men were in accord.

He slowed the car down to the speed limit when they came to a few buildings flanking a small town.

"Wake up, Hans. I'm nearing the turnoff to the school. Do I go up the main road?"

Hans straightened up and looked at the road. "Yes, sir, for about a mile then we'll turn right on a side road. We'll leave the car there and walk the rest of the way to the fortress."

Falco turned and looked at the young man, "How bad is the walk from the school to the fortress?"

"Not bad and not very far. It's a narrow path that gets a little slippery in the rain. You have to be careful and watch your step."

Conversation and the last rays of light faded as they neared the mountain range.

LAS COLINAS, TEXAS

PARRINO'S PATIENCE WAS AT an end. "You heard what I said, follow Falco and Davenport. Stay with them and make sure they complete the job. If they screw up, your orders are to take over. I've waited long enough."

His temper was barely controlled when he hung up the phone, Falco had not done his job and his grandson's death had not been avenged. It had been over a week since he issued the command to even the score for Joey's death. Tears rolled down his face, his only grandson murdered and nothing was being done about it.

The old man shivered and his shoulders tightened up. He left his desk and went over to the fireplace; it seemed like he was always cold. What good was he if he couldn't protect his own, if his orders were not obeyed instantly? He held trembling hands toward the burning logs.

The younger men were not like the old guard. The Mafia was changing, even the money didn't come up the chain like it used to. He had decisions to make.

Parrino stirred the fire and sat down in his chair to wait.

Superstition Mountains, Arizona

OTTO FLEICHER PRESSED DOWN on the accelerator and the car flew through the small town. He should be at the chairman's fortress in about thirty minutes, maybe a little less. Once he left the highway, the dirt road leading up to the gate was slow and tedious. There was no other way except the path from the school and it would take just as long. Besides, he didn't feel like walking that far.

The thought of leaving excited him, he'd waited a long time for this day. Last week when he saw the boy, it awakened something in him. He remembered he had a son, and he raged at what had happened to him. Davenport had taken his son away, no, that wasn't right. His brow creased in a frown, it was the chairman who took his son. The chairman took away his memory and his son. Well, his memory was creeping back, and he was getting his son back tonight. He knew where the chairman had hidden the boy.

He almost missed the road to the fortress; he slammed on the brakes and turned. The car skidded onto the dirt road hitting every rut and pothole in its path and weaving from side to side. Trying to gain control of the car, he roared in pain.

"Damned dirt trail…"

His face contorted, he slowed the car down to a crawl and eased around the potholes. The pain in his side gradually subsided, but not his rage.

Chapter 49

THE THREE MEN WERE lost in their thoughts. No sound broke the silence except for rain beating on the windshield. Davenport turned up an unmarked road that led to the school, it was barely more than a dirt path cut around scrubby trees and boulders. Parking lights did little to illuminate the dark as he tried to stay in the ruts.

"If I remember right, it's about two miles up the mountain."

"Yes, sir, it won't take long to get there," Hans said.

Falco couldn't sit still; his last conversation with Parrino was worrying him. It had been a week since Joey was killed and the old man was furious. He didn't tell Davenport how angry Parrino was or that the local Mafia would be following them. He watched the side mirror; there was a car behind them with no lights. He felt sure Davenport knew.

"Pull to the left just beyond that boulder," Hans said. "The guards could be at the school. We'll walk the rest of the way, it's not far."

Davenport parked and handed Kevlar vests to Falco and Hans. "Put this on under your jacket, Hans, it's a bulletproof vest." He watched the young man put it on before turning to Falco. "The vest will stop most bullets, but it won't stop Fleicher's razor blade so don't depend on it for that."

Davenport checked the gun in his shoulder holster and the one in his belt then picked up the rest of his gear. It was time to go. They left the warmth of the car and stepped into drizzling rain.

Hans led the way toward the school, the men followed single file. When they neared the school, he motioned for them to stop. "We're close, watch for guards."

Davenport went ahead of them threading his way through the trees and bushes, his hand gripped the pistol in his belt. A cleared area around the building came into view and he stopped in the shadows. The building was dark and no guards were in sight.

"I don't see any guards," Hans said. "They may all be at the fortress. We can stay in the shadows and slip over to the path that goes down the hill. Do you want to do that?"

"Lead the way, Hans."

Staying in the shade of trees and bushes, Hans led them around the side of the school and over a low rock barrier. "It's downhill from now on. The path is narrow so we go slow and in single file. Stay as close to the right as you can, the left side drops off in places and is slippery in the rain."

Falco groaned, "I knew there would be problems, it's always something in these damn mountains."

"Just be careful," laughed Davenport. "You'll be all right, you've handled worse. It can't be as difficult as the ravine we climbed getting to the ghost town."

Hans led the way, Davenport brought up the rear sandwiching Falco in the middle. The ledge was muddy and a few places crumbled under their feet. It took about twenty minutes to make their way down the mountain. When they reached the bottom Hans stopped and whispered, "There's an electric fence surrounding the fortress. I know the code for the gate and we can go in through the kitchen."

"Let me look first, you and Falco stay in the bushes." Davenport flattened against the wet ground and crept forward ignoring the pain in his leg. He crouched beside a boulder. The back of the stone building bumped up against the mountain. A door was straight ahead, probably the one to the kitchen that Hans mentioned. On his left between the door and the mountain was a staircase going up to a small balcony. The right side of the building had to go to the front entrance. He waited and watched for a few minutes. Two guards walked to where the building joined the mountain then returned to the front. Davenport slipped back to where Falco and Hans waited.

"I saw two guards patrolling the area. Hans, is there a way around the back of the building?"

"No, sir, it's built into the mountain."

"Then guards can only come from one direction. That simplifies getting in," Falco said.

"Other than the two guards, the only sign of life was three lighted windows. Two upstairs and one downstairs beside a door, I assume it's the door to the kitchen."

"Yes, sir, it is," said Hans.

"From what I can see, this place is an actual fortress," Falco said.

Davenport nodded and stood up in the shelter of a large boulder and trees. He attached a miniature jamming device to the shoulder of his jacket. "This will block the security cameras. They won't be able to capture our images, but you have to stay close to me." Suddenly he turned toward a creaking branch and whispered, "Get down."

A third guard on the outside of the electric fence came into view. Adrenalin fueled Davenport. The man Jennie didn't know, the other Davenport, smiled as he stepped out of the bushes and extended his hand. It took the guard by surprise and he reached out to shake hands. Davenport stared into the guard's eyes while speaking in a low voice. The pressure on the guard's hand slowly bent him over. Davenport's thumb pressed down hard on a nerve until the guard crumpled all the way to the ground.

He gave a thumbs-up to Falco and Hans. "He's out for an hour or more. Punch in the code for the gate, Hans. Stay low and run to the staircase, get up against the building where it's dark. Go."

The men breathed heavily when they got in the alcove under the stairs. They waited for the two guards to come back. A cold wind blew against their faces, the temperature was dropping. It was a tense few minutes before the two guards came back around the side of the building. Davenport nodded at Falco and pointed to the nearest guard.

"Take the guard nearest you, Falco, don't let him yell. I'll get the one on the far side."

The guards paid no attention to the stairs as they walked by. When they passed the staircase, Falco and Davenport stepped out and circled the men's necks with their forearms dropping the two guards to the ground without a sound.

"How many guards are here?"

"Six. There should be three more," Hans whispered.

Davenport looked over at Falco and held up three fingers.

The kitchen door was locked. Davenport pulled a slender wire from the pack attached to his wrist and pushed it in the lock on the heavy steel door, the door opened and the men stepped inside. The cook was stirring something on the stove and she turned to look at them.

"I'll talk to her," Hans said. "She won't be a problem, she hates it here. The chairman won't let her leave."

CHAIRMAN HOUSER SLID OPEN a panel on the wall next to his desk and adjusted the screen. He scanned the exterior of the building then looked at every room starting with the front entry hall.

"Damn cook," he muttered. The kitchen camera wasn't working; she must have hit it with the broom again. He closed the panel and turned back to his desk just as the study door opened and his nemesis stepped into view.

The chairman's face drained of color, he didn't like surprises. None of his cameras showed an intruder, the alarm system had not signaled a break in. That blasted man had sneaked in again. He was like a damn ghost, one that never forgets anything. Davenport's recall was intimidating. Houser's hand shook as it went to the Spear of Destiny in the side pocket of his chair. He took a deep breath and said, "What took you so long? I've been waiting."

"I've come for my grandson. I'm asking you to be a gentleman and tell me where he is." Davenport walked toward the chairman. His voice lowered, "This is the only time I'll ask nicely."

The chairman punched a button under his desk to call his guards. "What makes you think I'd tell you after all the problems you have caused the *Brotherhood*?"

Davenport stopped in front of Houser's desk. "You shouldn't have touched my family." He stared at the chairman until the man squirmed. "It's just you and me, Houser. No need calling your guards, they aren't coming."

The chairman looked anxiously around the room then back at Davenport. "Have a seat and let's talk." He motioned to the one chair in front of his desk.

"You don't really think for one minute I'll fall for that, now do you? I know all about that chair."

"It was worth a try, you're here alone." The chairman's hand shook as he pointed a gun at Davenport. "Please, be seated."

"What makes you think I'm the only game in town?" Davenport laughed and leaned on the desk. "Here's the deal. I've left a detailed expose with a trusted source. It tells everything that the *Brotherhood* has done plus all your future plans and timetable. I've also included the names and addresses of all the members including you." He leaned a little closer. "You know I know everything, and I never forget."

Hands flat on the desk, Davenport bent low and stared straight into Houser's eyes. "If I don't leave here with my grandson in one hour, the papers will be sent to the President of the United States and all major newspapers, radio and television stations by breakfast tomorrow. Make no mistake, Houser, it will happen unless I make a phone call to stop it. Now, play nicely and put the gun away. Where's my grandson?"

Houser sneered and kept the gun pointed at Davenport. "You don't really think the newspapers will print it, you know better than that. I own all the newspapers and the stations, or have you slipped up and forgotten that little fact?"

"I have forgotten nothing, they will print it. The President of the United States will see to it. Now, where's my grandson, or do I have to get physical?"

Houser blinked rapidly as his eyes swept the room, "I see no backup."

Falco stepped into view and stood in the doorway checking out the room. He twirled his knife when he started walking toward the chairman. "The man asked you where his grandson is. I didn't hear an answer."

Houser turned a shaking gun on him and pulled the trigger, but Falco's knife was already in the air. It hit the chairman's hand sending the bullet into the wall. Houser yelled and yanked the knife out of his hand. Davenport grabbed the gun and knife.

Without warning, the door behind the chairman burst open and crashed against the wall. An inhuman scream filled the air as Fleicher exploded into the room.

Fear flew over the chairman when he saw Fleicher's bloody face. The man should have been dead. He grabbed the remote control with his bleeding hand and held the button down.

Fleicher roared like an animal and flew at the chairman slashing him with his razor blade. Houser tumbled out of his chair and fell to the floor under the desk with the activated remote clutched in his hand.

Crazed with pain, Fleicher spun around the room. His arm extended and holding the razor in front of him, he slashed wildly at anyone he could reach. The men dove for cover trying to get away from the razor blade; it seemed to be everywhere at once. Fleicher's knees buckled and he stumbled against the chair howling like an animal in pain. The razor dug a hole in the chair triggering the explosive that was hidden in it...

The chair blew up as gunshots rang out...

The howling stopped, but Fleicher kept spinning around and slashing at anything within his reach…

Another shot pierced the air…

Fletcher went down. In the last second before darkness silenced him, he called out, "My son…"

Then all was silent.

No one was left standing.

Flames and smoke from the burning chair permeated the room.

No one uttered a word. Falco slowly pulled himself off the floor and used his jacket to wipe blood off his face; one of Fleicher's wild slashes got him across the face and another in his thigh. He limped over to Fleicher, flipped the man over and checked his pulse. The man who murdered Parrino's grandson would kill no more.

Davenport sat up next to the fireplace. Blood was running down his face and he was rubbing the side of his head where it hit the fireplace when he dove away from the razor. Surveying the carnage of Fleicher's insane attack, his eyes went from Falco's bloody face to Hans' bleeding arm. Fleicher got them all, but they had survived.

"This looks and smells like a war zone," Davenport said coughing. He struggled to his feet making his leg throb.

"You were right, Davenport, that man wasn't like anyone I've ever encountered. That's the craziest thing I've ever seen, and I've seen a lot of bizarre stuff. He slashed at anyone or anything he could reach. He got us all."

Falco stopped and looked around the room shaking his head. "I wasn't sure we were going to stop him."

"I wasn't either," Davenport said. He picked up a pitcher of water from the chairman's desk and poured it on the smoldering chair. "The chairman, he's got to tell me where my grandson is."

"He's in bad shape, you better try fast," said Falco looking down at the chairman.

Davenport hobbled around the desk to Houser. The chairman was bleeding and not moving. He was alive, but he wasn't going to cause any more trouble. Davenport yanked him to a sitting position against the desk and his head rolled about. A spear was sticking in his chest.

"Talk to me, Houser. Where's my grandson?"

The chairman's lip curled in a sneer.

It inflamed Davenport and his jaw clenched tight. Blood ran down the side of Davenport's face and dripped on Houser. He shook the man until his eyes opened.

"Where is my grandson?"

"You'll…never…find…him…" Houser's voice grew fainter with every mumbled word.

Davenport leaned over him trying to hear what he was saying.

"…isn't… over…" He coughed and blood ran out of his mouth down to the spear in his chest. "Chancellor… in… control…"

"Who is the chancellor? What's his name? Where's Nicky?" yelled Davenport.

The chairman's head fell forward as he bled out.

Davenport leaned back and watched the man draw his last breath. The Spear of Destiny had taken revenge on the man who stole it.

Chapter 50

THE DOOR BEHIND CHAIRMAN Houser's desk burst open again and three men wielding guns stormed inside. Wind and rain blew through the open door and papers flew off the desk and landed all around the room.

"Freeze," yelled Falco pointing at Joey's assassin on the floor. "It's finished, it's all over."

Momentum carried the men into the middle of the chaos, guns leading the way and looking for a target.

"Stand down," roared Falco stepping in front of them. "It's over. The assassin is dead."

The three men froze in their tracks when they saw a man on the floor with a spear sticking out of his chest. Their eyes darted around the room going from Falco's bloody face to blood dripping off Davenport's chin to a young man holding a bleeding arm and ending on a chair that was smoking.

"What the hell happened here? We heard gun shots and an explosion, but this looks like a bloody massacre."

"An encounter with the man who killed Joey," said Falco. "It wasn't pretty. I was warned he was a crazy bastard, but I've never encountered anyone like him before. He was wild, howling like an animal and slashing at everyone with a razor blade. We could have used your help then. What took you so long?"

"Sliding along the narrow slippery path was slow going, but the main problem was getting over that damned electric fence, then we found several bodies and had to secure them, they were starting to wake up." The men walked around the room taking in the chaos. "It's a bloody mess in here," he said staring again at the spear sticking out of the chairman chest.

"You can tell Parrino the man who killed Joey is dead." Falco laughed and wiped blood off his face. "I told him we didn't need you, but since you're here, make yourself useful and take some pictures for Parrino," he said pointing at Fleicher. "He'll want to see proof."

"Are you positive he's the killer?"

"Oh yes, no doubts about that."

"Who killed him?"

"I'm not sure," Falco said. "For a few seconds during the attack, I didn't know if we were going to stop him." They rolled Fleicher over and counted four bullet holes in his chest.

"Looks like we all took a shot at him. I shot twice and Davenport shot once before Fleicher got him with that damned razor. I don't know where the fourth shot came from. I was too busy trying to stay out of Fleicher's reach."

Hans was beaming as he came into the room with a basin of water, towels, and bandages. "I think I made the last shot, sir. When I heard the shooting, I grabbed a gun the chairman kept hidden in the hall table. When Otto came at me, I shot him and he went down."

Davenport took hold of Hans' arm, "Well done, son. You can do one more thing for me, do you know where Houser has my grandson?"

"There are several rooms carved into the mountain and I think he's in one of those. The cook told me she takes meals there. There's a secret door in the bookcase in one of the back rooms. I can take you there, but first, we need to clean you gentlemen up."

"Are any more guards back there?"

"I don't think so, only a woman and a child from what the cook told me."

One of the Mafia men spoke up. "We passed three guards already down and put three others out of commission. You won't have any trouble with them. Are there more around?"

Davenport gave them thumbs up. "That's six. Hans, are there any more guards?"

"No, sir, that's all. There were two at the school and four here."

"Davenport nodded. "Then it's over. Show me where that back room is, Hans."

"May I suggest, sir, it would be best if you clean up first. You might scare the boy with all that blood running down your face."

"I guess a few more minutes won't matter."

Falco picked up a towel and tossed it to Davenport. The men cleaned up and Hans put bandages over the cuts on their faces.

"I'm ready, let's get my grandson," he said limping toward the door.

Falco caught his arm. "One more question, Davenport. How do we get out of here and back to town? The cars are up at the school."

"You could drive the chairman's cars," Hans said. "There are several in the garages adjoining this building and he doesn't need them now."

"That'll work. Now, can I get my grandson?"

DAVENPORT AND FALCO HAD started down the hall with Hans, the Mafiosi following close behind them and checking out the building, when the phone in the study rang. Davenport stopped and sent Hans to answer it.

With his hand covering the phone Hans told Davenport, "It's the chancellor, sir. I don't know his name. I told him the chairman was unavailable."

Davenport grabbed the phone and listened. A voice was demanding to speak to Chairman Houser.

"That's not possible, Houser is dead."

"Are you sure?"

"Absolutely, he has a spear sticking out of his chest."

The voice laughed, "That's good news. Is this Davenport?"

"Yes, you might want to know I'm releasing all the *Brotherhood's* plans to the president and the major news media around the world. Everything will be made public in a few days."

The man continued to laugh. "It doesn't matter anymore, new leadership has taken over and new plans are being made."

"Who are you, your voice is familiar."

"It should be. I'm married to your wife, and I want her back."

Davenport slammed his fist against the desk; he knew who the voice belonged to.

"The old regime is dead, it died with my father. You didn't know my father was the chancellor, did you, Davenport," the voice mocked. "And now, thanks to you, I don't have to worry about the chairman. He and my father are dead and gone and out of my way. I've been groomed for this job all my life and my time has come." The man paused waiting for a comment.

Davenport remained silent.

"Cat got your tongue, Davenport? Well, you don't have to talk, just listen," he said manically. "The family business, better known to you as the *Brotherhood,* is now mine. It's all under my control now. I'll be calling the shots from now on."

Davenport was sickened by what he was hearing. He shifted his weight to his injured leg, it buckled and he grabbed the desk to keep from falling.

"Was that a moan I heard, Davenport?" He paused and waited a minute, but Davenport didn't answer. "Your past work is down the drain, Davenport, it was all for nothing," he sneered. "Everybody failed to realize who I am. My father trained me well and I'm drafting a new set of plans and timetable that you know nothing about," the gloating voice continued.

Davenport's face froze as he listened to his enemy rant on and on.

"Long live the new king of the *Brotherhood*. That's me, Davenport, in case you haven't been listening. I'm giving you fair warning, I will get Jennie back and she will be my queen. I have all the power I need at my beck and call. All I have to do is pick up a phone."

The line went dead and fury swept over Davenport. The snake had grown another head. This time it was a viper, and it was very, very personal.

Nathan Scott had become the chancellor and was in control the *Brotherhood*.

Chapter 51

THE ATOMOSPHERE IN THE room became menacing, no one moved or uttered a sound. An involuntary shudder swept over Davenport as he replaced the phone. The game had changed. His hand dropped to a heavy glass paperweight and his fingers curled around it. He hurled it at the wall beside the desk.

The men stared at him then at the wall when a section of paneling moved. It slid open exposing a small screen that was focused on the kitchen. Reaching over, Davenport punched a button and the scene changed to a bedroom. He kept pressing the button and looked at other rooms in the fortress and the grounds surrounding it. The last click showed a woman and a little child sitting in a rocking chair.

"Hans, is this the room you were telling me about?"

"Yes sir," Hans nodded his head.`

"That must be my grandson; it looks like he is safe enough for now." Davenport turned his back to the room and went to the open door. He sucked in the cold fresh air as he stared out at the dark night. After a few tense minutes, he closed what was left of the door Fleicher had busted. Wind continued to blow through the already cold room.

Davenport cleared his throat and faced Hans and Falco. "That call clarifies a lot of things. The man on the phone was Nathan Scott; he said his father just died. His father was the chancellor, the invisible man who's been calling the shots behind the chairman. He was the real power in the *Brotherhood*, and the man I've been trying to find all these years." Davenport looked at Falco. "This was the man from Hungary who's been promoting and funding the one-world government movement that started back in the 1950s."

"He's dead, so what happens now?" asked Falco.

"It means the *Brotherhood* has sprouted another head. Scott has stepped into that position. With his father's death, he said he inherits the *Brotherhood*. He is now leader and in control of this group of power-hungry men."

Old ways took hold of Davenport and an emotionless man shoved the chairman's body out of his way. He sat down at the desk.

"Gather all the papers that blew around the room. I want to see if there is anything here that will tell me where the chancellor's headquarters are." He rifled through each drawer placing a few papers on the desktop and shoving others back in the drawers. Falco and Hans handed him the papers they gathered up and he sorted through them.

"Hans, find me something to put all this in. I'll have to study it later."

Davenport stood up and stared at the chairman then he leaned down and pulled the Spear of Destiny out of his chest. He wiped it clean on Houser's shirt and placed it in the briefcase Hans handed him.

"That's the Spear of Destiny. It must be returned to the Hapsburg Museum in Vienna, Austria." He shoved the stack of papers on top of the spear and handed the briefcase to Hans. "Take care of this for me. Don't lose it."

"Falco, you and your friends check out the garages and find a couple of cars we can use. Bring them up to the front of the fortress. We'll leave in fifteen minutes."

Davenport was cold and unapproachable when he left the room. "Hans, lead the way to the back room. I'm going after my grandson."

No one stopped Davenport this time.

Chapter 52

"YES, MR. PRESIDENT, I UNDERSTAND. The situation is quite clear now."

General Thurman left the oval office and two Secret Service agents escorted him to the elevator. He was reviewing every second of the fifteen minute meeting with the president. It had been a long time coming, but he finally had the entire picture of what had taken place in Arizona and what was going to happen from now on. The president made it abundantly clear—with the exception of one impossible problem.

"There is no way under the sun I can keep track of everyone under these conditions," General Thurman muttered pounding the side of his leg with his fist. One thing was out-and-out obvious, what he heard today was not going to make his job any easier.

Davenport would continue to receive his orders directly from the president, no surprise there, and it was no surprise Owen Blakely would be working with Davenport. However, what blew the lid off was when the president said two more agents would be working with them, and those agents would remain nameless.

"Nameless, that's a hell of a thing to tell me. How am I to keep track of and support two people whose names I don't even know," he mumbled as his face turned red.

He got in the car and told his driver to take him back to the Army Command Center.

After that shock, the president dropped an even larger bomb. Nathan Scott had taken over leadership of the *Brotherhood* and was the new chancellor. The former chancellor was Scott's father and he died naming Scott his heir. Scott was emotionally unstable and unpredictable. He did things his way, regardless of orders or established procedures. You never knew when he would blow up or what he would do. However, it did explain how he got out of the prison in Leavenworth.

The general's aide was known throughout G-2 headquarters for his calm composure in any situation, but this was going to change that. Even Reaves could not stay calm at this news, he had never trusted Scott. The only good news in the entire affair was that the Mafia cleaned up the mess at the chairman's fortress. It now looked like any other old, deserted building in the Superstition Mountains.

Davenport's new orders were to stop and apprehend Nathan Scott, whatever his real name was. The president said they still didn't know the name of the former chancellor so that means no one knows Scott's real name. The general's orders were to provide protection and backup for Davenport and his team, the nameless team. The general leaned back in the seat and sighed. His shoulders drooped.

The car zigzagged through the traffic making its way back to the command center.

Reaves needed to restock the bar, looks like they both were going to need a drink or two. "Probably more," he muttered. He sighed again when he entered the building and headed for his office. He wanted that drink now.

The general sat down in his chair and closed his eyes. *Where do I begin? How on earth do I protect and provide backup for two people whose names I don't know? Nope, having what the president called the entire picture is not going to make my job any easier. It just became impossible.*

Chapter 53

FALCO AND HANS CLIMBED a narrow spiral staircase and stopped at a small window near the top of the ancient castle that Davenport called home.

"I didn't know places like this still exist outside of movies," Falco said, his voice echoing off the rock walls. The stone was rough when he touched it. "It's a strange feeling to think someone lived here centuries ago and climbed these same stone steps."

The two men continued to the top of the tower. Fortified ramparts and rock barriers stretched out as far as they could see and surrounded the castle grounds, all designed with defense in mind. Falco and Hans stared at the rock walls, walls that had been standing guard for centuries, walls that Davenport had updated and electrified.

"I studied about castles," Hans said. "The tutors Chairman Houser arranged for me made sure I knew about castles and their history, but I didn't know I'd ever get to see a real one."

Falco had never paid much attention to history, but being in the castle made the past come alive and he was curious about the people who lived here a hundred years ago. He could even imagine a few ghosts roaming about. Nothing in their past had prepared Falco or Hans for the sheer size of the castle or for the towers, turrets, circular rooms, dark dungeons and narrow passageways. It fascinated them and they had explored every day, but there were still parts of the castle they hadn't visited.

The place Davenport chose to make his home intrigued Falco, it caused him to wonder what it would be like to be free to choose where you wanted to live. He'd never been that free. Now that he thought about it, Davenport wasn't a free man either, he was a hunted man with a contract on his head. Maybe no one was completely free, he thought looking at Hans. Hans was captive of a mind that remembered no past.

"To be free," Falco shook his head hard, that kind of thinking wasn't smart for a man in the Mafia. After the problem of Fleicher was settled, Parrino had given Falco two more orders. He was to stay with Parrino's grandson and the boy's mother long enough to make sure they were safe and well cared for, which is what he told Davenport. He did not tell him about his second task, Parrino wanted to know exactly where Davenport's compound was located. He knew Davenport wouldn't tell him and he hadn't been able to figure it out. All he knew was Davenport's plane landed at a private airstrip somewhere in the British Isles and then they boarded a helicopter. There were no signs anywhere, he had looked vigilantly. So far, he had no clue where he was. He only knew he was in Scotland, somewhere in the mountains in a castle. That wasn't good enough, it would not satisfy Parrino.

Eight weeks ago when the helicopter settled on the ground, a man with a heavy accent named Duncan and a bossy old doctor that Davenport called Doc Fitz met them. Doc Fitz saw the bandages on their faces and immediately herded everyone into his infirmary so he could check their wounds. "I need to see what you've done to yourselves this time." And every day since they arrived, he'd checked each of them saying, "Nae helpful if ye get blood poisoning, wounds like this have to be kept clean. Who knows where that man's razor blade had been."

However, nobody was as bossy as nurse Scully, she even bossed Doc Fitz. Falco smiled as he thought about them, they were quite a pair. His smile faded when Parrino came in his mind.

"It's cold up here, Hans, time to go below. Parrino is pressuring me to figure out where we are. If you hear anything, please tell me, I have to find out before we leave for the states. The media frenzy has finally moved on to other things and Davenport says he'll fly us home the first week of January."

Falco turned and started down the spiral staircase. He wanted to talk to Duncan; maybe he would tell him the address of the castle and the name of the nearest town.

"Remember, we have a tree trimming party tonight," Hans said following Falco. "Mrs. Davenport says it's traditional and we'll decorate a tree with ornaments. I don't remember ever doing this or celebrating Christmas, but it's possible I did before Houser erased my memory. Of course, I've seen pictures in books and it looks like fun. Have you ever decorated a tree?"

"Every year of my life, Hans, you have a lot of catching up to do. This will be the first of many fun times for you. Have you decided if you want to come home with me or stay here with Jennie and Josh?"

"No, sir, I keep going back and forth. Mr. Davenport tells me you are in the Mafia. I hear what he says about it, but I don't understand most of it. I don't know what I should do. When I look at Mrs. Davenport, I get a warm feeling. I think she must be like my mother, she makes me feel good. I like it here and I feel safe. It's very confusing."

Falco had been having that same thought lately, he'd been wondering what would happen if he never went back to the Mafia. He closed his eyes, *crazy thinking*, he had to quit doing that. That was really dangerous and he was going to get himself in trouble. Nobody ever leaves the Mafia. Shrugging his shoulders, he turned and studied the young man who had become like a son to him. Maybe Hans should stay here, he would be safer.

"This is Christmas Eve, Hans." He patted the young man on the back. "No more serious talk, next week is soon enough."

Chapter 54

IT WAS CHRISTMAS EVE. Memories of her husband flooded in and tears slipped down her face. Kris swiped at them and stomped her foot, "I will not cry anymore." She opened the window and let cold air blow in her face. Her hand touched Jeffrey's ring that hung on a chain around her neck. "No more tears, Jeffrey, but I'll never forget," she whispered.

After her collapse in Phoenix, she'd decided crying didn't help. It was reinforced when they went back to Dallas to bury Jeffrey. She never wanted to feel as lost and out of control as she had when she stood beside her husband's casket at the funeral home in Dallas.

Kris stared out the window. The memories of that day wouldn't go away; they were seared in her mind. She couldn't forget what the *Brotherhood* took from her. They had murdered her husband and wrecked her life.

Remembering her vow to Jeffrey her eyes darkened, she had promised him she'd get the ones who killed him. Fleicher was dead, but the rest of the *Brotherhood* was not. They had to be held accountable even if it meant going back to the United States. Never again would she be as helpless as she was that horrible day at the funeral home...

"Jeffrey looks like he could speak."

Kris whirled around and there he was—her stepfather, Nathan Scott. He was standing beside her in the funeral home, her stomach came up in her throat and she couldn't speak. How dare he come here?

"You look like you've weathered the storm pretty good, daughter."

"I am not your daughter, what are you doing here? Dad's looking for you," Kris looked anxiously out the door of the small viewing room for her dad. *"He'll be back in a few minutes."*

"I figured your mom would be here with you."

"No, she's not. What do you want mom for?"

"She's my wife. I made a promise to Davenport that I intend to keep."

"What promise?"

Scott smiled. Chills went through Kris and she backed away from him. She looked down the hall. *"Dad will be back any minute; he had to talk to the funeral director."*

Scott grabbed Kris' arm and pulled her close to him. *"Tell Davenport I was here and I will be nearby no matter where you go or what you do until I get my wife back. I'm in charge now and I have all the power behind me that I need. It will happen."*

"Take your filthy hands off me," Kris shivered and jerked away. She slapped him hard across the face.

His hand came straight up and slapped her in return.

Kris stumbled backwards, almost falling. She straightened up and said through gritted teeth, *"Do not ever mess with me or my family again."*

The man sneered and rubbed his cheek. *"And what will you do, my pretty little widow, slap me again?"*

Kris' heart turned to stone. A new plan formed in her mind as she stood face-to-face with the man who had betrayed all of them. Her voice was low and cold and her eyes pierced his eyes. *"If you ever try to touch me or my family again, you better not miss. Because the next time I will be ready for you, and it will not be a mere slap in the face."*

Scott laughed out loud and walked away from Kris. She could hear him laughing when he disappeared out the door of the funeral home…

THE MASSIVE GRANDFATHER CLOCK in the great hall chimed four times bringing Kris back to the present. Scott's laughter was ringing in her ears when she looked at the clock, her hands clenched tight, her face hardened, and anger consumed her. There would never be any peace or rest for her or Laurie as long as the *Brotherhood* and Scott were at liberty.

Owen Blakely understood; he knew how she felt. Scott had tried to kill him by shoving him off a speeding train. She and Owen had become friends and he'd been teaching her self-defense tactics ever since she got to the Compound. She had a plan and feeling helpless wasn't part of it. Plans always made her feel better.

"It's Christmas Eve and I'm in control now," Kris said aloud, her labored breathing gradually slowed. This was not the time for bad memories and anger.

She concentrated on Sophie and Nicky. They were so excited about Christmas she had to smile. They'd been eating cookies and running non-stop around the tree all day; they had eaten way too many sugar cookies. What Sophie was excited about was Santa Claus coming in the morning. Nicky was too young to understand, he was just following her.

"I have to make this evening fun for them. I'll have a wonderful time with the children and my family." She would not think about the past tonight, or about the future. Laurie was getting stronger every day, and they were safe with mom and dad and friends. It was a new beginning for all of them. Tonight they would laugh and enjoy being together, and she could play with the children.

Kris turned and went up the winding staircase to find Sophie. She relaxed and smiled when she remembered she had promised her daughter she could wear her new red dress Christmas Eve. Sophie would look so cute.

LAURIE WATCHED HER SON Nicky play with his toys. He was too young to know what had happened to him and she prayed he never would. It was enough she knew. When she woke up in that coffin and found she couldn't get out…Laurie's breathing quickened and her stomach threatened to erupt. She fought to relax her shoulders, to remember she was safe, to control her breathing like Doc Fitz had taught her to do. No more panic attacks.

She focused on Nicky and his toys. She was okay, Nicky was in front of her playing with his toys and she watched her son. She had to quit thinking about being buried. Daddy got her out of that horrible coffin. Her hand hit the arm of the chair, "I'm safe and far away from that place," she said out loud. "The monster, that evil man is dead. I have to remember I'm at home with mom and dad." She breathed deeply and concentrated on Nicky.

"It sneaks up on me," she mumbled. "I don't mean to think about it. This is a new day, I'm in Scotland and I can walk, not very well, but I can walk. And I can talk again. Doc Fitz says my strength will come back and I'll be feeling much better in a month or so." Nicky watched her as she talked; she picked him up and cuddled him. Her heart was filled with love for her little son.

"We're safe, Nicky, the bad man is dead."

Her mind kept bringing up those times when the evil man showed up; she could hear his horrible voice telling her she was dead. It also replayed Kris' voice talking to her and telling her she was alive and daddy was coming to get her. Even when she didn't know who Kris was, her voice made her feel safer.

She had survived. They were safe in Scotland with her mom and dad, but her Joey was dead; the thought of him brought tears to her eyes. She didn't even get to go to his funeral and say goodbye. Their plans and the babies they would have together were gone, but she had Nicky. She hugged him tighter.

Her thoughts centered on her husband. "Someone has to stop those evil people who killed Joey and Jeffrey. They have to pay for what they did." She rocked Nicky and breathed slow and deep.

Every time she talked to Doc Fitz he told her that time heals all wounds, physical and emotional, that she had to be patient. He didn't understand how hard it was to do that, but she wasn't crying as much as she had at first, so maybe.

She looked up when she heard a knock on her bedroom door and a smile crossed her face. She put Nicky on the floor and pushed herself up. She picked up her cane and walked slowly to open the door.

"We're ready, Jack."

She smiled as Nicky ran over and grabbed hold of Jack's leg.

Chapter 55

"MERRY CHRISTMAS, JOSH DAVENPORT said as he and Jennie watched snow floating past their bedroom window. He put his arm around his wife and drew her close. His mind was reliving the past months, it was a miracle they were all alive and in Scotland. After so many years of being alone and longing for his family, it felt like a dream.

Jennie watched a range of emotions cross his face. Doc Fitz had doctored all of them and the physical injuries were almost healed, the emotional ones would take a little longer.

"It's almost time to decorate the tree. Are you ready?" Josh asked.

"Just about," she hugged him then turned and gathered up several packages she had wrapped.

"We have a few minutes before we meet everyone. I have a question for you, if you could have anything you want for Christmas, what would it be?" asked Josh.

Jennie put the packages down. "You know the answer to that, it's what I've wished and prayed for ever since I got here last spring. I want you to quit putting yourself in the line of fire. I want you in bed beside me every night and at the breakfast table with me every morning for the rest of our lives. I want you to quit chasing evil men and stay home."

Davenport picked up the cane he'd been walking with ever since he got back to Scotland and limped around the room. His injured leg was better, but it had gone too long without care and the infection was slow to heal.

There were lots of things he regretted, but getting Laurie out of that grave was not one of them. He would do it again. It meant everything to him to have his daughter safe and getting better every day. It was due to the good care of Doc Fitz and Patty Coleson, the ICU nurse who flew to Scotland with Laurie when she was unable to move. Patty had stayed and helped Doc and Scully for a month before returning to Fort Worth. Doc had asked her to stay with them at the castle saying that if all these people keep getting injured, he could use her help.

Davenport watched Jennie and he knew the time had come. He wasn't as mobile as he needed to be to keep working for the president. Doc said his leg was healing and he should be grateful he even had the leg. Davenport was trying to be patient, but stepping down was not in his nature and it rubbed him the wrong way. He had no choice now; he was trying his best to do it without complaining.

Owen Blakely was ready and more than capable of doing missions for the president. Davenport closed his eyes and massaged his forehead. It was gut-wrenching to step back and let someone else do his job, particularly since Nathan Scott was in charge of the *Brotherhood*. He wasn't sure he could ever say the words, "I'm stepping down."

It was time, he took a deep breath and said, "Well, honey, I can't wrap it up and put it under the tree. But, I can tell you that Owen is taking over my job. I will be his phone contact and help him with what I can from here. He won't be alone as I always was, I'll be available by phone and can provide backup. We cleared this with the president yesterday."

Jennie threw her arms around him, "Finally! Thank you, Josh. I don't need packages under the tree, I just need you. This is the best Christmas present ever."

"There are some other plans you won't be so happy about, however, that news can wait until after Christmas."

"Oh, Josh, what now?"

"Tomorrow is soon enough to tell you. For tonight, just remember, I'm not leaving anymore." He smiled and reached for her hand, "I'm giving you fair warning, I'm not sure I can do this gracefully. You're going to get tired of me underfoot."

She studied her husband's face as she said a quick prayer that her suspicions were wrong. She'd been watching everyone for days and knew something was brewing they weren't telling her about. She hoped she was wrong, but she didn't think she was.

"You know I hate it when you start something and don't finish." She turned and picked up the packages then smiled at him "Since this is Christmas Eve and we have a party to go to, I'll let it go this time. Tomorrow, Josh, you have to tell me everything."

Jennie pulled his head down to hers and kissed him. "I promise you, I won't get tired of you." She handed a couple of packages to him and they left the bedroom and went down the hall to the library. It was their favorite room in the castle and they'd decided it was the perfect place for the Christmas party. Jennie paused in the doorway to enjoy the homey feel of the decorated room. She, Kris, and Hans had put up all the decorations with Laurie watching and making suggestions. Josh had cut down the tree and it stood in the corner of the room near the fireplace. It felt like home and, for the moment, she was content.

"No more talking business tonight. Let's just enjoy our family, we're all together and we have two grandchildren who will entertain us tonight." Jennie laughed, "And you, sir, have to play Santa Claus. The costume is on your desk in your office."

Chapter 56

Christmas Eve
December 24, 1983
CAMERON COMPOUND, SCOTLAND

THE LAST RAYS OF the sun dropped behind the mountains as Jennie and Josh Davenport entered the library. "It feels like home, Josh," Jennie said looking at the stockings hanging on the mantle. "This is the first Christmas in six years we're all together."

Home, the word brought visions of past Christmas Eves when their daughters were young, visions of toys and laughter and love. Happy and sad feelings mingled in her as celebrations in Texas ran through her mind, particularly the bad years when she thought Josh was dead. Tonight was their first Christmas Eve in the castle, they were a family again and new memories would be made. A stray tear crept down her face.

Jennie checked the room making sure everything was in place. Garlands with lights twinkling in the green leaves adorned the fireplace and spread across the bookcases. A huge spruce tree stood waiting to be decorated; boxes of ornaments and decorations were sitting beside the tree. A large bowl of popcorn and a ball of string sat on a side table.

At the far end of the long room, a table was covered with fruit, finger sandwiches, cookies, gingerbread, mincemeat pies, cakes, and candies. Darcy was still adding food to the already crowded table. A huge punchbowl sat at one end with cups all around it. Darcy and Duncan had created a feast for the Christmas Eve party. The two were planning dinner for Christmas Day and were being very secretive about it. All they would tell Jennie was there would be roasted turkey and lamb along with a mixture of American and Scottish foods.

Josh headed for the bar where Duncan was pouring a drink for Tony Falco. Jennie went to her favorite place beside the fireplace and watched the flickering fire. Darcy had put chestnuts in the fireplace to roast, Jennie had never done that and she wondered when they would be ready to eat. Through the French doors, she could see snowflakes floating around the balcony railings. The moon was already coming into view and the lake sparkled in the soft light with the snow falling on it.

Jennie turned when she heard someone come in. Hans was excited and grinning as he joined the men at the bar; they stood talking in low voices. The scars on the faces of Josh and Tony were fading, but she could still see them. They would always carry those; they were a reminder of a night no one liked to remember. Pictures of the grave where Laurie was buried flashed through her mind. She sat down on the hearth and closed her eyes as she said a prayer of thanks for her family. She prayed nothing would interrupt tonight.

Hans was excited about decorating the tree. This would be his first time to celebrate Christmas and she had explained the meaning of it to him. Jennie couldn't help but think about his parents, how sad to have lost him at eight years old and not know what happened. It was heartbreaking. He hadn't decided whether he would stay with them at the castle and let Josh try to find his parents or go home with Tony. She was hoping he would stay.

Jennie's heart swelled with love when Laurie walked in with Jack, she was laughing and happy. Nicky was hanging on to Jack's hand. *Miracles*, she thought, *they really do happen.* Her daughter was walking and her memory was good. There were a few gaps, she still didn't remember falling off the bridge, but she didn't need that memory anyway. She grew stronger every day. Herman, Molly, Doc Fitz, and Scully followed Laurie in.

"Now, sit ye down, Laurie. Don't ye be tiring yourself out tonight," Doc Fitz ordered.

"Quit scowling at me," Laurie laughed. "I won't overdo, Doc, I promise."

Herman put his arm around Laurie and hugged her. He and Molly led her to an overstuffed chair next to the fireplace and stood talking with her. Nicky was already pulling toys out of the toy box and dropping them all around him. Jennie had to laugh; she had seen him do this before. He was hunting for the little cars.

"I don't want that weak-minded bourbon of yours, where's my single malt whiskey?" Doc Fitz said glaring at the men around the bar.

"Calm down, Doc, I've got it right here. I took it to my room," Scully said handing the bottle to him. "For medicinal purposes," she added when Doc scowled at her.

Jennie was standing by the tree when Kris came in the room laughing and talking with Owen. It was good to see Kris relax and have fun. Sophie ran ahead of them and lifted her arms to Josh, he picked her up and tossed her in the air. Sophie giggled and yelled, "Again."

The tree looked forlorn without decorations and Jennie chose an ornament out of the nearest box and hung it on the tree. She motioned for Hans to come join her.

Having everyone here was a dream come true and her heart soared in spite of a nagging feeling it wouldn't last. She couldn't get rid of that thought, no matter how hard she tried. She hated it when premonitions came; they hung over her head like a dark cloud.

Jack handed the bowl of popcorn and string to Laurie along with a cup of punch. "Make yourself useful and string this popcorn."

"Let's see what we can do in five minutes," Laurie said looking at Jack. "I bet I can make a longer string than you can." He grinned as he drew a chair close to her and sat down. He grabbed a handful of popcorn and tossed it in his mouth. "String it, Jack, don't eat it," Laurie laughed.

Herman kept glancing at Molly and smiling. Jennie was trying to figure out what that was about when Herman tapped on the table. He waited until everyone quit talking and looked at him. "Molly and I have some news. I had a call from the police department in Dallas this morning." A wide grin spread across his face, "I've been offered the job of police chief." He paused then grinned bigger, "I accepted. Molly and I will be going home after the holidays."

Josh turned and looked at Herman, "You know the *Brotherhood* will be after you."

"I know, I haven't forgotten," Herman said. "I know the players now, especially Nathan Scott. I'll be in a position to help you deal with the *Brotherhood*. Ever since I found out the chief was part of them, I've known I had to do something." He picked up Molly's hand. "Molly and I have talked this over and we've decided our place is in Dallas. We love it here, but we really miss our daughter and the rest of our family."

"I understand, I was without my family for years and it's hard to live that way," Josh said. "I wanted to be sure you knew what was ahead of you." Josh looked straight at Herman, "This time you won't be in the dark, you know my number in case you need me."

Herman laughed and nodded.

Josh raised his glass, "To Herman and Molly, we love you both. You and your family have a standing invitation to visit or move back anytime. Consider the castle your second home, you know there's several areas of this place that are unused—you can have an entire wing for your family."

Duncan came in the room clearing his throat, "Mr. Blakely, you have a phone call in the study."

Owen put down his glass and left the room. Kris' eyes darkened as she watched him leave. She took several steps toward the door then stopped and slowly turned back to Herman and Molly.

"I'll miss you," Kris said putting her arms around them. She took a deep breath and stepped back so she could see them. "I mean it. As daddy said, you are family and I will miss you both." Kris looked longingly at the food on the table. "Since we're standing here, I think we should eat. I missed lunch today and everything looks delicious." She picked up a plate and started piling food on it, but her eyes kept straying to the door as she waited for Owen to return.

Jennie sat down near Laurie and watched the activity in the room, particularly Kris. The feeling something was about to happen grew stronger when she heard there was a phone call. She'd lived through many of those calls this past year and she knew who was calling. Even though nothing was said, Josh followed Owen when he left.

When you feel the wind blowing, it's coming from somewhere and you need to be alert. Josh had told her that after her nightmare about their daughters and that time Kris and Laurie had been kidnapped. Her head throbbed, the wind was blowing and something was happening again, she lowered her head and rubbed her temples.

Everyone was laughing and talking, even Doc and Scully were having fun tonight. Jack stirred the embers in the fireplace and added a log to the fire. Laurie was stringing popcorn and had already finished one long garland. Jack took it and wrapped it around the tree. Herman and Molly filled their plates and were talking with Kris. It looked like a normal Christmas Eve, but Jennie knew better. That phone call signaled trouble.

Jennie was on edge by the time Owen and Josh came back. She tried to brace herself for whatever was coming. Owen stopped at the table and got a cup of punch before turning to the expectant faces around the room.

"I know you're all anxious to hear what that call was about. It was the president. It appears the *Brotherhood* is stirring up trouble again, and he needs help back in the States." Owen glanced at Josh before continuing and Josh gave a slight nod. Owen turned to Jack. "Jack, make sure the helicopter is ready and alert Heathrow to have the plane gassed up. The good news is we don't have to leave until after Christmas dinner tomorrow."

Kris put her food down and joined Owen and Josh. The three stood next to the table talking. Jennie's shoulders drooped, she knew, and she wasn't sure how she could stand what was coming next.

Jack talked with Laurie for a few minutes then got up and filled a plate and took it to her. He went back to the table and stacked another plate with food and sat down beside her. They ate and talked quietly.

"Jennie, you should get something to eat." Josh leaned down and kissed her and put out his hand. "The food looks great and Darcy has worked hard on this feast."

"I seem to have lost my appetite, Josh, but I'll try." She took his hand and looked at his face which told her nothing. "I know what you're going to tell me tomorrow," she said as she stood up. "It's evident on their faces. Kris is going with Owen, isn't she?"

"Yes, Jennie, she is." He watched his wife's face as he continued. "She made that decision long ago. There was no way to change her mind; you know how stubborn she is. Kris and I have talked long and seriously about it, it's what she feels she has to do. She didn't back down even when I explained how dangerous it is. So, for the past two months, Owen and I have worked with her. She's young and strong and smart. I believe she can defend herself."

"I know how determined she is when she makes up her mind," Jennie said. "She's always been stubborn. She told me before we left Texas she had promised Jeffrey to find his killer. I was expecting this; I just didn't want it to happen."

Jennie put a sandwich on her plate and filled a cup with punch. Laurie came to the table and joined her mother. She leaned her cane against the table and picked up a piece of cherry pie.

"It'll be all right, Mom. Kris will be fine. I've been watching her train and she's ready." Laurie took a bite of pie. "Mom, there's no way we can let these people do what they did to us without fighting back."

Laurie finished her pie and sat the plate down. She took hold of her mom's hand and said, "You have to know sometime so we may as well get it over with right now. When the next assignment comes, I'll be going with Kris and Owen."

Jennie gasped and dropped her plate.

Doc Fitz's head jerked up when he heard Laurie's words. "In a pig's eye ye will, my girl. Ye will stay right here until I pronounce ye fit to go."

Laurie laughed. "Relax, Doc, I'll wait until you say I'm ready."

She looked back at her mother. "Kris and I have decided that together we can help. Think about it, Mom, we can communicate in ways the *Brotherhood* will never understand." Laurie paused and held both Jennie's hands. "Maybe this is why we have this ability."

Nobody said a word. Tension filled the room.

Falco watched everyone for a few minutes then he tapped on the table. "Listen up. You need to get rid of those serious faces, nobody's going anywhere until tomorrow. This half naked tree will not decorate itself so quit standing there, that tree needs a lot of help. Get up and get busy." He handed an ornament to Hans, and they turned to the tree. Kris and Laurie picked up ornaments and motioned for everyone to join in.

THE AIR IN THE room grew heavy and the walls felt like they were closing in. Jennie slipped out on the balcony and breathed the cold air. Davenport followed and put his arms around her drawing her to him. He didn't try to make it better, he just held her.

"I knew, Josh. I've tried to prepare myself for both of them doing this, but I didn't think it would begin this soon." She shivered and Josh led her back inside. The fire popped and crackled as they stood in front of it absorbing the warmth, both lost in their thoughts.

Davenport was just getting to know his daughters as grown women and he knew what they would face if they joined the fight against the *Brotherhood*. That wasn't what he wanted for them. He hated to see Kris and Laurie get involved with the *Brotherhood,* but he understood their need to fight back. They were well aware of the risks.

Davenport had been expecting a call, it was inevitable. The *Brotherhood* would not stay quiet forever. The day after he picked up his grandson at the fortress, the president had released the expose and the media went crazy. The *Brotherhood* stayed silent for two months while the media frenzy was going on. During this time, several double agents in Fort Leavenworth were ferreted out. The NSA, CIA, and G-2, well, those groups were another story. The only thing he could do was to hope and pray all the traitors in those divisions had been found.

Davenport's thoughts centered on Nathan Scott and he kicked the stool in front of him. Pain shot down his injured leg and it gave way. He grabbed the nearest chair and fell down with a thud. The media exposure had not stopped the *Brotherhood*. It was just a temporary delay while they regrouped under the command of Nathan Scott. He wasn't as powerful as the old Chancellor or Chairman Houser, but the president told him Scott had managed to rally his father's worldwide organization under his leadership. Scott had named himself Commander Scott and was making new plans for a global takeover with the United States first on his list. It was starting again. This formidable power-hungry group was back creating conflict and division not only among the people, but also in Congress.

Davenport glared at his injured leg, right now he was useless, and that bastard Scott was using the organization to search for Jennie. He pounded his fist on the arm of the chair.

Jennie watched her husband's face harden and her heart broke. She wanted him home, but not this way. Lost in her thoughts, she stood motionless for a while as tears escaped down her face. She wiped them away and knew what she had to do. She leaned down and kissed him, "Give your leg a little more time to heal. You'll join Blakely and our daughters when it does."

He looked at her with surprise written all over his face. Jennie held her hand out to him and pulled him up. "We're all together tonight, and that is something special to celebrate. Josh, you're going to be all right. Your leg will heal." She paused for a second then added, "I will be all right, too." Hands together, they went over and joined the group gathered around the tree.

Sophie and Nicky were running around with cookies in their hands and singing. Jennie loved having all of her family in the same room together. "It's Christmas and Falco's right, no more serious faces. It's time to have fun. Let's finish decorating this tree before Sophie and Nicky eat more sugar and get anymore wound up."

Sophie was bouncing all around the room and singing *Santa Claus is coming to Town.* Nicky sang and ran behind her trying to keep up, what he was singing was anyone's guess. The mood lightened, the children's excitement was contagious.

DAVENPORT SAT DOWN IN a chair near the tree and massaged his aching leg. He watched everyone decorating the tree and listened to them talking. Kris and Laurie had lost so much, but they were still able to laugh and enjoy their children. The children didn't know they weren't at home and it didn't matter to them. What mattered was they were with their mothers. "Little children..." he murmured as the hint of a smile slipped across his face.

He stood up and tested his leg to make sure it would support him then limped to the tree and hung several ornaments on it. He had tried for so long to figure out a way to go home. In the deepest recesses of his mind, he knew that had never been a real possibility, but this felt like home for the first time in many years.

Davenport grabbed a couple of sandwiches and went to his office where Jennie had hidden the Santa Claus suit. The lights were twinkling on the tree when Santa came in the library. Sophie ran straight at him yelling "Santa Claus." Santa looked over at Jennie and winked. Nicky followed, but was slower than Sophie. He wasn't sure who this red-suited person was. Santa leaned down and gave Sophie a doll and Nicky a truck. Sophie giggled and bounced around the room hugging her doll. Nicky sat down on the floor and pushed his new truck back and forth.

LATER THAT EVENING, SNOW was piling up on the balcony outside the double doors and moonlight was making the darkness disappear. Christmas carols were playing softly and the lights on the decorated tree were twinkling. Everyone had eaten and settled down around the warmth of the fireplace. The children were almost asleep in their mother's arms. Davenport watched the scene with different eyes, eyes that were at peace for the first time in a long time.

Maybe the illusion of home is all that matters. That was all the children needed.

Davenport went to the bar and opened a bottle of his favorite wine, Mouton Cadet Rothschild, and poured a glass for everyone.

He smiled and lifted his glass. "To my family and friends, to a day I didn't know would ever happen again. I wish you a blessed Christmas."

"To Owen and Kris and Jack, we wish you safety in the new assignment and a quick return to us."

Doc Fitz stood and looked at the group who he thought of as his family. "Hasten ye back to us," he called out loudly as he lifted high his glass of single malt whiskey. "And, if possible, come home in one piece."

Everyone laughed.

Tension left Davenport's face as peace spread through him. *Maybe home was not so much a place, but simply a moment in time when family and friends are gathered together.* He smiled and put his arm around Jennie drawing her close. He felt a contentment he hadn't felt in a long time. The battle wasn't over, he knew the *Brotherhood* wasn't going to give up and go away. But what he thought could never happen again had happened.

Tonight he was home. And for now, that was enough.

Author's Note

This is a story of fiction, well, most of it anyway...
To the best of my knowledge, The *Brotherhood*, Illuminati, Inner Circle, and European Alliance do not exist as represented in this story. The events and people, including the president, the general and his aide, tales of NSA, G-2, the Dallas police chief, Mafia, and Fort Leavenworth are merely figments of my wild imagination.

For the part that is real...
Places such as Hensley Field in Grand Prairie, Texas, John Peter Smith Hospital in Fort Worth, Texas, Dallas/Fort Worth Airport, Sparkman Hillcrest Funeral Home in Dallas, Texas, Luke Air Force Base in Phoenix, Arizona, and the Superstition Mountains in Arizona are real locations. The story about these places is once again my imagination.

The Superstition Mountains are located about 35 miles southeast of Phoenix and east of Apache Junction, Arizona. The mountains have been the subject of interesting stories, Indian lore, and legends of lost treasures of gold. There are abandoned ghost towns, hiking trails, and many tales about the Lost Dutchman Mine. The aura of ancient civilizations and the old west permeates the Superstition Mountains.

The Spear of Destiny is said to be the one that pierced Jesus' side. The Spear passed through a succession of Roman emperors and then to Charlemagne, who carried it into battle. Legend said he was invincible as long as it was in his hands. Every Roman emperor after Charlemagne wanted it. It was said that whoever held it would be undefeated in battle.

History tells us that Hitler arrived in Vienna by plane two days after the invasion of Austria in World War II. One of the first things he did was go to the Hoffburg Palace Museum and open the case and take possession of the spear. With the Spear of Destiny in his possession, Hitler was convinced he was unstoppable in his aim to conquer all of Europe, however, the Spear failed to bring Hitler the victory he had dreamed of. His ambitions were shattered and his empire was on the brink of collapse. In the chaos the Spear of Destiny, one of the great treasures of Europe, disappeared. After the war was over, an attempt was made by the US Troops to find and return the stolen items to their proper locations. The Holy relics and the Spear stolen by the Nazis were found (and that's another story for another time) and returned to the Hapsburg, Museum in Vienna, Austria. Today, they are back in the same room they were stolen from.

But the question remains—is the Spear of Destiny real? After all, one uncomfortable fact, even for Hitler, is that it isn't the only spear claiming to be the Spear of Destiny. There are competitor spears in different locations that claim to be the spear. There is one in Echmiadzin, Armenia, one in Poland which is almost certainly a replica, and another in St. Peters' Basilica at Vatican City. They are all said to be part of the spear that pierced Jesus' side. The question remains unanswered. However, here's an interesting point for you to reflect on—Hitler understood that it didn't matter if the Spear was real or not. What matters is what people believe it to be.

Remember, there are always elements of truth in every book of fiction. After all is said and done, there is nothing new under the sun!